SIZE MA

Low, black, and mena...
tling with sensors and p...
anything, a walking warship.

It moved on six multipli-articulated legs. Its front consisted
of a blunt, turret-like head, flanked by a pair of rotary-jointed
grasping appendages terminating in movable claws.

Emerging soundlessly from a steep-sided valley of depths
lost in blackness, it climbed a hill of regularly spaced ridges
alternating with darker furrows. A fibrous growth, like coarse,
springy grass, covered the surface, which yielded slightly
under the robot's weight. It reached the top of the rise and
paused to survey a landscape of peculiarly rounded mounds
and folds, picked out bloodred in the gloom by the glow of a
distant red light which formed the numerals *3:17:04*.

The device was no bigger than a cockroach. It stood atop
the highest of a chain of wrinkles formed where the bedspread
was pulled around the figure lying asleep. After checking its
direction, the mechanical insect resumed moving, following
an ascending fold onto the slowly breathing form, higher to
the shoulder, and from there onto the smoother expanse of
sheet. Inches from the sleeping man's ear, the device halted
again to identify its target, gauging angles and distances.

Then it moved fast for the area beneath the ear lobe, where
even in an autopsy a small puncture would easily be overlooked. The claws had anchored to the epidermis and the tiny
needle discharged before the alarm message registered in the
sluggishly responding brain.

The figure stirred, turning its head. "Uh . . . Huh? . . ."
An arm freed itself and slapped, but the tiny assailant had
already jumped two feet back down the bed. It dropped to
the floor and exited via the gap beneath the door.

The man lay puzzled in the darkness, rubbing his neck as
his faculties returned. For a moment he was restored fully to
wakefulness; then his body went utterly limp. . . .

By James P. Hogan

BUG PARK

JAMES P. HOGAN

BUG PARK

This is a work of fiction. All the characters and events portrayed in this book are fictional, and any resemblance to real people or incidents is purely coincidental.

A Baen Books Original

Baen Publishing Enterprises
P.O. Box 1403
Riverdale, NY 10471

ISBN: 0-671-87874-3

Cover art by David Mattingly

First printing, May 1998

Distributed by Simon & Schuster
1230 Avenue of the Americas
New York, NY 10020

Library of Congress Catalog Number: 96-51550

Printed in the United States of America

TO

MELINDA MURDOCK

for being such a great and cheerful friend

The help of the following is gratefully acknowledged.

Arlan Andrews of Sandia National Laboratories, New Mexico
Kevin Dowling of the Robotics Institute, Carnegie Mellon University, Pittsburgh
Dale Gee of Lucas NovaSensor, Fremont, California
   —for advice and technical information on microengineering technology and structures.

Sandra Lockney-Davis and Ed Barnett of Pensacola Junior College, Florida
Steve Bortone, University of West Florida
   —for help and information on microbiology and microscopy.

John Toutonghi of Seattle
Sally McBride of Victoria, BC
   —for help with Northwestern and local geography.

David Cherry of Edmond, Oklahoma
Patricia Hoin of Campbell & Hoin, Atlanta, Georgia
Terry Kilgore, Homicide Division, Pensacola Police Department
   —for help regarding police and legal matters.

Kenneth Roxburgh of Pensacola, Florida
   —for sharing some of his background in the U.S. Navy

Captain Greg Segur of St. Louis, Missouri
Robert Cohen, owner of the motor yacht *P'zazz*, Long Beach, California
Jim O'Sullivan, captain of the *P'zazz*
Tina Hogan, Gordon Grant, and Skip Odell
   —for help with understanding more about boats, marine technology, and navigation

PROLOGUE

Low, black, and menacing, its angular metallic surfaces bristling with sensors and protuberances, the robot resembled, if anything, a walking warship.

It moved on six multiply-articulated legs projecting outward and downward from its underside in pairs, like sprung arches. Its front consisted of a blunt, turret-like head, flanked by a pair of rotary-jointed grasping appendages terminating in four-point, independently movable claws.

Emerging soundlessly from a steep-sided valley of depths lost in blackness, it climbed a hill of regularly spaced ridges alternating with darker furrows. A fibrous growth, like coarse, springy grass, covered the surface, which yielded slightly under the robot's weight. It reached the top of the rise and paused to survey a landscape of peculiarly rounded mounds and folds, picked out bloodred in the gloom by the glow of a distant light. The red "moon" illuminating the nocturnal landscape formed the numerals *3:17:04.*

The device was no bigger than a cockroach. It stood atop the highest of a chain of wrinkles formed where the bedspread was pulled around the figure lying asleep. After checking its direction, the mechanical insect resumed moving, following an ascending fold onto the slowly breathing form, higher to the shoulder, and from there onto the smoother expanse of sheet. At the edge of the sheet, inches from the sleeping man's ear, the device halted again to identify its target, gauging angles and distances.

Then it moved fast for the area beneath the ear lobe, where even in an autopsy a small puncture would easily be overlooked. The claws had anchored to the epidermis and the tiny needle discharged before the alarm message registered in the sluggishly responding brain.

The figure stirred, turning its head. "Uh . . . Huh? . . ." An arm freed itself and slapped. *"Wassat?"* But the tiny assailant had already disengaged and jumped two feet back down the bed.

The man lay puzzled in the darkness, rubbing his neck as his faculties returned. For a moment he was restored fully to wakefulness; and then a heavy, muggy feeling came over him. He sat up, fumbled for the light-switch in the red glow cast by the hotel room's clock, but couldn't coordinate sufficiently to find it. He swung his legs out and grabbed for the phone, but crashed instead into the bedside unit, upsetting the tray with the coffee pot and chinaware from his room-service meal.

He put a hand to his head. "Oh Christ . . ."

His legs buckled, and he slumped down onto the edge of the bed again. For a few seconds he tried futilely to resist whatever was happening to him; then he slid down and crumpled to a sitting position on the floor. His body went limp and keeled over.

At the foot of the bed, the tiny robot dropped to the floor. It crossed to the protruding corner formed by the bathroom, from there to the small vestibule area, and exited to the corridor via the gap beneath the door.

The eyes staring sightlessly upward slowly glazed over in the dim red glow from the clock, obliviously counting away the seconds.

CHAPTER ONE

Kevin Heber had never really believed in love at first sight. It was something that he had always taken on faith about the world of adulthood, like the work ethic, the appeal of unsweetened black coffee, or the notion that Wagner's music might really be better than it sounds. Not that he had devoted a great amount of contemplation to the subject. Being an active and healthily curious fifteen-year-old with rapidly expanding horizons on how much there was to do in life, he was more preoccupied with trying to fit a constellation of interests that was constantly growing, into a residue of twenty-four hours which, after deductions for even minimal eating, sleeping, and necessary chores, seemed to be all-the-time shrinking.

Well, it probably wasn't really love, he told himself—not if the things that adults liked to tell smugly about life's complications always getting worse, never better, were to be believed; or the words of the songs that they got sentimental over, that dated from somewhere in that vague span of time between the appearance of personal computers and the last ice age. But any reaction that could make him turn his head away from the screen not once but a second time, and fixedly,

3

just when he and Taki had found the error that had been hanging up the tactile-array interrupt routine, had to be somewhere on the same emotional continent.

He watched as she stepped out of the white Buick that had just parked in one of the visitor slots downstairs, opposite the company's main entrance. A stocky Oriental was straightening up from the passenger side. "Wow!" Kevin murmured. "Look who just showed up with your uncle."

Taki, hunched on the stool next to him, glanced away from the sheet of printout and down through the lab window. He was second generation Japanese-American, the same age as Kevin, almost as smart—when he wasn't thinking up bad jokes—and the only other person able to see the world the way it really was, i.e. the way Kevin saw it. "Her name's Michelle Lang," Taki said, looking back at the printout. "She's his business lawyer."

Kevin blinked. *"She* . . . is a lawyer? . . ."

"Yes, I forgot—he said he was bringing her here today to meet your dad and see the mecs for herself. She's from a law firm somewhere in the city." Taki indicated a block of code with his pen. "What if we moved those lines outside the loop?"

It was an instantly captivating, indefinable quality that combined looks, dress, and poise that did it, Kevin thought to himself, propping an elbow on the worktop and cupping his chin in a hand. "Style" would be the word, he supposed. She was tall and slim for her size, with long, off-blond hair tied back in a ponytail from a tapering, high-boned face that was eye-catching in an angular kind of way, though not really the Hollywood or fashion-model concept of beautiful. She was wearing a tan two-piece with a contoured skirt that enhanced her ample proportion of leg, and carried a brown leather purse on a shoulder strap. No briefcase. That appealed to Kevin straight away—a lawyer who didn't have to be in uniform all the time. And there was something about the unhurried way she turned after closing the car door and stood for a moment surveying the Neurodyne building curiously that set her apart from the typical visitors who hurried inside as if intimidated by the thought of being watched from a score of anonymous office windows. With the touch of haughtiness in the way she tossed her head, she could have come to buy the place.

Ohira, by contrast, black hair cropped short, crumpled suit draped awkwardly on his broad figure, looked more as if he might have come to deliver something to it, were it not for the giveaway flashes glittering from his fingers. He took a last draw from his cigarette, crushed out the butt with his shoe, and joined the lawyer behind the car. They walked together toward the main entrance to the building and disappeared beneath the forecourt canopy.

"It would speed things up a lot," Taki said.

Kevin pulled himself back from thoughts of lithesome goddesses and fair-skinned mountain maids. "What?"

"If we moved those lines of code outside the inner loop. It would speed up the scan sequencing."

"Move which lines?"

"These. The ones I'm pointing at."

"Oh, sure. I was wondering how much longer it would take you to spot that."

"Yeah, right." Taki moved the keyboard closer and began entering the changes.

Kevin looked around at the laser heads, control consoles, and other equipment filling the partitioned space of the Micro-Machining Area. Patti Jukes, one of the technicians, was at the bench on the far side, manipulating something under a binocular microscope. Larry Stromer, the supervisor, stood nearby, cleaning a batch of substrates. It was quiet for early afternoon, which was why Kevin and Taki were able to use one of the computer stations. There was definitely something to be said for having an easygoing scientist for a father, who just happened to own the company, Kevin couldn't deny.

Then he looked back out the window at the Buick— sleek lined, a creamy off-white with black side-stripe and trim, looking sexy, gleaming, and racy. And there were times when it seemed that the fascination with technology that he had grown up with could result in existence becoming too restricted and narrow.

Life continually pressed its confusion of opposites, such as the conflicting advice that young people were assailed with. On the one hand, they were urged to make the effort to broaden their outlook; and then, at other times, to concentrate on what they were good at and not waste the best years pursuing futility—and usually by the same people. The easiest thing was to agree with everything and not take too much notice of either line. After all, wasn't it another of the standard dictums that nothing teaches like experience?

He sighed, turned to the other screen that they were using, and called down a simulation routine to test the patch.

Eric Heber's office was on the top floor of the building, oriented to frame Mount Rainier's snowy, thirty-mile-distant peak in the window to one side of the desk. According to Ohira, he had moved here out of Seattle when he set up his own company three years previously.

Michelle could see the attraction of being located a half mile off the Interstate, here at the south end of Tacoma: a guaranteed stress-reliever after the urban congestion, easy to get to from any direction, and handy for Seatac International Airport. Also, it was less than half an hour by car from Heber's home, which Ohira said was somewhere just west of Olympia, the state capital. It seemed an ideal situation—close to town and his work, yet in easy reach of the Olympic Peninsula with its mountains and forest, and the Pacific Coast beyond; and the big city was always there in the other direction when he needed it. Michelle guessed him as somebody who knew himself and lived for his own values without too much concern for others' expectations.

His office seemed to corroborate the image. It looked more the office of someone at heart the maverick scientist that Ohira had described, than the successful company president that Heber had ostensibly become. The modular walnut desk and credenza, glass-fronted bookcase, and coffee-style conference table, along with the tubular chairs and other accessories were all appropriately matched and imposing—but that was just background scenery that his secretary or a hired designer could have taken care of. The testimonials to the daily routine enacted center stage spoke differently: Files, papers, microelectronics parts, and gadgetry littered the desk; the rolled-gold twin pen set and digital clock-calendar had been moved to the top of the file cabinet to make room for a high-power magnifier; and charts tabling the physical and chemical properties of materials, an industry guide to chip manufacturers, and a whiteboard filled with scrawled math expressions, phone numbers, and reminders had found places between the marquetry designs and chrome-framed art prints adorning the walls.

Eric Heber himself was around forty, wiry, with crinkly yellow hair, fair skin, a thin nose, and gray eyes that peered keenly behind gold-rimmed spectacles. Ohira had mentioned that he was German born. He had taken off the lab coat that his two visitors had found him in, and sat looking relaxed and casual in a sky-blue shirt and tan slacks as he regarded them over his desk. Ohira sat with his hands planted on his knees, his rugged Oriental face expressionless. Michelle's law firm had represented his family's various business interests for six years. He still put her in mind of a godfather—or whatever the equivalent was—of the Japanese *yakuza*.

She leaned forward in her chair, using tweezers to hold a device no larger than a match head in the light from the desk lamp, and examined it through a magnifying glass in her other hand. It was vaguely humanoid in form, silver and black, with two legs and a pair of jointed arms—though there were additional attachments and interchangeable auxiliary parts on the outside. Its head, she observed, was more of a dome than head-shaped.

"That's a general-purpose tool-operator that goes back about half a year," Heber said, watching her. "We've come down a bit further in size with some experimental models since then. The idea was to implement full tooling and fabrication capabilities on a series of intermediate levels down to true nanotech. It's like the fleas with the littler fleas. Once you're equipped at a certain scale, you can use that to construct a next-smaller scale, and so on." Although a soft accent was discernible, his English was flawless. Michelle guessed that he had migrated at a fairly early age. "In the early days, people thought it would be possible to do everything using the etching techniques developed in the chip industry. That worked well enough for making simple rotors and other things with only a few moving parts. But as things became more complicated we found that you have to have precision manipulation. God might be able to put things together with pure willpower, but we humans need a little help."

Michelle already had the feeling that she could enjoy working with Heber. He was not pompous like some scientists she had met, and he kept things simple without losing a touch of humor. She thought that was important. Humorlessness, she had found, was usually a sign of people who took themselves too seriously, which invariably meant they would never admit to being wrong—nor even, in extreme cases, to the possibility that they *could* be. An attitude like that made insufferable clients—as well as bad scientists.

"This is amazing," she said, turning the micromec over beneath the glass. "I've read about these and seen them in documentaries. But it really doesn't come home to you until you hold one in your hand, does it?"

"It's nothing compared to feeling it in your head," Ohira grunted. "You wait. You'll see."

Michelle moved the tiny figure against a white-paper background to see the details more clearly. The dome of a head suggested a picture she had seen somewhere of a deep-sea diving suit—an impression reinforced by the stockiness of the proportions. "Walking tank" would be a better metaphor than "robot," she decided.

Heber seemed to read her thoughts. "The only reason they're fat like that is the things we have to fit inside. For the strength they need at that scale, they could be quite slender."

"Surely there still can't be the kind of complexity in this that we're used to seeing every day," Michelle said. "If I opened this guy up, I can't believe that I'd find all the cogs and springs and other kinds of gizmos that there are . . . well, in my car, for example."

Heber smiled and shook his head. "The physics changes, which means it's often better to do things in different ways. Simply trying to reproduce what we do at the everyday level doesn't always work too well—electromagnetics is a good case in point. For motors and actuators at the microscale, we make far more use of electrostatics. Another technique that works well at smaller scales is what's called peristaltics, which means moving things by means of an induced wave motion. For example, some crystals expand and contract when you apply an electrical voltage across them. So, you can walk one piece past another." Heber made a bridge on the desk with the thumb and little finger of one hand, then advanced it by sliding the thumb closer, anchoring it, extending the little finger away, and repeating the motion. "Kind of a solid-state muscle. It harnesses molecular forces, which are very strong. So you can amplify the range through linkages in the limbs and get a finely controllable movement. Clean and simple, really. Not at all like your car."

All Michelle could bring to mind to ask just at that moment was, "Does it ever need an oil change?"

She meant it as a joke, but Heber nodded approvingly. Evidently not such a dumb question. "Friction works completely differently at this scale. Some surfaces just don't seem to stick or wear at all. In other cases, a tiny electric current works better than any lubricant. It's a whole new science that we're learning about."

Michelle replaced the mec in its cell in the plastic box that Heber had taken it from, containing examples of several models. Heber closed the lid and returned the box to his desk drawer. "Anyway, those are just dummies to show what they look like." He rose, closing the drawer. "Let's go downstairs now and see the real thing."

CHAPTER TWO

They descended two floors and came to a set of double doors part way along a corridor. Heber led them through into a brightly lit open area where perhaps a dozen people were busy at desks, screens, and white-topped benches. Gray and blue equipment cabinets lined the walls and formed improvised partitions around some of the work spaces. Heber led the way to the far side of the room, lined by windows, where a half dozen or so padded chairs with armrests were grouped near more cubicles and screens. Two men were seated in the chairs, each wearing an open-frame headset studded with terminals buried in multicolored wires; also, each had a kind of collar attachment resting on foam shoulder pads. The head frames and collars connected to electronics mounted behind the seat-backs, which in turn sprouted tangles of leads going off to the surrounding equipment. One of the men's eyes was closed; the other's were open but showed no indication of seeing anything. They were engaged in a dialogue that made no sense.

"Hold it over a bit more—more to the left."

"Any good?"

"Nah, it's slipping again."

"Maybe I can wedge it. . . . How's that?"

11

"Better. . . . Okay, keep it right there."

Michelle gave Heber a mystified look. He enjoyed her befuddlement for a moment, then waved her over to the bench standing alongside. On top was a maze of wires and meaningless apparatus arranged around a number of tray-like constructions, about the size of shoe boxes but shallower. They had glass tops and were lit internally to reveal what appeared to be mechanisms of some kind. But the contents looked strange and were organized peculiarly. Instead of the kinds of components that would be found, say, behind an automobile instrument panel or filling a radio, everything was delicately fabricated and spread out across the floor, as if something incredibly intricate had been disassembled and its parts laid out on display. The first thing to suggest itself to Michelle was a scale model of an exhibition hall for machines; then she wondered if it could be some kind of extended mechanical computer. Moving along the bench, she saw that while the different boxes all had the same general theme, none were identical. She gave up and looked at Heber inquiringly.

He turned his head toward the two men seated in the chairs. "Hello, Dean. Where are you?"

The one with his eyes open answered. "Is that Eric?" Apart from his jaw he didn't move, and his faraway expression didn't alter.

"Yes," Heber said.

"We're in three—aligning the rotary grinder."

"How's it going?"

"Oh, we're getting there."

Heber directed Michelle's attention to one of the boxes on the bench. A red 3 was stenciled outside on the end. Michelle peered down, but still she was unable to make any sense of what she was looking at. Heber swung a large, rectangular magnifying lens toward her—

one of several mounted on hinged pivot arms attached
to the bench. "Try looking with this," he suggested.

She did, and suddenly a portion of the scene leaped
out and took form. It was, indeed, as she had at first
conjectured: an incredibly detailed model of a factory
floor or some kind of machine shop . . . except that
this wasn't a model. Michelle didn't know too much
about machines, but she recognized the general form
of a lathe from ones she had seen in pictures and
museums; and a pillar drill would be difficult to
mistake. There were handles and clamps, tool holders
riding on screws. Everything was there in impossibly
realized miniature. . . .

And then she spotted the two figures hunched over
one of the machines, both silver and black like the one
she had seen in Heber's office. She blinked disbelievingly.
Even with Ohira having given her some idea what to
expect, it was still hard to swallow. "Oh my God!" she
whispered.

"Ahah, yes, I think you've got it," Heber said. He
raised his voice a fraction. "We have two visitors here,
Dean. Ohira knows us already, but it's Michelle's first
time. Can you show us which one you are?"

One of the micromecs centered in the magnifier stood
back and waved an arm. It lifted its head to look up.
"Hey, Grandma, what a big eye you've got!" one of
the men in the chairs said. Then the mec turned away
again and resumed what it had been doing.

"These are experimental machining setups," Heber
said, waving at the boxes on the bench top. "We're
making a production facility next door. Our factory is
a room at the back of the corporate offices—a lot better
than needing acres of real estate and having to handle
materials by the ton, eh?"

Michelle shook her head, awed. Ohira, who had been
watching phlegmatically, nodded his head at the figures

in the chairs. "You see, it's the way I told you. No ordinary VR helmets here. This connects straight into your head."

"DNC: Direct Neural Coupling," Heber said to Michelle. "That's what makes Neurodyne different."

She nodded. "I have read a little about it."

"Would you like to try it?" Heber invited.

Michelle moved her gaze to the empty chairs but looked apprehensive. "I'm not sure. I wouldn't want to get one of your little guys shredded or caught up in a wringer."

Heber laughed. "You're right. But I didn't mean right here. We have a nursery for getting people started." Without waiting for a reply, he addressed the man in the chair again. "We're moving on, Dean. I'll probably not be back today. We'll talk tomorrow."

"See you, Eric," Dean acknowledged. They left him talking arcanely again with his companion.

"It needs practice," Heber explained as they made their way between benches and cubicles to another part of the lab area. "The physics is strange at reduced size. Your weight gets smaller at a much faster rate than you do. Gravity becomes insignificant. Surface forces have more to do with how things move—or won't, as the case may be."

They came to a partitioned space where a man and a woman were in two more similar chairs. Michelle guessed them both to be in their late twenties. Another chair stood empty. The man was frowning, seemingly concentrating on something. The woman, who had yellow curls and was a little on the chubby side, laughed delightedly. Another man, dark haired, bearded, wearing a plain navy shirt and jeans, stood by the equipment behind them, surrounded by screens, checking readouts and adjusting settings on the chair panels. He looked up as Heber and the others approached.

"This is Doug Corfe, our chief technician," Heber said. "Doug—Michelle Lang, from the firm that takes care of Ohira's business legalities and other things that I don't understand. Doug's an associate of mine from the old days."

Michelle extended a hand, and Corfe shook it. He had clear dark eyes and a lean, sallow face that didn't immediately smile too much. Corfe nodded at Ohira, who grunted an acknowledgement. "Eric's here with a couple of visitors," Corfe informed the two people in the chairs.

Heber indicated a large table. On it was a system of wooden terraces at various levels, connected by ramps and steps. Michelle thought it looked like a model of an ancient pyramid construction site. Tiny mechanical assemblies and other objects that Michelle had difficulty making out were scattered about on it. There were more magnifiers on pivot arms along the table's edge. Curious, she moved one of them to look through it at a white, squarish shape standing atop several broad steps. "I don't believe this," she muttered.

"Why not? What's the best way of learning how to work with objects?" Heber said. "Build things!"

It was the shell of a miniature frame house, partly constructed. There were stacks of sheet and strip, piles of white "bricks" that must have been smaller than salt grains, even ladders and working platforms. Michelle picked out more mecs, standing motionless . . . and then, up on one of the raised platforms, one that was doing something. It seemed to be trying to fit a sliver of some material several times its own length into the unfinished structure overhead. From behind Michelle came the voice of the girl who had been laughing.

"This is weird. I didn't think I'd be able to pick it up, it looked too huge. But it's like nothing. You keep overcompensating—anticipating forces that you think ought to be there, but aren't."

Heber positioned another lens to watch. "You think it's easy to understand when someone tells you, but it's a different thing when you actually experience it."

"So I'm finding out." No sooner had the woman spoken when something happened suddenly, causing the mec that Michelle was watching to shoot off the platform and go skidding across the floor. *"Eeek!"* the woman in the chair screamed.

"But materials still retain their springiness, so you have to be careful," Heber commented, smiling.

The mec went through a few contortions and managed to right itself. "At least you don't break anything," the woman muttered.

"That's one of the benefits of losing most of your weight, Bel," Corfe said to her.

Bel sighed from her chair. "If only it were that easy."

Heber spoke to the man in the other chair. "John, how are you doing? Should we be able to see you somewhere?"

"Okay, I think."

"John's in the pipe maze." Corfe pointed to another part of the layout, at what looked like a patch of fuzz made up of hairs. On repositioning the magnifier, Michelle saw that it was a tangle of microscopic plumbing. There was another mec there, but with no movement discernible. "It's an assembly exercise," Corfe said. "A good way to teach motor skills."

"The monitor shows you what John's seeing," Heber said. Michelle looked up and followed his gaze to a screen that was showing something. It was a view of two multi-clawed hands, one maneuvering a part into place and then holding it while the other turned something against the joint. Michelle shook her head and looked away. Somehow, just trying to imagine the scale of what was going on down there was painful. Another screen showed arms hauling their way up a ladder. Presumably that was what Bel was seeing as she climbed back to her platform.

Heber looked back at Michelle. "Well, your turn. Want to have a try?"

"Sure, see what you can," Ohira said. "It'll prepare you better for what we've got later."

Of course Michelle wanted to try it. "You don't think you're going to get me out of here until I do, do you?" she told them.

Heber nodded. "Can you set us up, Doug?" he said to Corfe. "Is the other coupler ready?" Corfe nodded over his shoulder. Heber looked at Michelle and pointed to the unoccupied chair. She went over to it and sat down. Her first impulse was to make some joke about being electrocuted but she desisted, figuring they probably heard it from everyone. Corfe finished what he was doing and brought another collar over from a rack by the wall. It was hinged at the front, opening into two halves like the ends of tongs.

"It's cold!" Michelle exclaimed as she felt the lines of metal pickups closing against the back of her neck. Ohira sat down on a regular chair, patted his jacket pockets mechanically for his cigarettes, then thought better of it.

"The collar does two things," Heber explained while Corfe made adjustments. "First, it intercepts the motor signals going down your spinal cord. So instead of driving your muscles, they go out to the mec that you're linked to. Second, it injects feedback from the mec in the opposite direction, which your brain interprets as coming from your own body. It's a bit crude at present, but enough to give some feel for reaction forces, pressures in major joints, and things like that. The main problem is getting a sense of balance. There isn't enough mass to make an inertial system like the ones in our ears. You'll feel as if you're drunk until you adapt to it. After a while you learn to use vision to compensate."

"Comfortable, Michelle?" Corfe checked. She nodded as much as she was able. He turned away to get a headpiece for her.

"The feedback system also injects a signal to inhibit the voluntary motor system—a kind of electronic spinal block," Heber said. "Your brain does the same thing when you dream. So when you feel yourself moving it's really the mec, not you."

Corfe positioned the headpiece and made connections. Suddenly the scene inside the lab vanished and was replaced by a test pattern, something like a screen saver. "Does that look okay?" Corfe's voice asked.

Okay? It was outstanding—in a different league from any VR presentation that Michelle had ever experienced. There was no peripheral distortion, and the depth perception was perfect. The resolution of detail increased unerringly wherever she shifted her focus. She was *in* a world of moving colors and shapes. It was totally real. She tried turning her head; the pattern flowed sideways, then reversed when she looked back the other way. It worked the same vertically. The illusion was total. "It's uncanny," she said. "Are you telling me my head isn't really moving?"

Heber's voice answered. "You saw the others. The signals from your brain drive the display instead of your neck. Ditto for eye movement. No need for any optical tracking. . . . Okay, Doug, connect her through."

And Michelle found herself standing on what looked like a rectangular plain about the size of a football field, lit by a blaze of white light from above and seemingly standing in the sky like a mesa in a Western movie. Chasms separated it from other, similar, square-built massifs, giving the scene the appearance of a strange Grand Canyonscape composed from straight lines and right angles. On the top of the block opposite stood the partly-built shell house that she had looked down at through the lens.

"Now, maybe, you're starting to understand better what I've been talking about," Ohira's voice said from somewhere.

Michelle turned her head and saw a wall with wide steps leading to a higher level. Assorted objects lay scattered on the terraces: wheels, blocks, and other geometric forms; sets of bars and ladders resembling gymnastics equipment; pieces of mechanical assemblies. A larger form caught her eye at the edge of her vision. She began turning, felt instantly light-headed, and completed the movement in a slow, wary shuffle. It was strange. She knew that she was sitting still, yet she could feel her feet moving. She *was* moving . . . and found herself staring at a mechanical humanoid standing just several yards away.

At least, it seemed just yards away. It had no recognizable face or features—just a mushroomlike, multi-faceted turret studded with lens openings and sensor attachments, and a thicket of antennas above. It looked like a walking tool rack with accessories and appendages girdling its hips, and limbs more intricate than had been evident on the model she'd examined earlier. The mec remained motionless. It wasn't linked to anybody. But the surprise of seeing it so close had left her feeling jittery. She wasn't really *here*, she had to remind herself.

She looked down, and although she was prepared, she couldn't suppress a reaction of mild revulsion at the sight of the lobsterlike form that she had been turned into.

"A bit of a shock the first time, isn't it," Heber's voice

remarked. Of course—they could follow what she was seeing, on the monitor.

Well, this wasn't getting her very far, she decided. She concentrated her attention, took a step . . . and reeled uncontrollably, promptly falling over. Somebody laughed.

A huge shadow blocked out the light, and a pair of long silver jaws came down from the sky to close around her and set her back on her feet. "It takes a little while to get the knack," Heber's voice said. "We do have multi-legged models that stay upright automatically, but I thought you'd prefer something a little more familiar. Let's start again. This time we'll guide you through it. It's not as hard as you're probably thinking right now."

CHAPTER THREE

Eric called Kevin from the Training Lab to say that Ms. Lang was ready to leave, and they would all meet in a few minutes in the lobby.

Her face was softer, tapering to a chin that was more rounded than it had appeared from a distance through the window. And her mouth was wider and more full-lipped closer up, with an upturn at the corners that gave her a homier look. Her eyes, too, were bright and alert, silently interrogating, alive to every response. Face to face, she was altogether less aloof and daunting.

"This is Kevin," Eric said, introducing them. "And his partner in crime. . . . I guess you and Taki know each other?"

"Oh yes, Michelle and Taki are old friends already," Ohira put in, nodding.

"Kevin and Taki are kind of unofficial staff here at Neurodyne," Eric said. "That's another advantage of having your own company." He gestured. "Kevin, this is Michelle Lang, who takes care of Ohira's legal matters businesswise."

She smiled and took in his lean, wiry frame, tall for his age, clad in a pale blue shirt and jeans; narrow

21

features with sharp, mobile eyes; mop of fair hair, tousled and shaggy. "Hello, Kevin. I'm pleased to meet you at last."

"Hi," Kevin responded. He would have liked to elaborate further with something witty and erudite the way people in movies always seemed to be able to, but nothing of that description suggested itself. But then, people in movies had scriptwriters to spend hours thinking it up for them.

"That was quite an experience," Michelle said. "Now that I've had my reality expanded, I don't think the world will ever seem quite the same again. I suppose you must be used to it."

"It takes practice," Kevin said.

"You did just great once you got the hang of it," Eric said. "I think she's going to be a natural," he told Kevin.

Now that Michelle had seen the mecs, the plan was for them to drive to the house so that Kevin and Taki could introduce her to their "Bug Park," which was what Ohira had really brought her to see. Eric looked around the group. There were three adults and the two boys. "Okay, I guess I'll take Kevin back." He looked at Ohira and Michelle. "Whose car did you two come in?"

"Mine," Michelle said.

Eric nodded. "Taki, do you want to ride with us or go with your uncle and Michelle?"

"Oh, I'll stick with Kev."

"Of course he does," Ohira said. "What boy wants to listen to us talking about money and business?"

They began moving. "Do I need directions?" Michelle asked Heber as he held open one of the plate glass doors leading out of the building.

"Just follow me. Mind you don't fall down a hole in our local lunarscape outside the gate."

The road along from Neurodyne was being torn up

by backhoes cutting trenches; bulldozers were leveling the adjacent lot.

"We saw it on the way in," Michelle said. "What's happening?"

"Oh, they're expanding the office park—they call it a 'corporate campus.' We were one of the first companies here. It's to be expected, I suppose."

"What's the place next door going to be?" Kevin asked.

"Some kind of management training facility, I think." Eric waved a hand vaguely as they crossed the parking area. "That's another of the advantages of microengineering for you. With us, a factory floor is the size of a regular office. Nobody who's into any conventional kind of manufacturing would get a lease anywhere near this place."

"I still can't get over how nice it is to have my own legs back again," Michelle said.

With Eric's maroon Jaguar leading, they followed Interstate 5 west for a little over fifteen miles, exiting north when they had passed Olympia. The road became single track, and soon they were descending across thickly wooded slopes toward water, with occasional homes tucked among firs and pines. Kevin could see Michelle's white Buick in the passenger-side wing mirror, following them about a hundred yards back.

Cars were another subject of extreme significance for him right now. He was at the age where his visions of the unbounded freedoms that would come with a driver's license had grown to be matched only by the unendurability of having to wait another year to get one. Most unfair was the thought that he could probably handle a car as well as most adults that he knew—at least, he would if he could only get traffic experience.

Eric had been taking him out to unused lots and other deserted places since Kevin was ten. It was part of the way in which Eric had tried to compensate and keep life as full as possible after Kevin's mother died. The way he allowed Kevin and Taki to come into Neurodyne and use the equipment there was another instance. All the same, Kevin was conscious of an increasing distance between them since the times when they had built model airplanes together and gone out to the flats to fly them, or set up a telescope out on the deck at the house on a frosty night to marvel at Saturn's rings or the color bands of Jupiter. He told himself that with Eric running his own company now, and everything else that was going on, that was only to be expected. And Kevin himself was getting older. Perhaps he was being allowed to learn that the world was not his alone; that others lived in it too and needed to do things for their own reasons. If so, it seemed a good thing to be made aware of.

"Did you two get that driver routine sorted out— the one that was hanging up?" Eric asked as he drove.

"Yes, finally," Taki answered from the back. "There were a couple of glitches."

Kevin added, "We cleaned it up so it'll run faster, too. Maybe we can check it out later, after Michelle leaves."

"What's all this about *we* cleaned it up so that it would run faster?" Taki challenged. "*I* was the one who spotted it. You were too busy watching Michelle get out of the car."

"Ah, the truth tumbles out," Eric murmured, grinning.

"I just said she was something different to be showing up with Ohira," Kevin insisted defensively. "Besides, you only shortened the loop. Who was it who saw that we could replace the whole thing with a conditional sub?"

"And then attached the wrong interrupt. . . ."

"Only because you didn't update the device table."

"It was there, penciled in."

"Well, it would have helped if you'd *said* so."

"I did, but you weren't listening. You were too busy looking out the window."

A silence fell while the car negotiated a bridge over a creek. Kevin decided that he was getting the worst of things and changed the subject. Ohira ran a corporation called Theme Worlds Inc., which operated public amusement centers, theme-parks, and similar attractions. He was always looking for new ideas. As far as Kevin could make out, his aim in bringing Michelle along was to show her what Kevin and Taki had been doing, and let her judge the potential for herself.

"Is Ohira really serious about thinking that this could have real commercial prospects?" Kevin asked his father.

Eric nodded. "Oh yes, very serious. He's been trying to sell her on the idea, and now he wants her to see for herself what it's all about. No doubt he's hoping she'll get as fired up about it as he is." Eric was not exaggerating. Ohira's performance earlier had shown him about as fired up, externally, as he ever got about anything.

Kevin turned his head to look back from the passenger seat. "Did you hear that, Taki? They're getting serious about it."

"My uncle is always serious when money's involved," Taki said.

"So does that mean we could be onto a good thing here if we play our cards right, do you think?"

"I guess . . . if he meant what he said." Shameless in recruiting allies wherever they were to be found, Ohira had indicated that as far as he was concerned, since it was the boys who had originated the concept, they should receive an appropriate share of the proceeds if the project ever became a reality.

"You two might have taken your first step to becoming millionaires," Eric told them. They reached the cluster of mailboxes mounted on a log shelf where narrow trails diverging off among the trees led to the surrounding houses, and turned along the one with the sign saying HEBER.

Michelle's first impression of the house as she got out of her car after drawing up behind the Jaguar was of comfortably contained confusion—like Heber's office. It had begun as an original two-level structure, since sprouting an aggregation of decks and extensions that seemed to have lost their way in the surrounding greenery. To the right of the house and at the rear, the ground descended toward the edge of the water that they had been approaching. Michelle estimated it to be about a half mile across to the low hills forming the opposite shore.

One door of the double garage was open, revealing a gray Dodge van. A clutter of cabinets, stripped-down electronics frames, and assorted pieces of machinery took up the rest of the space. To the side of the garage was an extension, probably some kind of workshop, with a go-kart and a partly dismantled motorcycle under a carport roof. A blue Jeep was parked in front of the garage, and a brown Ford around at the side. Heber had said that his wife, Vanessa, would be home. Michelle guessed that he had used her car that day for some reason. Although they had not yet met, the image that Michelle had formed of her went with the Jaguar, somehow; the Jeep was definitely more "Eric."

Michelle and Ohira moved forward to where Heber and the two boys were waiting. "Most people expect something vast and imposing," Heber said, tossing out an arm as they began walking to the house. "Everyone seems to think that all corporation presidents live in something like the Taj Mahal behind security walls with electric gates. I suppose we're not really what you'd call very formal."

"I'd call it casual," Michelle told him. "Don't try to change it. It suits you."

"It gets more casual round back," Kevin commented dryly.

"The tidiest places I can think of are museums," Heber said. "But not very much gets done in them. Would you or Taki really want to live in one? I can't imagine either of you surviving half a day."

"Is that a lake at the back?" Michelle asked.

Heber shook his head. "Not quite. It eventually connects to the Sound, but through a maze of inlets. You'd need to know them to find the way out."

"I think it's wonderful—the sort of change I could stand for a while."

"Oh? So where do you live?"

"The city, right in the center. But that's where the firm is. I don't think I could stand a long commute twice every day."

"Yes, I understand exactly what you mean," Heber said.

The woman who greeted them at the door was short and mousy haired, fortyish perhaps, dressed in tan slacks and a lightweight patterned sweater—nothing at all like the person Michelle had pictured. As the arrivals entered, she chided Kevin about not leaving his laundry out *again*. Kevin returned some remark that Michelle didn't catch, and ducked with a laugh when the woman tried to tweak his hair. Michelle realized then that this was a housekeeper, or equivalent. Heber introduced her as Harriet.

"Will everyone be staying for dinner?" Harriet asked Heber.

"I don't think so—it wasn't the plan." He looked at Michelle and Ohira. "But if you want to change your minds, it wouldn't be a problem."

"Thanks, but I have to be in town tonight," Michelle replied.

"A coffee would be very welcome," Ohira said.

"How about a pot of coffee, sodas or whatever for Kevin and Taki, and some cheese or snacks or something?" Heber suggested.

"I'll see what I can rustle up," Harriet said with a nod, and disappeared along a corridor leading off to one side.

The interior echoed the easy informality that Michelle had read into it outside. In addition to the regular hallway furniture of coat stand, side table, and chairs, there was a case of bookshelves that looked as if it carried overflow from other rooms, and a grandfather clock wearing a sombrero. Some kind of early scientific instrument made of polished wood and brass hung on the wall, along with a couple of old, framed sea charts and other pictures. A gray cat, curled on one of the chairs looked up and regarded the intruders balefully, otherwise refusing to be budged.

"That's Batcat," Heber said. "It usually guards the house from there. When it isn't on that chair, it manages to be on the wrong side of every door, no matter how many times you let it through. Sometimes I think it has clones."

"Liquid cat," Kevin said. "It flows under the crack and reconstitutes on the other side—but never when you're looking."

"Why Batcat?" Michelle asked.

"Oh, I can't remember," Heber said. "Harriet got it from somewhere as a kitten. Why did we call it that, Kevin?"

"It could cross a room from one side to the other without touching the floor," Kevin said.

"Oh, that's right. I believe it, too." Heber led the way through toward the rear of the house.

The story as Michelle understood it was that Kevin and Taki had long ago become expert mec "pilots," and Heber had started giving them old prototypes and obsolete models to experiment with, which he let them modify for their own purposes. From these, they had built up a collection of what they called "battlemecs"— like tiny Heinleinesque power suits or computer-game war-robots—that they used for acting out combat games, performed in miniature over real landscapes. Apparently Taki had a lab at home also, and there was an area behind Kevin's house that they reserved for their exploits "in" these bug-size machines. They called it "Bug Park."

Ohira, always an entrepreneur, had become fascinated by these games that the boys had created, and wanted to develop the concept commercially as a novel form of entertainment for the public. The Circus Worlds, Water Worlds, and all the other familiar themes had become, in his opinion, boring. The visit to Neurodyne had shown Michelle the technology. Now Ohira wanted to give her a feel of the kind of thing they could do with it.

Michelle was less sure about where Vanessa stood with regard to the prospect. It seemed she was also a scientist by background, and, like Doug Corfe, had worked with Heber at a company called Microbotics, toward Redmond on the far side of Lake Washington, east of Seattle, which also produced microscale devices but of less advanced design. She had married Heber after the death of Kevin's natural mother, Patricia, and moved with him when he left Microbotics to start Neurodyne. Her attitude mattered because Ohira's plans would require licensed use of the Direct Neural Coupling technology that made Neurodyne's mecs unique. Even if the patents were filed in Eric's name, which Michelle thought would most likely be the case, Eric didn't strike her as the kind of person who would press matters if Vanessa had some objection; and if, on the other hand, the company owned the patents, Vanessa would almost certainly be a co-owner—which would make her agreement necessary anyway. When Michelle sounded out Ohira to see if he knew the situation, he had seemed surprised. It had never crossed his mind that what a wife might think could be relevant to business affairs.

Michelle could think of no particular reason why somebody in Vanessa's position should object to such a deal. But if her experience of human nature had taught her anything, it was never to take anything for granted.

Vanessa was waiting in a large, airy arboretum of a room, riotous with potted ferns and climbing plants hanging from hooks. Two armchairs and a couch finished in a soft, dark brown velveteen faced a brick fireplace, and a baby grand stood at the far end. The far wall consisted almost entirely of glass, looking out over the rear garden and the water through a screened-in porch. Although they were still on the same level as that on which they had entered, there were stairs on the far side leading down. Evidently, the slope of the ground toward the water created another level below in the rear part of the house.

Vanessa was what Michelle would have imagined a few hours previously, before meeting Eric. But the impressions of him that had been coming together in her mind since then had been steadily altering her expectations, with the result that now she found herself surprised.

Vanessa would have looked in place on the cover of *Vogue* or at a film-festival party in Cannes; her face was made for the title role in Cleopatra movies. She was tall and poised, with hair falling to her shoulders in a black wave edged with a hint of red where it caught the daylight from behind. Her dress was sheer and dark, woven with silver and blue metallic thread, sleeveless, high-collared, and figure-hugging. Her eyes had a peculiar iridescent quality, not taking on any readily definable color but reflecting the light in a way that seemed to alter the tint as they moved, like moiré silk. They regarded Michelle with interest and curiosity, but betrayed nothing.

"I'm pleased to meet you, Ms. Lang," she said after Eric had introduced them. "I take it you've had the tour of the firm. This is our off-duty side. Sometimes it's not all that easy to tell the difference."

"Oh, I think there's a world of difference," Michelle answered. "What's work there becomes a hobby here. And this location by the water is charming. Did you know exactly what you wanted and have to search for ages, or were you just lucky?"

"Eric had made his mind up to move out of the city when we left Microbotics—I assume they've told you that story?"

"Yes."

"It was Kevin who wanted to come out this way, to be nearer to Taki—Taki has family scattered all over the Olympia area. In fact, it was through one of Hiro's friends that we learned this place was on the market."

"Hiroyuki—that's Taki's father," Eric put in. Michelle already knew of him through Ohira.

"It's nice to hear of families being that close," she said. "Especially these days, when everybody you talk to seems to be lost among strangers. How did you all get to know each other? Was it professionally—when you and Eric were with Microbotics?" It seemed likely. The Japanese were also active in microtechnology.

But Vanessa shook her head. "Through Kevin and Taki. They discovered via the Internet that they were kindred spirits, and it developed from there." Michelle glanced at them. They were looking on and waiting patiently while the adults played through their formalities. She was warming to these two, she decided. "Anyway," Vanessa went on, "I gather that Ohira has brought you here because of this idea that he wants to popularize. Were you aware of the technology before you saw it at the labs today?"

"I thought I was. I did some reading when I knew we'd be coming here. But actually experiencing direct neural connection was something else." Michelle shook her head. "It's just . . . well, it seems practically real."

"DNC, you see. It makes all the difference," Ohira said.

"Wait till you've tried the Park," Vanessa told Michelle.

"Are you joining us?" Michelle wasn't sure what made her ask. Maybe it was that Vanessa's dress wasn't appropriate to showing casual visitors the back yard.

"No, I'm afraid you'll have to excuse me," Vanessa replied. "I'm meeting some people in town this evening. In fact, I ought to be leaving now. But I'm sure you'll be suitably impressed." She looked at Eric as he stood aside to let the two boys and Ohira cross the room to the stairwell. "Is the Jaguar okay?"

"Fine. I put some gas in it at lunchtime."

"Thanks. . . . I'm not sure how long I'll be."

Eric looked puzzled. "I thought you were away for a couple of days. Isn't this the seminar on neurophysiology, or whatever it is—the one where you're giving the presentation on DNC?"

"No, that's next week."

"Oh. I was planning on going back to the labs later. Doug needs some help with the new assemblers. I don't know if we'll be through by the time you get back."

"I'll see you when I see you, then," Vanessa said.

"Yes. Have fun." Eric turned to follow the others, and for an instant Vanessa's and Michelle's eyes met. Vanessa smiled politely, and nodded. But at the same time there was a coolness about the light in those hypnotic, blue-violet eyes that didn't match the set of the lips—a distancing effect, as if they were not looking at somebody standing a few feet in front of her, but watching a face being telephotoed from a thousand miles away.

Michelle smiled back, striving to inject a warmth that she hoped would look natural. Just reflexive cautiousness, she told herself. A reaction to a strange female entering another's family turf, probably not even conscious. That's all there is to it.

Then Vanessa left. Michelle followed Eric downstairs after the others.

CHAPTER FOUR

Disagreement over the DNC interfacing had led to Eric's decision to set up on his own. After the original micromecs were pioneered at Microbotics, where he had been head of research, a split of opinion had developed over which way to go with operator interfacing to best exploit the substantial applications potential by that time recognized to exist. Most of the senior management were for staying with the body-suit and force-feedback methods that they were familiar with—proven technology from the virtual reality industry. Eric, on the other hand, was convinced that a more fruitful future lay with perfecting the partly solved direct neural approach. When the decision went against him, he left and founded his own company, Neurodyne, to pursue his ideas independently. Now, Ohira thought that DNC would be the key to opening up a whole new market that the journal reviews and applications studies had missed completely.

The space they descended to at the back of the house was a mix of workshop and laboratory, with benches, tool racks, keyboards, screens, lumps of electronics draped in tangles of colored wire—the kind of thing that Michelle had come to expect by now. The windows along the outer wall looked out over the grassy slope leading down through trees to the inlet, where a boat dock was partly visible beyond a fringe of rocky mounds and bushes hiding the shoreline.

A large table supported an artificial geography of wooden plateaus, steps, and obstacles, which Michelle was now able to recognize as the miniature world of a mec testing ground, complete with several inhabitants. Some of them were bipedal, others more insect-like. In general, these were not as tiny as the ones she had seen earlier at Neurodyne. She remembered Eric saying that the models the boys worked with were older prototypes and test batches—precursors to the state-of-the-art models in the company's laboratories.

She also identified DNC headsets and collars—distinctly lab-lashup variety in appearance, with connectors bolted to panels of hand-cut aluminum, and bundles of wires secured with duct tape. Three chairs decked with more gadgetry and wiring served as couplers. One was a regular lounge recliner with the footrest removed and foam rubber pads where most of the upholstery was supposed to be; the other two looked familiar in pattern, their associated electronics mounted on hinge-down trays at the back. Michelle moved some cables aside to read a half-hidden label attached to one of the seat backs: USE SEAT CUSHION FOR FLOTATION DEVICE. She frowned and looked at Kevin questioningly.

He shrugged and made an apologetic gesture, as if some justification were called for. "We got them from Boeing's clearance basement. Ten dollars each."

"You can't beat that," Michelle said.

Eric grinned at her and patted the headrest of one of the two airliner seats. "Okay, Michelle, you know the drill by now. Get yourself comfortable, and I'll connect you up."

"I'm going for another ride?"

"Sure. That's what you're here for."

Michelle turned and lowered herself down into the seat. It was not as restful as the specially made model that she'd tried earlier, but she had endured hours in these on enough occasions. Kevin and Taki occupied the other two, Kevin taking the modified lounge chair. They seemed to have the connections and adjustments preset, slipping into the equipment without needing assistance.

Unlike the headsets that she had seen at Neurodyne, this one included plug earphones and a stem microphone. "We added sound to the mecs that the boys use here," Eric explained. "It's not something that we need in the labs, as you saw. But for the kind of thing they do, it adds a whole new dimension."

There was another visual test pattern and checks of field motion correlating with imagined head movements. "Does everything look good?" Eric asked. His voice didn't sound close by her as before, coming through the phones this time. "Can you hear me okay?"

"Everything feels just fine. . . ."

She had expected to find herself somewhere in the miniature landscape of straight lines and flat surfaces that she had seen on the tabletop. Instead, she was in some kind of large room, dark inside but with light coming through the wall facing her, made of what looked like frosted glass. A metal band that had been clamped around her waist as a restraint sprung open on release of a catch, freeing her. There was a warm, pleasant sensation in the middle of her back, roughly where her shoulder blades would be if she'd had any. She turned to investigate. After her familiarization that afternoon, adapting to being in a mechanical body again came more easily this time.

She had been standing in one of four vertical recesses in a block of whitish, waxy-looking material that formed most of the near wall and extended to the ceiling. Several rounded golden pads projected a few inches on the inside of the recess, a little below shoulder height. Another mec, with a squat, angular body and froglike, football-shaped head carrying eyes at the extremities, was inactive in an adjacent recess, secured as she had been by a metal band around the waist. It was painted yellow with black stripes, like a tiger. The remaining two recesses were empty. Oddly curving pipes snaked through the shadows to the sides of the room, down to the corners, and overhead.

The transition had been so sudden that it took Michelle a few seconds to accommodate to her situation. The "room" had to be a box of some kind— a receptacle that mecs were stored in. The pipes were wiring, she decided. And the gold pads looked like electrical contacts.

"Can anybody hear me?" she said.

"We're reading," Eric's voice answered in the phones.

"What's this funny feeling in my back? It's not unpleasant at all. Just . . . 'funny.' "

An image appeared superposed on her visual field of a dial-type gauge colored red at the left-hand end, amber farther toward the center, and the remainder of the arc green. A white pointer sat hard to the right, in the green. The caption below read *Charge*. Along with it were several other gauges, a thermometer symbol with its column again showing green, and more figures whose meaning was not obvious. "You'll start feeling cold in your back as you run down," Eric's voice said. "Neat, eh? We wanted to link it to the hunger response, which would have been even neater—but it never worked properly. You can activate the display yourself at any time." The superposed data vanished.

"Wag your finger sharply to cue the system, then point it to select STATUS from the menu."

Michelle was unsure what he meant. She extended a finger—one of three, formed from jointed, square-section metal segments actuated by rods protruding from grooves—and waved it vaguely. "Like this?"

"No, *sharply*. As if you're ticking someone off."

She tried again, this time as if she were trying to shake something sticky off the end. A bar of boxes containing words, like the pull-down menus on a computer screen, superposed itself on her view this time, listing STATUS, KEYBOARD, MAP, and other options, along with associated icons. She pointed to highlight STATUS, and then stabbed her finger in the standard manner used with VR systems. The display that she had seen previously returned. She wagged her finger once again, and it vanished.

"You've got the idea," Eric's voice said. "The other functions can wait till later. In the meantime, why not try a walk outside?"

"Which way's out?"

"Turn around."

Michelle looked down and at her arms to get a better feel of herself, and was curious to see that she was colored red and orange. She turned back to face the frosted glass wall and saw that it was opening outward and upward on an overhead hinge, like a huge garage door. Outside was a mountainside, green in the sunshine, and beyond it an ocean . . . except that it couldn't be, of course. She thought rapidly over what she could remember seeing, trying to make sense of the situation. "Where am I?" she asked. "Somewhere down by the shore?"

"Go and find out," Eric suggested. Michelle guessed that, as before with the lab setup, he had a monitor that reproduced what she was seeing.

She walked out into the sunlight. Although the mec was several times larger than the one she had used in the lab, the power for its weight was still enormously greater than what a lifetime of everyday experiences had conditioned her to think of as normal. It gave her a feeling of moving without weighing anything at all, of limitless energy and unbounded strength. Too much so. In her exuberance she forgot that coordination required a different "feel," and pitched full-length onto the white rocky ground outside. The jolt hit her solidly in the hands and knees. Strangely, she felt herself winded and gasping—whether through some reflex association or another of Eric's ingenious neural feedback connections she was unable to tell. Fortunately, he had not taken realism so far as to stimulate pain receptors. She turned over awkwardly, making metallic rasping noises on the rock, and sat up. There were no Great Tweezers In The Sky to put her back on her feet this time—everybody was still in the house, while the mec that she was occupying was God-knew-where, possibly hundreds of yards away. With her weight effectively nothing, getting up was more a matter of balance control than effort. What made it difficult was the light-headed and mildly nauseating feeling that came with having to rely on vision, without help from the normal internal balance sense. It was like having to consciously focus on coordinating movement after having too much alcohol, which probably accounted for the giddiness. But with some experimenting she succeeded in tottering upright again, and looked around.

The white rock looked artificial—a coarse, flat expanse stretching away on either side and ending abruptly in a straight-line edge a short distance ahead of her, like an elevated beach. Behind her and overhead, the "door" was a side of what she could see now to be a gray plastic box standing as high as a house, with molded ribs like cathedral buttresses and shiny metal screw-heads the size of garbage-can lids. Behind the box, the ground rose steeply, forming what looked like the side of a mountain: broken slopes of earth and rock interrupted by sheer cliffs, with plants the size of trees, though formed in the wrong shapes and with enormous leaves resembling pointed green sails. Beside the plastic box was a sequoia trunk without branches: a huge wooden cylinder transformed by height into a foreshortened tower rising far above her. She almost lost her balance again craning her head back to follow it, and saw a red-and-yellow pennant at its top, bright against the sky.

The "beach" that she was standing on, she realized, was concrete—a block, or a piece of block, forming a ledge in front of the gray plastic box. The box had to be a kind of movable base, at the moment placed somewhere down by the water's edge, that Kevin and Taki operated their battlemecs from—it would protect the mecs from the weather and save having to traipse down from the house every time the boys wanted to use them. Since the box was facing the water, Michelle guessed it to be on the mounds at the bottom of the slope that she had seen from the window, facing away from the house. She turned back and moved to the edge of the concrete block to view the ground below.

No doubt the effect was a result of the graphics, but the colors had a radiant quality that made the scene even more surreal. She was looking across a valley full of monstrous plants with impossibly exaggerated verticality, rising on the far side into a tortured, alien landscape of quarried rock bluffs and boulder-strewn ravines. Beyond was a green coastal plain, fringed by a distant sandy shoreline. Another mast rose from the far side of the mountain opposite, flying a pennant of white and blue.

At an intellectual level, Michelle knew that the mountains were just mounds, and the shore a matter of mere yards away from her; but the knowledge was overwhelmed by the torrent of raw, irresistible sensory perceptions flooding her awareness. The chasm of crags and gorges between the mound that she was on and another to her left had the impact of flying through a Rocky Mountain vista in a small plane. Trying to take in the gigantic tangles below was like gazing over the canopy of an entire Amazon of mutants. Stems of grass sprouting from below brushed the ledge that she was standing on, tubular, scaly trunks looking like leaning palm trees. She turned slowly to look in the other direction. And that was when she saw a real tree.

It was growing near the ledge from behind some heaped rocks below that looked like a part of Yosemite—probably no more than a foot or two away, but it seemed a city block. Its girth was as great as a football stadium's, an immense, vertical panoramic assault on the senses, of rust-red ridges and jagged black canyons flowing upward in a column that defied comprehension; soaring away, shrinking, paralyzing the mind—an Interstate highway stood on end; then it exploded out into a green galaxy filling half the sky. Michelle stood, unable to thread one thought after another into a coherent string. Miles above, a bird detached itself from a branch, emitted a cry that reached her from a different universe, and disappeared beyond the periphery of her vision.

"Impressed?" Eric said in her phones. "Getting the idea now, eh?"

In a way, she was sorry that he chose that moment to speak. She had just begun to get the feel of losing herself in the experience totally. Until now, having the earphones had helped. By cutting out local sounds inside the house they suppressed her awareness of the room and the others in her vicinity, and made it easier to create the illusion of really *being* the mec. She imagined that there was probably a way to switch out the voice channel; but to ask about it just at this moment didn't seem very gracious.

"It's . . . stupefying," she replied instead. "I know you told me. But it's unlike anything I could have dreamed."

There was a whine, sounding louder suddenly, and something whizzed by erratically overhead in a blur of wings. It was too fast to leave an image but seemed alarmingly big. Michelle changed her mind about wanting to be left to absorb her reveries in solitude. Suddenly she appreciated the anchor to reality that the sound channel gave her.

Ohira's voice came in. "Do you understand better now what I've been telling you? This could be a sensation, worth millions. And it's all thanks to Taki and Mister Kevin. They're great kids, those two."

Michelle had been so enraptured that she had forgotten about the boys. "Where are Kevin and Taki?" she said. "I don't see them anywhere. I thought they were in the other couplers. Shouldn't they have mecs out here too?"

"They're on their way over," Eric answered. "They've got several mec boxes scattered around down there. Explore around while you're waiting. They'll find you."

Ah, Michelle thought to herself. So that was what the sticks and flags were for.

To her left, the concrete ledge ended at a slope of earth and rubble leading down. She began heading in that direction. The surface was not as flat as it had seemed, but pitted and lumpy, like rocks set in a swamp of frozen oatmeal. She moved carefully, placing her steps, and crossed a dark area discolored by what looked like scattered pieces of coal. Past it, she climbed gingerly over a finger of grainy, coagulated mud, and reached the slope.

It was not steep, and opened into a broader fall of convoluted sand gullies choked with pine needles the size of telephone poles, and rocky screes that slid and shifted beneath her feet. Water had sculpted the sides into crazy formations that reminded her of hydraulic mining sites she'd seen once in California.

She was still descending, when a beetle-shaped body the size of an armchair emerged from a fold in the ground a short distance away. It was encased in shiny black plates that could have been forged by a medieval armorer, and rode on thick, jointed legs feathered with barbs and ugly bristles. Michelle froze involuntarily, but before she could register anything more, the creature had scurried away and disappeared again among the boulders.

If she had thought about such things, there would have been no reason for her to be shocked or surprised. But that was the problem: She hadn't *wanted* to think about the obvious reason why Kevin and Taki called their adventure ground "Bug Park." Instead, she had pushed it to the back of her mind in the illogical way that people do inconvenient truths, as if that might somehow change them.

Still keeping motionless, she directed her gaze slowly over the nearer surroundings. Other things were moving in dark caves of hanging roots; among sinuous growths looming all about her like thickets of twisted vines; watching from spaces underneath rocks and behind logs. She became acutely conscious suddenly of round, ominous-looking burrows that hadn't been made by rabbits.

Wait; calm down; get a grip. This wasn't really "real," she reminded herself. At the same time, she found herself wondering what kind of nerve it would take to carry on if it were real. A genuine pang of doubt assailed her that she would have been up to it. Now she was beginning to grasp what Ohira had been getting at. Seeing it was the only way. No amount of talk could have rivaled this. She felt herself suck in a long breath, even though the mec had no mouth or lungs, sensed the others watching the screen but saying nothing, and resumed moving.

The slope became more open. Descending required no exertion, but loose particle-rocks dislodged under her feet caused her to slide and stumble. She tried picking up what she took to be a thorn to use as a staff. It looked impossibly heavy and unwieldy, but she remembered Bel lifting beams in the tiny house in Neurodyne's Training Lab, and sure enough found that she could handle it easily. The thorn worked well, and soon the concrete block was high above her, looking, with its red-and-yellow flag, like a fortress built into a mountain face in a scene from a science fiction movie.

She came to an unearthly forest, where purple cables writhed among scaly trunks and leaning spires of grass. Then the forest was dwarfed in turn by an overhanging shoulder of some distant, leafy Everest. The ground became spongy, with white spears and curled pink tendrils thrusting up through a mat of fuzzy gravel poured over tangled, spring-like fibers. She entered shadow as leaves of a drooping plant blotted out the sun, hanging over her like rounded, lot-size lawns upended in some titanic earthquake. Each leaf carried its own tree of trunk and branching veins on its underside. The spaces between were thick with curved spines, which in reality must have been barely visible hairs, and pitted by circular depressions surrounding openings leading to the interior. In some places the holes exuded rust-colored growths—she guessed, some kind of parasite, spreading and joining into patches like seaweed on a beach.

Ahead of her now was a slope covered in shredded logs, suggesting the remains of a blasted forest. It rose to the base of a turreted castle of shattered wood, defended by pale crenelations of fungus looking like huge, fantastic corals beneath a fairytale sea. In places, the mound of earth and logs was moving. Michelle stopped and backed away warily.

Then a tearing, crunching sound made her look up. One of the leaves up over her head was missing a saw-edged piece the size of a door. As she looked, another portion of the leaf disappeared, and suddenly the face of a caterpillar—if the obscene globular shape that was virtually all mouth, with just points for eyes could be called a face—was staring down from the front end of an undulating green mass the length of a railroad car, studded with spikes and portholes. Michelle retreated farther, instinctively restraining herself from moving too suddenly, but at the same time unable to prevent her steps from quickening. She *knew* that she was seeing through a remote sensor, and she guessed that the monster was probably harmless in any case. . . . But her capacity for reasoned control was reaching its limit. Reflexes were taking over now. Finally she allowed herself to turn, and hastened in a new direction.

It brought her onto a house-size rock with a domed top. An impassable wall of dead leaves and pine needles lay to the left, while on her other side a ramp of sand scree and pebble-boulders led down. Scuffling and clicking noises came from ahead, growing louder as she moved forward. She crossed cautiously over the steepening slope of the dome until she could see down the far side of it . . . and found herself looking at an ant freeway.

There were hundreds of them, streaming in a two-way column: pinch-waisted bodies the size of hogs, jostling and swerving, occasionally bumping to exchange pieces of substances that some carried in their mandibles. Others bore triumphantly aloft pieces of leaf and other trophies. The flowing patterns of bustle and movement were hypnotic, and even in her agitated state Michelle was unable to pull herself away. She had heard that a colony was in reality, somehow, a single, extended organism, its cells freely mobile as individuals, yet at the same time totally subordinated functional parts of the whole. She had never really understood what that meant; but here, watching them, she could feel it, chilling and unnerving, as if she were watching an entire race that had become zombies; individually mindless, yet collectively with a sinister single-mindedness of purpose evident in the endless, mechanical, marching lines.

There was movement at the edge of her field of view. A scout on the flank of the column had detected her and was coming up the ramp by the side of the dome to investigate. And it was coming *fast*.

Michelle finally lost the control that she had been striving to maintain. She didn't care about this being an illusion, didn't stop to reason or intellectualize. She couldn't have if she'd tried. The flurry of clacking, Erector-Set legs and the sight of the tapered head with its huge eyes, antennas switching like whips, crushing mandibles extended, triggered her most basic, animal survival responses. The next she knew, she was plunging back through shoots and vines, moving faster than she'd thought possible, not sure if she had shouted out her terror. All that mattered was to get away.

A whine like a diving jet fighter came from overhead. She looked up to see a winged school bus coming out of the sky, straight at her. She certainly screamed then, but it streaked over her and came down among the overhanging leaves. One of the shoots sagged to reveal the green caterpillar that she had seen before, caged among the wasp's legs. It convulsed and squirmed, causing the whole frond of leaves to shake. Michelle saw the wasp's body arch, watched the sting drive into the quivering bulk. . . .

Get away, anywhere! . . .

She was back at the wood-chip mountain, scrambling frantically, causing logs and boulders to slide. The hillside burst open as the centipede emerged—amber and brown, armed with huge claws converging like pincers, and two trunklike antennas—a monstrous, loathsome, segmented train with waves of legs undulating in place of wheels. The avalanche of wood tumbled down around Michelle, bowling her over. A gigantic head studded with eyes loomed over her, ghastly beyond her worst nightmares, its sideways-gaping mouth open to expose slavering fangs. The horror overcame her. She had no voice, no will, was incapable of reacting.

Then another whine, higher-pitched than the wasp's, came from close by; there was a quick rasping sound, and the centipede recoiled as one of its antennas flew away. Something long and deadly flashed above where Michelle was lying, and the monstrosity wheeled away, rearing to meet a different threat. Michelle rolled clear with brief impressions of a bright yellow, upright creature dodging in an amazing leap, then lunging. The centipede grappled with its claws and tried to bite, reeling back as two of its legs came off.

It was another mec! Michelle pushed herself up, staring disbelievingly. The assailant was another mec, with black and yellow stripes again, like the other one in the box back on the ledge. It was brandishing something that looked like a chain-saw ten feet long.

Again, they closed. The mec evaded the snapping claws and sprung in nimbly to hack off another leg, causing the front part of the beast to lose support and lurch over. As it did, another mec, bright red this time, raced in from the opposite side, leveling a whirring lance even longer than the saw, and drove it into the base of the centipede's head. Coordinating perfectly, the striped mec swung the saw down at the back of its neck. The head dropped, almost severed. The remaining antenna flailed violently a few times, and then the rest of the body collapsed in a wave of shuddering legs that rippled down its length like a line of toppling dominoes. Some of the legs twitched spasmodically; then it was still.

Michelle hauled herself slowly to her feet. Somehow a shaking from her own body managed to communicate itself to her mechanical one. "Guys?" She found that she could only croak. Her mouth had dried up.

"Acme Pest and Dragon Control, at your service," Kevin's voice said in her phones. The tiger-striped mec saluted with its saw. "Hi. It's Kevin. Or in this outfit, better known as Tigger. What do you think?"

Its red companion withdrew the lance, revealing a rotary cutting end that bored like a drill. "No job too small. Saving pretty damsels a specialty," Taki said. "Meet the Red Lobster."

Just at that moment Michelle had never wanted to hug two people more in her life.

Eric's voice cut in. "I think that might be enough excitement for now. Michelle's showing a cold sweat here. Can you two guys get Carroty Chop back up to the box if we decouple her?"

"Sure," Kevin said. Michelle wasn't going to argue with that. . . .

And seconds later she was back in the chair at the house. Her breathing was coming in quick, panting gasps, and she could feel her pulse hammering. But she was her own size once again. She wouldn't have believed that something so basic could feel so wonderful. A few seconds more, and the helmet and phones were lifted away. Eric was grinning at her.

"Are you okay?" he asked, unfastening the collar. She nodded mutely but didn't feel it. He shook his head wonderingly. "Well, you sure believe in going for the spectacular, I'll give you that."

"So what do you think?" Ohira asked her. "What would people pay to visit a safari park like that? A big difference from looking at stupid giraffes and zebras, yes? You think these two kids might be onto something good here?"

Michelle's recent experiences didn't appear to have aroused much in the way of concern; but she'd worked for Ohira long enough not to be too surprised. She sighed inwardly and told herself not to worry about it. It was all part of the job. She was being paid for it.

Eric passed her a can of soda. She sipped it gratefully and nodded. "Yes, I think they could all be onto something big," she said, at last finding her voice. "Really big."

CHAPTER FIVE

Kevin sat in his room with a deck of cards, practicing fan flourishes, false shuffles, and top- and bottom-palming. Two days had gone by since Michelle's introduction to Bug Park. Michelle was downstairs, having come back to the house on her own to talk about patents and licensing arrangements with Vanessa, who had the most involvement with the legal and financial side of the business—Eric was at Neurodyne, anyway. She had been there for about an hour. Kevin had a video cartridge that he'd promised to copy for her, a collection of highlights from other Bug Park exploits, and had asked Harriet to make sure that Michelle didn't leave without picking it up. It would be an excuse for him to say hi again, too.

He and Taki had agreed that Michelle had given a pretty impressive first-time performance—an unusually generous assessment to grant to an adult still in the yet-to-be-categorized category. Taki's older sister, Nakisha, had frozen in terror at the sight of a clawed scarab beetle, and refused to have anything further to do with the enterprise since. Ohira never displayed much in the way of feelings or emotion, but Kevin had noticed that he did more observing from the home base than active exploring these days. And Vanessa thought only in terms of the scientific and industrial possibilities that had spurred the technology into existence in the first place. The thought of any involvement in public entertainment evoked the kind of attitude that she might have held toward a game arcade or a VR parlor. Kevin had overheard her describe it to one of her friends as "vulgar." Kevin wasn't really that surprised. It was typical of the coolness that she seemed to display toward all of his and his father's projects.

He felt sometimes that Vanessa avoided emotional closeness deliberately, which struck him as peculiar for somebody who had taken on the challenges of becoming a replacement mother. But adulthood was full of peculiar attitudes and rituals that he didn't understand, but which he presumed—more through a primitive faith that the world he was becoming a part of was a product of people who knew what they were doing, than from any solid conviction that he could attest to—would make better sense one day.

People of his age had generally discovered what they liked to do. And then convention seemed to require that they progressively abandon those things in order to spend what should have been their most enjoyable years pursuing "success," the object of which being, as far as he could make out, to make enough money to one day retire from it to do what they had always wanted to. The circularity of it all made about as much sense to Kevin as a solar powered tanning lamp, but nobody ever wanted to talk about it when he brought the subject up.

The phone rang on the shelf above the computer—Kevin and Taki could tie up a line for a whole evening, so Eric had given him two numbers of his own. He put down the cards, reached across, and answered. "Hello?"

"Knock-knock." It was Taki's voice.

Kevin groaned. "Who's there?"

"Acne."

"Oh, tacky, Taki. Okay, I'll buy it. Acne who?"

"A k-nee is a k-nob halfway up your leg. So, watcha up to?"

"Nothing much. . . . Oh, I got that motor running for the KJ-3, so we'll be able to fly it this weekend. There was some gunk in the fuel line."

"That's great, Kev. Hmm. But my amazing psychic powers tell me that other things have been preoccupying you more recently. I see shapes of diamonds, hearts, spades, and clubs. You're practicing your cardsharping, unless I'm very much mistaken. So, am I right or am I right?"

Kevin frowned, taken by surprise. "Hey, what is this?"

"And that book on MEGA-DOS that I lent you is right there by your elbow. If you're done with it, I could use it back."

Kevin moved the phone from his ear and looked suspiciously from side to side around the room, across to the window, and over his shoulder at the door. "Taki, what's going on? What kind of stunt are you pulling here?"

The voice on the other end of the phone chuckled. "Up on your bookshelf—the bottom one. Check about a foot along from the gap where the calculator and the stapler are."

Kevin turned his head, more puzzled than ever, and looked where Taki had indicated. Even with the directions, it was several seconds before he located the mec standing in a space formed where a couple of volumes were indented between *University Physics* and *The Guinness Book of Records*: one of the older, inch-high models, metallic gray with square black eyes. It was one of several that Taki had had over at his place for a couple of months. Taki was obviously decoupled from it now, since he was using the phone. But he could have left it live and be copying its visual output to a screen.

"Okay, I see you now." Kevin was intrigued, but at the same time baffled. Taki had been talking about developing a relay device that would enable mecs to be controlled from a distance—Taki's house was six miles away, outside the range of their regular transmitters, such as the one in Kevin's basement. "Are you at home?" Kevin queried. The first, obvious possibility was that Taki might have driven over with Michelle and brought the mec with him, sneaked in without announcing himself, and had used one of the couplers downstairs to send the mec up to Kevin's room as a prank. It was the kind of pointlessly silly thing that Kevin would have expected from Taki—if he didn't think of it himself first.

"Sure, I'm at home. Where else?" From his tone of voice, Taki was clearly enjoying himself.

Kevin frowned. "You've got a relay working? Are you saying you've cracked it?"

"Right! So what do you think? It works just fine, eh? I got it up between your bed and the wall, and from there to the shelf via the window drapes. Getting it up the stairs was a drag, though. Pronged feet are a must for getting around in houses."

That still didn't explain everything. "So how did you get it over here to the house?" Kevin asked.

"In Michelle's laptop. She was here showing my dad some papers before she went over to your place. It was lying open, so I hid the mec in one of the pouches inside the lid. A bit sneaky, I guess, but I wanted to see it work for real."

"I have to agree—but it's still pretty cool. Is that where the relay is too?"

"Yes. That's what I'm calling about. Could you get it out of there before she finds it, and hang on to it until I see you next? She's probably not the kind of person who'd get mad about something like that if she did find it, but why risk it?"

"Okay, sure—if I get a chance. You said in a pouch in her laptop?"

"Inside the lid. There's a row of elastic pockets for holding diskettes and stuff. The relay is in a black plastic pack with a rubber band around it—it's a two-inch card with some chips and a couple of batteries."

"I'll see what I can do. . . ." Kevin glanced huffily at the mec still staring at him from his bookshelf. "And we need to call a truce on this business right now, Taki. I don't think I like the thought of being spied on like this anytime, anywhere in my own house. So let's draw the line right here, okay?"

"Okay. You've got it."

There was a tap on the door, and Harriet stuck her head in. "Anyhow, I have to go," Kevin said, nodding at her and speaking into the phone. "I'll do that thing for you if I can. You take care, okay?"

"Thanks, Kev. Talk to you later." Taki hung up. Kevin replaced the phone and looked at Harriet.

"It looks as if Vanessa and Michelle will be finished soon downstairs," she said. "And Beverley called from the office with some figures that your father said you wanted." Beverley was Eric's secretary at Neurodyne.

"Oh, great. They must be the scaling constants."

"I haven't the faintest idea. They're written down in the kitchen. Oh, and speaking of kitchens, a tin of black, sticky, nasty-smelling stuff has appeared by the side of the sink. You wouldn't know anything about it, by any chance?"

"Oh, yeah, right. That's mine. I'll move it."

Kevin got up to follow Harriet back down. As he

turned to close the door, he looked across at the mec again. Just for a moment, he thought he caught it starting to wave at him. . . . But then again, he could have been mistaken.

He heard Vanessa talking as he and Harriet reached the bottom of the rear stairs. "Oh, Eric's up to his eyes in something or other all the time. But there's no need to tie him up with this. I'll have Phil Garsten call you first thing tomorrow morning. He can give you all the details." She was coming through the door from the den. Michelle answered, following immediately behind her.

"I'm glad I stopped by. Things still get done quicker face-to-face in the long run. Is Kevin in? I wouldn't want to rush off without saying hello."

"He should be about somewhere. . . ." Vanessa looked around as Harriet appeared through the archway from the rear hall. "Have you seen Kevin anywhere, Harriet? Ms. Lang was just—oh, there he is. Kevin, Ms. Lang is just about to leave. She wanted to pay her regards." Harriet nodded and disappeared in the direction of the kitchen.

Michelle smiled. "Hi, Kevin."

"Hi." The wheels in Kevin's head slammed to a halt. Again, the adult knack for instantly following up with something that didn't sound dumb eluded him.

Michelle smiled. "Well, you'll be pleased to know that I seem to have survived it all without mishap— no midnight screams or trips to a psychiatrist." She was carrying a burgundy attaché case, Kevin saw. There was no sign of a laptop.

"That's pretty good, I guess," he responded. Maybe they spent hours thinking things up and then waited for the right occasion. Or was it that they'd just had more time to collect material?

"Oh yes, and while I think of it—did you run me a copy of those movie clips that you told me about? They sounded fascinating."

She remembered! Kevin nodded a head of shaggy dark hair. "Yes. It's down in the mec lab."

"Do you want to run down and fetch it?" Vanessa said.

"Sure."

"I'll come with you and pick it up," Michelle suggested. She looked at Vanessa. "Then we won't have to keep you standing here waiting. I can go out the back way and walk around to the car. Kevin will see me out."

Vanessa made no protest. "Very well. Thank you again for coming over. I think it was quite productive. Were there any other points?"

"No, I don't think so."

"Goodbye, then."

"For now, anyway."

They shook hands. "If anything further occurs to you, give me a call," Vanessa said. She stood watching with a formal smile while Michelle and Kevin crossed past the plants and the grand piano to the stairs leading down. When they had disappeared from view, she turned away and retired to another part of the house.

Michelle was wearing a pale blue, pleated skirt with white blouse and navy top. Her hair was looser this time, held by a band instead of being tied in a ponytail. Kevin pictured her as the sun-bronzed, untamed Amazon queen, riding a white horse, her hair billowing, a bow slung across her back—and, naturally, one of those loincloths that they always had in fantasy-novel cover illustrations, showing all of those incredible legs.

They came into the lab, with its wall of window facing the slope behind the house, leading down to the shore of the inlet. Kevin went over to the corner where the video equipment was and retrieved the cartridge from a drawer. Michelle stopped to look over the tabletop mec world. "So what's new with these little guys since I was here," she asked. "Anything interesting?" That was what warmed Kevin toward her: like Eric, she found microspace fascinating in its own right and was able to lose herself in the wonder of simply experiencing it. Everything didn't have to be a matter of bottom lines and market sizes.

Kevin made a face. "Not really. We talked about trying a speck of depleted uranium mounted on some kind of sprung joystick as a balance sensor, but nobody could figure out how to interface it. Flies use something like that."

"Why uranium?"

"You need all the mass you can get."

Michelle thought back to what Eric had talked about at the lab. "Oh, is this to do with that business about mass and size shrinking at different rates?" she said.

Kevin nodded. "Mass scales down with the cube of size—being a hundred times smaller makes you a million times lighter. So inertial systems don't work too well when you get really small—for example, as balance regulators."

"You mean like the ones in your ear?"

"Right. It's probably why insects have six legs. A tripod is the most naturally stable configuration you can get. So what you do is stand on one while you move the other."

Michelle put the attaché case down on the bench and picked up one of the mecs from the table. She pulled up a stool and studied the mec through one of the benchtop lenses. "Is that why you came up with those weird weapons too—jumbo chain saws and drill-tipped lances?" she asked.

Kevin didn't normally go into technicalities with outsiders, but Michelle's interest seemed genuine. "Nothing that depends on stored kinetic energy works," he replied. "Hammers, axes, spears, missiles—anything that you swing or throw—they all behave as if they were made of Styrofoam."

"So what do insects do? That's right, they concentrate on things like stabbing and cutting and crushing, don't they?"

"Right. Exactly."

"Don't they spray chemicals around too?"

"Yes . . ." Kevin made a vague gesture in the air. "But it's kind of messy. We haven't really gotten into that."

Michelle leaned back from the lens. "How did this Bug Park thing start? Ohira says it was with you and Taki playing out combat games—the kind of thing you see on computers."

"That's about how it was. Being able to stalk somebody across real terrain was just a whole lot better than things faked on screens." Kevin nodded toward the window. "Especially with the kinds of landscapes you get down there."

"But wait a minute, you can't be serious. Those weapons of yours are totally destructive." Michelle indicated the mec that she was still holding. "These might be a bit out of date, but they're still pieces of high-quality engineering. You're not telling me that you hack them to pieces playing adventure games?"

Kevin shook his head. "Oh no. The real battlemecs have got buttons that you have to get at—like vital spots. If you can hit the other guy's first it deactivates him, and he's dead." He hesitated, wondering if a lawyer might have a problem about bugs' rights or something. "The, er, other stuff . . ."

"Oh, say what you mean. Chain saws and spin-tipped lances?"

"Right. That came later, for protection—when we found that all kinds of other things were likely to come muscling in on the act too."

"But it was more fun, right?" Michelle winked, daring him to deny it. That was the moment when Kevin found that he felt at ease with her completely for the first time. This adult was okay, he decided. He grinned and nodded back at her in a way that said *of course* it was more fun.

"Why the fancy colors?" she asked.

"Birds. They think you're something yucky and leave you alone."

Michelle sighed and nodded. "Obvious, really. Why is the obvious always the last thing we think of?"

"Probably because once you realize it's obvious, you quit looking. Who's going to keep on looking for an answer after they've found one that works?"

"Hm. I guess that's obvious too, really."

"Anyhow, we lost a few that way—before we started painting them."

"You don't mean the birds ate them?"

"Oh, I wouldn't think so. Probably they just got dropped in the water or around the neighborhood."

"I suppose if we went public, the place could be enclosed with nets or something," Michelle said distantly. In her mind she seemed to be involved in the scheme already. It was refreshing.

"It could actually happen, then?" Kevin said. "Dad says that Ohira is really serious."

Michelle put the mec back down on the table. "You bet he is. He could end up scraping quite a lot of investment money together to back it, too. He's got people back home interested. You know, it could turn out to be an even bigger hit in Japan. They seem to go in for things like that—you know, novelty."

"You think so? Taki and I have been having other thoughts as well."

"Such as . . . ?" Michelle looked interested.

"We've got a mec over at his place that we're trying

to get to fly. The wings are flexible and vibrate like an insect's. The trick is getting the twist right. When people tell you that old story about bees not being able to fly, what they don't understand is that those equations were for fixed-wing. Insects fly more like helicopters." Kevin waved a hand to indicate boundless possibilities as the tide of enthusiasm swept him on. "Suppose you could actually *be* a submarine in an aquatic environment, able to *see* parameciums and amoebas?"

"Great educational potential," Michelle said, getting into the swing. "A lot more than just entertainment, maybe—the way Ohira thinks."

Kevin cast an arm around. "How many people really know what else goes on in the houses they live in? It's a whole new world at mec scale, just like outside. It's unbelievable. You really don't want to know what's down there in your carpet. And when you get a chance, take a close-up look at the solid walls that you think keep everything out. Every school should have something like this. They tell you all about how corporations are structured inside, but how many kids get a chance to climb around inside a clock?"

Michelle stared at him, intrigued. "You know, Ohira has never talked about anything like that. I don't think possibilities like that have occurred to him. I'll bring it up next time I see him." She glanced at her watch. "Speaking of which, Kevin, I hate to break this up because it's absolutely fascinating, but I have to get moving. I would like to see more of Bug Park, though. When can we set up a date?"

"Well . . . any time that suits you, I guess. I don't have too many commitments."

Michelle stood up from the stool. "I'll look forward to that."

Kevin still had no idea where to find the relay that he had promised to retrieve for Taki. He thought frantically. "What kind of computer is that?" he blurted suddenly, nodding at the burgundy attaché case on the bench.

"That?" Michelle looked surprised. "It isn't a computer."

Kevin knew it wasn't, but the laptop had to be somewhere for Taki to have remote-guided the mec. He waited in the hope that Michelle might pick up on the subject, but she just came around the table and picked up the video cartridge that she had come downstairs for. "Oh, I thought it was a laptop," he said lamely. She didn't respond. He went on desperately, "Do you use one?"

"All the time for reference material and e-mail. You can't get away from them. It's out in the car." She began moving to the door.

Great, Kevin thought as he followed her. What was he supposed to do now? He drew alongside her as they crossed the yard. "What kind is it?" he asked—anything to keep on the subject.

"I'm not sure. Bell, I think."

"Oh. What model?"

"Seven hundred something. Does that sound right?"

Kevin tried to look astonished. "That's really amazing! Do you know, I was having an argument about those with somebody just the other day." He hoped it didn't sound as stupid as he felt. "Does the internal phone come out on an ansi or International PIN configuration connector?"

"Kevin, would you believe?—I have absolutely no idea. Neither do I care."

"Could I have a look? It would only take a second."

"Well, sure . . . I guess." Michelle gave him a strange look. "If it's really that important."

They came around to the front of the house, where the white Buick was parked in the driveway. Kevin stopped and pulled off his sweater. "Wow, it's hot all of a sudden. Don't you think it's hot? Or maybe it's just me."

Michelle unlocked the doors. "It's down by the seat there," she said, indicating with a nod.

"Oh, right." Kevin opened the passenger door and lifted out the laptop while Michelle climbed in the far side of the car. "Now let's see, what have we got?" He unzipped the case, slid the computer partway out, opened the lid for no reason that he could have explained if she'd asked, and made a show of flipping open covers and peering at the connector arrays inside. All the time, his fingers were searching feverishly through the pouches inside the case. He found the plastic pack containing the relay card and slipped it into the folds of the sweater draped in his other hand. "Okay, right, that's it." He reclosed the case and put it back on the floor in front of the seat. Michelle leaned across to peer out at him.

"Did you find what you wanted?" she inquired in the kind of tone she might have used to ask if he were feeling well.

"Yes, thanks. . . . It's what I thought." He closed the passenger door, and stooped to wave as the car pulled away, sending Michelle an inane grin before he could stop himself. *Taki, you'll pay for this,* he vowed savagely. He waited until the Buick had disappeared from the driveway, then turned and trudged back to the house.

CHAPTER SIX

Doug Corfe's experiences had left him with a generally pragmatic approach to life.

His background before working for Eric Heber at Microbotics had been Navy. After enlisting and going through the Naval Training Center at Great Lakes, Illinois, he had been selected for electronics school, graduated in the top five percentile, and spent two years as an electronics technician in attack submarines. That qualified him for the Navy's scientific education program, in which he did well enough to be sent to Cal Tech, where he got his electrical and electronics degree. He then received a commission as ensign, applied for flight training, and was sent to the Naval Air Station at Pensacola, Florida. After a year's duty as a Navy Flight Officer based at San Diego, he transferred to carriers and left the service four years later having made full lieutenant.

His experiences said there was no such thing as a dysfunctional piece of equipment that couldn't be fixed, and few problems that would admit to no solution. It was just a question of looking hard enough. In dealings with people, he valued directness and simplicity. While there were exceptions, his inclination was to mistrust those who seemed unable or unwilling to put plainly what they had to say. Too often he had found obfuscation a sign that somebody just didn't know what they were talking about, or wasn't being honest about something.

It was not surprising, therefore, that he had taken well to working with Eric, who, heedless of the scientists vying for status in the fast-growing environment that Microbotics offered at the time, had shown no interest in campaigning for self-glorification but saved his energies for the work at hand instead. So when the schism developed over whether to go with conventional or DNC interfacing, it had been almost predictable that Eric would be the one to defy what eventually emerged as the consensus, and perfectly natural that Corfe would move with him when he left.

Things had been different with Vanessa, who seemed completely unprepared for the development, and Corfe could remember some acrimonious exchanges between her and Eric when Eric announced his intention to head off on his own. But they were married by then; and Eric could be astonishingly stubborn once he had made his mind up. Here Neurodyne was today, maybe a fledgling yet as corporations went, but after three years its feathers had sprouted. It was about to fly high. . . .

Provided, that was, that nothing happened to prevent the company from capitalizing on the unique technology that it now owned.

After all, DNC was a completely new way of connecting between things going on in people's heads and events in the world outside. It hooked straight into the brain, bypassing the normal buffering functions of the senses. Some people found that a pretty scary thought. While others, apparently, made it their business to ensure that as many people as possible stayed scared.

Corfe had suspected in the early days that hostile interests were at work, playing upon such fears to undermine confidence in the new company. He had tried alerting Eric, but Eric had been too immersed in his work and was too innately trusting to give serious consideration to the thought. After twelve years in the Navy, Corfe, having made his point, didn't argue with the boss.

Although the initial fuss did eventually die down, it had never really gone away. Every now and again some journalist would dig up one of the earlier articles and gnaw on it again like an old bone, or a scientific editorial might make a passing reference when commenting on a newly alleged hazard that had absolutely nothing in common. It was as if somebody, somewhere had been keeping things at a simmer, waiting for . . . what? Now the latest signs were that it was all about to build up again, just when the news was starting to go around that Neurodyne was poised to clean up a market reckoned to be worth billions. Just coincidence? Corfe didn't know. And the same restraints that had checked him before made him reluctant to go back to Eric, harping the same tune all over again. Besides, this kind of thing really wasn't in his line of expertise.

But a new person had recently appeared on the scene who might have better ideas on how to handle this kind of situation. It was, after all, a legal matter at the bottom of it all, wasn't it? He pondered for a few days on how to go about broaching the subject. Finally he called Kevin's number.

Corfe's only regret in marrying the Navy was that the eventual divorce had left him without any children of his own. But at thirty-five he still had time to put that right. In the meantime, he was getting some good practice, having become something of a second father to Kevin when Patricia died. It would have been as well in any case; teenagers with minds as active as Kevin's needed two fathers.

"Hey, Kev, it's Doug. How's things?"

"Oh, hi, Doug. Fine. What's up?"

"Listen, do you have any plans for Friday?"

"I don't think so. Let me check with Taki. Do we—" A blur of voices followed as Kevin talked away from the phone. Then, "No, it looks okay. Taki's got something going on in Seattle, anyhow."

"Is he at the house?"

"No, I'm at his place. The call was rerouted. So, Doug, what did you have in mind for Friday?"

"Mack called. He's got a used outboard that sounds right for the boat—twenty horsepower for under two hundred dollars. How would you like to give me a hand mounting it?"

"Sure. Sounds great."

"Okay, I'll pick it up and be over at the house at, say, five-thirty. We'll make the cutout and line it with fiberglass, and I'll come back in the morning when it's all dry to mount the motor. Betcha we'll have it out on the water by lunch."

"In that case I'll plan on a late lunch. Okay, Doug. See you Friday at around five thirty."

It was an old fourteen-foot hull that Eric had picked up from a yard in Tacoma as an intended renovation project to get into with the boys, and had put off repeatedly as other demands rolled inward in their relentless tide. Kevin and Taki had scraped the bottom, stripped off what was left of the paint, and recoated it to at least keep it together until some new initiative should make itself known from the adult world. Since then, it had remained upturned by the end of the dock behind the house, providing shade and shelter for a menagerie of things that rustled and scurried on the ground below, and a grandstand from which to view the world for contemplative gulls above.

Corfe stood over the stern, measuring and marking the cutout to be made in the transom. Kevin, in jeans and a tracksuit top, sat on a crate, sorting out the items they would need from the toolbox.

"We'll need that rasp with the wooden handle too," Corfe said, glancing across.

"Got it." Kevin turned over other items in the toolbox curiously and held up a two-handled gadget with pivoted fingers and a serrated piece that looked like some kind of ratchet. "What's this thing?"

"For autos—a valve spring compressor. To take the tension off until you've got the keeper in."

"Neat." Kevin picked up the container of polyester resin that Corfe had brought and studied the instructions on the label.

"How are things with that lady lawyer who was at the labs?" Corfe asked, plugging the drill into an extension cord from a power point set in a concrete post at the end of the dock.

"Pretty good from the sound of things. She's been here at the house a couple of times. Getting to be one of the family already."

Corfe inclined his head to indicate the rocks and mounds at the bottom of the slope down from the house. A stick with a red-and-yellow pennant marked the location of one of Kevin and Taki's mec boxes. Another fluttered a few yards from it, blue and white. "Eric tells me she gave Bug Park a try too. How'd she get on?"

"She really got into it," Kevin said. "I mean right away—like somebody who really wanted to find out what it was all about. A lot different from just freaking out, like Taki's stupid sister."

Corfe handed Kevin the drill and indicated the places

he had marked for the corner holes. While Kevin was attending to those, Corfe unfolded the fiberglass cloth. "What would you say about her as a lawyer?" he asked. "Does she seem like a good person to handle this scheme that Ohira's talking about?"

Kevin shrugged. It struck him as an odd question. "I don't know, Doug. Evaluating lawyers isn't my line." Corfe watched his face for just a fraction of a second too long before looking back down at what he was doing. Kevin got the feeling that he was trying to work around to something but not quite sure how to go about it. "What are you getting at?" Kevin asked.

Corfe seemed about to reply, but then sighed and shook his head. "I don't know if it's something that I should be involving you in. . . ."

Kevin waited, decided on provocation as the best ploy, and grinned tauntingly. "Oh, I get it, Doug," he drawled. "You fancy her, right? You want me to see if I can get you fixed up. Can't say I blame you, though. . . ."

"Oh, come on. You know better than that." Corfe's voice was clipped, impatient.

"Okay, what is it, then?"

Corfe conceded with a throwing-away motion, but carried on working. "Ever since we set up the firm, there have been things going on that I don't feel comfortable about. . . ." He screwed up his face. "Hell, no. More than just not comfortable—things that I'm damned suspicious about. I've tried talking to your dad, but you know what it's like trying to get him to pay attention to anything outside what he wants to be involved in. And it isn't something that I know how to handle. I think it needs somebody like a lawyer."

"What kind of things?" Kevin asked, dropping the flippancy.

Corfe looked up. "Before Eric quit Microbotics, when they'd just developed their first line of mecs, there was a big disagreement over which way to go with future interfacing. Eric was in charge of research. It wasn't every day you get this kind of edge on the big guys like IBM, GE, and the rest—he thought they should play the higher stakes and go straight for DNC. But the top management wanted to play safe and stick with what they already had."

Kevin nodded. And so Eric had left to go his own way, set up Neurodyne, and done it himself. Kevin knew the story.

Corfe went on, "Now that Eric's got DNC working, Neurodyne looks set to cut those other guys out in a big way from an area which so far they've practically had monopoly control over." He waved toward the pennants with the shears that he was using. "Look at this thing that Ohira is talking about—a whole new market that nobody thought of before. You can bet that won't be the only one either. . . . Well, I was with Microbotics too, don't forget. I've worked with those people, and I know how some of them operate. They're not the kind who'll just sit back and let something like this happen."

Kevin paused from fitting a blade into the saw. "What do you think they'll do?"

"Try to discredit the technology—by spreading scare stories, getting it bad press to frighten investors into pulling their money out and keep new ones away. That's what I'm pretty certain they tried before."

"Before? You mean when my dad quit?"

Corfe nodded. "It happens a lot more than you probably think. It didn't work then, but that doesn't mean they won't try again. Lots of stuff was printed and circulated around at the time. It's just waiting to be resurrected."

Kevin thought for a moment. He knew that around the time that Eric left Microbotics there had been some controversy over alleged dangers of DNC, but he had been too young at the time to really follow it; and in the years since, life had been too full of other things. "You mean those stories that were going around about DNC screwing people up in the head? Way back. Is that what we're talking about?"

Corfe nodded. "That's right."

"I thought it was just one of those alarmist things that hack science writers with nothing better to do pick up. That's what Dad says."

"I know he does. That's what he's always thought. I wanted him to get the thing out in the open and fight it, but he said it would die a natural death faster if we just left it alone. I think he was wrong. It never really went away, and I don't think it will until it's killed—dead in the water."

"What actually happened?" Kevin asked.

Corfe made the first cut in the transom, then switched the saw off to speak. "Right after Eric set up Neurodyne, stories started going around saying that the reason why Microbotics had decided against DNC wasn't that management had chickened out, but on account of unexpected side effects. But the stories weren't true. I was there, and I *knew* that the things they talked about hadn't figured in the debate at the time. They were concocted afterward."

"What kind of things . . . for instance?"

"Okay, I'll give you an example. One report that got a lot of press was about a couple of technicians who were supposed to have developed neural disorders through being involved in the early work at Microbotics. But I happened to know that one of those cases had always suffered from that condition. It ran in her family. The symptoms had been there before any work on

DNC was ever started . . . but the reports didn't tell you that. And the other guy had a drug history. He'd kicked the habit by then, but he still had flashbacks. As far as I'm concerned, anything that ignores facts as basic as those is no different from plain lying."

Corfe completed cutting out the piece and lifted it clear. Kevin picked up the container of resin and peered at the directions while he reflected on what Corfe had said. "Shall I pour some of this out?"

"About a pint. But don't add any of the catalyst until I tell you."

There was a short silence. Finally, Kevin said, "Did anyone else know about this? I mean, you can't have been the only one. Didn't anyone else try to point this out?"

"Not openly. As far as the public knew, it all blew over and went away." Corfe gestured with his free hand. "After all, Neurodyne's here today. The funds didn't dry up. . . . Right at the last moment, something made them back off. And I think it had to do with Jack. Did you know much about him?"

"Jack? You mean my stepmother's ex?"

"Right: Jack Anastole."

Kevin made a so-so face. "Not a lot, really. I guess they split up before she had anything to do with my life."

"Jack was a lawyer too—in fact, he used to be the partner of Phil Garsten, who handles your family affairs now. Now Jack told Eric once—back when all this business was going on that I was telling you about— that he had proof there were people out to discredit the DNC concept. Said he could name the names, had it all documented—everything. That was enough to make even Eric sit up and take notice." Corfe finished smoothing the edges of the cutout and began lining it with the layers of fiberglass cloth that he had cut.

"And?" Kevin prompted.

"Suddenly, nothing. We thought Jack was putting a case together to expose the whole thing. But instead, he quit the partnership with Garsten, disappeared with a lot of money, and set up his own practice somewhere back east. That was when Eric decided that Jack never had anything, and that he—Eric—had better things to do than waste any more time on it."

Kevin thought through the implications. Why the sudden, apparent truce? If Jack possessed evidence solid enough to deter whoever had been behind the campaign from pursuing it further, what had dissuaded him from using it? He voiced the obvious. "You're saying that Jack was bought off?"

Corfe nodded. "I'm pretty sure of it. All the years he was there, as a potential threat, we never heard more about it. But the moment he isn't around any more to make trouble—" Corfe broke off and eyed Kevin uncertainly. "I assume you *do* know about that? . . ."

"Yes, I heard about it." Two months before, Jack Anastole had been found dead in a hotel room in Seattle after a heart attack.

Corfe nodded and went on, "The moment he's not around to make trouble any more, suddenly it looks as if the whole thing might be about to become news again. There's a piece in *Science* this month that asks if all direct neural work—in other words read ours, here at Neurodyne—ought to be put on hold until the risks have been officially checked out."

Kevin felt genuine alarm for the first time. "You mean us? Somebody could be trying to get Dad shut down?"

"Just so." Corfe nodded his head slowly and gave Kevin a somber look. "I think the people behind it now are the same ones who tried it before—because Eric has cracked DNC and he's about to run rings around them. And what we've seen so far is only on account of supposed concern over people who work at Neurodyne. Imagine how much more attention it'll get when the world finds out that Ohira wants to make it a public attraction."

CHAPTER SEVEN

"Hey, pull up, pull up! Watch that power line."

"I see it, Taki. What's the matter, don't you trust me all of a sudden? See—all perfectly under control."

"Oh God, he's going under!"

"Sometimes I think you pick up a bit of that neurosis from your sister."

"There's a duck taking off. The noise has scared it. You'll never—"

"Wheeeee! . . . Never what, Taki?"

"Jeez! I don't care what you say—balance sensors or not, I still feel sick."

"Look at this tree coming up. Wow, it's like a mountain. This is way better than Disney."

Since they were too young to fly real airplanes, they had settled for the next best thing and fitted one of Kevin's models with onboard controls to override the radio-actuated system so that they could fly it as mecs. After some initial setbacks and a bit of trial and error, the experiment seemed to be working out just fine. And they didn't need cubic miles of space to contend with all the restrictions and legalities that that would have entailed. The inlet of water at the back of the house provided as much of a world as they could have wanted.

"Take it up higher so we can switch places. It's about time I had a turn," Taki called via the intercom.

"Okay. Let's follow the road and see what's going on around the neighborhood. Boy, wait till Ohira sees this!"

Inside the house, Vanessa came into the front hall carrying a box containing a loaded slide carousel for her presentation at the neurophysiology seminar being held that weekend in Seattle, and in her other hand, a brown leather briefcase. She put the briefcase down beside the overnight suitcase, plastic bag containing books and files, and hanging bag already piled by the door, and the carousel box by the folders and several large envelopes stacked on the hall table. "Let's see," she said, checking over the items, "change of clothes for tonight, cosmetic bag, background files, journals . . . *notes!* I need my notes for the talk." She took the briefcase and went back to the den just as Harriet came down the back stairs with Vanessa's coat and purse.

"You did say the blue coat?" Harriet checked as she paused on the bottom step to let Vanessa pass.

"Yes, that's the one." Vanessa slipped it on, took the purse, and went into the den and over to the desk. Outside the doorway, Harriet's footsteps receded to the front of the house.

"Is this all? Shall I take these things out to the car?" her voice called distantly.

"Yes, please," Vanessa called back as she sorted through papers. "The stuff other than the bags can go on the back seat. It isn't locked. Be careful with the yellow box." *Notes, references, prints of slides. Better take the papers by Christie and Rolands, too. . . .*

In the front hallway, Harriet picked up the suitcase and plastic carrier, tried taking the loose folders as well, but they didn't feel very safe. So she put everything down again and stuffed the folders into the carrier; and since there was still room to spare, she slipped the envelopes in as well. Along with them and not really noticing, she put into the carrier a folded black plastic bag, secured with a rubber band, that had also been on the hall table, and which Vanessa hadn't noticed either. That felt better. She picked up the items again, found that she could now manage the hanging bag as well, and hauled all of them out through the front door.

A harsh roaring sound, rising in pitch to a whine and then falling again, made her look up as she began crossing to where Vanessa's Jaguar was parked. One of Kevin's model planes, red with yellow wings, fin, and tail surfaces, was circling above the open area at the end of the driveway. Taki was visiting and had been busy with Kevin in the workshop all day. The plane dived to pass low overhead, making Harriet flinch as she dropped the bags by the trunk, wondering for a moment if it was out of control and about to crash, but it climbed again and banked away over the garage. She looked around as she opened the rear door of the car to put the plastic carrier and the yellow box inside as Vanessa had said, but she was unable to spot where the boys were operating the plane from. Probably they were up at one of the windows, or hidden, chuckling, in the greenery somewhere. "Young monkeys," she muttered. "Always up to some kind of mischief."

Vanessa came out of the house with the rest of her things and opened the trunk. Inside were a couple of boxes of assorted paraphernalia belonging to Kevin and Eric, but enough room for her bags. Harriet handed them to her, and she hoisted them in. If the stuff in the boxes was important they wouldn't have left them there, she decided, and closed the lid. For once, Eric didn't seem to have a particularly pressing schedule this weekend. In fact, he'd said he might show up at a barbecue that Hiroyuki was throwing for his countless relatives to show their assimilation into American culture. Vanessa was happy that she would be away. It meant she wouldn't have to make excuses.

A noise like a motor boat that had been rising and falling grew louder, and Kevin's red-and-yellow KJ-3 swooped over a tree and disappeared around the side of the house.

"It's the two rogues," Harriet said needlessly. "Don't ask me where they are, though. That thing has been buzzing around since I came out, but I still haven't been able to spot where they are. It looks as if they're having fun, though."

"Yes," Vanessa agreed distantly. She paused as she was about to climb into the car and checked mentally for any last-minute things she might have forgotten. "If Eric does go over to Hiroyuki's tomorrow he'll probably take Kevin with him, so you might as well use the day for yourself," she told Harriet.

"Thanks. There are a few things I need to catch up on."

"If the washing machine man stops by before you go, there's a check for him tacked to the board in the kitchen."

"Okay."

"And I've marked a few things in the Dillards catalog that I'd like ordered."

"Will do."

Vanessa got into the car and closed the door, then lowered the window. "Oh, and if that woman calls again about wanting me at her sorority dinner or whatever it was, could you tell her it clashes with a prior commitment? I just don't have time or very much inclination for these sewing-evening get-togethers."

"I'll take care of it. In fact, I've still got her number. I'll call her. It'll sound better that way."

"Good." Vanessa agreed with a quick nod. "I'll probably be back sometime late on Sunday, then. If anything changes I'll let you know."

"Fine. Have a good time." Harriet stood back while the Jaguar pulled away, then turned to walk back to the house.

She had never been able to make up her mind about Vanessa—never quite knew if she admired her for taking on the burdens of filling the gap in Eric's and Kevin's lives, or resented her for not bringing more warmth and involvement. But then, she thought, who was she to criticize a professional contending with expectations and responsibilities that somebody like Harriet had no personal experience of and could know next to nothing about? Maybe a person like Eric needed intellectual companionship in the home as much as some husbands needed someone to criticize TV shows with and tell politics to over breakfast—although for what her opinion was worth, Harriet didn't see much evidence of intellectual companionship to a degree that she'd call stirring, in any case. Eric was always wrapped up in the lab, and Vanessa was always wrapped up in . . . well, Vanessa.

But that was their business. Harriet's concern was more about Kevin. After her own two grew up and left home, she had missed the unique ingredient that having young people around, even with the mess, emotional penduluming, and perpetual impecuniousness kids bring to a home. So when she and Frank separated, she had answered an ad and moved in to manage the domestic scene when Kevin's mother died, before Eric moved to Olympia. Although she had never known Patricia, she pictured her, from the things Patricia had left behind and the way Eric and Kevin sometimes talked, as someone who would have gotten involved and messy when Kevin and Taki painted their boat, and been more curious about where they were flying the plane from.

In fact, something like the lady lawyer in many ways, now that Harriet came to think of it. And *she* was a busy professional with responsibilities too, wasn't she? It would brighten up the place a lot, Harriet reflected as she went back inside through the front door, if just a little bit of Michelle would somehow rub off on Vanessa.

Michelle was getting more used to the idea of a factory workshop small enough to sit on a tabletop. She stood with Eric in one of the production areas at the rear of the Neurodyne building, looking down through a magnifier into one of the glass-topped shoe boxes, where two fly-size mecs were working at a bench surrounded by tool racks and trays of parts. The technicians operating the mecs, helmeted and collared, were in coupler chairs nearby, talking intermittently to each other in the way that Michelle still found disconcerting. The object they were assembling was a scaled-down mec a tenth the size of themselves. Even through the magnifier, Michelle was unable to make out any detail. She found it almost unbearable to try and imagine the scale at which it was happening—the mental equivalent of eyestrain.

"A misconception that many people have is that making things small automatically means being very precise," Eric commented. "In fact, it works the opposite way round. Suppose that your technology sets a limit on the tolerances that you can work to—a micrometer, say, which is forty millionths of an inch. Suppose that gives a snug fit between parts for a mechanism when it's built, let's say the size of a salt grain." Michelle nodded that she followed. He went on, "Now, if you make your mechanism ten times smaller, the same tolerances would result in a relative precision that's ten times sloppier. So it's not just a question of making everything smaller. You have to achieve correspondingly higher precision as well."

"You mean, all your reference standards have to be reestablished," Michelle said.

"Exactly. You have to recreate the whole system of dimensional gauges, flatness gauges, machine lead-screws, and so on to produce a new regime of precision tooling. Your entire engineering practice has to be exported down to the reduced scale."

Michelle watched him looking down into the compartment like some cosmic lord contemplating the strange realm that he had brought into being. She could understand why Corfe had abandoned his normal taciturnity to come and talk to her. The chances of seriously awakening Eric to the possibility of a criminal conspiracy directed against him would be about as remote as the far side of the moon.

"I'm still amazed that you can have that kind of complexity on such a tiny scale at all," Michelle said. "It makes you wonder why we're as big as we are in the first place."

Eric smiled without looking up. "Erwin Schrödinger asked the same thing."

"Who's he?"

"Was. One of the pioneer quantum physicists. He concluded that it has to be that way for a world that makes sense to be possible. The illusion of causality only takes over above a scale large enough to swamp out quantum weirdness. . . . But you're right. It still doesn't explain why we're as big as we are."

"That was your field originally, wasn't it?" Michelle said. "Before you turned commercial and got into microengineering. You were more of a physicist to start with."

Eric looked up and eyed her with mock severity through his gold-rimmed spectacles. "What's this? Have you been checking up on me?"

"No. Just talking to Doug. He said you were excommunicated from the church for being a heretic, and that was why you got out of the academic scene."

"Hmm."

"What did he mean?"

Eric didn't answer immediately, but moved away from the bench to glance briefly over the status display for the two operating couplers. "Every generation of scientists eventually becomes impervious to any ideas that challenge the ones they were raised on," he replied finally. "They stop being the impartial seekers after truth that they're supposed to—if they ever were in the first place—and turn into high priests defending the entrenched dogma."

"So why didn't it happen to you?"

"I don't know. Maybe I was born between generations—too late to be a bishop in the established church; too early to start my own. So I changed to a different religion and ended up at Microbotics." Eric grinned as the irony struck him, and swept an arm to take in the surroundings. "And now here I am, doing the same thing again. Maybe it's just in my nature." Michelle would have been curious to learn more, but Eric changed the subject. "Anyhow, I don't think that was what you wanted to talk about." He turned to her and waited. Michelle shifted her eyes to indicate the two technicians in the couplers and returned a questioning look. Eric nodded and led the way around a partition to an equipment bay where the sounds of motors and extractor fans soaked up their voices.

"Back when you quit to set up on your own, there was this business about DNC having side effects," Michelle said. "I'm concerned about it."

"My word, you are being thorough with your homework," Eric commented.

"It's what I'm paid for. So what's the real story?"

Eric made a dismissive gesture. "You just said it—that was years ago now."

"Yes, but it never really went away, did it? And it could be coming back. Isn't there something in *Science* this month about a call for putting direct neural work on hold?"

"You know about that too, eh?" Eric nodded and looked impressed.

"I have to know the truth. If there are any grounds at all for suspicion about this technology, we can't risk using it in a project that would involve the general public."

Eric drew a long breath and exhaled it sharply, as if determined to put this to rest finally. "The truth is that there was never a scrap of truth in it. There were some overactive imaginations at work, coupled with sensationalized journalism. That's always a bad combination. When you peel away the hype, it all boiled down to two cases of mental disturbance that turned out to have nothing to do with DNC."

"Yes, Doug told me about those."

"Then what else do you want me to add?"

Michelle raised a conciliatory hand. "Well, no disrespect or anything, Eric, but one person's assurance isn't really enough in this kind of situation. I'd need to go through the records you have of exactly what was said at the time, and any references that pertain. Also, it would help if you could point me to other specialists in the field who could give an opinion."

"Yes, yes," Eric said, nodding several times. "Of course you can have all that. . . ." He read the expression on her face that said there was more and let his eyebrows ask the question.

"Do you really think that was all there was to it?" she said. "Or could those imaginations and those pieces of journalism have had a motive?"

"Oh, I see. You *have* been talking to Doug, haven't you."

"Just doing my job," Michelle reminded him.

"Jealousy at Microbotics. Fear of being left behind. A scheme concocted to discredit the technology. . . ."

"It wouldn't be the first time that something like that has happened," Michelle pointed out.

"Practically anything you can name has happened, but that doesn't mean every piece of tabloid gossip is right," Eric countered.

Michelle hesitated, wondering if it would be diplomatic to bring up the subject of Vanessa's previous husband just then. But Corfe had been particularly anxious to make known his suspicions regarding Jack Anastole's involvement. She could hardly get this close and shy away now. "Wasn't Jack supposed to have had documented proof?" she said finally.

"Oh, you know about him too?"

"He said he had evidence that something like that was going on—the names, everything."

Eric flashed a humorless grin. "That's what he *said*. And for a while I took him seriously. But when the time came for him to produce it, it all suddenly evaporated. And so did he—but I suppose you know all that too."

"Isn't it possible that he could have been bought off?" Michelle ventured.

Eric showed both palms and made a face. "Anything's *possible*. But any scientist would be suspicious of a proposition contrived for no other reason than to explain away a lack of evidence. So should any lawyer." He looked at her challengingly, as if to say that as far as he was concerned that wrapped it all up. Michelle bit her lip.

"Why would he make something like that up?" she persisted.

"Who knows? Perhaps he didn't actually make it up—not consciously, anyway. More likely he had his suspicions, just like Doug, got all fired up to build a case around them—and wishful thinking did the rest, for a while. But by the time Jack came to see things more soberly, he'd implicated some influential people at Microbotics and elsewhere. When he realized there was nothing in it, he accepted a peace offer and made himself scarce until the dust settled."

Michelle waited for a moment and then said neutrally, "Who's contriving explanations now?"

Eric's head jerked up sharply. He could have reacted with pique, anger, or a curt denial. Michelle tensed inwardly. But instead, his face creased into a grin of admission that she found warming. "Okay, you've got me," he conceded. "So, I take it that you buy into this conspiracy theory of Doug's. But, then, we've already agreed that lawyers have to be suspicious of everything, haven't we?"

As it applied just then, Eric's observation was even truer than he realized. As a result of the further research she had done and her subsequent reflections, suspicions had begun forming in Michelle's mind of possibilities a lot more serious than just a disinformation conspiracy—suspicions that she had so far not confided even to Corfe. She studied Eric's face, looking for a clue to whether this was the time to broach them. For clearly, Eric hadn't made the connection, any more than Corfe had.

"Very much so," she agreed. "As you say, about *everything*."

Eric caught her tone. "What is that supposed to mean?"

"It does seem . . ." Michelle reconsidered her words and began again, articulating slowly. "If there was . . .

something, to what Jack was claiming, there are people who might construe what happened to him, when it did, an extremely fortuitous coincidence. . . . Wouldn't you agree?"

Eric's mouth opened as he started to respond, then closed again. He frowned at her, as if replaying in his mind to be sure that he hadn't misheard, then screwed his face up incredulously. "You can't be saying that . . . No, this isn't you. It's Doug again, isn't it?"

"No," Michelle said. "These are my own thoughts—based on what I've heard and read, what I know of how the world can be." Eric was still struggling to take in what she was saying. She went on, "Let's just assume for the moment that Doug is right about Jack being bought off when he went east, and look at things in that light. Three years later you've got DNC working. Everyone in the industry is saying that Neurodyne is on its way to the billion-dollar league. And what happens? All of a sudden Jack's back in town. Isn't it a pretty likely bet that he was here to renegotiate the price? But what it really said was he was going to be a security risk permanently." Eric was shaking his head; but Michelle was committed to seeing it through now and continued, "And then he's found dead in a hotel room, supposedly of a heart attack—forty-two years old, normal weight, swam and played tennis, no history of coronary complications, nothing in the family. If you were in Ohira's position, wouldn't you fire me if I *weren't* suspicious?"

"Oh, I can't believe it. It's too preposterous." Eric snorted and waved the whole idea away. "This isn't Chicago a hundred years ago, for heaven's sake. Are you sure you don't watch too many movies? . . . If it didn't involve a recent tragedy, it would be a joke."

Michelle stared back at him without smiling. "I very much hope I'm wrong," she said. "But until we can be certain of that, I'd say it's something you ought to think about. Anyone capable of going to extremes like that isn't going to stop at just creating some bad publicity for a piece of technology."

The mec and the relay had been in a black plastic bag secured with a rubber band. Kevin searched behind the cushions of the couch in the living room that Taki had been sitting in earlier, then craned his neck over the top to peer down between the back and the wall. "Well, that's just great, Taki. I risk untold wrath and retribution to get it back for you. I guard it with my life for days. And now you've gone and lost it again in a couple of hours. What kind of appreciation is this for being the best friend you've ever had?"

"Well, it's your fault for distracting me with all that stuff about game strategies." Taki stepped back from the table and looked back across the room to the door. "I went there to put the book down, and later I went out through the hall and back to the kitchen. . . . It'll be in the last place we look, you wait and see. Things always are."

"Well, of *course* it'll be in the last place we look. Do you think we're gonna keep looking after we find it?"

Taki wandered through to the front hall. "You don't think it could have gotten mixed up with all that stuff that your mom and Harriet were loading into the car, do you?" he said, looking around. Vanessa had been gone a couple of hours by now.

"Harriet said she hadn't seen it," Kevin said, appearing in the doorway behind. It was her night off, and she had gone for the evening too. "Did you put it down out here?"

"I can't remember."

Batcat, the only other resident to be home just at

the moment, uncurled on its favorite chair, stretched, sat back on its haunches, and blinked at Kevin several times. Not for the first time, Kevin got the uncanny feeling that the animal was telling him he was stupid. The cat straightened up, stretched again, and then jumped down off the chair. Kevin watched as it entered the piano room through the open doorway and crossed the floor toward the stairs leading down to the rear lab.

"Taki, we're being stupid," Kevin said.

"Oh, I see. It's *I* risk wrath and anger, but *we* are being stupid. How come?"

"What's the obvious way to find out where a lost mec is?"

Taki thought, shrugged. "Put an ad in the Lost Mecs section?"

Kevin nodded in the direction the cat had disappeared in. "Go downstairs and activate it from a coupler, then look around and see where you are." Taki spread his hands. What more was there to say? He followed Kevin to the stairs, and they went down to the lab.

CHAPTER EIGHT

Kevin was enveloped in blackness. Although his attenuated sense of touch did not enable him to distinguish fine details of structure or texture, he felt himself confined and his movement restricted. It was about what he'd expected the inside of a folded black plastic bag to be like. And Taki said he'd wrapped the mec in another piece of plastic inside that.

"Any luck?" Taki's voice said in his ear.

"Well, I'm through, but mummified. Now I have to try and get out of this stuff."

There seemed to be light of some sort coming from the outside. . . .

"Is there—"

"*Shh.*"

And the muffled sound of a voice—a woman's.

"I'm not anywhere in this house, and that's for sure," Kevin said.

"How could it not be in the house? That's crazy."

"Well, either it got taken out by mom, or it got taken out by Harriet. Nobody else has been here, have they?"

"Oh, okay. . . . I guess so."

"Logic, Taki. Logic."

Bending his body forward to create space in front

of him, Kevin brought his arms together and gripped one of his claw hands with the other. He released the wrist catches, enabling the hand to come free, and clipped it into a receptacle in the mec's accessory belt. Feeling farther along, he located a blade attachment and secured it in the empty wrist socket. A couple of slow slicing motions through the inner wrappings, one vertical and one horizontal like a papal blessing from the Vatican balcony, gave him some working room. Then, cutting a layer at a time and using his claw hand to clear the way, he made an incision through the outer bag.

The light was coming from somewhere on the floor. . . . No it wasn't—he was upside down. He could hear more clearly now, but the voice that was speaking was now a man's. Kevin pushed aside the curtains of waxy blanket, thrust his head and shoulders through, and twisted until he could view the world right side up.

"There are plenty of places in Bellevue to eat," the man's voice was saying. "Or Trev could rustle up something here. Whatever you prefer."

"Oh, let's go out somewhere. I could use some air and exercise after driving." The woman's voice again. It sounded like Vanessa's.

A high, narrow canyon above opened to a yellow-brown sky. One side of the canyon was a smooth, maroon colored wall, most of it in shadow but the top part catching the light. The other side was dark and bumpy, curving toward the top like the wall of a cavern. Kevin had just recognized the maroon wall as a regular office file folder, when Taki's voice said, "I think you're in a plastic bag of folders and stuff. I saw it on the hall table." It meant that Taki had tuned in on the lab monitor.

"I thought you said you didn't leave it in the hall," Kevin accused.

"I said I didn't remember."

The man's voice came again. "Let's get the business out of the way while we're here. I don't like discussing it in public places, anyway." His voice fell to a more suggestive tone. "Besides, that way, we can get more relaxed over dinner for later."

"I've brought copies of the QA reports that I told you about. The figures for—" The voice that sounded like Vanessa's grew suddenly louder, but Kevin missed the rest as an enormous hand closed around the top of the maroon wall and lifted it away. For a moment the canyon mouth above yawned wider, bounded now by a green folder back from where the maroon one had been; then the green wall leaned and toppled, crushing down the plastic side opposite to transform the vertical canyon into a cave, and tipping over the package containing Kevin in the process. Now he was underneath the green folder, looking up toward the light over a hump formed by the bowed-over underside of the bag. He squirmed and kicked to extricate himself from the plastic, and then crawled up the hump. From the top, beyond the opening between the folder above and the sagging side of the bag below, he could see part of a room. Still keeping to a crawl on the swaying surface, he moved closer to the rim to take in more of the surroundings.

Slight though it was, his weight was sufficient to make the edge of the plastic dip suddenly, taking him by surprise and spilling him out onto a surface of matted ropes covered in tangles of wiry fibers. The lip of the bag sprang back and hung above him, high and inaccessible.

"Very clever," Taki's voice remarked. "Now how are you going to get back in?"

"Shut up. If I want your opinion, I'll give it to you."

The woman was Vanessa, standing with her back to

him and talking to someone that Kevin couldn't see. The room had a luxurious, expansive feel about it even from Kevin's diminutive perspective, with opulent furnishings and gold inlaid designs set into wood-panel walls—but just at that moment he wasn't of a mind to ponder on such details. He was out in the open below the plastic bag, which was resting on a bench seat covered in a coarse, hairlike fabric, its back buttressed by cushions, extending away like a long cliff to a padded arm. If Vanessa turned back to get something else from the bag now, she couldn't miss seeing him. He picked himself up from where he had tumbled, and scurried into a hollow between two of the cushions. Sure enough, Vanessa turned, and a huge arm came down, causing Kevin to pull back into the darkness of the hollow. She took the green folder and straightened up the bag, speaking over her shoulder to her companion at the same time.

"I don't think he's going to change his mind about it, and we can't risk being too pushy. Honestly, I've made all the suggestions that I think would be prudent."

Kevin had a glimpse of a man with yellow hair, wearing a red shirt, as Vanessa turned away again. "Then we'll have Phil go ahead and draw up a codicil. It's probably the safest way, anyhow. . . ."

"It's your mom," Taki said illuminatingly.

"No! Really? My God, it is! I'd never have guessed. How *do* you figure these things out, Taki?"

"Well, *excuse* me. Jeesh. . . ."

The thing was to get away from the seat and the bag, the whole area where people were likely to be moving. Beside the arm of the bench was a U.S. flag furled about a polished wooden staff that stood attached to the wall by a brass bracket. Beyond was what looked like the end of a wooden wall cabinet, ornamented with carvings and shell inlays. Kevin thought it might be possible to get up onto the cabinet by climbing the folds of the flag. He exchanged the blade for his other claw hand again, then set off, worming up behind the cushions to get to the top of the seat back. The fabric afforded easy holds on both sides. His biggest problem was with protuberances of the mec's body catching in the threads.

Kevin waited until Vanessa had her back to him again, blocking the man's view, and then raced along the top of the seat and leaped into a fold of the flag, kicking the prong-tipped feet into the weave and gripping blindly with the claws. The flag was made of flimsier material than the seat cover, with a harder, finer-woven thread more difficult to grasp. He steadied himself, then started climbing—or, more accurately, floundering—his way upward through a near-vertical billow of stationary surf, unable to avoid making tremors that he prayed wouldn't give him away. Taki, for once, seemed to appreciate his predicament and kept quiet. Eventually, Kevin reached the top part of the mast where the folds became tighter and easier to wedge into, and made the last few inches to the top of the cabinet by bridging across the angle between the end and the wall.

The man with Vanessa was asking about new theoretical work on neural dynamics.

"You stick to organizing the finances," Vanessa said. "That's what you're better at. Don't worry about the scientific side. Leave that to me."

"I was just curious."

"I think you might find this more interesting."

"What is it?"

"Open it and see. . . ."

At last, Kevin had reached his haven. The top surface of the cabinet stretched away before him safe and secure in shadow, high near the ceiling. Along its length were carved heads and figurines, ornamental pieces in copper and brass, decorative plates, and a couple of replica dueling pistols mounted on plaques. To Kevin they looked like an avenue of gigantic sculptures staring down over the void. He moved cautiously to the edge and settled in the darkness behind the base of one of the figurines to observe the surroundings fully at last.

He wasn't good at estimating the ages of people over about thirty but the man talking with Vanessa looked to be in the range that was usually selected for sports equipment and fast-car commercials. Certainly, he had the looks. His yellow hair was styled collar-length, covering the ears, eyes clear and candid, tanned features, fine and strong-lined. He stood loose-limbed and athletic, wearing a bright red short-sleeved shirt with white edging, and white, lightweight, casual slacks. He was scanning through the contents of the green folder and saying something about forecasts and percentages that Kevin didn't follow.

The room itself, as Kevin had registered vaguely but not had time to think more about until now, was low-ceilinged, with round-backed chairs and a bulging couch, sculptures and art works set on tables or mounted in backlit niches, and carpeting patterned in black, browns, and gold. A marble-topped bar with mirrors behind stood below a long window at the far end, and across from it, a glass-fronted cabinet exhibiting sculptures and crystal.

"What do you make of this place?" Kevin asked Taki.

"I'm not sure. A pretty nifty kind of house. . . ."

"It looks like it should have pointy arches and snake-charmer music, somehow." Then Kevin noticed that the window partly visible behind the half-closed drapes high on the wall opposite, through which he could see lights reflecting off water, was rounded at the corners.

"Wait," Taki's voice said. "What was that?—back to the right of where you're looking now."

"Where?" Kevin moved his gaze back to the right.

"Back a bit more. . . . There, on the end wall."

There were two doors in the end wall, the right-hand one closed, the other open to what appeared to be steps going down.

Mounted on the wall as a centerpiece between the doors was a carved wooden crest in the form of a composition of scrolls and ropework framing the inscription *Princess Dolores*.

"It's a boat," Taki said. "Didn't the guy say something about Bellevue? You must be up on Lake Washington somewhere."

"This is wonderful, Vanessa," the man in the red shirt was saying. "I hadn't realized it could be worth so much." He made a face, accompanied by an empty-handed gesture, and then smiled. "Will I still be able to afford you when you own all this?"

Vanessa moved close and pressed her head against his shoulder. *"We'll* own it." She looked up and murmured something close to his ear that didn't come through on the audio, and the man slid an arm around her. Kevin watched with rising discomfort. At least, it wasn't his natural mother, so he was spared having to deal with that. His strongest reaction was a feeling of indignation on behalf of Eric. Taki, discreetly, refrained from comment.

"Let's go out to the bar on the fantail," the man in the red shirt said to Vanessa. "I'll mix us a couple of drinks. Then we'll take a short drive. I think I know just the place." He slipped his arm from her waist and took her hand. They moved to the end of the cabin bearing the carved crest. The man opened the door to the right that had been closed, and showed Vanessa through.

"You could try getting the mec down," Taki suggested. "A bit of noise getting back into the bag won't matter now."

Kevin was thinking the same thing. Vanessa would find it later, of course. But she wouldn't even need to know that it had been out of the bag. It would just be a case of something belonging to the boys having inadvertently found its way into her luggage. He turned to go back the way he had come. . . .

And that was when he became aware of a freezing sensation in his back, almost painful. He had been too preoccupied with events to notice it building up.

He flipped on the SYSTEM menu and selected STATUS. The mec's charge was almost exhausted, pointer down in the red arc, which was pulsing. Almost certainly there wouldn't be enough to get back down to the seat, then have to either fight up the outside of the plastic bag or cut through into it. He deactivated, and all of a sudden was back at the house, sitting in a coupler in the downstairs lab.

"I don't think I'm going to be able to do it," he told Taki, who was perched on a stool by the bench alongside. "It hasn't got enough juice left. I think maybe we're just gonna have to write off another one."

Later, Kevin called Eric at the lab. His outrage had abated, and he had decided that adult business was something best left to adults. It wasn't as if Vanessa was related in any way that made it his problem to get involved in personally, anyway. Even if it were, he had no idea what he was supposed to do.

"Dad," he said. "Would it be okay for Taki to stay over tonight? We really got the plane working properly today, and we're right in the middle of making the mods permanent. And Mom and Harriet have both left."

"Sure," Eric said. "In fact, it would work out better. We can take Taki with us to Hiroyuki's for the barbecue tomorrow, and it will save anyone having to pick him up tonight."

Kevin nodded, giving Taki a silent thumbs-up sign. "That's what we thought too."

"Oh, and Michelle was here at the lab again today," Eric said. "Apparently Ohira forgot to invite her. I thought that was a bit unforgivable since she's hardly a stranger to the family. So I said she could come along with us too. She'll be stopping by the house at about noon."

"Great," Kevin said. He frowned to himself. Had he imagined it, or was there just a hint of a swagger in Eric's voice? A note of feeling quite pleased with himself, in fact.

"Okay, I shouldn't be very much longer. Put three steaks and some veg on the timer for about eight. Then after dinner you can show me what you did on the plane."

"Sure. Will do. We'll see you later, then." Kevin hung up. "It's okay. You can drive back over with us tomorrow." He looked back at the phone and contemplated it for a few seconds. "Good for you Dad," he muttered, then nodded approvingly.

CHAPTER NINE

It was late Friday evening in downtown Seattle. In her apartment on the Eastlake side of Lake Union, Michelle pushed herself back from the computer in the cluttered room that she used as a home office and stretched her arms back past the sides of the chair. In the dimmed lighting, the blue from the screen picked out her features, while the rest of the room reflected the subdued hues of city lights glowing on the far shore through the half-open drapes. Far to the left, the floodlit Space Needle stood as a backdrop, its flickering image mirrored on water.

New York had been a city of lights and water too, but there the water was a separate element, surrounding the city but as a thing apart, defining where a different existence began, like a dark, besieging force. Here, the water insinuated itself and mingled with the lights, was part of the city and its life.

The remains of a burrito-enchilada combination that she had called out for earlier in the evening lay in a foil tray with sauce cups, wrappings, crumpled napkins, and an empty Heineken can on the coffee table behind her chair. She'd had a dinner date with Tom tonight, but called and taken a raincheck on the pretext of an urgent case due on Monday that was going to take the whole weekend to prepare for. She didn't think he believed her, and she didn't really care that much. She just wasn't up to another evening of being subjected to a not-very-subtly-put line that a better life was waiting if only women would learn to loosen up a little more, like men; in other words, if she took the initiative and asked, he'd be agreeable. Instead, she had spent the time delving deeper into the matter that had taken up most of her afternoon.

The collation summarized on the screen was from an information search and retrieval service located in St. Louis, that she subscribed to—electronic news clipping. The volume of information generated by a modern society was simply too overwhelming to attempt tackling raw and undigested. Michelle had already read the items listed. They revealed more clearly than anything she had learned from Corfe the new upsurge of fears concerning DNC that seemed to be circulating among the technical community. In fact, she was probably already ahead of Corfe. Although it was he who had first alerted her, she didn't think he was aware of the full extent and the virulence of what was going on.

There was an article in another scientific journal dredging up all the old material from Microbotics again, plus making the totally spurious speculation that perhaps DNC was able to mimic the action of known chemical causes of neural malfunctioning—thus, by implication, linking DNC to a whole lexicon of mental disorders on the basis of no factual evidence whatever. An editorial in the same issue created horrific scenes of mass-demented children and teenagers if DNC were to be let loose in the Virtual Reality marketplace, while a suspiciously portentious letter in the *Wall Street Journal* called for a government-enforced moratorium.

The subject had surfaced on three West-Coast TV channels, the tabloids had picked it up, and a lively exchange was already taking place on the Internet. And, certainly not coincidentally, over the last couple of days Neurodyne's normally robust stock had taken a three-point dive.

She had no doubt now that it was being orchestrated. Perhaps it was the image in her mind of envious scientists in collusion with money-running-scared mobilizing the media against one man with courage and an ability that outshone all of them that offended her. She picked through her thoughts, looking for a way of telling herself that it was simply her professional sense of injustice that was outraged, no more.

But there was more, something more personal. It was a disquiet that she felt toward Kevin and Eric because of what she perceived as their vulnerability—Kevin on account of his years and his circumstances; Eric because of his unbalanced stance toward the world—technically masterful, politically a rustic—that she had felt strongly for the first time that afternoon. She visualized the two of them again in her mind, heads bent intently over one of their creations in the lab, the one virtually an early copy of the other. Just the two. Why didn't she see Vanessa there too, in her mental picture?

That was it. She felt herself getting uncomfortably close to the root, now, of what was bothering her. She got up, moved to the window, and stood staring out at the bright tower dominating the night and the neon lights dancing on water.

Because Vanessa did nothing to make herself a place there. She had accepted the part but not the character. Vanessa would probably have scoffed and said they didn't need it; that Eric had his machines, and Kevin, his bugs. But Michelle didn't see things that way. To her, such preoccupation with the immediate meant that they needed someone to watch the longer term for them even more. What else had Doug Corfe been trying to tell her?

She felt frustration at not having made any more of an impression on Eric in her first attempt that afternoon than Doug had been able to. Now that she had more information to work with, she was impatient to try again. And if she was going with Eric and Kevin to Hiroyuki's barbecue tomorrow, maybe she wouldn't have to wait until after the weekend.

But before she tackled Eric again, there was one other person she needed to talk to, who might, conceivably, know more than anything she could gather from the kind of information that she had been collecting. She came back from the window, turned on the desk lamp, and found the number that Vanessa had given her. Then she called the Hebers' family lawyer, Phillip Garsten.

"Hello."

"Is this Phillip Garsten?"

"Yes, it is."

"Hello. My name is Michelle Lang of Prettis and Lang. We're the attorneys for Theme Worlds Inc., who are interested in a possible joint arrangement with Neurodyne in Tacoma. I understand that you represent the owners of Neurodyne."

"The Hebers. That's right, I do."

"Is this a good time to call?"

"As good as any. My team in the game here tonight are about ready for retirement. What can I do for you?"

"Well, I was planning to get in touch with you next week anyway to review the situation—Vanessa Heber has given me some of the background. But I'll be seeing Eric and some of the people connected with Theme Worlds again tomorrow, and there was something I wanted to check with you first."

"Well, Joe Skerrill is Neurodyne's corporate lawyer. You sure you shouldn't be talking to him?"

"Yes, I know. But this is about something that I think involves you more directly."

"Okay. Michelle . . . what was it, again?"

"Lang."

There was a short delay, presumably while Garsten wrote the name down. "Okay, what can I do for you?"

"It's about the DNC technology that they use. I'm sure you're aware that there have been allegations concerning adverse side effects."

"That's bullshit."

"Possibly—of course we'll have to go into it all at the appropriate time. But what I wanted to ask about was a man called Jack Anastole. I believe he was a partner of yours at one time."

Garsten's voice took on a cautious note. "Yes, he was. What about him?"

"It's all right, Mr. Garsten. I am aware of the recent unfortunate incident. But it's my understanding that he claimed at one time to be in possession of documented proof that the claims concerning harmful effects of DNC had been fabricated."

It all seemed straightforward and clear-cut. Michelle had reasoned that if Anastole had worked with Garsten, there was a chance that Garsten knew or might have access to whatever Jack had known. Garsten worked for Eric and Vanessa now, and Michelle represented interests that stood to benefit equally if the claims could be disproven. They were all on the same side. There was no reason for Garsten not to share what he knew—or at least to acknowledge that he was in a position to help, even if he chose not to go into details over the phone.

But it seemed that either Garsten knew nothing, or if he did, he had reasons for not seeing things the same way.

"I'm sorry Ms. Lang, but there's not a lot I can tell you," he replied. "Jack had a lot of dealings with Microbotics that he handled himself. I don't know what he might have discovered."

Michelle frowned at the unexpected brusqueness. "Did he have any records that might still be available somewhere?"

"Not with us. He took everything when he moved east. I was as surprised as anyone when he showed up back here again."

"Did he bring anything with him, as far as you know?" A spur-of-the-moment question. It seemed a possibility if Anastole had come back on business that involved Microbotics.

"I've no idea. Whatever was in his hotel room, I guess. You'd have to talk to the Seattle Police Department about that."

Impasse. Michelle sought for a continuation, but there was nowhere to go from there. "Well . . . I guess we'll manage either way. Thanks for talking, anyhow. I'll let you get back to your game."

"Huh. Bunch of geriatrics, all of 'em. Not worth watching."

"We'll probably talk again next week."

"I look forward to that."

"Goodnight, then."

" 'Bye."

Michelle replaced the phone. Well, it had been worth the try, she told herself. And there was no harm done that she could see. No harm done; but there had been that evasiveness in Garsten's manner, and the instant apprehension at the mention of Jack Anastole's name—sensed rather than explicit in anything Garsten had said. Was Garsten involved in the conspiracy that she was now convinced existed? She stared at the screen, thinking. . . .

But there was nothing further to be done about it tonight. Lawyers needed to go on more than just hunches. She switched off the machine and her thoughts with it. Going through to the living room, she mixed herself a vodka with tonic, a splash of lime, and not too much ice, and settled down on the couch with the remote to find a good movie.

In his house in the Magnolia district on the west side of the city overlooking the Sound, Phillip Garsten sat pinching his mustache and staring at the phone for a long time. Finally, he picked it up again and called a private line, but there was no answer. He tried another number and raised Andrew Finnion, head of security for Microbotics Inc.

"Andy, it's Phil. Do you know where Martin is tonight?"

"On the yacht. He's entertaining. I don't think he'd appreciate interruptions unless the world's about to catch fire. Why, what's up?"

"I've just had an attorney for that Japanese outfit onto me, wanting to know things about Jack Anastole. It's a 'she,' and she's asking too many questions. I don't like it. I think we could have a problem. Can you get in touch with Martin and tell him I need to talk to him before Monday."

CHAPTER TEN

Hiroyuki headed a family-managed consortium of automatic vending franchises that dispensed everything from overnight kits and throwaway shirts to non-prescription pharmaceuticals and office supplies. He was perpetually rushing off to some remote part of the world to expand the empire, at which times Ohira would generally step in to watch over the domestic front and be on hand to deal with emergencies. As a result, Kevin had seen more of, and come to know better, Taki's uncle than he had his best friend's father.

Hiroyuki's house was situated roughly ten miles east of Eric's, on the other side of Olympia. A large, gaudy affair sprawling beneath a discord of green-tile roofs and gables, it boasted an impeccable expanse of billiard-table lawn with floral beds and borders at the front, and several acres to the rear that Hiroyuki had had landscaped into a private 9-hole golf course. There was a pool, and along with it a sand pit, swing set, carousel, play house, tree fort, and climbing frame for the private army of grandchildren, grand-nieces, grand-nephews, and seemingly limitless friends that appeared in swarms on sunny days. Hiroyuki liked it that way. He said that houses without laughing children around were like mausoleums, and he'd get to spend enough time in one of those soon enough, anyway.

Kevin estimated that at least a hundred people had shown up at the barbecue by early afternoon. Hiroyuki himself, attired in white cowboy hat and blue jeans to announce him an American, was searing steaks to the accompaniment of spectacular gushes of smoke and flame at the grill at one end of the pool, while his wife, Chi, and assorted other smiling relatives dispensed chicken, burgers, salads, and other fixings, including, incongruously, sushi, from a long table taped with red crepe paper. An adjacent table carried desserts and cakes, urns of coffee and hot water, icechests of fruit juices, sodas, and beers. A large tent and several awnings had been erected in case of rain, but they hadn't been needed. The younger children splashed and screamed in the pool, while teens and a few adults bobbed to music supplied courtesy of one of the cousins turned DJ, piped via loudspeakers fixed to the trees. Taki's older sister, Nakisha, was at the center of a bevy of Japanese girlfriends, all petite, all pretty, who were drawing the young males like kittens to a cage of canaries. Kevin and Taki were having to deal with a similar kind of situation in reverse.

Avril was one of the high-school cheerleaders and dated football players. She had honey-blond hair that hung halfway down her back, took a 32B bra, and that day was wearing jeans that looked as if they could have come out of an aerosol can. She had homed on Kevin with the determination of a prima donna at a critics' convention making it clear that *she* was not someone you ignored, and was making her pitch with calculated professionalism that provoked nervous glances from her father, fifty feet away, who was trying at the same time to follow the conversation of a chairwoman of a local education committee, a

Vancouver ferry captain, and an electronics designer with Boeing.

"Where'd you get the shirt?" she asked Kevin. It was a gray cord with black edging at the pocket and collar. "It looks neat. I'm tired of all these guys dressing country."

He shrugged. "Some store at some mall, I guess."

"It's like the one the guy on *Open Minds* had last week," Avril's friend, Janna, said. She was slightly shorter, with curly dark hair and big brown eyes, clad in skimpy white shorts and a tank top—an equiprobable calamity trying hard to happen.

"I don't know. I never watch it," Kevin said.

"You never watch it?" Avril looked incredulous, as if he had announced that he hadn't breathed for the last ten years. "But how can't you? Everybody watches *Open Minds.*"

"Well, that's obviously untrue, isn't it," Kevin said. " 'Everybody' would include me, and I've just said it doesn't."

"But it's got some really neat stuff," Janna insisted. "Like the one they did last week about the UFOs and aliens. Did you know we're being watched? They're up there all the time."

"Oh, really? Can't say I've noticed many lately." Kevin cocked an inquiring eyebrow at Taki. Taki shook his head. "Neither has Taki," Kevin interpreted.

"Well, of course you wouldn't," Janna said. "They don't want us to know, so they stay out of sight."

"Not doing a very good job, then, are they?" Taki commented.

"You're *supposed* to be open minded. That's what the whole thing is about. But people don't know how to be, see. That's why everything's like it is."

Taki nodded knowingly. "Oh."

Avril was studying Kevin's face. "Why don't you buy it?" she asked.

He sighed and gave an easygoing grin, at the same time ruffling his hair with his fingers. He didn't want to argue—it never achieved anything. In any case, why should it matter to him what somebody else chose to believe? It was their right, wasn't it? "Oh . . . I just figure that if we'd been discovered by anybody who's come all that way, we'd know. It'd be like some island in the Pacific or wherever when the Navy showed up on its way to somewhere in World War Two. I mean, you've got juke boxes and Coca Cola machines, guys with tractors building airstrips. You *know* you've been found. There isn't any doubt about it."

Avril's gaze flickered over his face keenly. Something seemed to tell her that she could find herself outgunned here if she pressed the point. "I don't buy it either," she declared, opting for safety, and at the same time shooting up several points in Kevin's estimation for astuteness at least. Janna seemed confused by the sudden desertion. Avril looked around for a way to change the subject and saw Eric talking with Michelle a few yards away. "Isn't that your dad over there?" she said to Kevin.

"That's right."

"I was listening to somebody talking about him," Avril went on. He owns some company around here, right?"

"A bit closer to Tacoma."

"They make these little robot guys that you control like VR, except it goes straight into your brain. You can make them walk around and do all this stuff, and you feel like you're really inside them."

"Hey, cool," Janna pronounced.

"That's close enough, I guess," Kevin agreed.

"Kinda like ESP," Janna said.

"And is that your mom too?" Avril asked Kevin.

"No, just a friend. My mom's at a seminar in Seattle this weekend."

"She's my uncle's business lawyer," Taki said.

"Who, his mom?"

"No, *her*."

"Oh, okay."

Janna was giving Kevin a quizzical look. "They have ESP and stuff like that on *Open Minds* sometimes as well. Don't you go for that either?"

Kevin started to answer; but almost at once, felt as if he was about to start lecturing, and checked himself. This was supposed to be a party, after all. . . . He stole a glance at Taki and winked. Taki returned a faint nod.

"Well, of course, ESP's different," Kevin said. "I can *show* you that's real. Has either of you got a quarter?" The two girls frowned at each other. "Or it could be anything, really."

"Oh, I dunno. Lemme see . . ." Avril unsnapped the flap of her purse and rummaged inside.

"Here." Janna produced a handful of coins from a pocket of her shorts.

"Look away," Kevin told Taki. Taki turned his back on them and surveyed the activity by the pool. Kevin faced the two girls, using his body to screen the coins displayed in Janna's hand. "Pick one," he invited Avril.

"What is this?" she asked suspiciously.

"Just point to one."

"Okay. . . ." Avril studied the mix of coins for a second. "That one." It was a quarter.

Kevin peered at it and addressed Taki's back over his shoulder. "How about this, Taki? Now, what is it?"

"It's a . . . quarter."

"Okay."

"Oh, my God!" Janna exclaimed.

"And the date on it is? . . ."

"I'm concentrating . . ." Taki's voice trailed off. They waited. "1982."

In fact, Kevin had already told him by wording the

question in the form of a magician's code that they played with. Taki turned back, beaming. Janna gaped in astonishment.

"I don't believe he did that," she stammered. "How did he know?"

Kevin shrugged and shook his head. "We don't know how he does it. Maybe it's something to do with Orientals. You know, them being more spiritual, all that stuff. . . ." He caught Avril's suspicious look. "But not only ESP. Watch this!" He walked the quarter along the backs of the fingers of one hand, first one way, then back the other. Or at least, it was *a* quarter. . . .

In fact, he had slipped Avril's quarter to Taki and was performing with another that he had quietly taken from his own pocket. While the girls followed what Kevin was doing, Taki leaned closer as if to watch, at the same time reaching surreptitiously behind Avril and dropping the coin into one of her hip pockets. Then he backed off and moved behind Kevin to stand by Janna, making it so natural and inconspicuous that neither of the girls registered that he had been near Avril at all.

Kevin tossed the coin from one hand to the other and back again, then held out both fists, closed. "Which?" he invited.

"I *knew* we were into tricks," Avril declared.

Janna tapped one of Kevin's fists lightly. He peeled back his fingers one by one, smirking all the time, and showed it to be empty. "The other one, then," Janna said.

But Kevin showed that to be empty too. Then he made a throwing motion toward Taki, opening his hand but sending nothing. Taki caught the imaginary coin and redirected it toward Avril.

She looked at them uncertainly. "What . . . ?"

"Oh, it went right through. Check your back pocket," Taki said.

Avril did, and produced a quarter. She held it up, mystified. "How'd it get in there?"

"Let me see the date on that," Janna demanded, taking it. "Oh, my God! Look. It is!"

"Say!" Avril exclaimed, wide-eyed. "I don't believe this. Know something? These two guys are really neat!"

Michelle smiled to herself and looked back at Eric. It was the first time that she had seen him off-duty and relaxed. The real Eric that she felt she was discovering had a disarming modesty about his accomplishments, didn't press his opinions, and took the world with a strong dose of humor that she sometimes needed a few seconds to recognize, all of which was delightfully at odds with the stereotypes she had absorbed of Germans. He should make time to be himself more often, she thought.

"Kevin and Taki seem to be very popular with the ladies," she remarked.

"Do them good, too. Young people should learn how to defend against predators before they're old enough to marry. Then they'll be more likely to find the right one."

Michelle decided that might be a topic best steered clear of. "What was that they just did?" she said. "Some kind of magic trick? I couldn't make it out from here."

"Probably. . . . As a matter of fact, they're not bad."

"I didn't know they were into that kind of thing as well."

"Oh, you name it, they're probably into it." Eric took a swig from a bottle that he was holding. "It ought to be taught in schools as standard. Fifth grade."

"What? Conjuring?"

Eric nodded. "It's a great way to learn that things aren't always what they seem, and to examine your assumptions about what you think is going on. What better grounding in science could there be than that?

Learning should be fun. Was there ever a kid that didn't love conjuring?"

The mention of science sent Michelle's thoughts back to their earlier conversation. "You never did tell me about your previous life as a heretic," she said, giving him a curious look.

Eric's eyes laughed through his spectacles, savoring his own unrepentance. "Why do you want to hear about that?"

"Lawyers are like scientists." She bit into a pickle and regarded him impishly. "They want to hear about everything."

"Oh . . ." He waved a hand vaguely. "I dared to question the High Church of Relativity. Science has its infallible popes too, you see. And when one of them has been canonized and made a saint, any suggestion that he might have been following a false god gets you immediate excommunication." Eric took another sip of beer, apparently weighing up how far he wanted to go into this; then he gestured with the hand holding the bottle to take in the scene around them. "Just imagine, the Earth we're standing on is hurtling around the sun at thirty kilometers per second. And the sun's moving faster than that through the galaxy. So why doesn't the wind tear the roof off the house and blow all these tents away?"

Michelle frowned, hesitating to state the obvious. Eric nodded encouragingly. "Yes?"

"Because the air . . ."

"The atmosphere is moving with us," he completed for her. "That's right. There's no catch. It's like when you're in a plane. You can talk easily to the passenger next to you in the cabin because your whole acoustic environment and its physics is moving with you. But try doing it sitting out on the wing."

"Okay. . . ." Michelle nodded that it made sense so far.

Eric shrugged in a way that seemed to say that was all she really needed to understand. "The Earth carries its electromagnetic environment along with it too, in exactly the same way." He used both hands to trace a vertical, streamlined drop shape in the air. "You can see it clearly on the field plots of data from space probes over the last fifty years. There's a huge bow shock-wave about ten Earth radii out, which the charged-particle flux from the sun streams around like water around a boat."

"You mean like a kind of . . . bubble?"

"Exactly—with us inside it, like the cabin of the plane. Well, about a century ago, before all that was known, a famous experiment was performed to measure the electromagnetic wind of the Earth moving through space. But it didn't detect anything."

"So? . . ."

"So they invented Relativity to explain why."

Michelle screwed up her face, checking for something she might have missed, then shook her head. "But why would it need explaining? They shouldn't expect to detect anything. It would be like . . ." she sought an analogy, finally settling for the one Eric had used, "trying to measure your airspeed inside the plane."

Eric nodded. "Exactly. But it's in all the textbooks. And the clergy have been taught not to question the written Word, you see."

Michelle looked at him disbelievingly. "Surely it can't be that simple."

"I really think it is. So do a number of other physicists. But they're not the ones in charge. Science has gone the way of the medieval European Church and sold out to politics. It doesn't pursue truth anymore; it promotes correct agendas."

"So are you saying that Relativity is wrong?"

"Not wrong. Just a needlessly complicated way of

interpreting what's going on. Ptolemy's epicycles weren't 'wrong.' You can still say that the planets move in loops if you want. It fits the observed data. But trying to figure out laws of motion to make it work would drive you crazy. We're still waiting for the new Copernicus to come along who'll be listened to—but in the meantime, we do what we can. In fact I'll be speaking on this at a conference that's being held up in the mountains over the holiday weekend. So wish me luck, eh?"

"Oh? Where's this?"

"A place called Barrow's Pass. It's a new, glitzy creation that doubles as a conference center and ski resort."

Michelle shook her head. "Vanessa away this weekend. You next week. Is it always like that? You don't seem to see too much of each other." She meant it as a hint to take a look at his life, without wanting to sound critical.

"We're like the two yuppies in the story, aren't we?" Eric said, smiling. "Did you hear about them?"

"Go on."

"They pass each other on the stairs of the house, both wearing suits and carrying briefcases. He's just come in; his wife is just rushing out. He shouts back at her, 'Where are you going?' She shouts, 'Tokyo. Where are you back from?' He says, 'London.' Then, just as she gets to the door, she stops and calls back up the stairs, 'How are the children?' And he answers, 'I thought they were with you.' "

Michelle laughed, but then her expression became serious again. "We joke about it, but it's not far from the way a lot of people are getting these days. Life is something that should be lived, not strip-mined. Don't you think so?"

Eric snorted. "That sounds funny coming from a lawyer. I thought they were supposed to be among the worst."

"We're like airplanes," Michelle told him. "You only hear about us when one flies faster, higher, or crashes."

Eric grinned, putting a foot up on one of the lawn chairs and resting an arm on his knee while he surveyed the scene around them. "Younger people still have their values right, though. They make friends for the right reasons, read things they like, and are healthily skeptical of eminent authorities. You know, sometimes I think that all of this so-called wisdom that we brag about acquiring as we get older is really nothing more than rediscovering the common sense that we had at sixteen."

"That's interesting. Did you think it up yourself?"

"No. I got it from Kevin, of course."

Doug Corfe had appeared from the direction of the house and been joined by the Vancouver ferry captain, who had left the group he was with earlier. Ohira detached himself from a mingling of people and children by the pool and came over, holding a paper plate piled with pieces of steak and chicken. Like Hiroyuki he was in blue jeans, his hair plastered in points around his forehead by a scarlet headband worn in place of the cowboy hat.

"Too dangerous for grown-ups back there," he said. "A man could get drowned in all that flying water."

"Kids relive their fish ancestry," Michelle told him.

"I think it's called recapitulation," Eric said. "Are you enjoying yourself?"

"I always say that I'm enjoying myself. If you can't tell a lie honestly, then fake it. I learn from American lawyers."

"Hey, wait a minute," Michelle protested. "I'll have to figure that one out. . . ."

Ohira gestured approvingly toward where Kevin and Taki were talking with Avril and Janna. "See there, my nephew has the right idea. He enjoys himself too."

Eric and Michelle shifted their attention just in time

to hear Kevin saying, ". . . I don't know. I'd have to ask my dad."

Eric straightened up. "What do you have to ask your dad?" he called across.

"Oh. . . ." Kevin moved over to them. Taki motioned to the two girls. They followed hesitantly. "This is Avril. That's Janna," Kevin said. "They were asking about the mecs. We wondered if they could come and see Bug Park."

"It sounds absolutely fascinating," Avril said.

Ohira nodded his shaggy bullet of a head. "It's a great idea," he pronounced. "We should get more kids' thoughts on what they like, what more they'd want to see."

Going in like a tempest was typical of Ohira when a new idea seized him. Michelle was less sanguine. "Wouldn't it be a bit premature?" she said dubiously, glancing at Eric.

"It's called market research," Ohira said. "Never too early."

"Sure, why not?" Eric said. "Let's do it. How about tomorrow? Vanessa will still be away in town. We'll have the place to ourselves. Could you manage tomorrow?" he asked the girls.

"Wow!"

"Great!"

Doug Corfe had moved closer with the ferry captain. Eric, however, failed to notice them as Michelle laid a hand lightly on his arm. "Do you think it's wise, Eric?" she said. "You know—in view of this DNC business. Can you really be sure that there's nothing to it?"

He gave her a pained look. "Oh, come on. I've been involved with this technology longer than anybody. Do you think I'd let Kevin and Taki anywhere near it if I had any doubts?"

"It's not just that. If this becomes a legal issue and

a court decides there was any risk and negligence at all, we could be put through a blender over it."

Eric's expression hardened. He shook his head. "Giving these people any credence at all is the first step to letting yourself be intimidated by them. I'm sorry. Don't take this personally, but I won't let lawyers start telling me what I can do in my private life, at my own house. . . ." Just for a moment, Michelle had the feeling of glimpsing another facet of the real Eric. Then, just as abruptly, he grinned and lapsed back to his more usual, easygoing self. "In any case, I'm not your client. Ohira is."

"And your client says we stick to our own business," Ohira said to Michelle. She held up a hand and backed off graciously with a so-be-it expression.

Eric looked away and noticed Corfe and his companion for the first time. He gestured with an arm to usher them closer. "Hey, Doug. Why are you standing there as if you don't know us? It's a party. What are you up to tomorrow afternoon? I could use a bit of help at the house. Kevin and Taki want to bring these young ladies over to see the Park."

"Aw, gee. . . ." Corfe looked apologetic. He motioned toward the man with him. "This is Ray Young, an old friend of mine. I knew him when I was with a marine radar company up at Bremerton for a while, just after I came out of the service. We'd just decided to get together tomorrow."

Ray threw up his hands. "Hey, Doug, don't go messing things up on my account. We can make it some other time. I'm not planning on emigrating anytime soon."

"What were you planning on doing?" Eric asked Corfe.

Corfe shrugged. "We hadn't exactly decided. Sink a few for old times somewhere, probably."

"Then that's easy," Eric said. "Nice to meet you, Ray.

How would you like to come along and join us at the house too?"

Corfe looked at Ray as if to say it was a thought. "You'd find it interesting, Ray," he promised. "And we could still take a few beers out on the water. Eric's place is right on one of the inlets."

Ray made a play of hesitating, then nodded. "Well sure, if it's not imposing on anyone. Thanks, I'd like that. . . . Thanks very much."

"What kind of things will we be doing?" Avril asked Kevin.

He moved his eyes to Taki, then back. "Did you ever try parachuting?" he asked her.

Janna looked alarmed. "Hey, wait. That sounds dangerous. I'm not sure I—"

Kevin grinned and shook his head. "Not our way. You'll just love it. Trust us."

CHAPTER ELEVEN

One of the seminar organizers standing at the rear of the auditorium made a *T* with his hands to signal time almost up. Vanessa acknowledged with a nod and turned her attention back to the bearded man near the front, who had another question. With his plastic bag packed with papers and brochures, and a wirebound pad on his knee that he had been scribbling in continually through her talk, he looked like a dedicated stalker of conventions.

"Dr. Heber. About side-effects again. Are you aware of the item in *Science News* this week about four more cases of neural disorder reported among DNC researchers?"

"Yes, I have read it."

A pause. "Do you have any comment?"

Vanessa did her best to convey skepticism without appearing complacent. "What qualifies as a neural disorder?" she replied. "Just overt dementia? Can it be suggestions of stress and not enough sleep? Or anything that strikes the person doing the survey as abnormal? . . . And four out of how many? Was a group size established, or did it just cover anyone they could rope in? And if we do know the size, and what a 'neural disorder' is,

how many would we expect in a similar-size group from
some other section of the population—the people in
this room, for instance? . . . You see my point. Without
controls and a measurable criterion to compare them
by, nothing is really being said. Superficially it sounds
scary, but it doesn't mean anything."

"But if it was shown to be significant . . ." the bearded
man persisted.

Vanessa looked at him and sighed inwardly. Why did
people ask questions that could have only one answer?
"If it were proved to be a problem, I'd agree it was a
problem," she said. Appreciative laughs here and there
greeted her answer. Although a couple of hands were
still raised, she seized the moment to wrap things up.
"I'm sorry, but we have had a time signal from the
back. There is something else about to start in the
room. If there are any more points, I'll take them out
in the lobby area outside. Thank you all for your
interest."

There was a polite round of applause. Seats creaked,
and a mumble of voices built up as the audience began
standing and dispersing toward the doors. Vanessa
recovered her carousel of slides from the projector
and collected her notes. As she stepped down from
the dais, a gaggle of people who had come forward
escorted her to the exit amid questions and proffered
calling cards.

The lobby was abuzz with intense-looking people
clutching program books and papers, talking from
seats or standing in the spaces between. There were
a lot of beards, heavy spectacles, tweedy skirts, and
sweaters. Vanessa spent maybe five minutes disposing
of the questions. Then, when she was free at last,
she made her way over to a table set up with urns
and an offering of snacks, put down the things that
she was carrying, and fixed herself a hot lemon tea.

A young woman announced herself as a reporter from the *Tribune* and asked if Vanessa would be willing to do an interview for the Science section. At that moment, Vanessa saw the stocky, mustached figure of Phil Garsten standing by the wall, waiting to get her attention. It was Saturday, and he looked casually off-duty in light blue slacks and a tan windbreaker. Vanessa gave the reporter the numbers of the house and her office, and invited her to call sometime next week. Garsten waited until Vanessa was alone, and then ambled over. He helped himself to a cup and held it to one of the urns.

"So, this is life on the wild side, eh?" he drawled while he ran the coffee. "The real Vanessa that we've never glimpsed before. What have I been missing? I haven't seen so much fun since my draft physical."

"Give me a break, Phil. Having to put up with these dreary people for a whole weekend is bad enough. I don't need a eulogy on life's ecstasies from you as well."

"We all gotta do what we gotta do—for as long as it takes, anyhow. How'd the talk go?"

"Oh, pretty well. Practically a full house."

"Good. Who was that cute chick?"

"A reporter. She wants to set up an interview. You know, I've been doing this for long enough, you'd think I'd have gotten used to it by now, but there's still that relieved feeling when it's over. You know—like when you've made it to the airport, got your boarding pass, checked your bags, and now you can unwind."

"Did you get questions?"

"Of course—it's getting to be a hot subject. And if you came to set your mind at ease, naturally I played the party line." Vanessa picked up the file containing her notes, indicated the carousel box with her head, and moved away as a chattering group approached the table. Garsten took the box and followed her to an unoccupied lounge chair by a low table. Vanessa slipped the folder under an arm and turned to sit against the back of the chair, regarding him over the rim of her cup. Garsten put down the carousel box. "But I don't think you're here to check on that," Vanessa said. "What is it?"

Garsten looked around and lowered his voice. "I got a call from the Lang woman at home last night." Vanessa drew a sharp intake of breath. Garsten nodded. "From the way she talked, it sounded like you two have already met."

Vanessa's mouth compressed into a tight line. "She was over at the house. One of these meddling bitches who can't just stick to her job. She has to get involved in everything. I felt trouble in the wind as soon as she walked into the scene. What did she want?"

Garsten folded his arms loosely, his cup resting in a hand. "Sounds like a pretty accurate assessment. She's checking out the background on the DNC story." Vanessa nodded. That wasn't surprising. She would have expected that much. It was Theme Worlds' lawyer's job. However, to bring Phil here, there had to be more. He went on, "And she was asking about Jack. She thought I might have a handle on what he knew. She's got her suspicions about what happened, too. She didn't press it, but I could tell. And she'll keep digging. I know her type."

Vanessa took a long breath and exhaled it into a sigh. She sipped her tea while her eyes took in the floor and shifted agitatedly over the surroundings. "Have you got a cigarette, Phil? . . . No, forget it—they won't let you, here. It means we don't have the luxury of as much time as we thought. We're going to have to move things faster."

Garsten nodded. "That's the way I figured it too. I

didn't bother you with it last night since you were . . ." he bunched his mouth and made a play of being delicate, "relaxing. But I talked to Martin this morning. I called him on the yacht about a half hour after you'd left."

"And what does he think?"

"Oh, he agrees. The longer things drag out now, the more likely the ball of wax will come unglued. He wants us to get together at the Mansion to talk about it."

"Who?"

"You and me. Andy. The guys. . . . Could you get away from here to make it there for lunch say?"

"You mean right now?"

"No, tomorrow."

"I guess so—I'll be clear by then. I'm not due back in Olympia until late, anyhow." Vanessa looked at Garsten curiously. "What is Martin thinking? To bring the whole thing forward?"

Garsten nodded. "ASAP. Didn't you say something about Eric going up to the mountains sometime soon?"

"The Barrow's Pass resort—next weekend. . . . Could you have things ready by then?"

"There isn't a lot left to do. One piece of paper to draw up and some details to file for the record. I assume there's no problem with the equipment?"

Vanessa shook her head and remained expressionless. "None at all."

"Well, that's what Martin wants to go over tomorrow. We're gonna get the show on the road." Garsten drained the last of his coffee. "Have you had lunch?"

"Not yet." Vanessa had planned on making do with just a light snack. Martin had promised somewhere exclusive for dinner that night. She would be staying on the yacht again, of course.

"Me neither," Garsten said. "Come on, I'll treat you—

and it won't even show up on your bill." He set down his empty cup and looked around. "Do we need to go out someplace, or can you get something here? Do academics eat real food? Or is it all bean curd and processed fish brains? . . ."

CHAPTER TWELVE

It had begun as one of Taki's crazy ideas.

Kevin lay hunched on his back. The rubber band
fixed around both him and the wadded-up pack
attached underneath held him compressed into a ball:
chin tucked in, knees drawn up toward his head with
his arms clasped around them. Or at least, the
swiveling ball-and-socket joint that functioned as a
chin, the piezoelectrically activated articulations that
served as knees, and the linked multi-axial appendages
that were his arms.

Greenery, water, and sky turned around him in a
blur as Taki's fingers, looking like hinged balloons the
length of freight cars, fitted him into an inverted arch
of dinosaur hide floating a mile above the ground. The
kaleidoscope stabilized with Taki's face filling his view
against a backdrop of sky. The mouth opened and closed
to say something that Kevin couldn't hear.

"All set for launch?" Doug Corfe's voice queried.
Corfe was down by the water with Taki and Ray, the
ferry captain, speaking via a portable phone link patched
into Kevin's audio.

"This is exciting," Avril's voice said on the same circuit.
She was in another coupler up at the house with Kevin,

124

slaved to the same mec for vision input only to share the ride. Eric was with them, handling things in the lab. Janna was there too, having to watch for the moment. Normally it would have been possible to slave both of the other couplers to Kevin's, but one of them had developed a fault.

"We're ready," Kevin said.

Trees and sky whirled again. Then, for a moment, Kevin was looking up at the sky between the arms of an enormous horseshoe. Two rails, diverging above him into a wide V, yellow in the sunlight, elongated as Taki drew back the slingshot. . . .

"Three. . . . Two. . . . One. . . ." Corfe's voice recited. "Liftoff!"

Kevin felt as if he had been hit from behind by a train, and then he was hurtling skyward past the treetops. Avril screamed.

He had tangled impressions of rocks and shore shrinking rapidly below. He could see the house, Harriet crossing the yard; a boat out near the far side of the inlet. Then he felt himself slowing toward the peak of the climb, and for a few moments hanging and turning like a miniature moon.

Then falling. . . .

"*Oooh*. . . . I think I'm going to be sick," Avril's voice wailed.

"Please don't." Eric, coming in on the lab mike.

"Where are you, Kev? We've lost you in the sun." Corfe, from the water's edge.

Kevin cut the band, freeing his limbs. He let himself fall for a few seconds to develop a slipstream, and then released the chute of baled silk attached to the mec. Looking up, he saw it billow out above him as it filled with air against the sky. "Yowee, perfect!" he whooped.

"Okay, we've got you now," Corfe relayed. "You're looking good."

Silence and peace, the freedom of a cloud; drifting between earth and sky. . . .

"Okay, I feel better now," Avril announced. "Say, you know something, guys. This is really nifty."

The tops of the trees were coming up and expanding around him. Below on the grass, he could make out the three figures of Corfe, Taki, and Ray, their faces upturned.

"Definitely replete with ample nift," Kevin agreed, overcome with the euphoria. There was a slight breeze along the shore. He experimented with pulling lines to spill air from the chute, and after a few tries succeeded in keeping on course, aiming toward where the figures below were standing. The figures grew into monstrous effigies the size of the Statue of Liberty, Taki waving, Corfe with arms outstretched, beckoning, heads tilting to follow him down. Then, for a moment, Kevin was floundering in a morass of pine needles and grass . . . and the folds of silk came down over him. He stabbed a finger to activate the Control menu and exited from the system.

"Very good. You've earned your wings—virtual ones, of course," Eric told him. Kevin snapped open the collar and removed his headpiece. Eric was already helping Avril out of her equipment.

"It needs the bigger mecs for the weight," Kevin said. "I don't think the 'chute would open properly if we tried it with anything much smaller."

"Then maybe you don't use a parachute with smaller ones," Eric said. "Perhaps you go to something like silk cotton-candy, like spiders do."

"Hm. That's a thought."

"Do I get a turn now?" Janna asked. "It looked great on the screen here."

"You wait until you try this," Avril told her as she stood up from the coupler. "It's like you're really there."

Eric called Corfe via the mike. "Is Taki coming?" Taki was due to take the next ride, with Janna as "passenger."

"He's on his way," Corfe's voice answered from a speaker.

"Well, we can go ahead and get you organized while we're waiting for him," Eric said to Janna. He motioned toward the coupler that Avril had vacated—it was one of the converted airliner seats. "Make yourself comfortable. It's nothing like the dentist's."

"It's a really weird feeling, looking at the house from the outside and knowing you're really in there," Avril said.

"Here's Taki now," Kevin said, looking out the window. "I'm going down where Doug is to watch it from the other end." Then, to Avril, "Want to come too?"

"Sure." She went with him to the rear door. He held it for her and followed her out. They crossed the gravel behind the house and began descending the slope toward the water.

"It must be great having a dad who's into stuff like this," Avril said as they walked. "Mine just watches football and works in the yard. So the yard's just something we all look at. No one's allowed to do anything in it."

"Yeah. My dad says something similar about museums and houses. But you're lucky in some ways. Most times he's involved with something or other up at the labs. I guess this weekend he just decided to take a break."

"How about your mom? Didn't you say she was some kind of scientist too?"

"Yes—she's my stepmother, actually. She doesn't get too involved in what we do here at the house. She keeps more to the business side of things. . . ." Kevin picked up a pine cone and threw it at a trunk, not really of a mind to pursue that subject. They passed Taki coming the other way.

"How was that for navigation?" Kevin said. "Right down at your feet. Let's see you match that."

"Huh. Doesn't look too difficult."

"Wait till you try it."

"A good slingshotter is what it takes—to send you up right in the first place."

Kevin and Avril reached the area by the water where the trees opened out, in front of the boat dock. Corfe had already repacked the chute and was securing it to the mec with a new rubber band.

Ray shook his head in amazement. "Well, I don't know. If that ain't the darnedest thing I've seen in years. And did it seem like you were really there inside that thing?" he asked Avril.

"It was unbelievable," she told him. "It's just like you *are* it. And that was only receiving the visual. I can't wait to try driving one."

"One thing at a time," Kevin said.

"Gotta have a try at this myself," Ray said.

"You will," Corfe promised him. A beep sounded in his shirt pocket. He fished out his phone. "Yuh? . . . We are, just about." He looked over at Kevin. "They're ready up at the house. Do you want to shoot it this time?"

"Sure." Kevin took the compressed pack of mec and chute, and held it up in front of his face.

"Taki and Janna are coupled through," Corfe announced, looking away from the phone.

Kevin leered at the mec. "Aha, I've got you in my clutches now, Taki. About that two dollars you still owe me, eh?" He tossed the mec up in the air, spinning it deliberately, and caught it again. A squeal that could only be Janna's floated down from an open window in the house.

"Here." Ray held out the slingshot. Kevin took it, placed the mec in the sling, and aimed high.

"Get set, guys," Corfe said into the phone. "Hold onto your hats. Three. . . . Two. . . . One. . . . *Fire!*"

It might have been some perspiration on the grip that caused it to twist in Kevin's hand; or maybe his concentration just slipped a little. . . . But he could feel the slingshot slew to the side as he let go. Sunlight glinted off metal climbing high above the trees—but it was wide of where he had meant it to go. The wait was excruciating. . . . Finally the puff of white blossomed high above and began drifting serenely back to earth. Once again, it had opened perfectly—but this time out over the water.

"Dang, I don't reckon he's gonna be able to do much about it," Ray muttered. "The wind's the wrong way."

"Taki doesn't sound too appreciative, Kev," Corfe said, looking up from the phone.

They watched helplessly as the chute descended. Then it caught on the end of a pine branch hanging out over the water. And there, it hung.

"Decidedly niftless," Kevin opined glumly.

Eric, Taki, and Janna came down from the house a few minutes later to survey the situation.

Taki talked about climbing the tree, but it was obvious that the branch would never support him all the way out to its extremity. Kevin wondered what there was that they could maybe lash together to make a long enough pole. Corfe suggested that they take the boys' boat out underneath the branch, where they could use a shorter pole. And then Eric had one of his brainwaves. "We don't need to mess around making poles at all," he said. "Taki might not be able to climb out to it. But Ironside could."

Corfe, Kevin, and Taki looked at each other. "Of course," Kevin said.

"It just might work, at that," Corfe agreed.

"I still get to do the climbing," Taki told them, getting his claim in right away.

"Who the hell is Ironside?" Ray asked everybody.

Eric answered. "One of the early Neurodyne prototypes. More of a DNC test-bed—before we started miniaturizing them. It would be big enough to carry the other mec that's stuck up there and bring it down."

Corfe, standing fists on hips, squinting against the sun, looked up at the tree limb again, then down at the water below. "You know, it mightn't be a bad idea to have the boat underneath, anyway," he said to Eric. "That branch is going to sag more. If Ironside comes adrift from it, we'd stand to lose both of them."

"Good thinking, Doug. Let's do that," Eric agreed.

Eric went back up to the house to find Ironside and bring him down to the tree; Taki went with him to direct it from the lab. The girls went too, no doubt in the hope of getting another ride. So much for feminine loyalty and attachment, Kevin thought to himself. He stayed to take the boat out with Doug and Ray.

Corfe untied from the dock, and Ray took the oars to row them the short distance along the water's edge. Kevin began unfolding a tarp to provide a soft landing if needed.

"Did I hear you say this is the boys' boat?" Ray asked Corfe as he pulled.

"That's right. Eric picked it up a while ago, somewhere along the Sound. We only fitted the outboard last week. It runs just fine."

"So I'll be running into you out on the water, then, eh?" Ray said to Kevin.

"Not for a while yet, I'd say," Kevin answered.

"Hah! More interested in those sleek young hulls

up in the house there. I was watchin'. Can't say I blame you much, either." Kevin just grinned. Eric came back out of the house, carrying Ironside and accompanied by Janna—Avril had evidently won the battle for riding with Taki. They started on their way back down to the water.

"A few feet more," Corfe told Ray, looking up at the tree. "That's it. . . . Right about here."

Ray gauged the distance to the shore and rested easy, dipping a blade occasionally to hold them steady. Kevin spread out the tarp and bundled it into a cushion.

"Do you remember the guy, used to run a sloop up at that yard we worked at?" Ray said to Corfe. "Had a funny, foreign-sounding name. Ellipse? Epileptic? . . . Something like that."

Corfe thought for a moment. "Mike Ellipulos."

"Yeah, that's him. Had a big black mustache."

"I think his name was really Michaelis or something," Corfe said. "Greek, wasn't he?"

"I thought it was Cypriot."

"Somewhere around that part of the world, anyhow."

"What happened to him? I still see his face from time to time—you know, places here and there, so I know he's still around. But he disappeared from the old circuit."

Eric and Janna drew up at the base of the tree opposite. "Okay, Avril's riding shotgun again," Eric called across the few yards of water separating them. "Taki should be on line now."

Corfe used the phone to check. "Yes, they're waiting," he confirmed. Eric placed Ironside as high as he could reach, in a secure-looking niche on the trunk. The mec was roughly Coke-bottle size, with an inverted conical head, and a pinch-waisted body that swiveled along the center joint. It gripped the bark and began ascending in short, smooth movements, apparently with little effort. Corfe said something into the phone. "Taki says it's a piece of cake," he told the others.

"Is that your boat, Kevin?" Janna called across.

"Right. We'll take you and Avril out in it later if you like."

"Great."

They watched the mec progress higher up the trunk, then slow as it searched for a route out from under the projecting limb. Corfe looked back at Ray. "It's funny you should ask about Mike. What made you think of him?"

"Hell, I dunno. Talking to you again, I guess. Why's it funny?"

"He ended up at the same place I did."

"You're kidding!"

"Well, not exactly at the same place. But working for the same people. He took the skipper's job on the boat that belongs to the president of the company that Kevin's dad and I used to be with—a guy called Martin Payne."

"Well, you don't say! What outfit was that?"

"Over toward Redmond—it's called Microbotics Inc."

Above them, Ironside had made it to the top of the limb and was starting to crawl outward. "Here he comes now," Kevin said.

"Okay, I've got him." Ray checked to the shore and looked up over his shoulder. "So what kind of a tub is Epileptic running?" he asked Corfe.

"Oh . . ." Corfe shook his head. "Some tub. I worked on it a couple of times when Mike needed help with the electronics. Payne's a multimillionaire already, not yet turned forty. It's a Delta Marine hundred-thirty footer." Ray whistled. "Twin twelve-hundred-horse diesels, satellite communications, computerized nav and weather system. The works, Ray."

Above, the branch began to dip under the weight

as Ironside came nearer to the entangled chute. The mec was head down now, spreading and clutching the fronds like a wary squirrel in descent mode. "Oh, I can't watch!" Janna cried, covering her eyes, then peeking.

"Go for it, Taki," Corfe said into the phone. "We're right here underneath you." He listened to a response, then finished what he was saying to Ray before the action overhead absorbed everyone's attention. "You might have seen it about. Payne throws big parties and likes to impress his friends with days out along the coast. It's called the *Princess Dolores.*"

For a moment Kevin just sat open-mouthed.

Ironside got to the chute and released it without falling off. But by then it was easier for it to just drop down into the boat rather than have to climb all the way back to the ground.

Kevin wedged Ironside in a space under one of the seats and put the smaller mec in his shirt pocket. But he was so taken aback by what he had heard that he left Ironside there when they tied up at the dock and all went back up to the house.

Later, he, Taki, and Corfe did take the girls out in the boat as promised. And when they came back from their jaunt across the inlet, he forgot all about Ironside once again.

CHAPTER THIRTEEN

The next day, Monday, during the midmorning break at school, Kevin called Michelle's office in Seattle from a pay phone in the entrance hall outside the general office.

"Good morning, this is Prettis and Lang law offices. How may I help?"

"Oh, hi. I'd like to talk to Michelle Lang, please. Is she available right now?"

"I'll have to check. Can I say who's calling?"

"This is Kevin Heber."

"One moment."

"Thanks."

A grotesque face, eyes distended and fingers stretching the sides of its mouth, appeared in Kevin's field of view, groaning and grimacing. Behind and to one side, another of the class morons was waving and poking a tongue in an effort to distract Kevin's attention. Kevin ignored them and turned the other way. He felt hesitant about getting involved in these adult-world complications. However, if Vanessa was on those kinds of terms with the president of the company that Neurodyne's success threatened the most, Michelle needed to know. Or perhaps Neurodyne's own legal representative would

134

be the better person to take it to, but Kevin wasn't even sure who that was. He didn't want to go through Eric because of the personal aspect of the situation. Garsten was the family lawyer, but not somebody that Kevin knew very well or normally dealt with. At least he felt he could approach Michelle. The attorneys could sort out between them who needed to do what or talk to whom.

"Hello, Mr. Heber?"

"Yes."

"Putting you through to Ms. Lang now."

Michelle's voice came on the line. "Kevin?"

"Oh, er . . . hi. I hope you don't mind me calling you at your office like this."

"That's okay if it's important. But if it weren't I guess you wouldn't be calling. So what's up?"

Kevin had rehearsed in his head what he was going to say; now he found he couldn't find two words to string together coherently. The clamor in the background didn't help. The best he could manage was, "This is kind of difficult, knowing where to start. . . ."

"That's okay. Relax and take your time."

He collected his thoughts and tried again. "It's to do with this thing that seems to be going on—all these stories and stuff about DNC."

"What about it?"

Kevin ran the fingers of his free hand through his hair. "Doug thinks that some of the people at Microbotics might be behind it—or at least, mixed up in it somehow, right?"

"Doug does, but be careful," Michelle cautioned. "We don't have enough at this stage to start throwing accusations around."

"But suppose it was true. Wouldn't we be suspicious of any of our people that we found were involved with them—really closely, know what I mean?"

"What do you mean by 'our people,' Kevin?"

"Oh, say, somebody from Neurodyne, maybe really high up in the company. Or very close to my dad. . . . Maybe both."

There was a short silence. Three girls were standing a short distance away, giving him dirty looks. One of them held up a quarter and jabbed a finger at her watch, telling him that they wanted to use the phone before classes restarted. Then Michelle's voice said, "Are we talking about Vanessa?"

Kevin nodded, looking away from the girls. "Yes," he said, getting the word out with difficulty.

"But Kevin, she did work at Microbotics for a long time. I'm sure she still knows people there. That doesn't really say a lot."

"This is different. We're talking about the president— I think his name is Martin Payne. And it isn't just to do with DNC and technology and that kind of thing. It gets more . . . kinda personal, you know. I wasn't sure what to do." He didn't want to get into a protracted question-and-answer session just then. Before Michelle could interrogate him further, he went on, "Don't ask me how right now, because it would take longer than I've got. But I can show you it all on tape." The video input to the monitor on which Taki had followed the events aboard Payne's yacht had also been recorded automatically. Kevin shrugged. "Or maybe getting involved in that side of it wouldn't be your business. I don't know."

"Hey, Heber, tell your life story some other time," one of the girls called over. "We need to find out what's on at the movies."

"Where are you calling from?" Michelle's voice asked.

"I'm at the school. We're on break, but I have to go real soon."

"Leave it with me for a while. I have to think about

this and look into a few things. Have you told Doug Corfe or anyone else?"

"No."

"So nobody else knows right now except you?"

"Only Taki. He was with me when the tape got made. It's a transmission from a mec that ended up in the wrong place. I only found out yesterday who the guy on it is."

"Where is this tape at the moment?" Michelle asked.

"At the house. I've got it in my room. It'll be okay there."

"Will you be there this evening?"

"Either there or at Taki's."

"Leave it with me. I'm not sure at this point what would be the best way to play this. But I'll get back to you, either by this evening somehow, or tomorrow."

Michelle was hired to look after the business affairs of Theme Worlds Inc., not to go getting involved in the personal lives of Mr. and Mrs. Heber. Although the situation contained what could have been considered simply an unavoidable element of overlap, she knew from experience how easily this kind of terrain could turn into quicksand for the unwary. She decided that she needed to consult with Ohira. It turned out that he had left that morning on an overnight business trip to Los Angeles. Michelle's secretary managed to raise him on his personal phone, in the departure lounge at Seattle-Tacoma International Airport.

"If it were just a case of her involvement in an operation to discredit the technology, it would be straightforward," Michelle said when she had outlined what she had learned from Kevin. "But this other side to it makes it messy. I didn't want to start figuring out an angle till I'd talked to you."

There was no pause for deliberating. One of the qualities that made Ohira a good businessman was a knack for cutting straight through to the essentials. "Why should she want to sabotage her own company?" he said. "Selling Neurodyne's secrets for money? That makes no sense. She's got money already."

"Then it has to be for the guy," Michelle answered. "See my problem now? This is starting to turn into a seven-figure divorce case already. That's getting away from what you pay me to do. I'm going to need your thoughts on it."

"If DNC dies, then we don't have any deal, anyway," Ohira said. "This woman could do it more damage than anybody. How can you find out what she's capable of if we don't follow up on the information we've got?"

"If it's getting this personal, I thought maybe you might want us to approach it through Garsten," Michelle said. "He is the family lawyer, after all."

"You've already talked to Garsten. He says he doesn't know anything. . . ." Ohira's voice trailed away while a distant loudspeaker announcement echoed tinnily in the background.

"Not about whatever Jack might have known, no—" Michelle agreed. She realized that Ohira had been thinking aloud more than inviting comment, dropped what she had been about to add, and waited.

"This man Garsten sounds very strange to me," Ohira said finally. "For years he worked with Mrs. Heber's previous husband as a business partner. And she brought Garsten in as her family's lawyer, yes?"

"So Doug Corfe says."

"So she and Garsten are good friends, presumably. But he tells you that he knows nothing about what this man Jack Anastole knew, who was his partner and her husband? That seems a very unlikely situation to me, Michelle. Not believable at all. I don't think I trust him, this Mr. Garsten."

Michelle was not inclined to argue. She'd had a

feeling of something not being right ever since her conversation with Garsten, but it had refused to take on concrete form. Now Ohira had crystallized it for her. "What do you want me to do?" she asked.

This time there was a pause. Michelle knew how Ohira worked. He had already made his mind up what he wanted to do. She could sense him searching for an angle.

"Taki's best friend, Kevin, is also affected by this. I'm really an uncle to both of them. So we have to look after the family, eh? So what I want you to do is, follow up on this Mrs. Heber wherever it leads, and keep information to yourself. If you get into any kind of trouble, then as long as everything's legal, you'll be okay. I'll say you were working for me."

It was what Michelle had wanted: a clear directive and indication that they agreed. She nodded into the phone. "Okay, I guess that's it from me. Is there anything else?"

"No, that's all. They're calling seats now, so I got to go anyway. It sounds as if you need to see this tape."

"That was why I wanted to catch you. We can get right on with that now. When are you due back?"

"Just tonight in LA. I'll be back late tomorrow."

"Okay, we'll talk more later in the week. Enjoy the flight."

The phone buzzed again as soon as Michelle put it down. She picked it up again. "Yes?"

It was Wendy, the receptionist. "Stanley Quinze is on the line again. I tried to get a number from him, but he insisted on holding."

"Okay, I'll take it. And could you try and get Doug Corfe at Neurodyne for me? Let me know if he's not there."

"Will do."

❖   ❖

For a long time, Kevin and Taki had been intrigued by the thought of getting mecs to fly. In their experiments, they concentrated, naturally, on the smaller models in their collection, thinning the casings to fragile shells and taking out all nonessentials to reduce weight. They designed flexible wing systems based on insect patterns, which used leverage to exploit the improving power-weight relationships that came with diminishing size and stored mechanical energy recoverably in elastic structures.

A further problem was with the dynamics: of somehow matching the speeds of slow human neural processes, evolved to suit the needs of slow, lumbering bodies, with the high-speed motions appropriate to insect-world physics. And even with some real insects, for example bees and mosquitoes, it turned out that the frequency of wing beats was a result of resonance, and was actually higher than the rate of the nerve impulses driving the system.

Their solution was a "software gearbox": a micro-program that would translate one cycle of operator-muscle contraction and relaxation—or at least, what was perceived as an operator's muscles working—into a hundred or more precoded wing beats. Hence, each voluntarily initiated beat would cause a set series of instructions to execute over and over at a rate too fast to follow individually. Since the boys wanted their four regular limbs to be available for normal use, they had programmed the wing drive to link to the neural circuits associated with the shoulder blades. Flying would thus follow from a learned process of precisely controlled "shrugging." That was the theory, anyway.

The trick, Kevin told himself as he stood poised on the edge of a cliff in Neurodyne's wooden-block benchtop test ground, was to imagine that he was swimming in a dense fluid that amplified the effects of his movements. In fact, they had tried to write the microprogram to make the feedback feel just that way, with the perceived force serving as an analog of the wing speed that was impossible to register directly. Then, what felt like deliberate motion of an imaginary limb in a tangible medium would be converted insensibly into the appropriate vibrations. Having got that firmly fixed in his mind, he extended his virtual appendages and launched off.

The problem, he admitted as he found himself spinning and gyrating erratically across the floor, was that the system also amplified every error a hundredfold before you could do anything to correct it. It was like the old adage about the computer as something that can make mistakes a million times faster than the worst imbecile on the payroll: by the time you got to know that something was going wrong, it was already history.

He flipped out of visual to become himself again, viewing the Training Lab from one of the couplers. There were several techs in the vicinity, engaged at various tasks. Patti Jukes was nearest, clicking through report screens on a terminal. "Hey, Patti," Kevin said. "Can you pick me up off the floor and save me having to get out of this? I'm a couple of feet to your left, by the bottom of the bench."

"Sure, no problem." The lab staff who had been with the company for any time at all were used to having Kevin around, and sometimes Taki also. Kevin knew most of them. Patti listened to classical music and owned a dog called Bach. Kevin had told her once that Beethoven had had a dog with a wooden leg. That was where he'd gotten his inspiration when it walked across the room: dah-dah-dah-*dah*.

Patti got up and picked the mec off the floor. "I wouldn't want you to get trodden on down there." She held it over the landscape of blocks and terraces. "Where do you want to be—back on the big flat one at the end?"

"Yes. Thanks." Kevin had come in after school to use some of the firm's microcode utilities that he couldn't run at home. Taki was at his own place that evening, ensnared in some family function that had proved impossible to escape from.

"The way you guys have done this is terrific," Patti said, examining the mec before she replaced it. "How's it coming along?"

"Oh, slow, but I think we're getting there. The problem is finding a program to give just the right wing twist. Right now, it's spiraling and losing lift. That's why I ended up where I did. You want to try it?"

"I'd love to, but not right now. Maybe later, when I'm done with this. Will you still be around after five?"

"Probably. . . . No, more than probably. I'm supposed to be riding home with Dad, and he's with a couple of prospective customers. You'll have time for dinner, then come back."

"Is Kevin in here?" It was Doug Corfe's voice, from the doorway. "Ah yes, there he is." He came on in and approached across the lab area. "How's the magnificent man in his flying machine getting on?"

"I think he's amazing," Patti said. "They're going to crack it, you know, Doug."

"Did Stewart put that new lens in the Liga?" Corfe asked her.

"I'm pretty sure he did. He looked like he was aligning it the last time I was in there. That was about an hour ago."

"Good." Corfe turned to Kevin. "Can we wrap it up for now, Mr. Wright-brother-the-second? I need to talk to you."

"Well, I'd say it's still mostly Mr. Wrong-brother at the moment," Kevin said. "What's up?"

"Well . . . let's go to my office."

"Oh—sure." Kevin removed the headpiece and collar, and stood up from the coupler. "Shall I leave all this as is?"

"I'd shut it down and pick up your stuff," Corfe said.

Kevin saved his updated files onto a removable disk pack, ejected it, and collected together his coding charts and notes. He put the mec in its container and stowed everything back in his school bag, which he had left on a chair. "That's it," he announced.

"Some other time, then, I guess, Kevin," Patti said.

"Okay, I'll settle for a raincheck."

"We'll have it working better next time, anyway. You wait. I'll see you, Patti."

"Take care, Kevin."

Kevin followed Corfe out of the lab. They walked a short distance along the main second-floor corridor to Corfe's office. Corfe waved Kevin inside and closed the door. "I got a call from Michelle today," he said. "She told me about this business with Vanessa."

Kevin was taken aback. "She told you about that? I thought it would be kind of confidential. I don't understand."

"It's okay. I went to see her about what's going on with DNC—we talked about it that day we were working on the boat." Corfe's manner was conciliatory. "Now, I understand—I don't want to go dragging personal things up where they're not needed, either. But if it involves a person whose interests, to put it mildly, don't exactly coincide with the well-being of this company . . ."

"You mean Payne?"

"Yes, exactly. Well, in her position, Michelle has to know."

There was no escaping the reality now that sooner or later this was going to blow up in Eric's face. Kevin sighed, felt bad about it, but still couldn't see that he'd had any other choice. The only alternative would have been to do nothing. And one of Eric's own favorite sayings was that many decisions in life were made automatically when the alternative was unacceptable.

"Okay. So what do you want me to do?" Kevin asked.

"She says you've got some kind of tape."

"Right. It's a video from a mec that accidentally got into one of her bags when she was leaving for that seminar in town last weekend. Taki and I activated it to try and find out where it was. It turned out she was with Payne on his boat—that one you said you worked on a couple of times."

Corfe looked puzzled. "Payne keeps the *Dolores* at a private dock behind his house in Bellevue. How could you activate a mec at that distance?"

"Taki made a local relay pack. It was in the same bag as the mec."

Corfe raised his eyebrows, thought about that, and nodded to himself, looking impressed. "I'm going to have to take a look at that."

"Sure—assuming mom gives it back."

"She's still got it?"

"I guess so. But the mec's still in the boat. It was almost out of juice."

Corfe showed his hands. "Well, there's not much we can do about that now. But in the meantime, Michelle needs to see this tape. Where is it now?"

"I've got it at home."

"Uh-huh." Corfe nodded as if that was what he'd thought. "I don't think we want to go showing it here or at the house. So how does this grab you as a suggestion? I drive you to the house now, and we pick up the tape. Then we go into town and run it for Michelle at her office. After that, if you want, you could leave it with her and forget you ever saw it."

Kevin squirmed uneasily. "I was going to ride back

with Dad tonight. . . ." he began. But it didn't say much, really. He and everybody else changed their plans constantly. Eric, if anybody, was worst of all.

Corfe shrugged and recited the explanation for him. "So I had something to do in Seattle, and you decided to come for the ride. Hell, it's true. You're not telling any lies with that."

"Couldn't I just give it to you at the house?"

Corfe seemed to give the thought some consideration, but then shook his head. "Not really. If it's a mec video, it'll need some interpreting. And if you were working the mec, you saw more than what's on the tape. You know that."

Kevin nodded resignedly. "Okay, Doug. Whenever you're ready."

Corfe picked up the phone. "I'll just put in a call first, to let her know to expect us."

CHAPTER FOURTEEN

Martin Payne's home, referred to by his friends as "The Mansion," was a multimillion-dollar piece of waterfront real estate in the hyper-select Medina division of Bellevue, opposite Seattle on the east side of Lake Washington. It had been bought with the proceeds from what was still an explosive growth industry, where the rewards went to the quick, the shrewd, and the bold, and the rest rapidly became wall fodder.

At least, that was the way Payne was fond of idealizing things. The frontier of technical advancement was still far west of any moderating influence capable of imparting much semblance of law and order. He had started the company twelve years previously to develop miniature, silicon-based sensors and actuators that could be fabricated into the same chips as the electronics to provide integrated subsystems, which had rapidly found application in just about every likely area, from industrial control and space instrumentation to smart cars and talking appliances. A big field was the growing interest in small robots, and it was a natural step for the company eventually to start producing its own line. It had changed its name to Microbotics five years previously.

The corporation's dazzling financial performance had been due to more than simply the excellence of its technical innovations and the free play of market forces as enshrined in the textbooks espousing the American system; if the truth were known, it was more a result of political concessions and other practices that the said system's official financial regulators would not have approved of at all—not publicly, anyway. But that was his function, Payne told himself. Weren't results the first thing that stockholders wanted from a CEO? He and what he graciously termed the "executive committee" took all the risks and were entitled to be compensated appropriately; the rest took their shares and didn't even need to know the details. And those shares were far from table scraps. The way he saw it, they had a pretty good deal.

The billiard room, with its walnut paneling, leather upholstery, gun rack, trophy case, and mural sword display, was a celebration of wealth, success, and masculine opulence. It boasted a full-size, English twelve-foot table and commanded a view of the lake through French windows opening to a flagstone veranda with gray marble balustrade. The pillar supporting the overhead rack for glasses at one end of the bar, where Vogl, the house steward stood mixing drinks, was part of a totem pole from one of the Northwest tribes, dating back a couple of centuries. Payne would have had to look up the name to bring it to mind again. The designer commissioned to take care of the interior of the house had provided a book that contained their background and history.

The game was snooker—begun with fourteen red balls, six colors, and a white cue-ball. Sinking a red wins a point and allows a try at one of the colors, which score higher. Downed colors are brought up again and reused until all reds are eliminated. Play is then to dispatch the colors in turn, finishing with black, which is the highest scoring.

Norbert Dunne, Chief Financial Officer of Microbotics, stooped over the table to line up on a red. "From what I heard this morning, some people might be getting nervous already. It seems Geddes and West might be pulling out." Dunne was a heavyset man with thinning hair going white, at present visibly feeling the heat, his tie hanging loose and vest unbuttoned. One of his most useful talents was an aptitude for turning publicly raised investors' money, which was protected by law and required to be used only for properly authorized expenditures listed on the balance sheet, into short-term privately accessible venture capital, which wasn't.

Victor Bazhin was an old friend of the committee's, a partner in a New York trading bank that had provided a lot of Payne's capital in the early days. He was lean, tanned, slightly built—in good shape for his sixty-odd years, dressed suavely but conservatively in a gray pinstripe, having come straight from a meeting with the directors that day. "Geddes and West might?" he repeated from the far side of the room. "Where'd you hear that?"

"Around," Dunne said, playing his shot.

"That would put Neurodyne in real trouble," Garsten said. He had driven across the bridge from the city to make up a foursome. "I'd guess that could hit them with another ten-point dive."

"You get my point now about timing," Payne said, addressing Dunne and Bazhin especially. The talk was about the DNC scare. Geddes & West was one of the large backers that had put funds into Neurodyne. If they pulled out it would send a message to the market that would start a stampede. For all its scientific trappings, imagery, and rhetoric, the stocks business was still largely computerized superstition.

"You're as good as family here, Vic," Payne said to Bazhin. "I didn't want to leave you in the cold. Norbert's setting up for us here to buy in to a tune of a mil each, minimum. A week from now will be the time."

"That's why G and P are about to unload," Garsten put in while he sized up the table. "They can feel the dirt sliding."

Payne watched Bazhin as he chalked the tip of his cue. He knew what Bazhin was thinking. Floating bad press in the journals to drive prices into the basement as a setup for a bulk buying operation was hardly a new tactic. And it wouldn't be the first time that fears would be found to have been baseless, and prices magically recovered, once the right interests were in control.

"Okay, I hear the message," Bazhin said as Garsten played. "But the big egg in this instance isn't the company per se, is it, Martin? What we're talking about is the technology. Having Neurodyne on a leash won't accomplish much unless the patents come with it. And I can't believe that's the case."

"Heber owns them personally, and leases exclusive rights to the corporation," Garsten said.

"You see." Bazhin gestured to Payne as if to say that made his point. "Eric's a smart guy."

"His wife, anyhow," Garsten said. "She's the business brains."

"Whoever." Bazhin waved it away. "But it puts us on time. Leases have dates on, and have to be renegotiated. Then what?" Meaning that Heber could put them through a laundry, or, with DNC given a reprieve by then, walk away and set up a new company that would be eagerly capitalized, leaving them holding a worthless shell.

Payne moved to a corner to take his turn. "You'll be safe," he told Bazhin, leaning over and sighting. "I'll get control of the patents too. Then Microbotics gets full rights, and we buy out Neurodyne as a subsidiary."

Bazhin frowned. "How are you planning on doing that?"

Colors rolled on the green felt to a rippling of clicks. Payne smiled as he straightened up from sinking a red and moved to line up for the pink. "I'm not at liberty to go into all the details. Let's just say it gets a little personal. You know how it is, Baz, some things aren't really appropriate to a conversation between gentlemen."

"Just don't go underestimating Heber again this time," Bazhin said. "Because somebody thinks thoughts into chips all day, that doesn't mean to say he can't be a fighter. It caught everyone off guard when he decided to walk and set up Neurodyne. If it's his company and his patents, a guy like that could still cause a lot of trouble."

Payne shook his head. "Just trust me for a little while, okay, Baz?" It wasn't necessary to spell out the implications. In the event, whoever controlled Neurodyne by that time would stand to come out of it very well—and with Microbotics's stockholders providing the funds. And the eventual yield would in turn recompense the stockholders for their involuntary generosity later, all in the fullness of time. It could work out very neatly. Bazhin nodded.

Outside the French window, the water reflected lights from across the lake. Payne's yacht lay moored stern shoreward at its dock to one side, white, sweeping curves picked out in a blaze of floodlighting.

Not only his company, but his wife, Payne added mentally. But he hadn't deemed it tactful to go into that side of things just for the moment. And besides, if all went as planned, in another week Heber would no longer be around to raise objections.

CHAPTER FIFTEEN

The towers of Seattle center were gouging the darkening sky into orange streaks of cirrostratus edge-lit by dying sun when Corfe parked in a side street off 4th Avenue in the downtown district. He had borrowed Eric's van from the house so that on the way, he and Kevin could pick up some timber moldings and a door that he needed for a job at his own place that he had planned for the coming holiday weekend. Not that the van had a lot of spare room to squeeze a door and a pile of timber into. The back was filled with electronics consoles, screens, and three operator stations—like one of the mobile surveillance and communications units that backup teams used in the spy movies. Eric had fitted it out as a mobile mec command center in order to give demonstrations to prospective users on their own premises. But using it would explain Corfe's going to the house from Neurodyne, and make it seem more natural that he should take Kevin along for the ride.

Michelle's firm was in a high-rise called the John Sloane Building. Corfe knew it already, having come here the previous week to voice his suspicions to Michelle about DNC matters. They entered via a revolving glass door. Kevin saw from a directory on one wall of the lobby that the offices of Prettis and Lang were on the fifth floor. The day receptionist had left, and a security guard at the desk signed them in. After calling upstairs to verify that they were expected, he directed them through to the elevators.

Everything about the building seemed to have been formed by sticking together rectangular blocks, like Lego, Kevin thought, looking around while they waited. Even the numberless, internally illuminated clock overlooking the lobby floor. Or was the enclosed space formed by some kind of inverse process of subtracting blocks from some primordial Lego continuum that had once filled the universe? He wondered if architects got their inspiration from their children's cereal boxes over breakfast.

Michelle was waiting for them when they emerged from the car. "Hi," she greeted. "I was beginning to get a little worried. It took you longer than I'd have thought. You'd have been going against the worst of the traffic."

"We stopped to pick up some stuff at a hardware place on the way," Corfe said.

"No problem with the tape?" she said to Kevin. He shook his head and patted the school bag that he was carrying. Michelle led them across a landing area and a short distance along a corridor to a door bearing a brass sign that echoed the firm's name. Inside was a reception desk facing a waiting area containing glazed parallelipipedal furniture vaguely suggestive of a table, couch, and chairs—probably designed by architects— and beyond that, a deserted area with desks and data terminals, file cabinets, other assorted office equipment, and a garnishing of potted plants to relieve the utilitarian blandness. A passage on the far side brought them to a door bearing Michelle's name. It opened into a private office occupying a corner of the building, with windows in two adjoining walls. There were law books and begonias, framed certificates and degrees, and a corkboard of photographs and personal mementos, combining a businesslike appearance with a feeling of hominess in the way that femininity seems uniquely able to achieve—reassuring in its orderliness, yet with enough clutter not to seem clinical. A tape player and monitor on a metal cart were set up by the desk, which faced the room diagonally across the angle of the two windows. Kevin handed Michelle the cartridge from his bag while Corfe pulled up two of the chrome-armed visitor chairs. Michelle loaded the machine and sat down. Then she opened a manila file folder that was lying on the desk and pulled across a yellow pad.

"First, let's get the background straight," she said. "Now, just exactly what is this tape, and where did it come from?"

Kevin explained how, the previous Friday, a mec that Taki had set aside to take back to his place had gone missing. (He didn't see any need to go into how Taki had gotten the mec over to Kevin's house to begin with.) Well, what was the obvious way to find out where a lost mec was? "Couple into it from the lab and look around to see where you are," he concluded.

"Makes sense," Michelle agreed.

"So that was what we did. It was last Friday afternoon. Mom was getting ready for that seminar over the weekend. The front hall at the house was piled up with all kinds of stuff. That was where Taki must have left it, and it got put into one of the bags somehow . . ."

Michelle raised a hand. "Was it out on its own, in a way anyone at the house would recognize it? Or was it inside something?"

"It was wrapped in some plastic with a relay card that Taki had been testing, then put inside a folded plastic bag with a rubber band around."

"Okay."

"Anyway, that's about it. I coupled in and sent out its ID code when we got to the lab. Taki was following on the external monitor. And this is what we got." Kevin nodded at the player where Michelle had loaded the tape.

"Did you start recording from the beginning?" Michelle asked as she pressed a button on the remote.

"Whatever goes into the monitor is recorded automatically unless the option is switched out," Corfe answered.

After several seconds, Taki's voice came over the audio. "Any luck?"

Michelle looked puzzled. "Is something happening? . . . What am I supposed to be seeing?"

"I'm still inside the bag," Kevin reminded her.

"Oh, right."

The voices on the tape continued.

Kevin: "Well, I'm through but mummified. Now I have to try and get out of this stuff."

"Is there—"

"*Shh.*" Tones of a woman's voice, muffled and unintelligible, then Kevin again: "I'm not anywhere in this house, and that's for sure."

"How could it not be in the house? That's crazy."

"Well, either it got taken out by mom, or it got taken out by Harriet. Nobody else has been here, have they?"

"Oh, okay. . . . I guess so."

"Logic, Taki. Logic."

The woman's voice was still audible intermittently in the background. "I take it that's Vanessa we can hear?" Michelle said.

Kevin nodded. Patches of light and shade shifted meaninglessly, but were getting brighter: the bow view from a whale coming up out of the abyss to check on the world. "Now I'm cutting my way out," Kevin commented. A wedge of shadow sliced downward, and a dark blur opposite resolved itself into a claw hand pushing aside a curtain to let in a flood of color. At the same time, Vanessa's voice was answered by a man's, louder and understandable now. They were talking about whether to stay and have dinner in, or go out. The view through the curtains enlarged into a vista of massive geometric shapes, which proceeded through a series of jerky turning movements to transform into strangely leaning cliffs: Manhattan from the ground, painted in pastels and seen in a distorting mirror. "It's the inside of a paper carrier bag full of folders and books," Kevin supplied. "Taki remembered seeing it on the hall table."

"This is Martin Payne with her that we're hearing," Michelle checked.

"Yes," Kevin confirmed.

Michelle had filled in some background on Payne while she was waiting—nothing sensational: items on file in the local press and business news; listings of companies with their directors and chief officers; things like that. She'd even found a good picture of him from a black-tie banquet with the mayor and city officials held a little over six months earlier. He certainly looked more what she thought of as Vanessa's type than Eric did.

She listened as Payne suggested getting business out of the way first. Vanessa's voice replied, "I've brought copies of the QA reports that I told you about. The figures—"

Michelle stopped the tape with the screen showing the huge hand withdrawing a maroon file, and looked at the other two quizzically. "QA?"

Corfe frowned and rubbed his nose with a knuckle. "Quality Assurance. She must be giving him test results on Neurodyne's latest models."

"That's what I figured too." Kevin said it as if he

were experiencing a sour taste. Michelle resumed playing the tape. The ensuing exchange between Vanessa and Payne confirmed Corfe's guess, although somewhat garbled by the foreground sounds of the mec extricating itself from its wrappings and then being tipped out of the plastic bag.

"Very clever. Now how are you going to get back in?" Taki's voice said.

"Shut up. If I want your opinion, I'll give it to you."

The view stabilized for a few seconds as the mec took in the surroundings from the seat that it had found itself on. "Oh yes, you can see it's Vanessa now," Michelle commented.

Corfe leaned forward to peer at the screen more closely. "Yes, that's the main salon on the *Dolores*, all right. I can see where they are now."

Kevin nodded. "It gets obvious later." The scene turned like a view from a carousel, then halted to focus on the space between two cushions. The space grew larger and engulfed the viewer, and then gave way to an angle looking back out, as if from a cave.

"Getting under some cover, Kevin?" Michelle said. "You bet."

Then Vanessa said, "I don't think he's going to change his mind about it, and we can't risk being too pushy. Honestly, I've made all the suggestions that I think would be prudent."

Then came the first glimpse of Payne in a red shirt and white pants as Vanessa turned away. He said, "Then we'll have Phil go ahead and draw up a codicil. It's probably the safest way, anyhow." Michelle raised the remote and seemed about to stop the tape again, then changed her mind. There was more, but lost behind more wisecracking between Kevin and Taki. Further fragments came through the scraping and swishing noises while Kevin climbed the folds in the flag.

Payne: ". . . way it's set up. Phil has already looked into that angle. . . . redirected in your favor . . ."

Vanessa: ". . . Kevin as it stands. As I said a moment ago, I've tried everything that . . ."

"I couldn't make out what that—" Kevin began, but Michelle hushed him with a wave.

Payne: "Who else . . . background to the situation . . . Eric's the only one who . . . contest anything . . . right there in writing, notarized and . . . not around to argue . . ."

Vanessa: ". . . wish there was a day when . . . sick and tired of . . . can rely on Phil."

Payne: ". . . worth it when it's over . . ." There was a blurred patch that included a word that sounded like "dynamics."

"The folds of the flag were muffling the sound," Kevin interjected. "If I remember right, he was asking about theoretical work."

The mec paused at the top of the cabinet in time to pick up Vanessa saying more clearly, "You stick to organizing the finances. You're better at it. Don't worry about the scientific side. Leave that to me."

"I was just curious," Payne replied, sounding short.

"I think you might find this more interesting." Vanessa handed him a green folder.

"What is it?"

"Open it and see."

There was a silence while Payne read. The mec found sanctuary in the shadows behind one of the figurines and began scanning the scene. Michelle nodded to herself as she recognized Payne fully now from the photograph. He was murmuring aloud as he read. ". . . not restricted to places like Florida and California. . . . Year-round market in northern states . . . capture twenty percent of existing VR in two years, annual growth rates of . . ."

Michelle sat up with a start. "That's from one of the

reports that I gave Eric from Ohira! They're talking about moving in on Bug Park." She shook her head disbelievingly. "The bitch! . . . Oh, sorry, Kevin."

"That's okay. I, er, guess you're right. . . . It's not really that big a thing—us, I mean."

Corfe was rubbing his palms on the arms of his chair and shifting agitatedly, containing himself with difficulty. "I *knew* there was something like this all along. . . . Look, I'm sorry, folks, but I'm about to start talking outta line here. I've kept it to myself until now, but . . ."

Michelle stayed him with a hand. "All in good time, Doug."

By now, Kevin and Taki were debating the nature of the room. Corfe nodded as the view of furnishings and art works flowed by on the screen. "There's an entertainment center in that cabinet," he remarked. "It was me and Mike Ellipulos who installed it." The view backed up and came to rest on the carved crest adorning the end wall. "There it is," Corfe announced. *"Princess Dolores."*

"This is wonderful, Vanessa." The view moved back to Payne as he finished his scrutiny of the file. "I hadn't realized it could be worth so much. Will I still be able to afford you when you own all this?"

Vanessa moved closer to him. *"We'll* own it." They exchanged a few more words about having a drink and then driving to a restaurant somewhere, and then left, Payne with his arm around her.

"That's about it," Kevin said. "The rest is just me and Taki."

"Did you see anything else that we ought to know about?" Michelle asked him.

"No. The mec was almost out of charge. I didn't think there was enough to get it back down, so I left it."

Michelle raised her eyebrows. "You mean it's still there?"

"It seemed better up there than having it run down out in the open somewhere." As Kevin spoke, the image cut out. Michelle stopped the tape.

"They didn't mention Microbotics or Payne's name anywhere," Michelle commented. "How did you establish who he was?"

"I didn't until yesterday," Kevin replied. "When Ray came to the house."

"The ferry captain who was at the barbecue," Corfe threw in.

"Yes, I remember him."

"He was asking about a guy that we both used to know at Bremerton," Corfe explained. "Well, this guy became Payne's skipper on the *Dolores*—still is for all I know. When I told Ray that, Kevin recognized it as the name on the plaque that we just saw on the tape."

"I see. . . ." Michelle sat back and contemplated the blank screen for a while, then scanned over her notes.

"What do you make of it?" Corfe asked after what seemed like a generous allowance for silence. When she didn't reply immediately, he offered: "Vanessa's been taking Eric for a ride. They're setting up for Payne to move in on the business, and then, hell, I dunno . . ." He exhaled heavily and waved a hand. "Eventually, she walks, I guess, and Eric gets left . . . with what, the crumbs and a lot of problems?"

Michelle looked at Kevin dubiously and bit her lip, as if unsure how much to say of what was going through her mind. Kevin met her stare with an unvoiced challenge, daring her to just try and concoct some excuse for getting him out of the way, like asking him to go next door for some sandwiches or something. Dammit, *he'd* gotten the tape; it was *his* dad. . . .

If she had any such thought she seemed to think better of it, and relented with a nod that was probably unconscious. "I think it might be more serious than that," she said. Kevin's and Corfe's eyes met for an instant, then shifted back to her. She checked her notes again. "Vanessa said something about trying to change somebody's mind. She had to have been talking about Eric. Let's see if I can find it." She rewound the tape to where the mec was heading for refuge between the cushions, then replayed from there, picking out selected parts of the dialogue between Vanessa and Payne. "There. Vanessa's trying to change his mind, but doesn't think that being pushy would be prudent. Change his mind about what? . . . Now Payne's talking: they have to have Phil draw up a codicil. That almost certainly means Phillip Garsten, yes? Then, a few seconds later, we get something being directed in Vanessa's favor, with a reference to Kevin that seems connected. . . . Eric's the only one, and then something about contesting. . . . Then a reference to something needing notarizing, followed by somebody not being around to argue." Michelle paused the tape and looked across the desk. "Is it suggesting anything yet?" Kevin returned a blank look. Corfe had the expression of somebody who would rather not have been thinking what he was just starting to think.

Michelle fast forwarded through Ohira's projections for the entertainment market and Kevin's visual inventory of the cabin. "Now listen to this again, but in the context of what I just said. . . . Here. Payne hadn't realized it was worth so much. He wonders if he'll still be able to afford Vanessa when she owns it. She says not me; *we'll* own it. What's 'it'? What are they talking about here?" She looked from Corfe to Kevin challengingly.

"I assumed it meant this business they'd just been talking about—the entertainment sector that Ohira has his eye on," Corfe said. His expression said that now he wasn't so sure.

Michelle looked skeptical. "The wording's not right.

You have markets, or you get them, take them, or steal them; but you don't *own* them. And in any case, people don't. Companies do. I don't think that's what they're talking about."

Corfe's brow knotted. "Okay. So what do you think they're talking about?"

"How about the whole technology itself—the DNC patents? Isn't that something that Vanessa could own—and then the two of them together if she ditched Eric and climbed aboard Martin's wagon?"

The suggestion only seemed to mystify Corfe further. "How? How could something like that come about?"

"Very easily," Michelle replied. "Eric owns the patents and leases them to Neurodyne. I checked it out today with Joe Skerrill. It's the kind of arrangement that you'd expect." Skerrill was Neurodyne's corporate attorney. Michelle paused. "But depending on how Eric's will is set up, if anything should happen to him, all rights could pass automatically to Vanessa. It could be as simple as that."

Corfe shook his head and waved her away. "No! I can't buy that. He couldn't have set it up that way. . . . I mean, Kevin's his flesh and blood, for heaven's sake. Vanessa's not even . . ." He floundered and left it there.

"You mean his will is more likely to name Kevin as the beneficiary?" Michelle supplied.

Corfe looked about as if searching for some other way of putting it, then nodded. "I guess that's what I mean. Yes."

"That could be changed," Michelle said. "In fact, thinking about it, I wonder what it was that Vanessa was trying to get Eric to change, but without being too pushy. What you'd do is," she spoke slowly and deliberately, sounding every syllable, "have a lawyer *draw up a codicil* to *redirect it in Vanessa's favor.*" Kevin looked up sharply.

"But what good would it do?" Corfe asked her. "If it wasn't what Eric wanted, he'd simply deny it."

"If he were there to," Michelle agreed. "But what if he weren't?" She met his eyes pointedly, then Kevin's.

Kevin stared at her disbelievingly. But even as the protest started to form on his lips, other snatches of what they had heard replayed in his mind. If such a document were ever produced *in writing, notarized,* Eric would be the only one who could *contest* it. And that was where the words *not around to argue* suddenly took on their full, ghastly significance. Corfe had seen it too and was looking pale.

"All it would need is a crooked lawyer who could be trusted," Michelle said.

The implication was inescapable. "Vanessa has known Garsten for years," Corfe mumbled woodenly. "She introduced him to Eric. He was Jack's law partner— her first husband."

Michelle nodded. Her face was grave; her voice became very somber. "Exactly. And look what happened to Jack," she said.

CHAPTER SIXTEEN

It was getting late, and everybody was hungry. A few blocks away was a diner called Chancey's, that Michelle sometimes used for lunch. She locked up the office, and the three of them left the building together. Since the evening traffic had eased, they decided to take her car, which was in a basement parking slot. They found a table free in a secluded corner, and after they had ordered, Corfe was able to vent some of the feelings that had been smoldering earlier.

"Look, I don't know if this is the way to be talking in front of Kevin, but it's something I have to get out. To tell you the truth, I've had my doubts about Vanessa for a long time. But I've always kept them to myself because . . ." he waved a hand vaguely, "well, you know how it is. When there's families and friends involved, you don't go saying things that could start all kinds of bad feelings."

"I think we're a bit past the point where much of that matters now, Doug," Kevin said. He hadn't contributed very much to the talk since they left Michelle's office. He was still in a state of self-induced nervous anesthesia, not reacting to what it all meant until his mental shock absorbers had dulled the impact.

"What kind of doubts did you have?" Michelle asked Corfe. "From how far back?"

"All along—ever since I knew them both at Microbotics. She never struck me as the right kind of woman for Eric. . . . Or should I say Eric was never the right kind of man for her?"

"How do you mean?"

Corfe gulped down a swig of coffee and made a face. "She has always struck me as a social climber—you know, a taste for the high life, needing to be seen with the right people. That was what was wrong with Jack. He was okay for her in the early days: made enough bread to get started on, had some good connections. . . ." Corfe shrugged. "But once she got established on her own feet as a scientist, he didn't have the right image any more."

"And Eric did?" Michelle sounded surprised.

"In those days, yes—the way she saw it, anyhow. And you can understand why. He was head of research, with lots of awards and published papers—the corporation's rising scientific star. Vice presidency and a place on the Board within the next few years for sure. So Jack becomes history, and she signs up on a new ticket to ride high with Eric."

Michelle picked at her salad and nodded that it made sense now. "Instead of which, he picks a fight and walks out on their chance to join the rich and famous. But that's Eric all over. I saw a glimpse of it when I was talking to him on Saturday." She bit her lip but was unable to suppress a half smile. "I get the feeling that might have been when Vanessa started discovering the real Eric for the first time."

"I think you might be right," Corfe said. "And . . ." he turned to Kevin, "again, no offense, Kev . . . I think that deep down inside she's never forgiven him for it."

"And now she's about to change partners again," Michelle mused between bites.

"Martin Payne, yeah. CEO of the company; a million in checking before he's forty; grease line into City Hall; yachts, mansions, tuxedos, and diamonds. That's Vanessa's world all right."

Michelle thought distantly about that. "So how far back do you think it might go, this thing with Payne?" she asked. "Is it something comparatively recent—since she found out that Eric's always going to spend more time in worlds that he creates inside his than he will in executive jets, for instance? Or could it go all the way back to when they were at Microbotics? Could she have been an insider for Payne all along? . . . Is it possible, even, that she married Eric in the first place for no other reason?" Corfe could only shake his head.

What Kevin couldn't understand as he listened was that nobody was talking about *doing* anything. He felt he wanted to stand up and bang the table and stop it all by shouting at them: *Don't you understand? These people kill! They killed this guy Jack, and now they're going to kill my dad, and maybe me too! What are we going to DO?*

But in real life people didn't do things like that, not in a restaurant. So he sat. He chafed and fretted. And he said nothing.

He was finally able to make his point when they were in the car, on their way back to where Corfe had parked the van. Michelle's response only confused and frustrated Kevin further.

"Of course I understand your feelings," she said. "But there isn't any case for having anyone arrested. If mere suspicion were grounds enough, ninety percent of the country would be locked up. The only hard evidence we've got of anything is that Vanessa visited the president of a company she used to work for. Sorry, Kevin, but that's hardly a crime."

"And that's it? You mean that's all anyone can do? We wait till my dad gets shot, then we file a complaint?" Kevin was incredulous.

"We don't know for sure that they had anything to do with what happened to Jack," Michelle said. "We might be making it up in our heads. It could have been a heart attack, exactly as it seems. I'll talk to the coroner's office and the city police this week and see if I can get more details. If there are grounds for suspecting foul play, it would help our case a lot."

"But—but what about the alteration to Dad's will that they're going to fake?" Kevin protested, leaning forward from the rear seat. "What did Payne call it, a codicil? It's right there, on the tape."

"What codicil? Show it to me. And the tape doesn't say anything about Eric's will. It doesn't even mention Eric. It could be Vanessa talking about changing her own will to leave her jewelry to Batcat. Now, show me a piece of paper with Eric's signature on it, and with him there to say it's a fake, and you've got my attention. But short of something like that, we're just going to have to work at it a piece at a time, the hard way. That's how the real world is."

"Well, surely . . ." Kevin looked from one side to the other, as if the answer might be written in neon somewhere outside the windows. "We have to at least warn him. Don't you want me to tell him about this when I get back . . . or can Doug come inside and tell him?"

Michelle eased the car to a halt behind the van. "I don't think so, not tonight," she said. "It would be too much of a risky thing to discuss in the house with Vanessa there. Besides, I'd really like to have more to go on than there is right now before bringing it up with Eric. In the meantime, it's essential that he continue to act naturally." She turned in the driver's seat and looked back. "I know it's a serious business, Kevin, but let's try not to panic. After all, there's no indication that anything's likely to happen soon."

Michelle left for her apartment shortly afterward. Kevin and Corfe, in the van, drove back to I-5 and turned south.

By this time, Kevin was feeling subdued. His reaction earlier had been more of a reflex. Only now was a real awareness of the truth beginning to seep through in diluted doses that his emotions could handle. It was like watching layers of scenery being carried off the stage at the end of the performance, progressively revealing the reality that had been there all along. If what Michelle was saying was right, it meant that the woman who had eaten meals with him, taken him on trips, helped plan his school schedule, shared his home—whom he had come to look to as the nearest he would ever have to a natural mother—had all the time, calculatingly, been part of a collusion that intended to kill his father and steal his—Kevin's—inheritance. He suspected from the absence of any really violent reaction that the true enormity of it had not percolated through fully, even yet. Even so, he tried to detach a part of his mind to see if it could observe the rest and tell him how he felt about what had.

The most unbelievable part was not being able to do anything. This feeling of apparent helplessness was something he couldn't accept. He felt like a rabbit in a cage with a snake, having no option but to let it pick its time. How could such a situation come about? With all the ritual and ceremony and rules and procedures that adults heaped upon the world, how could something as basic as being able to demonstrate that a murder was probably being planned not trigger some kind of preventive action automatically?

And until something did happen, was he supposed to magically have the insight to know what to say, how to deal with all the situations that might conceivably develop domestically in the house? He felt like a psychic dowser who was supposed to know how to avoid buried mines—except he'd never claimed to anyone that he was psychic.

Eric and Vanessa were both home when Kevin got back. He found Vanessa in the den, composing something on the computer screen. She was deep in thought, and didn't become aware of him at once when he appeared in the passage outside the room. He stood, studying her through the open doorway, almost as if he should have expected to see some kind of alteration about her, some kind of visible change. But there were no horns poking through the dark hair, suddenly; no hump between her shoulders, fangs sprouting from her upper jaw. She looked, as always, calm, dispassionate, utterly composed and in control. Other words tumbled in his mind like clothes in a dryer: resolute; capable; indefatigable, undeflectable. A Terminator locked onto its goal.

She looked up suddenly. "Oh, Kevin! You're back. I didn't hear the van come in."

"I walked up the driveway. Doug took the van on to his place to unload the stuff that we got. He'll stop by in the morning and pick up his car." He was conscious of her bright, uncannily reflective eyes interrogating him silently, giving him the spooky feeling that it was futile to think he could conceal anything that had transpired. She knew. It was written plainly. She could read everything straight out of his mind.

"What did you get?" she asked him instead.

"Some wood, a door, and some bits and pieces for a room he's remodeling—hinges, screws, and stuff." Kevin noticed Vanessa's briefcase to one side, along with some folders and the slide carousel box that had been in the hallway on Friday. He didn't see the plastic bag that had been aboard the yacht. Just to prove that she could read his mind, Vanessa said, "Oh yes, I found something when I got to the seminar that looked as if it might be yours—something electronic, wrapped in plastic. It must have got mixed up with my things when we were loading the car."

"Oh yes." Kevin did a good job of feigning surprise. "It's Taki's. He was looking for it on Friday."

"I put it in one of those boxes of yours in the trunk of the Jaguar. Are you ever going to remove them?"

"Have you got the keys? I'll get them now."

"Oh, do it tomorrow sometime. Taki called, by the way. I told him you'd be back later. Can you call him back?"

"Sure. Was it about the relay?"

"Is that what it is? I don't know. He didn't say." Vanessa's eyes had strayed back to the screen and began scanning over what she had written. "Have you eaten? There are some cold cuts in the kitchen. Or there's the last of a stew that Harriet made that needs finishing."

"I had something with Doug in town . . . thanks. You, er, look busy. I'll let you get on with it. Where's Dad?"

"Downstairs, I'd presume. Yes, I do have a lot to do. Goodnight, in case I don't see you again."

" 'Night."

Kevin turned from the doorway and made his way down to the lab at the rear, trying to tell himself that this wasn't really happening. He'd read somewhere about lucid dreaming, that was so real you couldn't tell the difference from being awake—he'd even experienced it himself a couple of times. Sometimes he had "woken" up from such a state only to find out later that he wasn't awake at all, and then gone through it again and ended up with no idea if he was really awake now, or what was going on. But if this was a dream, then so must everything else have been all the way back to thinking he'd been in a mec on Payne's yacht. What yacht? Who was Payne? How did he know they existed? Neither of them had figured in his life before a few days ago, when everything had seemed so serene. Maybe they weren't real, then, and life was still serene. And maybe the stories about DNC were true, and this was what it did to you inside your head. Probably just as likely.

Eric was hunched on a stool at one end of the large bench, studying some graphs in a molecular circuitry catalog and comparing numbers with the content of an e-mail item showing on a screen. He looked over as Kevin came in from the stairs. "Ah, so you're back. What happened to Doug? Did he go straight on home?"

"Yes. He's got some stuff to unload. He'll pick up his car in the morning."

Eric looked him over briefly through his spectacles. "So, did you have a good time?"

"Well, I guess it was . . . something different. We ate out too."

"Fine. I talked to Patti Jukes just before I left. She told me about the mec that you were almost flying today. It sounds as if you've almost got it licked. That's terrific."

Suddenly everything seemed almost normal again. "A microprogrammed transmission is definitely the way to go," Kevin said. "The trouble is it gives coarse control-tuning. I think we're going to have to *learn* to fly. It doesn't look like something that'll precode easily into an algorithm."

"Well, if gnat-size brains can get the hang of it, I'm sure you will too, in time. I've got some papers on insect simulations that you ought to read. One of them has a good section on wing dynamics that might help you get the microprogram right. I'll dig them up tomorrow."

Eric's innocence as he sat there talking about mecs and flight dynamics, his utter unawareness of all that had been said that night, was affecting Kevin. It seemed to symbolize the whole pattern of Eric's life. He wanted to reach out, put an arm around his shoulder, and tell him to be careful because Kevin cared; and so did Doug, and Michelle, and they'd all be looking out for him, and everything would be okay. He wanted to spend more time with Eric, do all the things they kept promising each other they would do, and usually ended up putting off. People were always saying that time went faster as you got older. Kevin wondered if he was beginning to experience it already.

"Maybe we could look at it together this weekend," he said.

"I have to go to this thing at Barrow's Pass," Eric reminded him.

"Oh, that's right. I'd forgotten. What's happening there? Tell me again."

"It's a sort of conference on basic physics. I'll be playing Giordano Bruno to the Bishops of Relativity again."

That was an aspect of Eric's interests that Kevin had never gotten involved in, although he knew it had been Eric's prime subject when he was an academic physicist. All Kevin knew was that according to Eric, most of the experimental "proofs" cited in the text books were derivable from classical physics and said nothing exclusive about Relativity at all. That was something he'd have to sit down and find out more about, he kept telling himself—and putting off.

"When will you be leaving?" Kevin asked.

"It's the holiday weekend, and I know I have to be there on Saturday. So either in the morning, or maybe Friday evening. I'll need to check the schedule again before I—" A phone on a shelf by where Kevin was standing rang. Kevin picked it up.

"Hello?"

"Knock-knock."

Sigh. "Hi, Taki. Okay, who's there?"

"Winnie Thupp."

"Winnie Thupp who?"

"And Tigger too! Ho-ho. I take it you're back."

"No, actually I'm an aural hallucination. Mom says you called earlier. I was going to call you back. What's up?"

"The opposite of down. No, seriously, about flying mecs. Have you still got the ones that you were going to take to the lab today, or did you leave them there?"

"I've got them with me, in my bag. Why?"

"Oh, good. Can you bring them with you to school tomorrow? I think I might have figured out a better way of structuring the microprograms. If you come over to my place after school, we could try it out on them."

"Sounds good. I was just talking about that with my dad. He's got some papers on insect simulations that he says we ought to look at. Oh, wait a minute—I think they're at the firm." Kevin looked across at Eric. "Taki wants me to go on to his place tomorrow after school. I can't get those papers before then, can I?—the one that talks about wing dynamics, anyhow."

"I could fax it to Taki's," Eric offered.

"Dad says he'll fax it to us at your place."

"Okay. That settles that, then. Where were you tonight?"

"Oh, I went for a ride into town with Doug to pick up some stuff. We ate at a restaurant, saw a lot of traffic, highways, buildings, bridges. You know—the breathtaking, unfolding, urban extravaganza. Oh, and I've got your relay. It's in the trunk of Mom's car."

"Great. Maybe you can let me have that too. Okay, well, it's late. See you tomorrow."

"Be good, Taki."

"That's what everyone keeps telling me. I tried it. It's overrated."

Kevin smiled tiredly into the receiver. "Goodnight, anyhow." He hung up.

Eric was studying the screen again, bringing up another piece of e-mail. Despite what had been said earlier, Kevin was tempted to tell him all about what had been said that night; then he'd be able to stop worrying, and Eric would know as much as all of them. They were alone. Vanessa wouldn't come down to the lab now. . . .

But as he began mentally rehearsing how he might go about it, all of a sudden he found he was just too weary. The seeping in his brain had built up to a saturation that would need a night of sleep to absorb. It occurred to him then that if the entirety of the adult world was paralyzed, then *he* might have to be the one to do something. Just at the moment, precisely what was far from obvious. But in the morning a lot might seem clearer.

CHAPTER SEVENTEEN

Kevin was up uncharacteristically early the next morning. He had finished breakfast before Eric was halfway through his eggs and hash, ready to escape the trapped feeling that he anticipated might seize him when Vanessa came in.

"You seem very bright and sprightly this morning," Eric remarked, buttering toast.

"It's those girls they had over on Sunday," Harriet said over her shoulder from the stove. "Life here will never be the same now. Which one do you fancy, Kevin? The tall one, the blonde, I bet."

"Oh, I don't know. . . . One life at a time's enough," Kevin answered, grinning faintly.

"Where do they live?" Eric asked.

"Avril's on this side of Tacoma. Janna . . . I think she's somewhere around there too. I'm not sure exactly."

"Hmm. Sounds as if we might be seeing more of them." Eric winked at Harriet as she refilled his coffee cup.

Kevin shrugged neutrally. "Maybe."

"Good morning," Vanessa's voice said from the doorway. She came into the kitchen, make-up on, hair tied back and high, dressed to go out.

"Very nice," Eric complimented.

Vanessa acknowledged with a wisp of a smile and a nod. "Just a cup of coffee for me, Harriet," she said. She remained standing by the breakfast bar.

"Not hungry?" Eric said. "If it's a diet, you don't have anything to worry about." He indicated her appearance generally with a motion of his head. "You look as if you're off out somewhere."

"I have to go into the city."

"What, again?"

"Just to check the shops, and a few chores. I'll probably have lunch. Somebody told me there's a new Scandinavian place opened at the Center. I might try that."

Kevin was unable to comprehend her nonchalance— even though there was no reason why it should be any different today than any of the days that had preceded it. Confusion and the claustrophobia that he had feared began taking hold of him.

"Can I have the keys to the Jag, then?" he asked Vanessa, at the same time standing up. "I'll get those boxes out of the trunk before I go."

"Oh yes, I'd forgotten about those," Eric murmured.

Vanessa looked mildly surprised. "Well, certainly. They're in my purse, in the den. Can you get them?"

"Sure." Kevin tried to think of something more to say, couldn't, and left the room awkwardly.

"He seems quiet, not his usual self this morning," he heard Eric say as he left the kitchen.

"Definitely the signs," Harriet pronounced.

Kevin found Vanessa's keys and went out the front door. The morning had a sharp nip, with frost on the grass and a clear sky. He felt as if he had walked out of what had suddenly turned from a home to a prison, into a different world.

He crunched across the gravel to the Jaguar, which

was in front of Corfe's bronze Chevrolet, and opened the trunk. The black plastic bag containing the relay was in the top of one of the two boxes of gadgets and tools, standing among other items of Vanessa's. The rip in one side didn't seem to have been investigated, although he wasn't exactly sure how he expected to tell. Despite all his experience with mecs, it was still a strange feeling to find himself looking at the same cuts that he had made himself and crawled through, days ago and miles away. He lifted out the boxes and started to close the trunk again. Then his motion slowed, and he let the lid rise open again as a new thought struck him suddenly.

If it hadn't been for the mec finding its way onto Payne's yacht, nothing that he had discussed last night with Michelle and Doug would have been known. He had never thought of using mecs as intelligence-gathering devices before, and that one, brief, fortuitous episode had proved how amazingly effective they could be. In that case, why be restricted to that one lucky episode? Michelle had said they needed more information, and one sure thing was that in times ahead, Vanessa would be going to the right places to get it. Why not prepare for future opportunities in advance? He didn't exactly feel the ethical constraint at such a thought that he might have a week ago.

He leaned inside and checked the back of the trunk space. The sides and floor were carpeted; the overhead panel beyond the lid, bare metal. The farthermost recess, high at the rear, was lined by a foam-backed rubber strip, molded into the angle and glued to exclude drafts. Kevin reached up and checked along with his fingers. The rubber was not solidly anchored all the way along. Behind it he could feel gaps between the structural bracings. The gaps probably opened through to space behind the rear seating. He straightened up and looked at the house. All was quiet and still. Kevin picked up his two boxes, carried them inside, and went on down to the lab.

He sorted through the mec boxes on a shelf at the back and picked a black one about cigarette-pack-size, built to hold three of the smaller mecs, and checked that its batteries were good. For mecs he selected two: Tigger, the chain-saw wielder; and Mr. Toad, which with its huge eyes would make a great spy. Then he renewed the batteries in Taki's relay, rewrapped it in the plastic, and put it, along with some packing foam and adhesive tape, a Stanley knife, screwdrivers and a few other items that he might need, in a portable tool carrier. To these he added the flashlamp from its hook by the stairs, then went out via the rear door and back around to the car.

He cut a slit through the rubber high up in a corner at the back of the trunk, where only deliberate searching would have found it, and probed through with a screwdriver to explore the other side. Bringing his face up close and peering through with the flashlight, he verified that it was the space behind the rear seatback. He taped the relay to the metal behind the flap of carpeting that he had loosened, extending the antenna that Taki said worked better in confined metal spaces behind the rubber strip. He secured the mec box next to the relay, leaving the incision open so that a mec emerging from the box would have access both ways, forward or backward. That way, he reasoned, it would be possible to "bug" (he rather liked the double meaning), say, a purse or coat left on a seat in the passenger compartment, or a bag placed in the trunk.

The sound of a motor came through the trees, and Eric's van appeared from the driveway just as Kevin was finishing up. He waited while it drew up alongside the Jaguar. Corfe switched the motor off and wound down the window. "Hi, Kev. Being an early bird today, eh?"

"Not really. I always figured that stuff about birds is an example of vertebrate chauvinism. Nobody ever thinks of it from the worms' point of view: Early worms get eaten. I'm with the worms." It was a tired line that he had voiced before. He was speaking mechanically, his expression distant, still preoccupied with the unreal charade that was playing itself out inside the house.

"Watcha up to?" Corfe asked.

"Oh . . . just taking some stuff inside."

Corfe cocked an eyebrow pointedly. "How is everything in there?"

"Just . . . like normal. I can't believe it. It feels eerie."

"I know what you mean. Is Eric up?"

"Yes. He's in the kitchen."

"Maybe I'll come in and have a coffee and say hi. Like me to drop you off at school afterward?"

"Sure."

Corfe climbed out and closed the van door. They began walking up to the house. Kevin decided that until there was something specific to use his planted mec spies for, he couldn't see any good reason to mention them.

CHAPTER EIGHTEEN

"Hello, Ms. Lang?"

"Yes."

"Thanks for holding. Yes, I have the record here: Jonathan Charles Anastole, age 52, died March three this year. The cause of death registered here was myocardial infarction. There's no indication of anything unusual. The exterior examination showed a couple of minor abrasions, but nothing that would be associated with cause of death. No organ abnormalities. . . . Blood alcohol negative."

"Is there a toxicological report—poisons, neural agents, that kind of thing?"

"Those tests are specific. We wouldn't normally screen for them unless there was a reason to be looking for something like that. It wasn't requested in this instance."

"I see. Thank you."

"Would you like me to fax you copies of the death certificate and autopsy report?"

"Yes, if you would, please."

"The company is Prettis and Lang, you said? What is the fax number there? . . ."

❖   ❖   ❖

In movies and things like that, yes. But movies were made to escape into from unadventure and uniformity. Things like this didn't happen in real life.

". . . is it, Heber?"

Kevin shook himself back to real life. "Excuse me? . . . Oh, I'm sorry. What? . . ." Somebody with terminal-phase brain atrophy giggled at the back of the classroom.

"Jazz" Jarrold spread his hands, turned his eyes imploringly toward the ceiling, and went through his mime of mock martyrdom that always made Kevin feel that he'd missed his historical niche and should have been around at the time of the old silent movies.

"Heber, what is it? I work hard, I try. . . . I do my best to discharge the mission that the taxpayers of this fine Evergreen State of Washington have entrusted me with. What do I have to do to get your attention?" Kevin thought of saying, "how about making the subject interesting instead of trying to be the subject"; or, "project something we'd be motivated to want to emulate, instead of acting like an ass." Instead, he conceded with a weak grin and showed a hand apologetically. Jarrold took a step to stage left and turned with a flourish. "Oscar Wilde said that we live in a society that is overworked and undereducated. I'm trying to make a humble contribution to correcting that deplorable situation, and I would appreciate what measure of cooperation it is in your power to muster, particularly since you are the intended beneficiary of the endeavor. *We* were discussing the works of the Baroque composers. Where were you—lost in computerdom again? So, could I have a little of that attention? Forget code and think coda, bass and not Basic. . . ." Jarrold paused, his eyes gleaming evilly with some inner inspiration that had just struck him. "In fact, you could say . . ." he was visibly fighting rising excitement as he strove to string the words coherently together, "it's the way to avoid growing up with . . ." Kevin saw it coming in its full awfulness a split-second before its triumphal delivery: "your Bach being worse than your byte!"

At least the rest of the class had the graciousness to groan with him.

"Good morning, this is the Ramada Inn, Patrice speaking. How may I direct your call?"

"Hello, Patrice. My name is Michelle Lang. I'm an attorney with the Prettis and Lang law offices. Could I talk to the general manager, please?"

"That's Mr. Willens. . . . He's not in his office. Just one second. I'll have to page him."

"Thank you." . . .

"Guy Willens here."

"Mr. Willens, my name is Michelle Lang, with the Prettis and Lang law offices here in Seattle. I wonder if I could talk to you for a moment about an incident that happened at the hotel about two months ago."

"What incident was that?"

"A man was found dead in one of your rooms. His name was Anastole, John Anastole."

"What did you want to talk about?"

"I'm trying to check some details as to the circumstances in which he was found—who made the registration; if anyone else was using the room; whether the door was secured internally. That kind of thing."

"I couldn't release any information like that. I'd have to refer you to the police department."

"Would it be possible to tell from your registration records if—"

"You have to talk to the police. We have a set policy with such matters. I'm sorry, but I can't help."

"I understand. Well, thanks for talking, anyhow."

"You're welcome. Have a nice day, ma'am."

It should have been obvious. What was she trying

to do anyway, for heaven's sake? She wasn't that kind of attorney.

"Michelle."

"Yes, Wendy?"

"I've got Joe Skerrill at Neurodyne. He's on the other line now. . . ."

The yellow Ford was signaling to move in ahead, crossing right for the approaching exit ramp. Vanessa accelerated into the gap, forcing it to slow down and pull in behind. "*My* lane, lady," she murmured.

Sometimes she thought her whole life had been an obstacle course of people thrown in her way to stop her being what she was and getting where she wanted to go. The world operated to a double standard. She imposed no restrictions, made no demands, held nobody back from actualizing whatever potential lay within them to be expressed. The powerful would take unless the weak could organize to stop them, in which case *they* became the powerful—and then, as far as she was concerned, the laws that governed the play were the same. Meeting hard opposition to curb what others saw as "excesses," she could understand, even respect; but please, not some appeal to "right," "goodwill," or any of the other forms of guilt-based moral socialism in which the weak and the inept laid claim to a share in the winnings they could never earn for themselves.

And when, in a genuine effort to spare otherwise inevitable ugliness, you contrived to have somebody who had become a liability moved far away and set up comfortably for the rest of what could have been a much more protracted lifetime, what did he do but come back again, insisting on making more trouble! It was a different league now, with different stakes, from the one that Jack had played in three years ago.

Jack had never risen beyond the class of specialist hired hand—looked after well enough and paraded in all the right places, there when Microbotics needed that awkward legal corner smoothed over a little; but one of the outside flunkies just the same.

Eric had been a passport to the inside—stimulating intellectually too, which was a relief. And for a while it had seemed they were bound for the inside summit, which lay in the global stratosphere—until he turned out to have scruples where men worthy of the name had balls. Typical of scientists: eager to dispense wisdom on the running of the world, but only from the safety behind someone else's throne; posturing verbally to compensate for what they lacked the nerve to risk physically. Or they ran away to build their haven beyond the empire's borders—which would last until the first legion of reality caught up.

Vanessa could have done without the complication of Kevin's being in the picture. But, materially he would still be better off than most—and perhaps even more so than otherwise, since this way the patents would be used more aggressively and effectively. He could even come out of it better in the long run—made of sterner stuff. It was hardly as if tragedy didn't happen every day, in any case. Sometimes it was just somebody's misfortune to be in the way. She could hardly rewrite the script of the world back to Day One.

As Payne's wife, she would come into joint control of a sizable portion of Microbotics, which, boosted by ownership of the by-then-reprieved technology and the deal that Ohira was talking about, would have appreciated to an impressive sum, indeed. Then, life would have acquired some truly interesting dimensions of possibility, cosmopolitan in scope and properly suited to her tastes. The only proviso was that in the meantime her spouse would need to overcome his narcissism and learn that there were greater things to aspire to in life than sailing his floating playpen and entertaining starlets with more boobs than IQ points. Otherwise, sad though it would be in some ways, one day, she might have to get rid of Martin. . . .

"Homicide Division."

"Hello, my name is Michelle Lang. I'm an attorney with the Prettis and Lang law offices in Seattle. I understand that one of your investigating officers was called to the scene of an incident that happened about two months ago. Could I speak to him, please?"

"What incident was this?"

"The deceased's name was Anastole, John Anastole. He was found dead in a room at the Northgate Way Ramada Inn on March third last."

"Anastole? Spelt *O-L-E*?"

"Yes."

"I'll check. . . . Here we are—Jonathan Charles Anastole?"

"That's right."

"That would be Officer Kollet. . . . Yes, he is in. Putting you through."

"Dave Kollet."

"Oh, hello. My name is Michelle Lang, with the Prettis and Lang law offices in Seattle. I wonder if you could help me with some background details of a case that you were called out to at the Northgate Way Ramada Inn about two months ago. A man by the name of John Anastole was discovered dead in one of the rooms."

"Just one moment. That was Prettis and Lang, in Seattle?"

"Yes. We're a law firm. I'm one of the partners."

"And we're talking about a John . . ."

"Anastole."

"Got it. Okay, well, I'm going to have to take your number and call you back on this. You're Ms. Lang, right? And what number are you calling from? . . ."

The premises of Microbotics Inc. were located among the space-age industrial developments and office parks north of Bellevue, just off Route 520 before Redmond. They consisted of a five-story metal-and-glass office building facing lawns, shrubbery, and the main parking lot; a laboratory block to one side; and two manufacturing units, which included stores and shipping, at the rear.

To avoid making her presence needlessly conspicuous, Vanessa drove past the visitor area in front of the main building and parked in the employees' lot at the rear of the lab block. She had called ahead, and Andy Finnion, Microbotics' head of security, was waiting for her. He was thickset and powerful in build, with iron gray hair cropped short above a lined, craggy face. His former background was with the city police department, which made him an invaluable accomplice to Payne's political and quasi-legal machinations. He worked competently and inconspicuously, and asked no questions. If he had one outstanding characteristic it was loyalty. Vanessa had always treated him as one to be particularly careful with.

"How was the drive?" he greeted as he held the door for Vanessa to get out.

"Bearable, I suppose. I think the geriatrics are all out on the road already, practicing for the holidays."

Finnion took her inside through a side entrance of the lab block and up to a room on the top floor. Martin Payne was there already, with the equipment set up ready for her.

The body-suit was a close-fitting mesh designed to stretch over skin contours, laced with a piezoelectric web that performed the two-way function of converting body movements to outgoing signals, and incoming feedback to pressure changes that would register as forces. The helmet was VR standard. A cabinet by the wall contained computing and conversion electronics, control console and screens, and a radio transmitter-receiver system connected to an antenna on the roof. In addition there was a secretary's desk, several office chairs, and incidentals.

Vanessa ran a startup routine and went through a couple of screens of initialization. Then she checked over the body suit and tested its connections. "It should all be okay," Payne told her. "We put it through a full run downstairs an hour ago. Phil is up in the mountains. I just talked to him on the phone."

Vanessa nodded. She indicated a door across the room from the one through which she and Finnion had entered. "What's in there? Can I use it to change?"

Payne pushed it open. "Just a small office. Sure, it's empty." Vanessa went through and closed the door. She took off her coat and hung it behind the door, then began changing out of her dress, into the body suit.

In the room outside, Payne paced across the floor and back, saying nothing. Finnion went out into the corridor and lit a cigarette.

"Ms. Lang?"

"Yes, this is Michelle Lang speaking."

"Oh, hi. This is Dave Kollet from Homicide Investigation calling back. Sorry it took so long. I got hit by something else just after we finished talking. A guy of eighty-five, with one leg, falls off the roof. His daughter insists it couldn't be an accident. She wants us to look into it. We get 'em all."

"Yes, Mr. Kollet."

"Okay, I have the case here. John Anastole, body discovered at the Ramada, March three. Now, what kind of questions did you have?"

"Well, I was interested in establishing more of the background circumstances. For example, if the door to the room was secured on the inside. Whether there were any signs of other occupancy. Perhaps damage to anything in the room. That kind of thing."

"Uh-huh. Can I ask you, Ms. Lang, what your interest is in this case?"

"I think the best way to put it might be to say that the deceased's death was of some financial advantage in certain quarters. I wanted to check whether there might be grounds for any suspicion."

"I see. Well, I'm sure you'll understand that this isn't the kind of information that we disclose over the phone to people we don't really know. Sorry for the inconvenience, but it will be necessary for you to come to the office in person if you want to pursue it further."

"Now I almost feel as if I'm a suspect."

"Ms. Lang, in our business, *everybody* is a suspect."

Sigh. "Yes, I understand. Very well, when would be a good time? . . ."

The teledirection program was running and would activate the VR interface as soon as the link was established.

Vanessa settled back in one of the office chairs and positioned the helmet. Finnion steadied it while she made fine adjustments and secured the chin harness. Payne stood watching, holding a phone. "How's it feel?" Finnion asked.

"That's fine," Vanessa said. She verified the graphics with a visual test, then executed a sequence of body and limb movements to check the motor control and feedback loops. The suit driver routines were set to high gain, meaning that slight body actions and muscle flexings would be sufficient to evoke the full range of perceived motions and tactile responses. Dramatic posturings and flailings weren't necessary. In fact, for most normal movements and gestures, with high-gain settings it was seldom obvious to observers that an operator was moving at all. Vanessa pulled down a menu of options, highlighted REMOTE LIVE, and selected the channel that she had pre-initiated.

The test pattern vanished, and she was on a floor of spongy fiber matting, inside a square arena formed by walls that appeared to be about twenty feet high. There was a stack of flat slabs inside the arena, and a sloping ramp. "Okay, Martin, I'm through," she said. Through the circuit patched into the audio, she could hear Payne punch a number into the phone.

Above the arena wall on one side was an underview of the armrest of a seat, with a protruding elbow clad in a yellow twill sleeve. Beyond that, like the vault of a cathedral interior, she could see the inside of a car roof and the top portion of one of the windows.

A ring tone sounded on the circuit. The elbow above her extended to become an arm, which then moved high above her like the jib of a crane, carrying a telephone handset. Phil Garsten's voice said, "Hello?"

"Phil, it's Martin. Vanessa says we're through on the link. You should be seeing some action now."

The mec was a horizontally postured design with six-legged, insect-like locomotion—the same one, in fact, that had dispatched Jack. The operator's arm sensors were coupled to the manipulator appendages, leaving each lower-body system to control a triplet of two-on-one-side, one-on-the-other legs working as a unit. Developing a steady walking rhythm required something of a knack, but there was no balancing act to worry about as with bipedal mecs, and Vanessa found it easier. She walked a slow circle in the upturned cardboard box lid on the passenger seat, pushing and pulling on each limb in turn and flexing the manipulators.

"It looks like it's working just fine to me," Garsten's voice said. Vanessa looked up. His face, curiously distorted by perspective, was filling half the view above and peering down at her, the arm holding a phone to one ear. "Jesus, this is weird," he said. "Just watching this thing moving down here, right next to you, is enough to give anyone the creeps."

Vanessa exercised the mec through a few more movements, then experimented with climbing the stack of calling cards and the matchbook. Everything seemed to be working fine. So, they knew the setup would work over an extended range—ninety miles, anyway, which was the distance to where Garsten was parked on a rocky shoulder by the side of a winding stretch of mountain road on the way to Barrow's Pass.

"Can Phil drive for about a mile?" Vanessa said aloud. "I want to try it with the car moving." Payne relayed the request to Garsten over the phone.

"Sure." High above, Garsten's face receded and turned away as he sat back in the seat. The arm transferred the phone to somewhere beyond Vanessa's field of view, then came back and turned the ignition key.

When the tests were through, Vanessa, Payne, and Finnion could go for lunch. That would give Garsten time to get back to Seattle and turn the "special" mec over to Vanessa. And they would be set. Today was Tuesday. By Saturday it would be all over.

CHAPTER NINETEEN

Kevin stood to one side with Sam and Josh, both also from his grade, watching the daily boarding mêlée around the school bus. When God had finished creating people, He found Himself with lots of legs and pimples left over, Kevin decided. So He threw them together in clumps and called the results teenagers.

Vanessa thought that Kevin ought to attend private school. It had the right social image. Eric said that learning how to mix and get along with anybody was more important.

"Would you get a load of that assignment," Sam grumbled. "Five pages! What do I care about the dumb English and their dumb king? They should have chopped all their heads off, like the French did."

"When do we get to see this boat of yours, Kev?" Josh asked. "Are there any islands along the inlet? Maybe we could fix up a swimming party at one of them."

"Let me think about it," Kevin said. "I've got a lot going on right now."

Taki appeared, picking his way through the throng, a blue school-bag slung over one shoulder. "Ah, Kev. I was beginning to wonder if you were in today. I was looking for you at lunch time but couldn't find you."

"Oh, there was something I needed to get finished." Actually, Kevin had spent the break in the library. He had wanted to be on his own and think.

"Did you bring the mecs?"

"I've got them here." The two that Kevin had put in Vanessa's car were not the flying versions that he and Taki were trying to develop.

"And the relay too?"

"Er, no. There's something else—"

"Gee, darn it, Kev. You said last night that you would. I wanted to try adding something tonight."

"Something else has come up that I needed it for. I'll tell you about it later."

He had to talk to somebody, he had decided—about the whole situation. Somebody who could share his viewpoint as an equal without going into lecture mode. While he knew that Michelle and Doug were on his side, adults had this propensity for letting themselves be hemmed in by rules. Their reflex seemed always to see only the restrictions by saying, "You *can't* do anything *because* . . ." Negative. He wanted to talk to somebody who could listen and say, "Hey, we *could* do something *if . . .*" Positive. That was what being American was supposed to be all about, wasn't it?

"See you, guys," Kevin said to Sam and Josh. He and Taki boarded the bus behind two girls talking about the clothes that you could buy in thrift stores. One of them had a happy face on the seat of her jeans, that someone had stuck there. Kevin followed Taki to the back, where he found a seat wedged next to a younger boy with freckles, nursing a cage containing a bat that he had brought in to show the class. Kevin wondered if it might be possible to equip a mec with sonar and process the echo signals so that they could be perceived as vision. Now *that* would be really neat, he told himself.

He said to the kid that it was a weird looking bat. The kid blew a bubble of gum at him and didn't answer.

The bus pulled away and began threading its way through the suburbs: white oblongs, regularly spaced; each surrounded by its patch of green with flowers; no people. Eric always said they looked like graveyards.

Hiroyuki's house had what had once been a basement family room, which Taki had taken over bit by bit like an encroaching plague and transformed into his private workshop. It included a mec control setup, with a coupler in the form of a barber's chair that one of the innumerable relatives had acquired as part of a job lot at an auction and had no use for. Taki sat hunched in it, legs crossed and arms wrapped around his knees, the mec-control headset and collar set aside on the cubicle adjacent. One of the winged mecs lay on the bench beside him. Above the bench was a shelf with parts, drawer units containing components, and an assortment of mecs, including several of the larger, earlier models. Kevin sprawled on the bar stool in front of a console. Both of them had managed to keep the winged mec aloft semicontrollably—more or less—for periods of up to several seconds, which was an encouraging step forward, but that had been earlier. For the best part of an hour now it had been inactive and eventually forgotten as Kevin divulged the full meaning of the events that Taki had witnessed the previous Friday and recounted the further developments that had taken place since.

Taki's initial astonishment changed to disbelief, and then was replaced by a temporary numbness that echoed Kevin's own before the full shock of what he was hearing sank in. His features still betrayed a hint of part of him trying to reject it when Kevin concluded, ". . . I figured there might be more chances like on the boat last Friday—to find out more about what's

going on. Or at least, if they happened, we ought to
be ready for them. So I fixed a box with Toad and
Tigger inside in the trunk of her car this morning—
it's right up at the back; you won't see it unless you go
looking. And that's why I don't have the relay. I put
that in with them too."

Taki's features, which had communicated nothing
for the past several minutes, expressed skepticism. "Isn't
that a long shot, Kev? Who's going to sit there in the
car and shout about all their plans, just to oblige you?"

"No, I know. We'll still have to send them with her,
or maybe someone else, when she goes places—like
on the boat. But at least they'll be there."

Taki nodded distantly.

Kevin shrugged. "And who knows? There's always
the chance that we might pick something useful up
in the car."

Taki didn't seem hopeful. "It's still passive though.
It still means sitting and having to wait for some kind
of lucky break that may not even happen. The odds
aren't something that I'd want to bet money on."

Kevin sighed and showed both his hands imploringly.
"Hell, Taki, what else do you want in the course of
one whole day? It might not be much, but it's more
than anyone else has been able to come up with. Give
me a break, for heaven's sakes. It'll get better. We'll
work on it." The tension that had been building in
him vented itself in his voice. The strain he felt showed
on his face. It didn't matter that what he had done
was grab wildly at a straw, with chances of achieving
anything useful probably as near zero as made no
difference. He had *done something*. Taki understood,
nodded, and didn't press the point.

"I just don't believe it can be that much of a problem,"
Taki said. "I mean, what about the police? Isn't that
what they're there for? What's the use if all they can

do is show up to draw chalk marks around dead bodies? Aren't they supposed to stop people being turned into dead bodies in the first place?"

"You'd think so. I said more or less the same thing to Michelle and Doug, but she says it isn't so simple." Kevin massaged his brow with a hand. "When did grown-ups ever come up with anything simple? Half of them would lose their jobs."

"But it's right there on the tape," Taki insisted. "They're gonna change your dad's will to cut you out, and he won't be around to argue about it. What else could it mean?"

"That's what I said too. But when you really listen to it, it doesn't actually *say* a hell of a lot. Most of what you think you hear is in your head. It doesn't mention any names except 'Phil,' which could mean anything. And even assuming it is Garsten—which it is, obviously, although how do you prove it?—we don't have anything he's actually done that we could show as evidence—no document or something. It's all guesses."

Taki shook his head. "And Michelle won't even go talk to the police? I still can't believe it."

"Well, that could be on account of her job somehow, too, I guess."

"What about Doug, then? Won't he even try? He always struck me as the kind of guy who doesn't mess around—who'd go right in and tell it like it is if he thought there was a chance it might do any good."

"Hm." Kevin rotated the stool he was sitting on through a half circle toward the far wall, then back to face Taki again. "I think he might want to do more than that," he said in a serious voice.

"What do you mean?"

"Well, from some of the things he said this morning when he ran me into school, he doesn't seem to think that involving the police solves much, anyway—it would just put everyone on their guard, and they'd just lie low for a while. The risk would still always be there. It wouldn't have gone away."

"What *does* he want, then?"

Kevin shrugged. "An answer that'll be more permanent, I guess."

Taki stared, clearly trying hard not to show the alarm that he just as clearly felt at the way this was starting to sound. "Like what?"

"He doesn't know."

A silence fell while they mulled over what had been said, both looking for a constructive continuation and not finding one. Taki unfolded his legs, reached out to pick the mec up off the bench, and turned it over between his fingers, regarding it thoughtfully. "What do you think we should call it?" he asked, looking up. "Now we're getting it close to working, it ought to get a name to celebrate."

"I dunno. Any ideas?"

"How about, maybe, Icarus or Orville?"

"I vote for Icarus. It's got wings."

"Okay, Icarus it is. Hi, Icarus. Now we have to get the colors right. What colors did Icarus have?"

"I'm not sure. White sheet-things and ballet tunics? You know, Greek kinda stuff."

The phone rang on the console behind Kevin. "Oh, flip it to speaker mode," Taki said. "I can't be bothered to get up." Kevin turned and pressed a button. "Hello?" Taki said.

The voice of Taki's older sister, Nakisha, came through, giggling. "It's your *girlfriends* in Tacoma."

"Hey, wait a minute. No. We're—"

Click. "Hello? Is this Taki?"

"Oh . . . hi, Janna."

"Hi. Avril's here with me. She's helping me paint

my room. We just thought we'd give you a call to say what a terrific time we had with you guys over at Kevin's on Sunday. Those little mecs are absolutely incredible! We haven't been able to stop talking about them. The things you could do with them are just endless. Your uncle's got the right idea. They'd be an absolute sensation. There's no question about it."

"Well, I'm glad you enjoyed yourselves. . . . It was fun."

"You sound as if you're on speaker."

"That's right."

"Your sister said Kevin was there too. Hi, Kev. Are you there? Can you hear me?"

Kevin sent Taki a resigned look. "Hello, Janna. I'm here. Yes, just fine."

"Wanna say hello to Avril?" Before Kevin could say anything, the voice changed.

"Kevin? Hi, this is Avril."

"Hi again. Got your balance back yet?"

"Wow! I was beginning to think I'd never walk straight again . . . but it might have been more the boat. Do you know, we had such a good time. And you guys get into such really interesting stuff."

"Part of the service. We try to please."

"What do we have to do to borrow a couple of mecs? We could be a real sensation showing something like those around."

Kevin glanced at Taki and rolled his eyes upward. "I wish it were that easy. You'd need to have the gear to control them, for a start."

"Okay, I know, I know. Just kidding. Janna wants us to enroll in an electronics basics class next semester. What do you think?"

"Sure, why not? I think it's a great idea."

"Would we be up to it?"

"There's no other way to find out, is there? Go for

it. You'd be surprised what you can do. Think positive."

"Did you do any more yet with those mecs you said you were trying to get to fly?"

"That's what we're working on right now."

"Hey! Can we get to try those too?"

"Well, give us a chance to get it working right first." Kevin directed what was meant to be an exasperated look at Taki, but Taki was staring fixedly at the shelf where the mecs were and seemed to have floated away on thoughts of his own.

"We're with this club here that's having a hike up in the mountains next Saturday," Avril went on. "And we thought you and Taki might want to come along. I asked the guy who's organizing it, and he said it would be okay. Do you think you might be able to make it? Do you like going on hikes? We'd really love to have you along."

"Sure . . . when I can fit them in." Kevin looked over at Taki again for an input. No response.

"Have you got something else fixed for the holiday weekend?"

"Oh, I like the idea. But there's a lot going on right now that I can't really go into. I don't know if it's going to be possible to get away."

"You will let us know, though? You've got the number, right?"

"You bet. . . . And thanks."

"Great. Well, I seem to be hogging the phone here. I'm going to sign off and let Janna say a few more words. You take care. So we'll hear from you soon, Kev?"

"Right. Bye for now."

"See you, Taki. . . ."

Then Janna was back. "Hello, is this still Kevin?"

"Wait a second. I'll kick him. . . . Taki. . . . Taki, your *girlfriend* is back. Aren't you gonna talk to her?"

"What? . . . Oh, hi again, Janna. This is Taki. Sorry, I got a bit carried away by something."

"Do you think you might be able to make it Saturday?"

"Saturday?"

"The hike."

"What hike?"

"The hike that Avril just—"

Kevin interrupted. "It's okay, I'll tell him about it. Don't worry. He's having one of his withdrawals. You know, Orientals—retreating into the inner world. Meditation, contemplation, all that stuff."

"Are you serious?"

"No."

"Gee, then maybe it's not a good time. You sound like you could be pretty busy."

"Well, now you come to mention it, actually there is that, you could say so, yes. . . ."

"Okay, we'll leave you to it. But you will let us know before the weekend, yes?"

"You've got it."

"So long then, Kev. We'll see you around, anyhow. *And goodbye, Taki.*"

"See you, Janna," Taki managed from the background. The voice gave way to a steady, echoing tone, which ceased as Kevin reset the phone.

"Is it hot or cold there?" Kevin asked, turning back. "What color is the sky? Which planet are you on, Taki?"

Taki stared back at him for several seconds, his mouth making silent chewing motions. Then he said, "So, this guy Garsten hasn't been very helpful and left documents lying around for anyone to use as evidence. I think that's really inconsiderate of him. But you know, Kev, I bet there is one place they'll be—if they exist. And it wouldn't mean having to sit around waiting for someone else to give you what you want. You go there yourself and get it."

"Where's that?"

"Inside the computer in his office. He's bound to have one."

For a moment, Kevin started to sit up and look interested. Then he slumped down again, as if having expected better. "Oh, great. So what do we do, dress up as meter readers so we can sneak a look, like in some stupid movie? . . . And I'm sure he leaves it on a dial-in line overnight, with the files organized to be accessible just so as people like us can hack into it. Come on, Taki, get real. Even if you're right, what good does it do us?"

Taki got up from the barber's chair and walked over to lift one of the mecs down from the shelf above the bench. It was one of the older "telebot" designs, like Ironside—heavy-powered, sturdy, about the size of a quart can. Its name was Sir Real. Taki set it down on the console, facing the screen and keyboard like an organist confronting the controls of a gigantic Wurlitzer.

"What are you doing?" Kevin asked, straightening up again on the stool and looking baffled.

Taki moved the mec closer to the keys, estimating the range of its arm with his eye. "Can you move into the coupler and tune in?" he said to Kevin, still distantly. "I want to try something. I've just thought of another way of getting at what's inside somebody's computer."

CHAPTER TWENTY

Eric exited from on-line and stared at the desk-side screen in his office, now showing the general options menu. Another four points down. So the rumor about Geddes & West had been right on the mark. If this started a general run, it could get serious. No, it was a bit late to be thinking things like that—this was already serious.

Maybe the three-day closing of trading over the holiday would provide a cooling-off period and avert a panic? He shook his head, even as the thought began to form— he was honest enough with himself to recognize wishful thinking when he saw it. This was still only Wednesday morning, and with the aid of electronics these things could avalanche in hours, if not less.

On the other hand, the technical dispute at the back of it all might generate enough uncertainty to slow things down. He had been getting calls all week from reporters and journalists asking for comments, and his initially patient denials and explanations were beginning to sound more curt. Medieval superstition had not gone away with the advent of technology and its supposed accompanying rationalism; it had merely been computerized.

It couldn't be a coincidence that all this should be starting to happen again just when the company seemed ready to soar. Everything that was going on had the same feel and imprint about it as the events of three years ago that he had believed were over. Except that this time it had a more sophisticated touch. Whoever was behind it had been doing a lot more background research this time; or somebody was leaking information.

He still couldn't comprehend the spite of mentalities that would undermine what they had been unable to equal, the cowardice of trying to tear down now what they had been unwilling to risk themselves. But it seemed a truer picture of human history than the one he had tried to construct around himself, in which integrity and merit paid in the end. He had an uncomfortable feeling that perhaps he was just waking up to a fact of life that would already be self-evident to somebody like Kevin, and Kevin had been too kind or too polite to bring to his attention.

If true, then there probably wasn't very much that he could do about it, he decided. People were largely born what they were, and even if that weren't strictly the case, he was long past the age when nurturing or good intentions were likely to make much difference. He'd read a theory somewhere that the same peculiarity of makeup that enabled people to excel in one direction always created some compensating inadequacy somewhere else. He should have taken more notice of Doug in the early days, he told himself, for whatever use that was now.

The phone on his desk rang. He steeled himself for another reporter. "Dr. Heber, what is your reaction to the allegations that have been appearing recently concerning . . .?" Or, "Can you state categorically, Dr. Heber, that there are no adverse side effects whatsoever?" But it had to be done, of course. If not he, then who?

He sat forward and picked up the phone. "Yes, Beverley?"

"I've got Michelle Lang on the line for you."

"Oh." Eric's eyebrows raised. "Very well. Put her through."

"Hello, Eric?"

"Yes. Hello there. What's new in the legal parts of the world? Or did I phrase that badly? Are there illegal parts?"

"I think I'm beginning to see where Kevin gets it from. As a matter of fact it's more social. I know this is short notice, but are you doing anything for lunch?"

"Well, I was originally scheduled to spend it with a couple of entomologists from San Francisco who are interested in using mecs to observe working insect colonies from the inside." Eric shrugged to himself. "At least, they were interested. They've canceled the trip. I guess we slipped down on the priority scale. Why, are you due out this way?"

"I can be," Michelle said. "And I want to talk to you— preferably before the holiday."

"Well, I'm glad somebody does, apart from jugular-seeking reporters. What time did you have in mind?"

"I'm flexible. How about twelve-thirty?"

"Sounds good. Would you like to meet here?"

"That would be fine. Oh—and by the way, I mentioned what you said about Relativity to a physicist I know at the university. He said you're crazy, it's all been proved experimentally, and haven't you ever heard of mass . . . what was it? I've got a note somewhere here . . ."

Eric smiled. "Mass-energy equivalence," he supplied.

"That's it. And there was something else about—"

"Don't tell me. Velocity-dependence of mass, and time dilation," Eric said.

"Is that what it was? Okay, if you say so."

"I have heard that before. Well, you can tell him that all those can be derived from Maxwell's equations and the conservation of momentum by classical methods, and don't say anything that's unique to Relativity at all. Einstein himself admitted it in his later years." Eric waited a second. "Was that all?"

"From me or from the physicist?"

"From the physicist."

"Yes, I think so."

Eric made a face. "Then tell him I'm disappointed. If he comes up to Barrows Pass this coming weekend he'll hear more objections than those—and some interesting answers, too. Ask him to explain the aberration of VLB interferometers. And what about laser ring gyros?"

"Slow down, Eric. I'm still at the beginning. Who was it again with the equations? Maxwell, was it? . . ."

"Don't worry about it," Eric said, laughing. "I'll write it down and give it to you at lunch. We'll see you here at about twelve-thirty, then."

On her drive south from the city, Michelle tried to analyze her own thoughts and ask what, exactly, she was hoping to accomplish. Her honest answer was that she wasn't sure. She felt frustrated at the little headway she had made the day before, the only tangible result being faxed copies of Jack Anastole's autopsy report and death certificate, which were public-domain information anyway and could have been obtained by anyone. Her real intention, she supposed, was to sound out Eric's state of receptiveness, and, depending on his reactions, maybe plant some thoughts that might germinate over the holiday weekend. In that way she would have done as much as was possible for the present to create the circumstances for things to progress further in their own time. If nothing more happened for the remainder of the week, it would not have been entirely wasted.

She arrived at Neurodyne shortly before twelve-thirty. As she parked in the visitor area, she noticed that both the Jeep and the Jaguar were in the reserved slots, which meant that Vanessa was also on the premises today. Michelle tried to anticipate what complications that might be likely to precipitate. Would it not seem odd for Michelle to be visiting Eric, not Vanessa, when she and not he was involved most in the firm's legal matters? Worse still, he might invite Vanessa to join them, which would negate the whole point of Michelle's coming here.

Michelle was still hurriedly composing some alternative reason in her mind for being here, when Eric appeared in the lobby—alone. Outwardly he was his usual affable self, and said he'd had Beverley call ahead to make reservations at a seafood restaurant in University Place, a marina waterfront center on the shore of the Narrows; but in his eyes and his voice, Michelle detected hints of strain.

When they left the building, Eric showed her to the Jaguar. "What's this? Don't you think the Jeep is appropriate to taking a lady to lunch?" she teased as he held the door for her to get in. "It really doesn't matter. I'm not that much of a snob really."

"Vanessa's taking the Jeep into the shop to be looked at this afternoon," he told her. "She says the transmission's playing up, or something."

"How is she today?" Michelle asked as Eric climbed in the other side and closed the door.

"Tied up with Joe Skerrill—I think. Something to do with the DNC patents. It all means about as much to me as Swahili. I haven't seen her all morning."

Which put paid to that particular worry. Michelle

settled back in her seat, feeling more relaxed. The road outside the gates was still as Michelle had last seen it: machines digging trenches for sewer pipes; earthmovers leveling the adjacent lots. "That's another advantage of being in microengineering," Eric commented as they threaded their way between cones and warning signs. "Expanding to larger premises isn't a problem. You just open up another room."

On the way to the restaurant, he talked about the bad press that DNC was getting and its effects on the company's fortunes. Neurodyne stock was down alarmingly, and investors were getting nervous. A couple of big ones had actually pulled out. It was the first time Michelle had heard him admit that it was probably being engineered deliberately. He didn't seem to understand how people could try to suppress through fraud and disinformation what they were unable to compete with legitimately. Michelle couldn't help but get the feeling that he had never before seriously entertained the possibility that the world could be that way. He was ready to grant, too, that certain among the top management at Microbotics—and perhaps some of their financial associates—were probably behind it. The journalists and hack scientists who figured more visibly were dupes or hired hands. At least, this changed outlook could make her task easier, Michelle reflected.

The head waiter knew Eric and had saved them a window table facing the water—not that there was especially much to look out at; it was a moody day, with dark piles of cloud low down to the west and gray overcast everywhere else. Choppy waves roughened the Sound, with a stiff wind flapping the lines and rigging of the boats at their moorings. Eric decided that the day called for something hot and ordered the steak and mushroom pie.

"Bowdlerized American version," he commented, now back to his usual self, eyes twinkling through the gold-rimmed spectacles. "In Europe it's steak and kidney."

"Sounds dreadful."

"You see—expectations predetermine taste."

Michelle settled for the grilled salmon.

When the waiter had gone, Eric produced a slip of paper with the phrases scrawled on it that he had used over the phone when they touched on Relativity, along with a few lines of explanation. "Do we need to go into this now?" Michelle asked as she took it.

"I hope not."

"Good." She folded the paper and tucked it into her purse. "You know, you and he are going to have to talk to each other direct if you want to take this further. This is as far as I go playing the messenger."

"What's his name?"

"Fred Wainer."

"At the university, you said?" Eric thought for a few moments and shook his head. "I know a few of the physicists there, but I don't think I've heard that name."

"His field is nuclear."

"Oh, that might explain it, then. How did you meet him? Was he an expert witness in another great lawsuit that you handled? Millions of dollars at stake, and a threat to national security? Espionage treachery, murder, mayhem—the stuff of great novels and blockbuster movies?"

"No. At a dance."

"Um." Eric broke a roll and started spreading butter on the pieces. The wine waiter stopped by. They decided to stay with a glass each—one house Burgundy, one Cabernet.

"Actually, most lawyers' work is pretty mundane," Michelle said. "I'll let you into a professional secret.

All the business about titanic clashes of intellect, and rapier-like cuttings and parryings of reason that you read about—it's all invented to satisfy the expectations of the faithful. At the bottom of it all, we're really a religion too—just the way you said science is getting to be."

"Oh, really?" Eric looked interested. "How's that, now? Tell me about it."

"Almost all human disputes and misunderstandings are easily settled as matters of routine. The conditions of sale of an airline ticket; who pays for the broken part; whether these bank charges are in order—clerks and counter assistants take care of it, according to the rules."

Eric nodded. "Very well."

"The cases that aren't quite so clear get referred upward to management, and the problems that don't get solved at some level or other there are relatively few. Those few are the ones you call in specialist help over—say, by turning it over to the legal department. And it's only the instances where the lawyers can't work out a solution—which again are the exceptions—that ever get near a courtroom at all."

"Okay. That makes sense. I agree. And? . . ."

"When the courts can't decide, it goes upward again, until finally you reach the summit for a ruling: the ultimate law of the land; the Supreme Court, the Pope, the British House of Lords . . . I don't know what they have in Germany. Whatever."

"Yes?"

Michelle shrugged, as if the rest ought to have been obvious. "That's it. That's the big secret."

Eric shifted his eyes from side to side as if fearing eavesdroppers, then whispered, "What is?"

"The issues that make it to that kind of level for a decision are inherently undecidable. They *can't* be resolved by any system rules or reason that humans are capable of devising. If they could they would have been already—somewhere lower down the hierarchy where the requisite technical expertise exists. They're beyond all that."

"So what do we do?"

"What we do is use robes and ritual to solemnly camouflage the truth that the most illustrious in whom we place our ultimate trust might as well flip a coin for all the sense they're going to be able to make of it now. But the people go away happy that great wisdom has been dispensed and justice done, and the important business of life carries on."

Eric seemed fascinated. "And what's the important business of life?" he asked.

Michelle shrugged. "Feeding kids; making shoes; painting fences. Things like that."

They paused as the wines arrived.

"But isn't someone going to notice sooner or later that the coin can come down heads one time and tails another?" Eric said.

Michelle nodded. "Yes, precisely—so you have to make sure that doesn't happen. When the Oracle is asked the same question, it needs to deliver the same answer. Hence the legal obsession with precedents."

Eric sipped his drink and thought about that. "Yes, you're right. Most of what's called science works the same way. Bad data is defined as any result that doesn't fit the theory."

Michelle looked surprised in her turn. "So what happened to all this business we hear about rigorous proof by experiment?" she queried. "Doesn't it work that way? I mean, if your theory's not right, your plane won't fly. Isn't it so? How can a bad theory in science survive?"

Eric beamed, evidently having expected just that.

"Easily. Because science that works stops being science and becomes engineering. So you could almost say that science doesn't really exist. It's a bit like the present instant that separates future from past—an infinitesimally thin dividing line between unproven speculations and planned obsolescence."

"You make it sound almost insignificant," Michelle chided.

"Not really," Eric said. "It's simply a boundary. What we know is inside; what we don't is outside. Just because it's thin doesn't make it unimportant. Some of the most interesting things happen at boundaries. Take surfaces of planets. Wars, politics. . . ." He made a nonchalant, throwing-away motion. "What else is sex but a meeting of epidermises?"

Michelle smiled and shook her head. They sat back as the waiter arrived and set their plates. "Is there anything else I can get you?" he asked.

Eric shook his head. "No, I don't think so, thank you."

"Enjoy your meal." The waiter left.

"Anyway," Eric went on, "charming and delightful as all this is, I don't think you came here to exchange philosophies. So is it my body that you're really after? Or was there something else?"

Michelle admitted to herself that she had been putting the subject off. The fact was, she did enjoy talking with him. The bizarre tangents that his mind was apt to fly off on, always provocative, never in an expected direction, were fascinating—a refreshing relief from the dreary, predictable ego-centered or defensive monologues she was so used to hearing. For a moment she found herself questioning if it was really that vital to have the conversation today that she had told herself she had come here for, or had that been an excuse? . . .

Definitely not, she ruled. She was too much the

professional for that. Her sole motive was business.

"You pretty much brought it up yourself on the way here in the car," she said. "The business that's going on concerning DNC. It isn't an accident. You've said as much in effect yourself now."

Eric didn't pretend to be totally surprised. "So are you saying there's something we can do about it—apart from simply sticking to the facts? Lies always come unraveled in the end, you know."

"Yes, but that doesn't necessarily mean they're ineffective. They can still do a lot of damage while you're waiting for the loose ends to show. . . ." She was stalling, she knew. Eric chewed, watching her and waiting. She set down her fork to appeal with both hands. "My job is to be suspicious about everybody. In this instance, that means anybody in a position to be able to threaten Ohira's interests. With the situation we've got, the first questions in any cop's mind would be about people with previous connections with Microbotics." She paused, then, to emphasize her point, added, "Connections to things that matter. I'm not talking about any former janitor who worked there."

Eric's eyes widened in astonishment, his fork poised in midair. "My God! Surely you don't mean me?"

"I guess what I'm trying to say is that I can't exclude anybody. But I'd certainly hope not you—it wouldn't make any sense."

Eric frowned, then looked puzzled. "Well, Patti Jukes was there—but only for a short while, as a low-level technician. That only leaves Doug . . ." He snorted and smiled at the absurdity of the thought. "And Vanessa."

Michelle kept a sober expression. "I can't exclude *anybody*," she repeated.

"Don't tell me you're serious?"

"I just want to make the suggestion, and have you accept it, that we can't afford to ignore any possibility."

There. It had come out somewhat lamer than she had intended, but to someone of Eric's perspicacity it would make the point.

And as she watched, the shutters slammed down. He shook his head curtly, managing only with an effort to stop short of overt anger. "No, that's not possible. Please, I don't want to discuss this. Let this one ride."

The data didn't fit the theory. So what was Michelle to do now? Was this really the time to go wading in with a two-by-four and tell him she had a tape; that his son had been spying on his wife, who was not only betraying his business but had a lover too—and oh yes, by the way, they were planning to murder him? If he was this blocked to the small test that she'd tried, what would pushing it further achieve, other than produce an emotional standoff that would push any chance of their resuming on a constructive note only farther into the future? Better to let it rest for now. Leave the thought to soak in; give the spinal-cord reaction time to die away. Wasn't that, after all, as much as she'd told herself she had set out to accomplish?

She backed off with a sigh and enough of a smile to be conciliatory. "Of course, I understand how you feel," she replied. "But you have to understand me too, Eric. I just wanted you to be aware that from where I see things, nothing is impossible."

Eric nodded, made a face, and raised a hand to show that he concurred. There was still some visible ruffling of the feathers . . . but the situation was defused.

They had the time, Michelle reminded herself. There was no indication of anything drastic about to happen soon.

CHAPTER TWENTY-ONE

Doug Corfe sat in his second-floor office in the Neurodyne building and stared at the far wall, as he seemed to have been doing for half the afternoon. And that wasn't good enough. There was work to be done. But he couldn't get the situation with Vanessa off his mind. Eric and Kevin were too close, too much like family for him not to feel responsible. And even if that had not been the case, it wasn't something that a person of his makeup could sit by and let happen without at least trying to do something.

But do what? His mind seemed to oscillate between extremes like a beach ball rolling from end to end on a teeter-totter. Part of the time he felt that Michelle was being too cautious—weren't they talking about somebody's *life* being at stake here, for heaven's sake? He would go to the police himself if she wouldn't—and who cared whether or not there was enough evidence to make a case, who could prove what, or about all the other lawyer's technicalities? Several times he had been on the verge of calling them right there, from his office. . . .

And then, like a view of a wire cube, his perspective would shift, and the whole line of thought would appear as no more than a sop to his own conscience—fooling himself that it would mean anything to passively pass over to others what he had already been told would do no good. At that point he wanted to throw aside all caution completely, and would find himself seriously entertaining fantasies about arranging an accident himself—and then shake himself out of it.

Maybe something not quite as drastic, then. Weren't there supposed to be professionals who specialized in making sure that messages got received clearly—messages like, "Too bad, what happened to Martin's nice boat; guess what might be next if anything happens to Eric."? . . . But no, it was just another fantasy. He wouldn't even know where to start, even if he were serious. The result of it all was that he was still sitting there more than halfway though the afternoon, with nothing done that was worth speaking of, when Kevin called.

"Hi, Doug. Sorry to interrupt you at work, but I think it's important."

"I wasn't doing anything that you could call interruptible. Anyhow, if it's about what I think it's probably about, it's important. What's up?"

"Well, er, I don't think it would be a good idea to go into it now. But could we get together maybe this evening and talk about it?"

"Sure," Corfe said. "Did you have anywhere in particular in mind?"

"Probably best not at the house. I was thinking, maybe over at Hiroyuki's. Could you pick me up later?"

Corfe frowned into the phone. "Hiroyuki's? Why there? Wouldn't that be almost as bad?"

"It has to do with an idea that Taki had last night—you know, to solve our problem. Well, I don't know about solve it, so much, but do something that might help, anyway. We tried it out over there, and—"

"Wait a minute, Kevin. An idea that Taki had? You're not saying he knows about this situation?"

"He's okay, honest. It won't go any further. . . ."

"Oh, Jesus Christ!" Corfe groaned and covered his brow with a hand.

"I know him better than I know anyone, really. He's the only person I can talk to who's on the same wavelength. I had to talk to somebody. It's bad enough for you, Doug, from what you were telling me, and we're not talking about *your* dad. Just try being in my position for a day and see how it feels."

"Okay, okay." Corfe couldn't find it in him to argue. He'd known Kevin long enough to believe it wasn't something he would have rushed into lightly. And besides, it was done now. The worst thing they could do would be to start falling out among themselves with accusations and recriminations. "Give me a chance to get clear here." Corfe snorted to himself. Get clear from what? He'd said it through pure force of habit. "I'll stop by the house at around . . . say, between five and six."

"Sounds good to me."

After hanging up, Corfe remembered that Michelle had been at the firm earlier in the day. If what Kevin had to say concerned the case in general, then perhaps it would be an idea if Corfe took her along too.

It didn't make any difference, as things turned out. When he called Beverley, Eric's secretary, she told him that Michelle had departed back for Seattle a couple of hours previously.

While Corfe was driving to Kevin's a little over an hour later, he recalled a story that one of Ohira's friends had told him of an incident that had taken place some years before. One of Hiroyuki's female cousins—a widow in her fifties—became involved with a cult that practiced self-discovery and inner development. Their chosen path toward enlightenment and a higher mode of living involved groups getting together, usually at weekends, sometimes for a full week, at varying venues, and to feel that she was getting into the spirit and contributing her share, the cousin commissioned an architect to design a substantial extension to her house. The architect also offered his services as a consultant to choose a suitable contractor for the work, supervise the quality and performance, and generally act on her behalf to make sure she got value for the substantial amount of money involved.

All did not go well. Extras that were supposed to be optional suddenly became essential; time frames escalated; one estimate after another was exceeded. Ohira became suspicious and hired a consultant of his own to do a little checking on the side. It turned out that the architect's whole operation was a scam. He himself was the real contractor, paying himself under the table, while at the same time gouging on prices and cutting costs through substandard materials and shoddy work. At the same time, he had committed so little to writing, and the widow had kept so few records, that Hiroyuki's lawyer was dubious that much could be made to stick in court.

That was the point at which the architect received a visitation from some polite Oriental Gentlemen in business suits. They read their list of grievances, suggested a figure that they thought would constitute reasonable compensation, and gave an assurance that if it were met, they would consider the matter closed. The architect told them, in more verbose terms, to go to hell. The deputation expressed regret at their failure to communicate their position clearly, and withdrew.

In the course of the next two months, the architect had two cars burned out by vandals; his front lawn was moonscaped by an agricultural weedkiller; his garage was demolished by an earth mover that mysteriously moved itself from a nearby construction site. Haunted, perhaps, by the ghost of Christmas Future, he underwent a Scrooge-like change of heart and settled with the widow for a more-than-generous figure, upon which his run of bad luck ceased as promptly as it had begun.

Maybe, Corfe thought as he drove south on I-5, God did indeed work in strange ways, and was guiding him to the right people. In this new light, what Kevin had said about figuring something out with Taki that he couldn't go into over the phone suddenly began to sound as if it could take on a whole new meaning. Had they taken it upon themselves to involve Ohira? Surely it wasn't possible, Corfe told himself. Kevin couldn't be that far ahead of him already.

Working with mecs, Kevin had pretty much come to accept extraordinary experiences as a routine part of his life. Even so, this was one of the oddest sensations that he had ever known. Physically, i.e. in terms of motor control and tactile feedback, he was "in" one mec, while simultaneously monitoring himself through the visual system of another. It was like watching himself in one of the "out-of-body" experiences that the grownups' comics at supermarket checkouts talked about.

Taki's idea had been to use the mecs as a way of checking out Garsten's computer files. If the system wasn't as accessible externally via the phone lines as was always the case—conveniently—in movies, then the only other way was to go in. Doing so in person, however, would be messy and risky, and was very frowned upon. Also, it required some means of effecting person-size access, which was a good way to break things and leave all kinds of other traces. But from drains and ducts to packages and briefcases, there had to be a score of ways to get the little guys into a building. Once inside, how would they go about exploring the contents of a computer? Well, just as with any other kind of operator, it would involve pressing keys and looking at a screen to see what happened.

Smaller mecs couldn't provide the force necessary for pressing keys. That required one of the older, can-size, "telebot" models, which was why they were using Sir Real. The same mec could also observe the screen, but Kevin and Taki's trial runs to try out the idea had shown the process to be irritatingly cumbersome and slow—like running back and forth playing a theater orchestra single-handed while trying to watch what was happening up on stage at the same time. So Kevin had suggested using two mecs: the telebot to operate the keys, while another captured an integrated view of its movements and the results on the screen, and combining the two inputs into the sensory channels of one coupler.

It was like watching a puppet from a few feet behind, and having invisible wires attached to its limbs. And it was an improvement on using the telebot alone. However, although the view from the rearward-positioned mec did cover the whole keyboard, the portion immediately in front of Sir Real was obscured, which resulted in fumbling and awkward body-movements to clear the line of sight.

Kevin experimented with a few more lines, then selected the Control menu and exited. "It's better, but not as easy as you think," he told Taki and Corfe, who were with him in Taki's workshop. "The trouble is that I got used to touch-typing too long ago. I can't visualize where the characters are. It's my *fingers* that remember."

"I know what you mean," Corfe said. "Sometimes

you get the same thing with a phone number. You can't remember it to say it, but you can still punch it in."

"Yes, exactly like that," Kevin agreed.

Corfe had arrived at Kevin's earlier, all fired up with the strange idea that practically the whole of Hiroyuki's family was involved. He hadn't said what had given him such a notion, and had seemed a little let down for some reason when Kevin told him that he'd meant what he said on the phone, and Taki was the only person he had breathed a word to. This had puzzled Kevin, for Corfe had sounded aghast earlier at even that much—but Kevin hadn't quizzed him on it. Corfe had livened up again since they arrived at Hiroyuki's, and seemed enthusiastic about Kevin and Taki's scheme. As far as it went technically, anyway; he still hadn't committed himself one way or another with regard to actually implementing it.

"Maybe we could reposition the visual to look vertically down on the keyboard," Taki suggested. He picked up the monitor mec from the bench where it had been standing and looked around for something to provide a mounting.

"Why not just sit it on the edge of the monitor and invert the visual field?" Kevin suggested.

"Of course," Taki muttered. Then he frowned. "But then how will you see the screen?"

"Hm. A point," Kevin agreed.

Taki put the video mec down again. "Maybe we need two mecs for vision. Superimpose their outputs somehow."

"I've got a better idea," Kevin said. "I wonder if it would be possible to couple Sir Real's arm-control signals direct into the neural circuits for fingers. Then, maybe, you could drive it via your touch typing reflexes, and that way you wouldn't need a visual of the keyboard at all."

"Hey, that would be neat," Taki said. He sat back in his seat to think it over.

"In fact . . ." Kevin went on, taking it further, "the only visual you'd need would be the screen, and Sir Real already gets you that . . ." He nodded to himself. "So you can do it with one mec. That's all you'd need."

"Neat," Taki said again. "Decidedly niftful."

Kevin removed the head harness and collar and looked at Corfe. "Although . . . if we're talking about changing the DNC coupling tables, it would probably mean involving Eric. Could that be a problem?"

"Why should it?" Taki asked. "We can just tell him it's a project we got curious about. He doesn't need to know what we want it for."

Kevin shrugged and looked uncomfortable. "I don't know. It's just the thought of getting him involved in something like this, that's not very legal. . . . It doesn't feel right."

Taki looked as if he still couldn't really see why, but nodded anyway.

"Maybe you don't have to," Corfe said. "I've got a better way still."

"What's that?" Kevin asked curiously.

"We've got a new mec in the lab back at the firm that does just what you want. It's called Keyboard Emulator. We developed it to give operators in couplers general-system access through regular terminals. It plugs a cord into a regular terminal keyboard socket. The other end goes to a connector mounted on the top of its head like a hat. So there's no need to fool around hitting keys at all."

It sounded ideal. How it operated was still unclear, however. Were you supposed to "think" characters at it, somehow? Kevin wondered. No, that couldn't be right. DNC operated on definable motor outputs from the nervous system, not abstract concepts lurking in as-yet unmapped and impenetrable regions of the brain.

"So what do you do?" he asked.

"Pull down a virtual keyboard with two highlights that give you hunt-and-peck," Corfe said. He thought for a moment. "Although . . . I like what you're talking about better—direct linking to touch-type reflexes. Maybe that's something we ought to think about."

"It sounds fine for us as it stands," Kevin said. "How come I've never heard of it?"

"I told you, it's new." Corfe sighed. "Probably it shouldn't be let out of the firm, but in this situation I don't think I'd be too hung up about borrowing one for a night."

It was the kind of indication that Kevin had been waiting for. He looked at Corfe eagerly. "Does that mean you're in with us, Doug? You'll help us do it?"

Corfe held up a hand. "Hey, wait a minute. I haven't said anything definite yet. Borrowing a KE mec is the straightforward part—*if* we decide to do it. Breaking into this guy's office is something else."

All of Kevin's exasperation with the adult world came pouring back. He threw up his hands, and his voice rose. "But Doug, for two days you've been getting madder and madder about not being able to *do anything!* All the way here tonight—"

"Shh, Kev." Taki moved his eyes to indicate the house around and above them. "Keep it down, guy."

Kevin exhaled and moderated his tone. "All the way here you sounded like you wanted to start a war. Well . . . this is something we can *do*—something active, where we're not just sitting waiting for . . . for what? I don't know. What else have we got?"

"And soon," Taki put in. "We've got the holiday weekend coming up right ahead. Nobody's going to be around there then. It would be the perfect time."

They stared fixedly at him, as if daring him to find an objection.

Corfe agonized. Kevin could read his mind: loath to shoot the proposition down, but at the same time, way out of his depth.

"Okay," Corfe said finally. "So suppose you do get in there, and you're into his computer. What, exactly, are you hoping to find?"

Kevin glanced uncertainly at Taki. Taki returned a look that was about as helpful as a write-only-memory chip. They had been too preoccupied with the technicalities to really give that question much thought. "Well, this codicil . . ." Kevin said finally, to Corfe. "Or something that talks about it maybe. I'm not sure. . . ."

"You haven't got a clue, you mean," Corfe said. "What does one look like? Where would you look for something that talks about it? You see—you don't know. And neither do I." He had made his point, and he knew it. So did Kevin. Corfe's tone became stronger. "Okay, in principle I think you guys may have something. But I'm not the person to say if it has chances. We've got to bring Michelle in on this too. She's the only one who has the knowledge. And I'll contact her first thing tomorrow and go into town to put this to her if I can. That much I am willing to say I'll do. But beyond that . . ." He looked from one to the other and shook his head gravely. "It'll depend on what she says. Beyond that I can't promise."

Kevin nodded but looked away at the floor. The fervor had gone out of him. For a while he'd had visions of Corfe in a role as the leader who would cut through the morass of ifs and buts like Samson hacking a path through the hordes. He felt now as if they were on a circle that led back to Monday. As much as he liked Michelle, he just couldn't see her going with the proposition. Worse still, once she had ruled the suggestion out, any possibility of Corfe acting further on his own initiative would automatically have been eliminated also.

With that, the subject was exhausted for the rest of the evening. Kevin and Taki showed Corfe their progress with the flying mecs. Kevin managed to steer one on a full circuit of the room. That was something of an accomplishment to show, anyway.

Corfe called Michelle's office first thing the next morning—Thursday—as he had promised. Wendy, the receptionist, told him that Michelle was out until the afternoon, and had appointments scheduled then. Corfe left a message for Michelle to call him when she was free.

Vanessa went into the city again too. She told Eric it was to spend the day researching neurophysiological papers in the University Hospital library.

CHAPTER TWENTY-TWO

"You stick to organizing the finances," Vanessa said. "That's what you're better at. Don't worry about the scientific side. Leave that to me."

"I was just curious."

"There." Fozworth aimed the remote and stopped the tape. It was so brief that Michelle had missed it, but the expression on Martin Payne's face was not a happy one. Fozworth gestured toward the screen in a small conference room that they had found empty. "See the tightened jaw, narrowing of the eyes. . . . There's anger there, but it can't be expressed. Why not? Think where you've seen that look before: the lover rebuffed; the child ridiculed. It could be for all kinds of reasons."

"But he recovers quickly," Michelle said from a chair by the corner of the table.

"Oh yes, practically instantaneously. Masking his true self is reflex. Mark of a manipulator. We've got two of a kind here." Fozworth touched a button, and the figures on the screen resumed moving, with Vanessa handing Payne a file.

"I think you might find this more interesting," she said.

"What is it?"

"Open it and see. . . ."

Noah Fozworth was a behavioral psychologist at Washington State University. His specialty was profiling psychological types and identifying characteristic traits that matched lives of recognizable patterns. The police department, professional recruitment agencies, social welfare counselors, and others whose work involved betting on the fruit machines of human nature consulted him regularly. Michelle had met him a couple of years previously, through a private investigator who worked for one of her clients.

Fozworth was smooth and round everywhere, with a face rendered all the more moonlike by a brow that extended to the top of his dome, with a terminator of straight, brown hair running in a crescent from ear to ear. He was colorful and animated, and on every occasion that Michelle had seen him, dressed eccentrically—today in a canary yellow bow tie with port-wine cord jacket, which he had draped over a chair. But his advice had generally proved sound, and was always an education. Since there was little as yet in the way of hard evidence, she had come to Fozworth seeking reassurance that the suspicions she was beginning to form at least rested on credible groundings.

He stopped the tape again. "The remark about understanding the science was insulting. A direct snub. She's doing two things: asserting an area of superiority by putting him down; and staking out her own future territory. His real feelings are suppressed, maybe because they clash with his more immediate goals. Very likely, he's not even aware of them. But he can't stop himself reacting unconsciously." Fozworth waved an arm at the images, frozen once again. He had already watched the full sequence several times in silence. "And that's what will eventually bring those two into head-on collision. Right now they can't see it, or they're refusing to. But the match that will detonate the bomb one day is right there."

"So there's a pattern that you recognize, even in as little as this?" Michelle said.

"Plus the things you've told me. A mark of psychopaths is a need to feel superior in some way, which they'll express maliciously but always in a controlled way that lets them seem to be just the opposite on the outside." The arm waved again. "You just saw it. She as-good-as tells him he's dumb, and moments later she's nuzzling up to him. His feelings tell him one thing, but he sees another. That's the way people drive each other nuts. If he's a strong personality, he'll probably end up having her thrown overboard far out at sea one day when there are plenty of sharks around—if she doesn't poison him first."

"So you would class her as a psychopath? It's not something I'm imagining?" Now they were getting down to what Michelle had come to hear.

Fozworth started the player again but with the sound muted, and answered while he watched. "Almost a classical case. A compulsive need to control, destroy others, and take, while all the time disorienting them by masquerading behind a facade of perfection—which often expresses itself religiously."

"Is it something deliberate, calculated? . . . Do they sit down and plan it out this way?"

"Not really. It's just the way they are."

"Does anybody know why—what makes them that way?"

The video stopped. Fozworth started it on rewind, stood, and moved over to the machine. "Inner reality is tricky. We all think we know what's going on out there, including how we're responding—but how can you really be sure? All our awareness is ultimately inside. Very often, not everything about the way things affect us reaches our awareness. There are areas of denial, feelings that we block out, usually because we're taught that they're weak, inappropriate, unsuited for survival. With men in our culture it tends to have to do with expressing emotion; with women, their sexuality."

"You sound as if you're saying there's a bit of it in all of us," Michelle observed.

"Pretty much all aberrations are something taken to extremes that everyone has to a degree, but more or less keeps within acceptable bounds. With the kind that we're talking about, the denial leads to acute feelings of dissatisfaction and frustration. Since the real cause is repressed, they project it onto others and see them as responsible."

"They're not at fault, so why should they feel guilty?" Michelle said, taking the point.

"Quite. They're *punishing* the guilty. So they can pursue their objectives tenaciously and ruthlessly, without any impediment of sympathy or remorse. But they're quite capable of being outwardly the model of charming, caring reasonableness. That's what drives their victims crazy. They know what they feel on the inside, but they can't reconcile it with what they're seeing and hearing. Take a classical case: The husband's persuaded his heiress wife that she's sick and vulnerable in this big bad world, but not to worry because he'll take care of her; meanwhile, her broker's telling her that he's cleaning out their bank account."

"I don't think the husband in this case is in much danger of going crazy, Noah," Michelle said. Although she had described the situation, she hadn't mentioned names. If Fozworth had made any connections of his own, he hadn't mentioned them.

The tape stopped. Fozworth ejected it and turned

to face her. "No, he sounds pretty solid: intelligent, independent, trusts his own judgment. A good self-image." He held out the cartridge. The face in the moon was serious. "It's the kid that I'd be worrying more about," he said.

On the way out of the building half an hour later, Michelle called into the office for any messages. There were several routine items. Doug Corfe had called, wanting her to get in touch. The people she was due to meet at three o'clock wanted to know if she could make it for two-thirty instead. The other meeting for four o'clock across town was confirmed. That evening she was due to have dinner with an old girlfriend from New York who was visiting Seattle. Corfe would have to wait until tomorrow, she decided. She had meant to call him then, anyway. Nothing drastic was going to happen before the weekend.

Martin Payne, looking casually suave in black blazer and fawn slacks, white shirt worn open with blue silk cravat, stood with his hands on the rail of the after deck on the *Princess Dolores*. The waters of the lake stretching across to Seattle, and the sky, were gray. White gulls coasted and swooped around the dock extending from the lawns at the rear of the house.

There could be no doubt that he was the kind of man who was born to win. The twelve-million-dollar boat beneath him, the house, the company that he had built from nothing—they were surely testimony as tangible as anyone could ask for of that. He won because he knew the difference between an acceptable risk and a reckless gamble, and when having assessed the acceptable, having the nerve to see it through. And from knowing, when the signs were otherwise, that the moment was not yet right.

For three years he had been biding his time for the

present situation to ripen. Now, all of a sudden, the pieces seemed to be coming together of their own accord. Jack Anastole's sudden reappearance, which had seemed a problem at the time, had turned out to be the fortuitous event needed to set long-laid plans moving. And two months later, as if on cue, the meddling lawyer arrives on the scene like an essential catalyst to precipitate the final action involving Heber and ensure a speedy resolution to the whole business.

He had no qualms as far as Heber was concerned. DNC had been born at Microbotics before Heber even had thoughts of getting restless. Payne had paid for every step of acquiring the knowledge that Heber had stolen, from breaking dirt at the lab-block sites to buying the equipment and providing the research teams. It was *his* technology—Payne's! Any law that gave somebody like Heber any rights to it was a travesty—contrived by sheep to ensnare wolves and put them in harness for the service of all.

Payne rather liked the wolf metaphor. Wolves lived and survived by their own law. Those who couldn't run with wolves shouldn't mess with them. Heber had made his choice. Now came the consequences.

The sound of feet climbing steps came from behind. Payne turned from the rail, and Andy Finnion appeared from the aft fishing cockpit. Andy was ex-PD narcotics section, which was a sure indicator of "liberal" morality—the payoff scale made it certain that nobody was going to bring in any potential wrench throwers. A police background that entailed knowing where every wire in the city and state machinery led made him an ideal lieutenant on Payne's staff, and running Microbotics's security operation provided the perfect front.

"Mike's checked over the systems. Everything's okay except a switch for a pump that he'll get replaced today.

Restocking for the bar and galley stores will be delivered by noon tomorrow. He plans moving the boat across to Fox Landing tomorrow evening."

"Let's hope the weather holds out."

Apart from the gloomy skies, Providence must have been smiling at him, Payne thought. He'd planned the Memorial Day weekend Saturday-night party on the yacht weeks ago, turning into a cruise that would last through the next day to let the guests recuperate—or relive their favorite parts of whatever transpired; whichever. Fox Landing was the name of a dock at the back of the exclusive "Shoals," a marine club on the shore of Lake Union in the middle of Seattle, which formed part of the Ship Canal connecting Lake Washington to Puget Sound. The *Dolores* would be moved across to there late on Friday to take the guests aboard on Saturday. Payne really didn't want them swarming around his home in Medina, getting the idea that it was open house. People came there only by specific invitation.

"Vic Bazhin's decided to stay over the weekend," Payne said. "I didn't think he'd miss out. We'll need to organize some girls. Another half dozen should balance things out."

"I'll call the agencies this evening. Put in a reservation."

"Excellent."

Finnion looked past Payne and motioned with his head. "Isn't that her now?"

Payne turned to look back toward the house. Vanessa had appeared on the path leading from the summer house, presumably having just arrived and parked at the front. She was wearing a full, calf-length skirt with wrap-around coat and headscarf, along with sunglasses despite the leaden overcast.

"I hadn't allowed for her on the guest list," Finnion murmured. "Do you want her added?"

Payne shook his head. "I don't think so, Andy. It wouldn't look very becoming if the police had to trace her here to break the tragic news, would it? She needs to be at home to play the grieving widow."

"That makes sense." Finnion nodded. Then he grinned crookedly as a thought struck him. "Does that mean I should make it seven more girls?"

Payne tut-tutted, winked, and moved forward along the walkway outside the main salon to greet Vanessa at the port-side gate. Finnion followed. Vanessa walked quickly along the dock below, climbed the access stairs, and came aboard in a clatter of doe-skin boots. They went down a short flight of steps into the salon. Finnion closed the door leading forward—several of the crew were aboard, working about the vessel. Payne raised his eyebrows inquiringly.

Vanessa gave a quick nod. "Saturday's confirmed. I've told him that the Jeep is playing up, so he'll be using my car—the Jaguar. The special bug will be concealed among other gadgets and things in a couple of boxes that I'll leave down by the back seat. They'll be thrown all over the car in the wreck, so even if it's found at all, there'll be no reason for anyone to give it a second thought." She looked at Finnion for an opinion.

He pursed his lips while various improbable scenarios paraded through his policeman's mind. Finally he nodded, satisfied. "Nobody's going to be looking for a weapon. And if the weather breaks, it'll suit us even better. That road's treacherous enough even in an Indian summer." A fact of which Vanessa hardly needed reminding. It was she who had suggested it in the first place.

"And what's your schedule for Saturday?" Payne asked her.

"Ostensibly shopping in the city in the morning and

meeting a couple of old friends for lunch." She had to be away, in order to be at Microbotics in Redmond to carry out the operation. The matter-of-fact way she was able to talk about it chilled even Payne. "Then back to Olympia in the afternoon. After that, well, just play along with what happens." She ran an eye pointedly over Payne. "I presume *you'll* be busy with the party."

Irritation flared in him for an instant. What was she insinuating now—that he was just some kind of playboy, while she took care of the real work? Or was it a veiled reminder that the professional girls were strictly for Bazhin and the other guests? He could feel life becoming constrictive already. But until she—with the patents—became Mrs. Payne, that was something he'd have to practice living with.

He smiled and put an arm around her. "Someone has to look after those boring people. As you said the other day, taking care of finances is what I do best. In spirit I'll be with you all the way. . . . Andy, how about a drink to welcome our lost sheep back to the fold? . . . Soon-to-be so, anyhow."

Finnion opened a wooden wall cabinet that had ornaments and figurines lined along the top. "Aye, aye, skipper," he replied.

CHAPTER TWENTY-THREE

Monsters in old movies had scales and fangs, and lumbered about squashing cars, picking up trains, and causing heroines to put their hands to their faces and scream. Their modern counterparts symbolized fears of mutant technology more than mutant biology, and consisted, more often than not, of intricate assemblages of machinery and wiring directed by silicon brains that always made the eyes glow a sinister red.

The new Japanese release playing on the big screen in the game room of Hiroyuki's house had both. The big, green, natural, organic monsters had been awakened from dormancy on the ocean bed by nuclear-weapons testing in the Pacific, and "smart" battle machines were taking them on—apparently through some instinctual loyalty to their creators that none of the scientists depicted in the movie could explain, but which the scriptwriters evidently considered to be of deep, mystical significance. The heroines were now liberated, of course, and waded in wielding M-16s and Uzis with the best of the guys, thus doggedly emulating what their admirers had been denouncing as the worst of male traits for years. The screaming role had passed to Taki's younger sister, Reiko, and a half dozen other small members of the innumerable relatives watching in total immersion from the couch, the floor, and other seats around the room. Nakisha, in one of the armchairs, stared unblinking, but managed a restrained silence becoming to her sixteen years that showed she was above that kind of thing.

"Hey, look at all the arms on that guy. It's like a mechanical spider."

"It's like some of those miniature robots of Taki's. Is that what it was like, Nakisha? Did it feel like being one of those?"

"Did Taki really put you down next to a slug?"

"*Ooooh, yuck!* . . ."

"Shut up. It was horrible. I don't want to talk about it."

Kevin sat on a chair by the wall near the glass-paned doors behind them, half watching while he idly practiced materializing a playing card in one hand, then vanishing it again. Doug Corfe had gone for a drive into Seattle to reconnoiter Garsten's office from the outside. Taki had been called away for the moment to give his mother a hand with something. Ohira was on a stool at the back of the room, arms akimbo, hands planted solidly on his knees, watching the movie with a raptness that was unusual. It seemed to have triggered some distant line of thought.

Kevin rather took to the monsters, he decided. It wasn't their fault if they blundered around sinking ships and knocking gaps in city skylines, any more than foxes could help being partial to chickens. It was just the way they were made. He identified with them, he supposed, as another form of life that was misunderstood and looked down on—in the monsters' case, metaphorically—by grownups. There were days when he was sure that he too could find it a great reliever of stresses and tensions to go on a rampage of pulverizing a few downtown high-rises or picking up automobiles filled with the irritating kinds of people who played bullhorn radios in parks and left trash everywhere, and throw them into the harbor. Maybe grownups went out and dropped bombs on each others' cities for the same kind of reason. If that were true, it didn't seem fair that kids should have to be in them too.

Then the thought struck him that perhaps they could build miniature cities for stressed-out adults to crash around in and flatten, using monster-mec bodies designed specially for the purpose. They could even have other people—perhaps kids who liked being scared by monsters—in smaller mecs to run around and provide crowds of panicking inhabitants, making it all the more realistic, and presumably more satisfying. Then, perhaps, there wouldn't be any need for wars.

He was still musing over the thought as surely a touch of genius when Ohira got up from the stool and came over, at the same time making a sign to catch Kevin's attention. Kevin looked up. Ohira motioned with his head to indicate the doors. "I have been thinking. There is something I would like you and Taki to do for me," he said. Kevin held out the card deck that he was still holding in one hand and fanned it in an unspoken invitation. Ohira selected a card and returned it. Kevin shuffled it into the deck, gave the deck to Ohira, and then plucked the card he had chosen out of the air. He made it disappear again, showed his hand to be empty, and produced the card from the other one. "Very good," Ohira complimented. "It seems that everything young people do these days has to have screens and be connected to a nuclear power plant. You don't even need batteries." He waved again toward the door. Kevin got up and followed him out of the room.

The living room outside was bright and spacious, with a floor of gray and white marble squares with fleece rugs. Ohira turned and sat on the arm of a sectional divan filling one of the corners. "How would you like to be a movie director?" he said. "I want you and Taki to make a movie for me."

"So you're the producer?" Kevin said.

"If you like, yes."

It was a typical Ohira approach. He would get to the point eventually in his own time. Kevin, meanwhile, played along in his own typical way. "Aren't we going to talk about percentages, director's fees, contracts, bonuses? . . ."

Ohira's mouth turned upward at the corners briefly, but the rest of his craggy features stayed the same. "You see, always in too much of a hurry. You have all of your lives still before you, and always young people are in a hurry. We have most of ours behind us, yet we don't have to hurry and the things that need to, get done."

"I thought it was supposed to be good business. I was just going by what Hiroyuki says."

"Good business is getting paid what you are worth. A director is paid for his experience. First you get the experience; then you have something to sell. Being paid more than you are worth is bad business. Your customers don't come back again, and then you have no business."

Kevin grinned and put the cards in his shirt pocket. "Okay. So what's this movie about?"

Ohira waved a hand in the direction of the room they had just left. "I was thinking while I watched that movie that the kids in there are looking at, the part where you see the monsters over the trees."

"You mean where those guys with guns are looking for them—except they don't realize they've grown so much? . . . And then the slithery things come up out of the lake."

"Yes, by the river. I was thinking, suppose those heads looking down over the trees weren't monsters but . . . what do you call those long, thin insects that stand up on end and catch flies in arms that close like nutcrackers? Mantis, is it?"

"Oh, praying mantises."

Ohira nodded. "Yes, that's them. Then those hunters would really have something to hunt, wouldn't they?"

"Oh, I see. As mecs, you mean." Kevin pulled a face. "Their guns wouldn't be much use, though."

"The guns weren't much use to them in the movie there either." Ohira waved a hand. "But never mind the guns. You have other weapons anyway. But the point is we can add something extra to Bug Park, for the adventurous souls. Instead of just being tourists, they can go on safari too."

Kevin's brow furrowed for a moment. "You mean hunting bugs?"

"Sure. Why not? Think of the way that you and Taki have talked about some of your own experiences. Well, isn't it the kind of experience that a lot of people would be willing to pay for?" Ohira thought for a second and shrugged. "All the real safari animals are protected these days, anyway. Nobody can go big-game hunting anymore. So, we let them go little-game hunting instead."

Kevin sank onto a chair and stared at him. It seemed so obvious, now Ohira had spelled it out. How could it not have occurred to either him or Taki in all this time?

Ohira studied his face. "So what do you think?"

"I think it's brilliant," Kevin said. "It's got to catch on. . . . And how long would it take before malaria mosquitoes became an endangered species?"

"They couldn't. You'd never even make a difference."

"I was joking."

"And anyway, who'd care if they did?" Ohira raised his hands. "You see, every day we find more possibilities."

"So where does the movie come in?" Kevin asked.

"I want you and Taki to organize some hunting expeditions so we can put a movie together from the monitor videos for me to show to the other Theme Worlds directors. You know the kind of thing—lots of towering monsters and gaping jaws; the kind of thing that's making the kids scream next door there." Ohira thought for a moment and held up both hands in front of him, thumbs level as if framing a picture. "And I'd like a good still shot, maybe you two as mecs, posing with your arms folded and a foot each on the body of a dead beetle or something—you know, the way they used to with elephants. It would look good on the title page of a proposal."

"Okay, sure," Kevin said. "We've got the holiday weekend coming up. I'll tell Taki about it, and we'll see what we can do."

Kevin's answer had been mechanical. The eagerness with which he would normally have greeted such a suggestion was noticeably absent.

Ohira rubbed below an ear with a finger and contemplated him in silence. "There's something the matter, isn't there?" he said finally.

"What makes you say that?"

"Oh, some of this experience that I have that's worth something, and you don't have yet. You think more than usual, but you say less than usual. For the kind of person you are, that says there's a lot that would like to come out. If you and Taki want to tell me about it, that's all right."

Kevin bit his lip. He wanted to talk, even to somebody that he couldn't immediately see as in a position to be of help . . . but not without Taki around. And even then, the thought of Corfe's likely reaction was enough to make him not want to think further.

"Is it about Eric's company?" Ohira said after a pause. "I know that certain people have been giving him problems lately."

Kevin shook his head. "Thanks. . . . But it's nothing really."

Ohira's wide, strangely flat eyes lingered over him for several seconds longer, giving him the eerie feeling that they were able to read everything for themselves anyway. At length Ohira nodded. "If that is what you wish," he said. "But remember always that you are family here now as much as Taki is, just as your father treats Taki the same as you. And that means you have many friends who are here to help if there is trouble. We Japanese families look after our own."

"I'll remember that," Kevin promised.

Ohira looked at him for a moment longer, then nodded. "So go and make us a good movie, eh?" he said, standing up. "Maybe first we show it to some of that bunch in the next room. Let's see if you can get them really screaming."

Taki reappeared a short while later, and he and Kevin went down to Taki's workshop. As a test, and on the offchance that the time might be right to learn something new, Kevin used the coupler there to see if he could activate the relay that he had concealed in the trunk of the Jaguar—wherever it was. The relay responded, and moments later Kevin connected himself to Mr. Toad, one of the two mecs that he had left along with it.

The link functioned just fine. He emerged from the mec box and discerned immediately from the sound and intermittent lurching that the car was moving. Warily, he crossed through the space above the trunk and came up behind the rear seat cushion. The interior of the Jaguar loomed above him in shadow like the Hagia Sophia of Istanbul. Outside, it was dark, with not much in the way of other traffic or street lights. There was nobody in either of the rear seats, just a folded coat and the form of a briefcase, rectangular and clifflike, outlined above him in the gloom. By intensifying his vision, he was able to see sufficiently to follow the base of the seat-back to the corner. From there, using his back and legs like a rock climber negotiating a chimney, he wedged his way up the space between the seat and the car wall to the window ledge. As he gained height, he could see Vanessa in the front seat, driving. She was alone. The same feeling of unreality that had affected him before in the yacht, at "being present" as part of events happening miles away, seized him again. Outside was just darkness, trees rushing through the light from the headlamps. Taki was following on the monitor but not making any inane remarks this time.

Then Kevin felt himself thrown forward, then sideways, as the car slowed and made a turn—barely managing to jam a hand into the crack between the window glass and the sill in time to avoid being dislodged completely. Now there was light ahead, with dark shadows of what looked like trees on both sides. He braced himself more securely and turned toward the glass. Where would he find himself this time? . . .

Then, as the trees opened out, he recognized his own driveway. Harriet's car was parked just ahead, with Batcat coming out from underneath to be let inside the house. And why should he have hoped for anything else? Had he really expected that just when he chose to tune in, something would just happen to be taking place that would give them the great breakthrough? You needed scriptwriters for coincidences like that.

Vanessa turned in her seat, and her arm reached over to retrieve the things from the seat below where Kevin was clinging. He waited for her to leave the car, then returned Mr. Toad to the mec box and deactivated it.

Well, at least the system still worked. And that, he supposed, was something.

CHAPTER TWENTY-FOUR

Doug Corfe looked at Michelle across the desk in her office in the John Sloane Building in downtown Seattle. His decision to come here midway through Friday morning had been prompted more by desperation at the nearness of the weekend than by any clear intentions thought carefully through. Now that he had committed himself, it was important to go for the opportunity that the holiday presented; to pass up on it now would risk the appearance of fobbing Kevin off and of never having been sincere at all, which was something Corfe couldn't permit. After yesterday's experience, he hadn't been willing to just call and risk being asked to leave another message. This was something that he needed to put to Michelle face to face. That was about as far as he had taken things in his own mind. The rest, he'd more-or-less assumed, would fall into place once Michelle had the picture.

However, he could tell from her expression even before he had finished speaking that either he was putting the case badly or had picked the wrong time—or maybe the idea was just dumb. Whatever the reason, it clearly wasn't going over well. He stopped it at that point for a reaction.

Michelle spread her hands and looked from side to side, as if searching for words, then shook her head. "Doug, you can't be serious. It's just not on. We can't go breaking into another lawyer's office. I mean . . . it's just *not* something you can do. We'd be the ones who'd end up on criminal charges, with Garsten doing the filing. Then how would we ever be able to put a case of any kind together from that position? We wouldn't. Is that what you want?"

"What kind of case do we look like putting together as things stand?" Corfe answered. "You said there was no way to move without some kind of evidence of what these people are up to. Well, here's a practical way we might get some—if any exists to be got."

"It's not practical. It's totally impractical."

"Well, I haven't heard too many suggestions from any other direction," Corfe said hotly. He knew as he blurted the words out that it was the wrong thing to say.

Michelle contained herself with a visible effort. "Excuse me, but I do have other clients . . ."

"And I have a close friend who stands to be *killed*. You don't seem to understand. That's what doesn't seem to get through."

"Doug." Michelle's tone was sharp. "You just show up here unannounced. I've had to shoe-horn you in between appointments—there's one waiting in reception right now. Why on earth didn't you call?"

"It's Friday, and this is the holiday weekend. If we're going to do it, this is the time. I left messages all day yesterday. . . ."

"I was out working on this very thing yesterday. Yes, I understand perfectly well how you feel, Doug. Do you imagine I don't feel it too? As a matter of fact, I've put a hell of a lot of time in on it this week, despite having a full schedule to begin with. Do you realize how complicated this is? I'm a business attorney. I deal in contracts. We're probably going to have to call a criminal lawyer in on this, to build a case against somebody's family lawyer. That isn't the kind of thing that lawyers take to easily. And the client in question that we're trying to protect isn't even being what you'd call a hundred percent cooperative."

This time it was Corfe's turn to be hit the wrong way. He heard it as if Michelle were trying to blame Eric. "Have you shown him the tape?" he asked challengingly.

"No, not yet."

"Why not? Tell him the whole story. Don't you think that might help make him more cooperative?"

"And don't *you* think that maybe he's going through enough at the moment as it is? Look, I had lunch with him on Wednesday with a view to broaching precisely this subject. But I hadn't realized how dependent he is psychologically on Vanessa. It just didn't strike me as the moment to go kicking that prop away too, after everything else that's been going on this week."

Corfe shook his head stolidly. "We're not in a situation where we can afford luxuries like that. He's got to find out eventually—or not at all if we're too late."

"Of course he has," Michelle agreed. "But I'd rather it be at a time when he's in some mood to be receptive instead of showing every sign of being ready to start a fight over it. It was you who came to me and asked for help with this, Doug. I'd appreciate it if you'd let me handle it in my own way."

Corfe exhaled heavily and sat back. He was still prickly and far from satisfied, but it was equally clear that Michelle was not about to change her mind about anything just at the moment. Clearly, his coming here on impulse had done nothing to improve matters. But it had been something he'd needed to do at the time, as a safety valve. Michelle could very likely see that, but she wasn't showing it. The thought crossed his mind of how satisfying it would be if he went ahead anyway on his own, with Kevin, and they did manage to come up with something valuable.

"Okay, if you don't want to get involved, that's fine," he said. "Then I'm only going to ask you for one thing. Pretend I never talked to you, and just look the other way. If anything turns up that I think you ought to know about, you'll know about it. Is that acceptable?"

Michelle looked at him uncertainly for a moment or two. "You don't mean you're still going to do it?"

"I already told you, a very good friend of mine's looking to get killed. I'm not going to just sit around and do nothing. Nobody else is coming up with any ideas. We'll be okay. You enjoy your holiday." Corfe started to rise.

"We?" Michelle repeated. "You mean to include Kevin in this?"

"It was his idea, for heaven's sake—his and Taki's. How can I leave him out? Anyhow, it'll need at least two operators. Some parts will probably need a couple of mecs working together."

Michelle closed her eyes momentarily and sighed. "He's smart and a lot more mature than average, but he's still a kid, Doug. Do I really have to tell you that you can't go involving him in something like this?"

"He won't even need to be in the city. He can play his part from a remote coupler," Corfe replied obstinately. "Don't worry about it. We've already agreed, this isn't anything to do with you anymore."

"You do understand that what you're talking about is totally illegal?" Michelle said. "Even if you did come up with something, you'd rule out any chance of ever being able to use it in court. It would never be admissible as evidence."

Corfe paused at the door. "You're missing the point. This isn't for any court case. It's for Eric. We've both tried to make him take this seriously, but it doesn't do any good. Well, if it's going to need something like this to convince him, then okay, I'll risk it. Suppose something eventually did happen to him, and we still hadn't done anything. How would I be supposed to feel about that?" Corfe looked back, but Michelle couldn't answer. He left the office, closing the door behind him.

He crossed the outer room where a girl was typing at a screen while another took notes over a phone. Wendy, the receptionist, gave him a smile on his way out. A woman in a green coat and turban-shaped hat, looking impatient, was already rising to her feet as he passed through the waiting area. He came out of the main door of the Prettis & Lang offices and followed the corridor back to the elevators.

Well, he'd had to try, he told himself. He was still too charged with headiness and irked by the way the meeting with Michelle had gone to have any regrets. In fact, just the opposite: For the first time in days he felt resolved and purposeful. After almost a week of indecision and a debilitating sense of powerlessness, it came as a relief.

Compared to days gone by, people these days had become too passive, he decided. There had been a time when men stood up for their rights and took steps to protect themselves when they felt threatened. But somewhere along the line they had let themselves be turned into sheep, conditioned to dependence on impersonal authorities who as often as not were as impotent as they were indifferent. The thought of himself as somebody able to rise above such a situation was stimulating and invigorating. As he rode the car back to the ground floor, he felt a touch of the maverick quality that he sometimes sensed Kevin projecting into him. Good for you, for once, Doug Corfe, he told himself. Sometimes a man just has to do . . .

The day was gusty with squalls of rain sweeping the streets when he came out onto Fourth Avenue. He tightened his coat about him and walked a block to where he had parked—he had borrowed Eric's van again, in preparation for the weekend. It was a restricted loading-unloading zone only for that time of morning, but he had escaped getting a ticket. He got in quickly, half expecting a uniformed figure to leap from one of the doorways before he could start the motor. Just as he was about to pull away, his personal phone rang. He put the van back into "Park" and fished the unit from his pocket.

"Hello?"

"Doug?"

"Yes."

"This is Michelle."

"Oh. . . . Hi again."

There was a short pause. Then a sigh came through audibly. "You two guys aren't going to have a clue what to look for in there. . . . Look, if there's absolutely no way I can talk you out of this insanity, then we'd better try and give it the best chance of coming up with something. You're absolutely certain there'll be no question of anybody going into the building in person?"

Corfe's brow furrowed, then lifted as he realized what she was saying. "Does this mean you're in with us?"

"You're going to need help. . . . Look, I can't talk now; I've got somebody waiting. Can you find that place called Chancey's, that we went to with Kevin?"

"Sure, I think so."

"I'll meet you there. Can you give me, say, forty minutes?"

"Okay . . . and thanks. But you're right. There's absolutely no way I'm gonna change my mind about this."

"I'll see you, then."

A meter warden came around the corner ahead and approached, peering to see if there was anyone in the van. Corfe shook his head as if to say not this time, smirked, engaged gear, and drove away.

"Kevin won't need to be anywhere near," Corfe said across the booth after the waitress had brought Michelle's coffee and left. "I'll borrow Eric's van and control everything from a block or two away after the mecs go in—it's fitted out as a complete remote-command center. Kevin can stay back at Neurodyne and couple in from there, using the lab transmitter and a unit in the van as a local relay. In fact, some of the Neurodyne mecs need special software routines that will only run on the firm's machines, so someone would have to be there anyway. The place will be empty tomorrow. I can drop him off there on my way into town."

"And what about Taki?" Michelle asked. "You said something about him being mixed up in this too. I don't like that, Doug."

"No. It was just that he and Kev together came up with this idea of using the mecs."

"So you're not planning on giving him a part in all this tomorrow?"

Corfe shook his head. "Aw, come on. Credit me with some sense, Michelle. This is *our* affair. I wouldn't go dragging some other family into it."

"But Kevin has already told Taki about it, obviously," Michelle pointed out. "Are you sure it hasn't gone further?"

"Kevin says not, and I believe him. He and Taki have

got this special . . . 'thing.' I guess he needed somebody to talk to . . . like we all do sometimes."

Michelle sipped her coffee and ran over in her mind what had been said. "So when is Eric going up to Barrow's Pass?" she asked finally. "The last time I heard, it was still either tonight or tomorrow morning."

"Probably tomorrow, but that's okay. He'll leave by, oh, around ten at the latest. That'll still give me plenty of time to pick Kev up and go on into town."

"You're planning on doing this in the middle of the day, in broad daylight?" Michelle sounded dubious.

"The best time," Corfe replied. "Lots of activity and traffic. People about. Why wait until everything's quiet and risk being conspicuous? And in any case, it might not be so straightforward. We could end up needing the whole weekend for all I know."

Michelle thought it over one last time. Finally she looked up. "So I'd need to be where? In the van with you, I guess."

Corfe stared at her for several seconds. "Am I hearing this right? Are you saying you'll do it?" Despite it being the reason why he had come to her office, now that she had actually said it, he found it difficult to believe.

Michelle released a long sigh that acknowledged she was committed, at the same time shaking her head wearily in a way that seemed to say she couldn't think why. "I'll look at what's on the screens and make suggestions," she said. "I'm not sure I've had enough experience of driving mecs to be any more use than that."

"I understand that. But I wouldn't have asked more, anyway." Corfe laid a hand lightly on her arm as she started to look away. "And look, if anything does mess up, then you're out of it right there. If anybody ever needs to know, I'm acting strictly alone, on my own initiative. Kevin's back in the lab; you're out on the street. Neither of you had anything to do with it." He shook his head before she could say anything. "That's the number-one rule. This is my show this time, and I give the orders. I won't have it any other way."

Michelle started to say something, checked herself, and then nodded.

She picked up her cup again and went quiet as she ran over in her mind what would be entailed, searching for the snags. Corfe waited, saying nothing.

"Is this really going to be as straightforward as you seem to imagine?" she said finally. "For a start, what makes you think that Garsten will have obligingly left what we're looking for there in his computer for us to find? Lawyers are notoriously conservative people, Doug. They use paper and file cabinets a lot as well, you know. How is some little bug-size mec going to deal with things like that?"

"We've got larger mecs too—earlier models," Corfe replied. "You'd be surprised how powerful they can be at low speed. We use them for all kinds of tasks."

"But isn't getting larger ones like that inside going to be more of a problem?"

"How so?"

Michelle shrugged, frowning at the obvious. "You need to find a bigger hole," she said. "Or make one. We're getting closer to talking about breaking in again."

Corfe shook his head. "I don't think so. We've thought of a better way that won't involve anything like that at all. Or rather, Kevin did. For some reason it always seems to take a kid to see an obvious way of doing something. Why go looking for ways of trying to get them inside after the place is closed, when you can take them in while it's open?"

CHAPTER TWENTY-FIVE

The polished brass sign proclaiming the offices of
PHILLIP A. GARSTEN, ATTORNEY AT LAW was mounted on
the wall by the door at the top of five stone steps leading
up to what had formerly been a spacious, single-family
town residence in the First Hill district, close to the
Seattle University campus between Twelfth Avenue
and Broadway. The house had been restored to an
immaculate condition as a property investment, painted
pale yellow with white trim and a red tile roof. It stood
set back from the street behind a white picket fence
and secluding screen of shrubbery, giving it an air of
permanence and dependable confidentiality becoming
of the profession.

Corfe arrived thirty minutes after leaving Michelle
in Chancey's diner and coffee shop. He was carrying a
tan leather document case and a white plastic bag bearing
the name and logo of a local bookstore. The bag looked
heavy, stretching the grips as it hung in his hand. He
pushed the door open with an elbow and went through.
The entrance hall was opulent enough to bespeak success
and competence, but not to the point of daunting a
potential client contemplating the likely bill. The main
furnishings consisted of a redwood office suite and brown

brocatel-upholstered chairs, set against a background of beige velveteen overdrapes and a shag carpet with wood inlaid surround. A receptionist faced him across a desk equipped with paper trays, appointment book, computer terminal, and a sign saying that her name was Lisa.

"Good morning," she greeted, smiling. "What can we do for you?"

"Oh, hi. My name's Jeffreys. I called fairly late yesterday afternoon. I think it was you that I talked to."

"Yes, I remember—to see Mr. Garsten. You want to set up a boat business, right?"

"Well, to know a little more about the preliminaries of what would be involved, anyway." Corfe's eyes wandered around, absorbing the surroundings. "We made an appointment for eleven-thirty. I guess I'm a little early."

"Sure, I've got you down. Mr. Garsten is running slightly behind time this morning. Would you mind taking a seat in the waiting room? I'll buzz through that you're here."

"That's fine."

Lisa showed him across a hall and through a glass-paneled door into a room containing several easy chairs, a couch, and a couple of low tables with stacks of magazines. She invited him to make himself at home and be comfortable. He said he'd prefer to stretch his legs and stand. She said that would be fine, assured him it wouldn't be too long, and left.

Corfe wandered about the room, pausing near the door to register the layout of the hall and corridor outside, and the doors opening off. The waiting room had a window seat with doors below that might suit his purpose—although there was an external latch that could prove a problem if somebody closed it later before leaving for the weekend. There was a space in a corner behind one of the chairs that was unlikely to be checked; and feeling with a foot told him there was enough clearance underneath the couch. It really was that simple. He could accomplish his task and conceal the mecs right now, spend the rest of the time chatting innocuously, and then leave. The only trouble was, no terminal to the computer was located in the waiting room. That could make things difficult if the only access lay in other rooms that would possibly be locked. Better to keep his options open until he'd had a chance to see more. He went back out into the hall and asked if he could use a restroom while he was waiting. Lisa directed him along a passage leading to the rear of the house.

On the way, he passed two rooms with terminals on the desks inside. Beyond was a photocopying area with shelves of cardboard boxes and stacked paper, and a metal hanging-file cabinet with more boxes piled on top—all of them good possible locations also.

Naturally, the package that Corfe had brought contained the mecs that he and Kevin thought would be the most useful. There was always the chance, however, that as the weekend unfolded they might need to send in additional models to perform some specialized task, or for whatever other reason. A further objective of Corfe's visit, therefore, was to reconnoiter possible entry points. For obvious reasons, they didn't want to go disturbing any outside doors or windows.

On the way up to the house, he had noticed a grille low down on the side wall, that looked like a vent to the basement; that was a possibility. Now, in a room at the rear outside the restrooms that looked as if it might have once been a laundry, he found a blanked-off pipe that could have been a dryer vent.

On his way back to the front of the house he

deliberately took a wrong turn and discovered a coffee lounge with a wood stove and a pipe going up through the ceiling. If all else failed, there would be a chimney somewhere outside that a can-size mec would surely be able to reach without too much difficulty. Before he could investigate further, a clerk appeared from a filing room next door and directed him back to reception. Lisa was waiting in the front hall to say that "Mr. Garsten will see you now."

She showed him through a secretarial area with two desks. At one of them, a brunette was typing onto a screen. The other desk had a terminal too, although it was blank at the moment, the chair before it empty with a green cardigan thrown over the back. There were file cabinets along two of the walls, and a door leading through to what was clearly Garsten's office. *Here*, Corfe decided. This would be the perfect place.

Lisa knocked, ushered Corfe through. "Mr. Jeffreys," she announced. Garsten got up, beaming, and shook hands. He was short and ruddy faced, with straight, reddish hair brushed to the side college-boy style, and a close-trimmed mustache, failing completely to convey the sinister image that Corfe had half expected. More, if anything, he put Corfe in mind of a supermarket manager. Why, Corfe had no idea. As far as he could recall, he'd never met a supermarket manager.

The line Corfe had prepared was that he'd been invited to go into partnership in a boat-hire business and wanted to check on the legal requirements and implications before giving an answer. He had called his old friend Ray Young, the Vancouver ferry captain, the evening before, and as a result had been able to come armed with some plausible questions revolving mainly around liabilities, tax credits, insurance, and investment write-offs. He and Garsten talked for about twenty minutes. At the end of the interview, Garsten scribbled down the references to some pamphlets and guides that he thought it might be useful for "Jeffreys" to take away and study, and suggested they fix another appointment when he'd had a chance to go through them. They agreed to leave things at that point for now, and came back out of the office to the secretarial area.

"Carol, could you pull out a few things for Mr. Jeffreys," Garsten said to the brunette who had been there when Corfe went in. He handed her the list that he had jotted down. Then the phone rang in the office behind him. "That's probably somebody I've been expecting," he told Corfe. "Excuse me, but I'll have to leave you. Carol will show you out." And with that, he went back into his office and closed the door.

"Busy guy," Corfe commented, casually taking in the surroundings while Carol rummaged in her desk and on a shelf behind.

"It can get hectic. This is nothing, really. . . . Oh, it looks like I'm out of MTL4s. I'll see if there are any left next door. Back in a second." She went out into the hall, and Corfe heard her call something to Lisa. The other chair in the room was still empty. Corfe was left on his own. He blinked. Breaks like this didn't happen every day. In that case, all the more reason to make the best of them when they did. He looked around frantically.

A wooden cabinet of drawers stood by the wall behind the desks, below several shelves carrying books, journals, card indexes, and various office accessories. Between the cabinet and the far corner was a worktop with storage below for stationery supplies and assorted boxes. Stooping and peering in, Corfe saw there was an awkward-to-reach space back in the corner, where several cleaning cloths, several old binders, a broken Rolodex, and other odd items had been pushed in a jumble. He reached inside the bookstore bag that he was carrying and produced from it another, folded bag containing the mecs that he had brought with him to hide. The package included two telebots and an assortment of tools, besides the several smaller models that he and Kevin had agreed on as a minimum initial task force. He dropped onto one knee and placed the bag at the back of the space, out of sight behind the other things, and straightened up again quickly. There were enough books left in the bag that he was still holding to leave it unchanged in outward appearance. When Carol came back, he was back by the door, admiring a print of a 19th century schooner.

Corfe returned to the van, which he had left in a parking lot a few blocks away. From a console inside it, he activated one of the smallest mecs in the package that he had left behind, and in the course of the lunch hour was able to direct it up onto the worktop, and from there to a recess in the mounting bracket of a wall lamp, high up in the room where it would be unlikely to be noticed for the rest of the day. He then changed channels to activate another mec, and placed that one among the leaves of a potted plant on top of a file cabinet on the opposite side of the room. The second also contained an acoustic system that a couple of the engineers at Neurodyne were experimenting with, adapted from Kevin and Taki's models, and could thus pick up sound. Corfe left their transmissions on auto record and went off on foot to spend the afternoon amusing himself in the city.

From the positions that Corfe had selected, the two mecs commanded a clear line of sight to both of the secretaries' terminals and keyboards. The result was that by the time Corfe collected the van and left toward the end of the afternoon, he had not only successfully infiltrated the devices needed to commence the operation tomorrow, but he also had on tape the full sequences of codes and passwords for accessing Garsten's system. He also had an audio record of a lot of gossip and personal secrets between Garsten's two secretaries—some of it quite entertaining, but nothing immediately relevant to his purpose.

CHAPTER TWENTY-SIX

Kevin peered into a deep, crawl-size passage with floor and sides of streaky yellowish metal plastered with globs of oily mud. The ceiling consisted of massive, square-cut slabs of the same metal, set at varying heights along the length of the passage. All but the one nearest to him were wedged with props sawn exactly to length from pieces of paperclip. Reaching in with an arm, he braced one of his steel-jointed hands underneath the last pin of the lock in the old two-drawer file cabinet in Taki's workshop, and moved it upward in its guide, stopping every few inches—at least, what seemed to him to be inches—to work it experimentally to and fro and from side to side. He felt the friction reduce suddenly, and the lateral play increase. The top of the pin was at the shear line, where it would normally be positioned by its particular notch on the key. Unaided human fingers wouldn't have felt the change without years of training and practice. But to somebody mec-size, it felt like a boat lifting onto the water as it was pushed off a beach. Kevin used the scale that he had marked on a steel sliver to measure the height of the gap—one of the advantages of mec-scale physics was being able to hold up with one hand a block of solid metal which from its appearance ought to have crushed him.

"Six-eight-five," he told Taki.

"As good as done." At the foot of the cross-treaded wooden slat that Kevin was using as a ladder to reach the lock, Sir Real, an order of magnitude larger than the one Kevin was operating, stooped over the piece of 2x4 pine on the floor that he was using as a bench, and began cutting the last strut.

Grownups! Kevin thought to himself while he waited. For a whole week nobody had been able to do anything; now, suddenly, it was on for tomorrow, and everything was a panic. No wonder they dreamed up economic systems that were feast one day and famine the next, and went from boom to bust overnight.

Corfe had e-mailed him a message early that evening finalizing the plan. Eric had gotten involved in something late in the day at the office, and would be leaving for Barrow's Pass sometime between nine and ten in the morning. Corfe would collect Kevin from the house at ten-thirty, drop him off at Neurodyne, and go on into town to meet Michelle. The two of them would then proceed in the van to Garsten's office. The spearhead group of mecs was inside with some basic tools. Corfe had taped the access codes and passwords. How he had managed to talk Michelle into joining them, he hadn't said. He was adamant, however, that Taki wasn't to be involved tomorrow. Kevin had been unable to disagree about that.

"One length of sixty-eight and a half thousandths coming up." Below, Sir Real turned and moved back to the foot of the makeshift ladder. Kevin's perch shook as the larger mec began climbing. It still took a conscious effort to fight down his alarm reflex, although at his weight he could have fallen from the ceiling without damage.

The other nice thing about working through mecs was the convenience of remote coupling. While Taki himself was in his barber-chair coupler, there in his basement where the mecs were, Kevin was controlling the smaller mec from his own house several miles away. That was another new development. Whenever they had operated two mecs simultaneously in the past, such as in their forays against the insect world, they had used the multiple-coupler setup at Kevin's house. Coordinating them from different locations was something they had never considered until Doug proposed it for the operation at Garsten's office. It had seemed a good idea to try it out before going live tomorrow.

A huge steel hand, seemingly the size of a piano, appeared from below, clutching a metal rod as long as Kevin's leg. Kevin took it and wedged it into place like a pit prop below the pin that he'd been holding up. The other mec climbed higher, its head coming into view like a boilermaker's rendering of King Kong filling a window halfway up the Empire State Building. "Will that do it?" Taki's voice asked on the audio circuit.

"There's only one way to find out, isn't there," Kevin answered.

Sir Real produced another piece of metal from the accessories attached around its waist—an improvised key-blank, formed from a rectangular-section bar, with a cross-piece to turn it. Kevin guided the bar into the lock, steering it carefully past the struts that were propping up the pins. The struts and the blank, in effect, together formed a composite key. Kevin moved out of the way to one side, giving Taki room to apply force to the crosspiece. The lock's circular faceplate, looking to Kevin like the door of a bank vault, started to turn.

"I don't believe this!" Kevin exclaimed. "Taki, I think this is actually going to work!"

"See. Didn't I tell you to trust me?"

"How come you know so much about this kind of stuff?" Kevin asked.

"You would too if you had to live with a paranoid sister who locks up everything movable in closets and boxes. You have to learn about things like this, to get things you need."

"Why does she lock everything up?"

"I told you, she's paranoid. She thinks I'd take it."

There was a solid *clack* as the lock disengaged. "Jackpot!" Kevin said. "Now let's see if we can open it."

"Huh, what's this 'we'?" Taki said, scooping him off the ladder and transferring him to one of Sir Real's belt hitches. "What's a pipsqueak like you going to do? This is the real man's department."

"Was that meant to be a pun?" Kevin groaned, clinging on while the larger mec backed down the ladder to the floor.

"No—but it's not bad, is it?"

"No, not bad. Just terrible."

"I knew you'd like it."

They reached the floor. Sir Real set Kevin down and then shifted the ladder aside. Above them, the front of the file cabinet towered like a windowless gray skyscraper. From the handle of the lower drawer, a length of cord dipped across the floor like the cable of a suspension bridge and ran through a clothesline pulley secured to the leg of the bench standing a few feet away.

"Okay, then, let's see this great Samson act," Kevin said.

Sir Real picked up the free end of the line and took in the slack through the pulley. Then it turned to face the pulley, the line running through one hand and around its back to the other. It drew the line taut and leaned against it experimentally. "I need something to push back against," Taki said.

"There's the edge of the carpet just a short way back."

Sir Real looked back over a shoulder; then, paying out line as it went, moved backward until it could brace a foot. The mec crouched, took the strain, and then slowly straightened, using its legs and back. Above Kevin, the immense face of painted metal crept outward.

"You've cracked it! It's moving!" Kevin exclaimed. Taki paused to take in slack and then repeated the maneuver, pulling the drawer out another half inch.

Kevin wondered how much more they might have been able to achieve if they'd had more than a day to prepare. People were always making a fuss over there never being enough time to do things. Kevin had his own theory about that. Being God, knowing everything and existing forever, had to be a pretty boring way to exist, it seemed to him. It would be like reading a book that you already knew every word of. What made books fun was the uncertainty—wanting to know what happens in the part that you haven't got to yet. God must have gotten pretty tired of being God, Kevin thought. And so He had invented time to make the Universe more interesting.

Back in Kevin's own house, Eric sat down in the dining room with the plate of roast that Harriet had left for him, and read over his notes for the presentation he would be giving tomorrow. He had been through the routine many times before, and had no delusions that anything much was likely to change as a result of it. The minds of the orthodoxy were closed on the subject. Nobody questioned basics these days. What passed for science had degenerated into a competition of devising pretexts to attract funding from political bureaucracies. Who cared if an experiment performed a century ago had been accorded the wrong interpretation—particularly if it meant that a huge part of the theoretical work going on today, apart from creating platoons of jobs and helping to keep the paper mills busy, was largely a waste of time?

Eric was one of the few who cared. He cared because in his view, most of what was going on wasn't science at all. Science meant having an open attitude to what might or might not be, a simple, sincere desire to know what *was*. When no further examination was permitted of what had been decided was true, and inconvenient facts became non-subjects, then science had given way to fundamentalism. The spectacles featured in the news documentaries and magazines—bigger accelerators, faster computers, fancier satellites—were orgies of technology: maybe more refined and polished than what had gone before, but still essentially more of the same. Nothing was being discovered that was radically new. And whenever official eminences proclaimed this to be because there was little new left to be discovered, as happened periodically through the centuries and had once again become fashionable, it was invariably a sign of science in trouble and due for an overhaul.

"Ah, yes it is. I thought you were back." Vanessa came through the doorway from the kitchen. "You found your dinner?"

"Mm. Harriet left it in the microwave."

"Is it okay?"

"Just fine."

"I thought you'd be back earlier."

"So did I. We ran into a bit of a snag with feedback resonances." Eric indicated the rest of the house with a vague motion of his head. "Is Kevin around, or did he go over to Taki's?"

"He must have gone to Taki's," Vanessa said. "I'm

pretty sure he's not here. How about you? Have you decided whether you'll be staying till tomorrow, or will you be traveling tonight?"

"Oh, it's getting late now. I'll leave it until morning. Do you still want me to use the Jag?"

Vanessa nodded. "I would. There are a couple of boxes of things down by the back seat—brushes, paints, and craft things. Do you mind if I leave them there? Thelma left them when she was here the other day. I'll be seeing her again next week."

Eric shook his head as he ate. "No problem. I'll only be taking one bag. You sure you'll be okay with the Jeep?"

"I'll use the van if I need to go anywhere far."

"Um. I think Doug's borrowed it again—doing more work on his house over the weekend, or something."

"Oh, if I get stuck I can always call Harriet. I'll manage somehow." Vanessa looked around, remaining in the doorway. "Well, there's something I need to finish in the den. I'll leave you to your dinner."

Eric nodded as Vanessa turned away. Her footsteps receded across the kitchen and out the far side. Eric carried on eating in silence. Just for once, it would have been nice if she'd offered to get herself a coffee, sit down with him, and talk about something, he thought to himself.

Kitchens, dinners, which car to use, and boxes in the back. Vanessa had hoped this relationship might include some recognition of her worth as a scientist. Instead, she was supposed to become a full-time version of Harriet. Eric had done a smooth job of enticing her away from Microbotics and its realities of the kind he would never be able to deal with. She was expected to become part of this dream world that he had created to escape into, to be an accessory—a complement to his life, but no more. She sat down in the den, picked up the phone, and tapped in Payne's number. Well, Eric had picked the wrong person, she told herself as she heard the ring tone and waited. It was a harsh way to have to learn such basics, maybe. But she hadn't made the rules.

"Hello?"

Vanessa answered in a low voice. "Martin?"

"Hey! Where are you?"

"I'm at the house, so I'll keep it brief. He'll be leaving in the morning. Expect me at the lab by ten-thirty. Are there any changes of plan?"

"None. We're all set as agreed." There was a pause. "You, ah, don't have any . . . second thoughts, then?" Payne's voice held a curious note, a hint, almost, of disbelief.

Vanessa shook her head curtly into the phone. "What is there to think about?" she said, and hung up.

It was the first time that she had talked to Payne from the house, she mused to herself as she sat looking at the phone. But what of it? By the time the bill came in with its record of the call, it would no longer matter.

Martin Payne put down the phone, rose, and carried his drink slowly across the drawing room to the window facing out across the lake. The night was starless and murky, with swirls of mist smearing the lights on the far shore into watery blotches of color. The forecast for tomorrow was unsettled. He hoped the weather would hold sufficiently for them not to have to call off the planned cruise following the party.

So it was on. What had begun as an exchange of "hypothetically speakings" with Vanessa after their decision two months previously to eliminate Jack had in the space of one short, impossible week become reality. There had been times when Payne wondered if they repeated them more to flaunt their bravado at each other than from expectations of being taken seriously. Or at least, he suspected that Vanessa might have merely been playing a game. But it was he who had provided the quality of decisiveness to turn the remotely possible into actual. He trusted that she would take note and be appropriately impressed.

Of course, Vanessa liked to believe it was she who had provided the inducement and given him nerve— but that was to be expected in someone of her peculiar vanity. He hoped that Vanessa wasn't going to spoil things by turning this into a rivalry once the ugly part was over and the two of them had it all. Having to deal her out after all this would be a shame. But, one hurdle at a time, he told himself, looking over at the clock. He tossed back the last of his drink, went back to the phone, and called Finnion's personal number.

"Andy?"

"Yeah, it's me."

"Martin here. We're go for tomorrow. Double-check with the lab that we're set there. I have to leave right away to meet Victor and some people in town. Could you call Phil too, and let him know we're in business? Call me on my mobile number if there are any problems."

"Sure thing," Finnion confirmed. "Is everything okay there with the boat?"

"I talked to Mike ten minutes ago. He'll be moving it across the lake in about another hour."

"Fine. Have a good night out with the guys."

In the security manager's office at Microbotics out toward Redmond, Andy Finnion called up a directory screen and paged to the entry giving Garsten's number. Asking Finnion to question a decision from Payne would have been like arguing with a traffic cop over what the speed limit ought to be. If Finnion's years of police work had taught him anything, it was that you didn't dispute the motives of whoever gives the orders. The real world that most of the public never saw was a rough place, and the only art that mattered was staying alive and surviving. The reason why most people never had to worry too much about basic truths like that was that they were insulated from that world by a protective layer of professionals who took the risks for them. Being one of the professionals meant going by the code that professionals understood. The first part of the code was that you hung—or got hung—together.

Jack Anastole hadn't understood that. If he'd been content to stay East and enjoy a moderately good life, he'd have been left alone. His transgression had not been in being greedy—hell, who was there among them who wasn't there for what he could get? Where he'd overstepped the line was in coming back as an outsider threatening the integrity of the group in its obligation to protect its own, and that was not acceptable. It seemed that now Heber didn't fully understand the system he was part of, either.

The difference between Jack and Phil Garsten was that Jack had used his legal skills to attack the system, whereas Phil placed his at the disposal of the system. At one time they had been partners with pretty equal stakes. Today, Garsten was comfortably established with all the right friends, while the only case that Jack had was a wooden one. The comparison underlined Finnion's philosophy of life pretty strongly.

Finnion called Garsten's number but got only the answering machine. He thought for a moment, then said, "Phil, this is Andy. It's about six-thirty, Friday evening. Martin wanted me to let you know that both parties are on tomorrow. It looks like a busy day. Happy holiday."

❖   ❖   ❖

Garsten got the message a half hour later, when he arrived home after dining Chinese on his way back from the office.

The legalities were attended to, and once Vanessa and Payne became joint owners of the DNC patents and Payne's share of Microbotics stock, what Garsten knew would make him permanently indispensable and somebody they'd be anxious to be certain was kept happy in the future. It went without saying that he'd taken precautions for it not to be in their interest for anything to happen to him that might arouse suspicions—just in case the climate ever changed enough to give anyone ideas of staging another Jack or Heber. A businessman like Martin would understand all about insurance. Garsten had made a point of "confiding" the fact to Finnion one night when they'd been out for a few drinks. It was the easiest way of making sure that Payne would know without being direct with the risk of sounding threatening.

He thought through the plans as they had laid them, and couldn't see any flaw. However, there was one more detail that would round everything off neatly, he decided. Just in case something did go wrong, it would look better if there was something on record to indicate that he, personally, had had every expectation of business resuming as normal after the holiday. It didn't have to be anything especially startling; just enough to be able to point at, shrug, and show clean hands. After pondering for a while, he opened the phone book on his desk and turned to the L section. Then he called Michelle Lang's home number.

"Michelle Lang?"

"Yes."

"Oh, hi again. This is Phil Garsten."

"Mr. Garsten, hello."

"I hope I'm not gatecrashing on your holiday."

"No, it's okay."

"You see, I'm meeting a friend on his boat in the morning, and I'll be gone for the rest of the weekend."

"It sounds wonderful. What can I do for you?"

"You wanted to get together and talk about the Hebers and this theme-park idea. Well, I've just had a cancellation for Tuesday and wondered if we might fit it in then. The rest of next week's wiped out for me."

"Oh . . . what time on Tuesday?"

"First thing after lunch, say one-thirty or two. My office would be better, probably."

"I think that would be okay, but I'm not absolutely sure. Can I call you first thing Tuesday if there's a problem?"

"Of course. That would be fine."

"Well . . . then have a good weekend on the boat, Mr. Garsten. I hope the weather doesn't close in."

"Thanks. You too, Ms. Lang." Garsten replaced the phone and nodded, satisfied.

"The little details," he murmured aloud to himself. "Always remember to take care of the details."

"Hello, Doug? This is Michelle."

"Well, hey."

"Guess who I've just been talking to: Phil Garsten."

"Garsten?" Michelle could sense Corfe go tense suddenly, even over the phone. His voice took on a hollow note. "What's happened?"

"Nothing. He just wanted to talk about an appointment next week. Everything's still okay. In fact, I just wanted to pass on something that will set your mind at ease a little. He's going off with somebody on a boat in the morning—I wouldn't be surprised it it's Payne. So the office will be clear. I just thought you'd like to know."

There was a silence while Corfe digested what she

had said. "Why would he tell you something like that?" he asked finally.

"Oh, Doug, don't sound so suspicious about everything. It was the reason why he needed to call me tonight, that's all. Is everything else okay?"

"Yes. We've got the codes and passwords." Corfe's tone wavered. "Why are we doing this? . . ."

Michelle shook her head. How roles could reverse. Now that she felt confident and optimistic, finally, *he* was suddenly the one having doubts. "You know why we're doing it," she said. "Why ask a question like that?"

"I've just got this premonition that nothing's going to come of it. We're wasting our time."

"There's only one way we'll ever know," Michelle said. "Go and unwind, and then get a good night's sleep. I'll see you tomorrow."

Corfe paced around for a long time after he hung up. Now he could see dozens of ways for something to go wrong. The more he thought about them, the more impossible the odds of avoiding all of them seemed. Talking had been good for venting his frustration. But all his experiences of actual doing had prepared him for circumstances that were very different from those he faced now.

In his Navy years, there had always been the Book to spell out exactly what was to be done and how, and provided you stuck by it, you were protected. Other people had already made the decisions. Having to write his own Book and then stand by the consequences hadn't been part of the training.

Restless for some distraction, he sat down at the computer in a corner of his living room and dialed in for his e-mail. There was a message from Kevin, a response to one that Corfe had sent earlier. It read:
Will be ready in the morning at 10:30.

Tried out the remote hookup with Taki. It works just great. And we can get at hardcopy as well as what's on a screen. Another week would have been really useful. I've made a list of extras we might need. We can pick most of them up at the lab.

Bests,

K.

Corfe felt chagrined. Even the kid was sounding positive and set to go. He worked hard to pull himself together. It had been a mistake to come back home and spend this evening on his own with no plans for anything to do. He'd have been better off staying in town—perhaps could have gone somewhere with Michelle and let a little of her buoyancy carry over. It was different for people like her, who ran businesses, he decided. They wrote a new page of their own Book every day of the week.

CHAPTER TWENTY-SEVEN

Shortly before noon on Saturday morning, Corfe halted the van in one of the slots in the same parking lot that he had used the previous afternoon. The weather had brightened up, with the sun peeking through broken cloud, but the reports were of new squalls moving up from the south. The city was quiet, having a lazy holiday, the parking lot more empty than full.

After learning from Kevin that morning about Kevin and Taki's experiments the evening before, Corfe had agreed that they needed to send more tools and accessories into Garsten's office to tackle desk drawers and file cabinets. The van had its own collection of mecs that could carry the additional items in. But first, the ones that were already inside would need to check out the several possible entry points that Corfe had noted the previous afternoon, and find the most suitable.

Michelle shook her head wonderingly in the passenger seat next to him while he checked through the things they had brought. "I don't believe this. I started out trying to instill some respect in you for proper procedures. You end up turning me into a criminal. I'm a contract lawyer. This isn't what I do."

"Don't blame me, blame Eric," Corfe answered. "Everyone who comes near him ends up having their life turned inside out."

Michelle nodded. "You're right. And outwardly I've never met anyone more charming. How does he have this effect on people? Why do we end up doing things like this?"

"I guess because of what he stands for. And we all love him for it." Corfe picked up the van's phone and called the Test Lab at Neurodyne. Kevin answered a few seconds later.

"Right, we've arrived and we're in position," Corfe said. "I circled the block on the way, and it looks quiet. We're going to connect through now."

"Everything's quiet here in the lab too. I guess everyone's holidaying as we hoped. I'm coupled in, ready to go."

"Fine. We'll see you inside. Signing out." Corfe looked across at Michelle. "Okay, let's go."

They climbed back between the seats to the rear section of the van. Corfe drew a curtain across the front and turned on the interior light to reveal banks of equipment and screens, two operator positions on one side, and one on the other, and a regular seat facing rearward behind the partition. He motioned Michelle into the station nearest the rear doors and moved himself into the one next to her. "There won't be any need for you to couple in to begin with," he said as he flipped switches and tapped keys to activate the equipment. "You can work in conjunction with Kevin from here. I'm patching the video from one of the mecs already in the office to that monitor up there." He indicated one of the screens, then handed Michelle a regular telephone headset. "This carries Kev's audio channel, so you can talk to him. This other screen will let you follow what I'm doing from the mec I'll be controlling. I'll be on the same audio circuit as you and Kev. Want to check it out?"

Michelle put the set on her head while Corfe was attaching his own coupler collar and headset. "Hello, Kevin? This is Michelle testing. Can you hear me? . . ." Moments later she nodded. "Yes, he's there. We're through."

The inside of the van disappeared, and Corfe was in a colorful, cartoon-like visual world, facing a signboard showing a hierarchy of system menus and labeled boxes. He pointed at a DIAGNOSTIC branch and ran a quick test of vision and motor functions, then entered AUDIOSYS to make the connections.

"Can you hear me, Michelle?" he checked.

"I'd hope so. You're sitting right next to me."

"I meant through the phones."

"Yes. You're okay."

"Do you read, Kev?"

"Roger."

"Okay. . . ."

And Corfe was in darkness, entombed in a clinging plastic shroud. He freed his arms, worked them up over his head, and with some wriggling and tugging opened the top of the bag. He pulled the folds low around him and stepped over them to emerge into a shadowy vault of looming shapes and rectangles that he recognized as the storage space below the worktop at the back of the secretaries' area in Garsten's office. There was more movement in the bag, and the second telebot-size mec appeared—similar to the one that Corfe was occupying, but with different accessories. Corfe held the folds of plastic aside while it emerged fully. "Everything okay, Kev?" he asked.

"Check," Kevin's voice said on the audio.

"Still with us, Michelle?"

"I'm here. The pictures on the two screens are coming through pretty clear too."

"Good. Let's start by getting everything laid out where we can see it, and do an inventory."

Corfe walked to the edge of the cupboard's wooden base and jumped down to the floor. Kevin followed, dragging the plastic bag, now relieved of its major load. The carpet was like a field of closely packed tussocks of coarse gray grass, making the going bumpy. They stepped up onto the skating rink of plastic mat behind the nearer of the two desks, and passed beneath an office chair, looming above them like a gigantic tree of tubes and girders. Here would be as good a place as any to establish base camp, Corfe decided.

They laid out the remaining contents of the bag and took stock. There were: a half-dozen specialized mecs, ranging in size from a quarter-inch, to one of the new Keyboard Emulator models that Corfe had described at Taki's; a standard keyboard plug, with two feet of lightweight cable coiled like a hose; a miniaturized recharging unit with power cord; a selection of lines, pulleys, and attachment slings; assorted tools; a six-foot steel measuring tape.

The first thing, they had agreed, would be to get Kevin and Michelle working on the computer files while Corfe went off to look at entry points for the reinforcements. To operate the computer they would first have to plug in the KE mec, which required getting it up onto the desk. They stood looking up at it, towering over them like a hangar for zeppelins. There was no quick way up. They already knew that, of course.

"Okay, let's roll out the tape," Corfe said. "Now we'll see if this crazy idea of yours and Taki's works."

"We already tried it. It works," Kevin answered.

Taking a side of the case each, they carried the

measuring tape to the base of the chair and stood it on its side so that it butted against the castor and support bracket. While Kevin wedged the case to prevent it from moving, Corfe took hold of the protruding metal tag at the end of the tape and backed away until the markings showed that he had drawn out thirty-six inches. "That should do it," Kevin said, and locked the clamp to stop the tape retracting.

Corfe came back, and between them they moved the case out from under the chair and closer to the desk. Working together like firefighters maneuvering an extension ladder, they raised the tape carefully from the floor, moving it slowly so that it wouldn't kink and bend, and turned it until the top end leaned against the edge of the desk. "What we need now is something solid up on top of the desk to act as an anchor and keep the tape taut," Kevin said.

"Can you see anything on the screen, Michelle?" Corfe asked.

"There's a kind of metal desk organizer with lots of dividers and trays," she replied after a few seconds. She was looking at the screen that Corfe had pointed out before he coupled in, showing the view being picked up by one of the two small mecs planted high up in the office since yesterday.

"Let me see." Still retaining motor control of the larger mec, Corfe switched his vision to the channel that Michelle was watching. Hence, he was able to see down onto the desk and at the same time work with Kevin by touch to move the tape from below. The organizer was a chromed composition of stationery slots and trays for pens and other oddments, with numerous edges. Just the thing. "Okay, it's a bit farther to the left," he told Kevin.

With Corfe directing, they steered the tape above the organizer, and then extended it farther until it suddenly buckled over the edge of desk to fall across the metal dividers and edges. "Now we reel it in," Kevin said.

After a few tries they succeeded in snagging the end-tag. Pulling the tape tight, they now had a rigid ladder running up from the floor to the edge of the desk, and over.

Now it was Kevin's turn to switch mecs. Transferring to one of the small models that they had below, he wrapped a length of line around its body like a mountaineer's rope and inched his way up the swaying metal strip, using the mec's hands as clamps on the edges. Corfe switched his vision back to floor-view and steadied the tape from below. At the top, Kevin unwound the line, secured it to the desk lamp, and threw the other end down to Corfe, who was then able to walk himself up the drawer fronts, carrying the KE mec, and its keyboard adapter plug and cable with him.

"You know, if this fails, you guys could always get in a circus with that act," Michelle told them.

There were now three mecs up on the desktop: the small general-purpose type that Kevin had used to scale the tape; the larger, more powerful, telebot type that Corfe had taken up; and the Keyboard Emulator. Corfe unplugged the regular keyboard from the computer and replaced it with cord that he had brought up from the floor; the other end connected into the head socket of the KE mec, which Kevin now activated and brought around in front of the screen. Corfe tipped the power switch on the front of the computer box to "On," and the whir of the cooling fan starting came from inside. He crossed the desk and turned on the monitor, and a moment later the screen came to life to show the familiar operating system trademark and logo.

"We're in business!" Kevin announced.

"Bravo," Michelle complimented from the van.

"Teamwork," Kevin said from the lab at Neurodyne.

The cursor on the screen moved—presumably following a finger that Kevin was moving in virtual space. A selection of menus appeared. "Where would be a good place to start?" Kevin's voice asked on the circuit. "FILES, looks promising, yes?"

"Let's have a look at what we've got there," Michelle said.

The cursor moved over the screen, stopped, and then a box appeared with the legend: ENTER PASSWORD

"Okay, I think I've got this," Kevin muttered. "Give me a second to look up what we taped. . . ."

"Okay, can you do without me now for a while?" Corfe said.

"Sure. We'll be okay now," Kevin answered.

Decoupling from the can-size telebot on the desk, Corfe reactivated the other mec to find himself back down on the floor. He selected some tools and devices that he thought he might need from the collection they had laid out there, and departed for other parts of the house.

Michelle was not the only one who had been watching. Although Corfe had looked hard enough during his visit, he had seen no sign of internal surveillance, and had concluded that the building's protection was limited to standard measures for detecting external break in and entry. But some of Garsten's business was such that he didn't always want his clients to know that they were being observed and recorded. Also, he did highly confidential work for Martin Payne, and Payne owned a company that dealt in some pretty advanced technology.

Each of the principal rooms had a normal-looking mirror, wall plaque, or framed design concealing a miniature camera that could be remote-directed. And the bases of the ceiling-lamp fixtures contained sensitive motion detectors that responded to reflective metallic surfaces. Garsten had good reasons for not wanting either the police or any of the regular private security companies in any kind of proximity to his affairs. Accordingly, he relied on Microbotics for his security arrangements, and the alarm lines from his office went directly to the company's premises at Redmond.

Garsten was with Vanessa and Andy Finnion in the room at the top of the lab block where the equipment was set up, when a call came through from the supervisor currently on duty in Security, across in the main building. They were killing time, waiting for Eric to reach the hazardous stretch of road that they had picked for the "accident." All modern vehicles carried a satellite-linked positioning system, and it was simple for Vanessa to check the car's location by dialing a number that returned its current map coordinates. Payne himself had joined the yacht, now at Fox Landing, where he was finalizing preparations for the holiday weekend.

"Andy, it's Kyle here. We've got trouble. Can you get over here right away?"

"What is it? What's up?"

"Is Phil Garsten still with you?"

"Yes, he is. Why?"

"Bring him too. We've got an alarm condition from his office. You need to come and see this for yourself."

Finnion hung up, looking mystified.

"Perhaps I'd better come too," Vanessa said. There was time yet. Their last fix had shown Eric in the same place for almost thirty minutes, probably stopped somewhere for breakfast. Finnion nodded. They took an elevator down, left the lab block, and arrived in Security several minutes later.

Garsten's eyes bulged as Kyle showed them the current view from one of the live cameras and a replay of some of what had been happening. "*What are they?*" he protested in a strangled voice, pointing an outraged finger at the screen. "What's going on? . . . Goddamn robot things all over my office. . . ."

Finnion blanched. "Something's screwed up big. I need to call Martin. We may have to scratch the operation."

"No!" Vanessa's voice was tight but firm. "Think about it. Whatever's happening has nothing to do with the plan. Phil's office doesn't come into it. It's something else going on there, a coincidence." Garsten and Finnion glanced at each other. Maybe she had a point. They waited to see what she would make of it.

Vanessa stared at the screens, thinking rapidly. "The van has to be there somewhere. Whoever it is has to be doing this from the van. . . . It's no use us just going crashing into the building. All it'll do is alert them that we're onto them and scare them off." She shot a look at Finnion. "Andy, can you mobilize some of your guys quickly—you know, ones who can be trusted?"

He nodded. "We've always got an emergency crew on call."

"Get them over to Phil's office and comb the area for a dark gray Dodge van, registration 437 ECH, with antennas on the roof. It should be within a few blocks. Whoever's doing this will be right there."

Finnion gave a curt nod. "Okay. Kyle, rustle 'em out. Let's move it."

Garsten was still looking incredulously at the screen. "How in hell did they get in? Look at that. . . . Goddamn beer can walking down my hall!"

CHAPTER TWENTY-EIGHT

Corfe made his way to the rear of the house and found the place where the capped-off pipe that looked like a piece of old dryer vent entered from the outside. The inside end was covered by a painted aluminum plate held by four screws, which the mec removed without difficulty. Peering in, he saw that the way to the outside cap, about eighteen inches away, was unobstructed. There was no more to be done here for the moment. The mec would be best left where it was for the time being, to help carry the additional equipment away when it was brought through. "Okay, I'm done for now, and exiting," he announced.

"Did you find a way in?" Kevin's voice asked.

"I think so. It's time to tackle it from the outside. How's it going with you guys?"

"Oh, we're getting there. Talk to you soon."

Corfe called down the Control menu, exited, and was promptly back in the van beside Michelle. He removed the headset and collar, yawned, and rubbed his eyes with his fingers.

"Taking a break?" Michelle said.

"There's just a cap to take off from the outside, which

shouldn't be a problem." He looked up at the screen monitoring Kevin's video output, which was showing columns of names and numbers. "What do we have there?"

"We're going through the file indexes. The system's starting to make sense."

"Will you be okay on your own here for a while?"

"Sure."

"I might as well take the extra stuff over now. It shouldn't take more than thirty minutes at the most. You're sure you'll be okay?"

"Doug, stop fussing."

"You're right. It's nerves, I guess." Corfe indicated the canvas tool bag containing the additional mecs and other items to be sent in from outside, which he had placed inside the rear door. "Can you hand me that?" Michelle tried to reach, but couldn't turn her seat far enough. "It's okay," Corfe said. "I'll come around outside." He slid out of the coupler seat and opened the partitioning curtain to the front. Just as he was about to leave, Michelle said:

"Will I need to do anything with this?" She gestured to indicate the panels and controls.

Corfe thought for a moment. Then he took one of the van's complement of smaller mecs from a storage rack and put it down on the console in front of her. "Here," he said. "If you need to change anything, get Kevin to couple through into this. He can be the guide."

"Great. Thanks," Michelle said.

"Back soon."

"Good luck. Be careful."

Corfe squeezed between the front seats and climbed out via the driver's door. The street alongside the parking lot was quiet, the air cool and fresh after the mugginess inside. He drew in a long breath, stretched, and exhaled gratefully. Then he went around to the back of the van, retrieved the canvas bag from inside, closed the rear door, and walked away along the street.

The vent was at the back of the house, which meant going inside the fence and around. If that looked suspicious, it was a risk that just had to be taken. After a bit of searching, Corfe located the outlet and found that it was partly shielded by the shrubbery, which made him not quite so conspicuous, at least. He squatted down, and working quickly, removed the cap and transferred the mecs and other things from his bag into the opening of the pipe. Then he straightened up, and for the benefit of anyone curious who might be watching, made a show of inspecting the junction box where a power cable from a nearby distribution pole entered the house, and then scribbling in a notebook. Casting a final look around as if he had every right to be there, he returned the notebook to his pocket, picked up the tool bag, and departed back for the van.

Eric sat finishing his breakfast, listening to two men in the next booth arguing politics. The bearded man in the green sweater had decided that socialism was morally degenerate. The belief structure came first, determining what was acceptable as fact. Whatever accorded with it became a self-evident truth; anything in conflict was rejected as propaganda or typical of uninformed media. Finally, the white-haired man with him said, "I can't talk to you. You won't entertain any possibility that you might be mistaken. If it's not even conceivable, then there isn't anything to discuss."

After a few seconds of silence the other conceded grudgingly, "Well, theoretically I could be, I guess. . . ." Then rallied quickly. "But that still doesn't alter the fact that . . ."

But the one who'd asked the question had created

a chink. Now he could start probing it with wedges.

He faced the same problem, Eric thought to himself. It was a lonely business, waiting for one of Kuhn's paradigms to shift. The collective of the physics orthodoxy were literally incapable of seeing a fact that went against what in their minds had taken on the quality of self-evident truth. Hence, the very notion of questioning it was unthinkable. Eric had been through the routine many times, heard all the objections. Here, however, was an approach that he hadn't tried before.

"*Is it possible* that you might be wrong?" So disarmingly simple. Perhaps this time he would preface his talk with an appeal along those lines. Who could refuse to grant a modicum of open-mindedness in response to something like that?

He finished his meal, paid the check, and left, mentally composing various opening lines as he walked back to where he had parked the Jaguar.

They had found an index under Heber's name that contained references to various files and records. This looked more like it. Michelle studied the entries on the latest page that Kevin had routed through to her screen. "Now I need to check something back in the index," she told him. Just then, the display lost synchronism and broke up into streaky bands scrolling vertically. "Wait a minute, I've lost the picture here," she said. "What do I do now?"

"Hang on. I'll be there in a moment."

A few seconds later, the mec that Corfe had left on the console with Michelle moved a couple of inches and looked up at the controls beneath the screen. "Third knob from the left," Kevin's voice said in her headset. Michelle turned it. The scrolling slowed, then reversed. She turned the knob back a fraction, and the screen stabilized. There was still some residual judder. "Now try turning one next to it to the right a little," Kevin said.

A *clack* sounded from the rear door as the catch was released from the outside. Michelle turned her head as the door opened, expecting to see Corfe. But the man standing there in the dark raincoat was somebody she had never seen before: lean and muscular, dark hair slicked back above a sallow, unsmiling face. Two others were with him, one of them pocketing what looked like a phone. The one at the door jerked his head curtly. "Okay, it's over. Get out."

Michelle summoned as much semblance of outrage as she was capable of, given her surprise and the sudden shock. "*What the hell?* . . . Who are you? What do you think you're doing? Get *out* of here!"

The man sighed and produced a gun. Michelle stared at it disbelievingly. It took her several seconds to accept that this was really happening. "No, I don't think you understand," he said. "Either you come out the sensible way, or get pulled out with a hole in your leg. It's your choice. Don't touch anything in there." The tone and look on his face said that he meant it.

Michelle experienced a confused numbness. She got up and climbed shakily out of the van. The two men who had been standing back moved in on either side and seized her arms. A black Lincoln was blocking the back of the van. Another two men, she saw, had been positioned outside the doors at the front. Before anyone could say any more, a beige Cadillac came into the parking lot and pulled up behind the Lincoln. A short man with a mustache, wearing a camel-hair overcoat and black Tyrolean hat, climbed out and came forward.

The man in the dark raincoat closed the van door and turned, slipping the gun back into his pocket.

"There's just her," he informed the newcomer. "The gear inside is switched on. I've left it all as it was."

"Who else was with you?" the man in the hat demanded. "You weren't running this on your own?" Michelle glared at him and said nothing. He turned to the one wearing the raincoat. "We need to get her off the street. Take her back to Andy for now. I need to check out the office."

"Okay, put her in the car," the man in the raincoat told the two who were holding Michelle, then threw some keys to one of the other two by the van, who caught them. "Ollie, bring the van and follow us. Royal, you go with Phil to check out the office. We'll see you back at the firm."

The mustached man in the camel-hair coat began walking back to the Cadillac with Royal. Phil? Michelle forced the two who were steering her toward the Lincoln to halt. "Garsten?" she fired at the mustached man. He stopped and looked back. "You're Phillip Garsten. Just what in hell do you people think you're doing? Don't you realize you're going to have a lot of explaining to do?"

He didn't seem unduly perturbed. "Ms. Lang, I assume, is it? No, you're the one who's going to be doing some explaining." He turned and walked away.

One of the men holding her opened the door of the Lincoln, and then went around to the far side while the other followed her in. The man in the dark raincoat got in up front. Doors slammed in quick succession. The car moved forward a few yards to make room, and then waited for the van to back out behind.

Michelle, wedged between two sets of broad shoulders in the rear seat, wondered how the driver had come to be in possession of keys to the van. As the Lincoln pulled away again, the thought came to her suddenly that Vanessa had to be involved. Guns?

Abductions in broad daylight? Just exactly what was going on? A sinking premonition gripped her that she had gotten herself into something that could have consequences a lot more serious than breaking into offices. She shivered, drew her coat closer around herself and slid her hands into the pockets.

Inside one of them was something irregularly shaped and hard. It felt like a little metal bug. And as her fingertip traced over it, it moved. A mec! It could only be from the van—the one that Kevin had been operating. In the few moments while she was turning in the seat, before she got out, he must have seen what was happening and scrambled off the console and into her pocket. Michelle wasn't sure how much use that might be. She was still scared. But at least, she no longer felt totally on her own.

As Corfe came around the corner onto the street leading back to the parking lot, the first thing he saw was that the van wasn't in the slot where he had left it. A moment later he spotted it moving behind a black Lincoln that was coming out through the gate. The Lincoln turned away in the opposite direction, and the van followed it. Corfe came to a halt on the sidewalk, stunned. Then he realized that a beige Cadillac that had come out behind the van was turning the other way and coming in his direction. Something told him that he had seen that car before, causing him to retreat back around the corner and stand out of sight against the wall. Moments later the car passed, and he recognized Phillip Garsten at the wheel, accompanied by another man. Then he remembered: He had seen that car yesterday, parked in one of the "Private" slots outside Garsten's office. From the direction it was going, that could well be where it was heading for now.

He stood for what seemed a stupidly long time,

unable to fathom what it meant, utterly without a clue of what to do next. What was there to do? He didn't even know which direction to head. There was no point in going on the way he had been, since Michelle and the van were gone. And there was nothing to accomplish by going back to Garsten's office except to get apprehended himself too. Now he didn't even have a way of getting back, or anywhere else—even if he knew where he wanted to go.

It was all over, he realized sickeningly. What other conclusion was there? Michelle was very likely in danger. There was no time for any more games of pretend heroics. He had stuck a toe into waters that he didn't understand, and promptly gone in over his head. He stood on the corner of the street with his bag, looking first one way, then the other. He wasn't even sure which direction the nearest police station was in.

Wearily, he pulled his mobile phone from his jacket pocket and first tried calling Neurodyne to let Kevin know what was happening, but there was no reply. He pressed the Reset button and called Emergency.

CHAPTER TWENTY-NINE

Phillip Garsten stood looking around his office in bewilderment. The screens were turned on, and a bug thing with a wire coming out of it was plugged into the computer. Another bug and a beer-can robot were up on the desk; there was a piece of cord hanging down over the edge from the lamp; and there was a carpenter's tape and other junk all over the floor. . . . What in the name of God was going on?

He looked at the screen facing him, and his face darkened. It was showing entries from the Heber files. This was serious. He touched the smaller bug on the desk warily. It fell over. He nudged the larger one; it was just as inert. Of course, he told himself—they'd been controlled from the van, and the van was gone. All the same, he felt relieved.

What to do? His eyes darted around uncertainly while his mind worked. They had expected to find Heber's technical chief, Corfe, because Vanessa said Corfe was using the van. Without a doubt, Lang hadn't been working alone. Therefore, Corfe was still out there somewhere. Would he go to the police? Garsten didn't know. But one sure thing was that if they came here and found all this going on, a lot of inconvenient

questions would get asked. And with one thing leading
to another, all kinds of complications were likely to
develop that everyone could do without. Get rid of
the evidence and deny everything, he decided. First
leave everything clean; then consult with Martin and
Vanessa.

He went through to his own office—there was no
sign of anything amiss there—and returned with a large
leather briefcase that he used for carrying legal files.
Still handling them cautiously, he put the micromecs
inside, added the other things from the floor and the
cord that had been tied to the lamp, plugged the
keyboard back into the computer, and shut down the
system. Then he stood back to survey the room one
last time.

"Son-of-a-gun," he breathed. There were two more
of them. One was wedged in the bracket of a wall lamp;
the other was in the plant up on the file cabinet behind
Susanne's desk. How long had they been there, for
God's sake? Now he was getting really worried. He
scooped them down and put them in the bag just as
Royal came in from checking the outside of the
building.

"There was a cover off a pipe at the back," Royal
announced. "I found these in it." He opened his hand
to show several more bug-size robots and a small plastic
package. Garsten shook his head bemusedly and held
open the bag. Royal's eyebrows raised. "Was all this
stuff in here?"

"We had a mechanical zoo loose."

"Jeez!"

"Did you put the cover back on out there?"

Royal nodded. "Uh-huh. We'd better take a look at
the inside as well." He led the way back to where he
thought the place was, but Garsten had guessed where
he meant before they got there. The inside cover plate

was off, and there was another beer-can standing motionless to add to the collection.

While Royal resecured the inside cover plate, Garsten called Vanessa at Microbotics to let her know the situation and to say he was on his way. He and Royal gave the place a final inspection but found nothing more. They turned out the lights, reset the alarms, and left.

"You shouldn't have had them take her back to the firm, Vanessa. Now we're all implicated. It's a mess." Payne was talking over the phone from the yacht on Lake Union. He sounded agitated. Typical, Vanessa thought, controlling herself with difficulty. The minute the going started getting rough. Welcome to the real world, Martin.

She was back on the top floor of the laboratory block with Finnion. Eric was getting close to the target stretch now, where the road wound up a valleyside of sheer cliffs and gorges. Vanessa had changed into the VR body suit and had plugged in the helmet in readiness.

"Where else was there to take her?" she snapped. "Obviously she was working with Corfe, since he borrowed the van yesterday. We had to get her out of sight, off the streets."

"It means the whole thing's off," Payne began. "We're going to—"

"No, it does *not*. We're all set to go here. It's literally a matter of a few minutes now, and it'll be all over. We *can't* let it pass by now, Martin. There's no knowing when there might be another chance like this. Everyone's keyed up. We have to see it through."

"But she's *there* at the firm," Payne protested. "She knows I'm involved—Phil, all of us. Are you going to get rid of her too? This has got to stop. And in any case, Corfe's still loose over here in the city somewhere."

Vanessa sighed. "Martin, calm down and think about it. If Eric has an accident up in the mountains, there's absolutely nothing to connect us with it. That was precisely why we decided on doing it this way. Whatever Corfe and this woman are involved in has to do with something else."

"But what?"

"How can I know yet? Probably they're just meddling. But it puts them more in the wrong than us. She was involved in breaking into premises that this company has a perfectly legitimate contract to protect. So at worst, Andy stands to be reprimanded for letting his security people act over-zealously, that's all." Finnion nodded silently from across the room. "And I'm sure that with his connections he's well able to take care of something like that." There was a knock on the door. Finnion moved to open it. A man in a gray overjacket stuck his head in and murmured something.

"Well, I just hope you're right, Vanessa," Payne went on. Finnion caught Vanessa's eye. "I can't afford to risk any—"

"Just a moment, Martin."

"She's here—over in Security," Finnion murmured.

"Martin, they've got her here now," Vanessa said. "Phil should be on his way. Andrew will call you after they've had a chance to talk to her. But we need to take care of this other business first. It's almost time. I'll call you as soon as it's over." She hung up without waiting for an answer.

Finnion looked at the man who had brought the news. "We've got some business to wrap up here. Tell Kyle I'll be over there as soon as we're through. She's a lawyer, and we're probably a bit out of line, so lay off any rough stuff. Give her a cup of coffee or something."

The man in the gray overjacket nodded and left, closing the door.

They brought Michelle across the Evergreen Bridge and out to Redmond. She saw the Microbotics sign from the highway. The Lincoln took the next exit, followed a tree-lined avenue to the premises, and parked behind what appeared to be the main building. The man in the dark raincoat led the way up to a second-floor room with consoles and closed-circuit TV monitors that looked like a security center, to a small office at the back. Then he disappeared, leaving her with the two who had sat beside her in the car. They remained as uncommunicative as they had been through the drive.

Now she was even more scared. This whole facade of running a legitimate business was little more than a cover. The real moneymaking line that these people were in, that bought mansions in Bellevue and yachts like the *Dolores*, was stock manipulation and illegal use of investors' funds. Threatened with exposure, they had already shown themselves prepared to kill. And why hadn't it troubled them to bring her here? By the time Garsten showed up and told the other two to wait outside, she was close to having convinced herself that she was about to be shot on the spot.

"What do you think you're doing?" she demanded hoarsely. "You can't go grabbing people off the street whenever you feel like it. It's—"

"Do you think *you* can go breaking into buildings when you feel like it?" Garsten retorted. "This company happens to take care of my security. Legally."

"This still isn't some banana country where people run private armies. How long do you think you'll stay in practice after this?"

"Oh, you just let me worry about that. For now, I'm

asking the questions. What did you expect to find there?"

"Enough that you should be very worried." From the frown that crossed Garsten's face, Michelle knew she had scored a point. But just at that moment, all that really mattered to her was finding a way to stall somehow and make her situation safer. Even though a part of her knew that she was going too far, she carried on, unable to check herself. "I wouldn't let your friends here do anything rash, Mr. Garsten. We know about Jack Anastole . . . and the scheme you've been working on since. Don't make it any worse."

That evidently did it. Garsten looked as if he had been punched in the face. He seemed to lose the thread of what they had been saying, and glanced unconsciously at his watch. The transformation was so abrupt that Michelle was at a loss to know what she had said to produce it. Seemingly losing interest in her, Garsten went over to the door and opened it, still looking dazed. He said something to the two men standing outside and went into another office opposite. The two came back in, closing the door, and resumed standing guard.

Jack Anastole had been strictly Martin and Vanessa's affair.

Garsten had been just a go-between carrying messages. He hadn't even known what they were planning until after it was over. He could clear himself of the worst from that; there was no reason why he should have to go down with them over it now. He pulled across the phone and punched in the number of the room at the top of the adjacent building, where Vanessa had her stuff set up. Finnion answered. Garsten told him to put Vanessa on. Her voice came on the line a couple of seconds later.

"Whatever it is, Phil, you'll have to sit on it. We're almost ready to go here. I'm not available for anything until we're done."

"That's the whole point." Garsten spoke in a low voice, but urgently. "You may have to call it off. I think she may know everything."

"You mean about Eric?"

"I think so."

There was a short pause. "That's not possible." For once Vanessa sounded nonplussed.

"You haven't heard what she just said. I'm telling ya, hold off for Christ's sake."

A long, dragging silence followed. Then, "Get her over here," Vanessa's voice said.

Garsten went back out and collected Michelle and her two escorts. As they were leaving to go across to the lab block, Kyle, the duty supervisor, took an incoming call. "One moment, Mr. Garsten." Garsten stopped. Kyle drew him aside while the others waited.

"I've got the Seattle police on the line," Kyle muttered. "They're at your office now, with a Mr. Corfe. He's saying something about a stolen van, and that a woman is being held inside, but they don't have sufficient grounds to enter. Would you like to talk to them?"

Garsten groaned and shook his head. "Not now. I'm not here, understand? You're the security company responsible. Can you get over there and deal with it?"

"Yes, sir, I can."

"Do that. I'll clear it with Andy later." Garsten rejoined the others at the door, and they left together.

Something didn't add up, Vanessa could see. Although she was trying hard not to show it, the Lang woman was a lot more frightened than someone ought to be for just being caught raiding an office. She looked as if she thought her life was at stake.

They were in a storage room a few doors along from the room where the VR equipment was set up. Garsten and Finnion were with them, and two of Finnion's men were outside in the corridor.

"Jack, my ex-husband?" Vanessa said, when Garsten finished repeating what Michelle had told him. "What about him?"

"You tell me," Michelle shot back.

"And exactly what is that supposed to mean?"

"I think you know very well." Michelle's show of defiance seemed to require some effort. "And even if your friendly family lawyer gets you out of that, it would be just too much of a coincidence if anything happens to me too."

Vanessa was becoming aware then of a feeling welling up within her that she was not accustomed to, that she normally managed to keep under control and out of her mind. Only now was she beginning to realize just how much she hated this woman. "And what was this about Eric?" she demanded coldly, ignoring the remark.

"Just that we know all about your plans for him too. Husbands tend not to do very well around you at all, do they?" Michelle made what looked like a feigned tired look. "You might as well acknowledge it now and save yourself a lot of trouble, Vanessa. It's over. Let's be realistic."

Vanessa searched Michelle's face. If this was bluff, she was unable to tell. She went through the implications in her mind, one way, then another, touching on all the possibilities.

And what they added up to was, she couldn't risk it. She hadn't bothered answering Martin on the phone earlier about getting rid of Michelle because then the question had been too idiotic; but now, suddenly, there was no choice. There seemed a real chance that Michelle and Corfe had indeed unearthed something damning to do with Jack's death; therefore, they would have to be silenced. One was here already, and it wouldn't take long to track down the other.

The ironic part was that Michelle herself had brought it on them both by not keeping her mouth shut, which made her a fool on top of everything else. And that made all the other things that Vanessa had been holding back come boiling out. It might be quick when it happened, maybe just a bullet without warning. There might not be time then. But just in case, before it happened, Vanessa wanted her to *know*.

"You stupid little bitch!" she spat. "You had to, didn't you? You just had to! You couldn't leave it alone. Can you see what your interfering in what wasn't your business has done for both of you now?" Now Michelle was looking bewildered. Vanessa pressed on, "Yes, all right, *we* did it! Jack was another one like you: didn't know how to be satisfied when he was on to a good thing. He had to come back and interfere in what was over his head too." She paused for a moment, enjoying the incredulous expression spreading over Michelle's face. "Do you want to know how? You might as well, because you're not going to be telling anyone now. Well, just ask yourself, what can go in through a locked hotel-room door . . . or maybe *under* it?" She waited, then gave a satisfied nod. "That's right, honey. I think you're getting the picture now."

Michelle was shaking her head protestingly. "It still won't do you any good. Eric will—"

Vanessa laughed. "Forget Eric. He won't be around for much longer to be doing anything. In fact . . ." She looked at Finnion. "How are we doing?"

But before Finnion could say anything, Michelle gasped. Her face went pale. She was staring, horrified at the VR body suit that Vanessa was wearing. Its significance had just dawned on her. "Oh, my God, it's now! You're doing it today!"

Vanessa saw then that Michelle's own bluff had backfired on her. *Michelle hadn't known about that part.* Neither, then, would Corfe know. It followed, then, that if Eric went ahead and had his accident, neither would anyone else. They didn't have to postpone things at all.

Vanessa also saw something else. It was just a glint of light off something metallic, but enough for her to spot the mec ducking back into Michelle's coat pocket. With a masterful effort of self-control, she managed not to let her expression alter while her mind raced. Who was controlling it? It couldn't be Corfe—the van was here at Microbotics. Eric was on his way to the conference. But whoever it was had heard and probably taped everything. It could only be Kevin, relaying through the van, which meant he had to be in the lab at Neurodyne.

"I think our friend here could use a glass of water," she said to Finnion. "I'll be back in a moment." Finnion looked puzzled, but nodded. And forcing herself not to show undue haste, Vanessa left the room.

Outside in the corridor, she walked quickly back to the room where the equipment was and activated the communications software in one of the processors. She set it to call an access number into the Neurodyne research system, and it connected after about twenty seconds. This was a system that Vanessa knew intimately. Working deftly, she identified the control computer handling the DNC coupler that Kevin was using. He was still coupled in, with the executive program running. Vanessa typed in a patch of code and sent it over the link to disenable the exit routine. It meant that the operator would be locked into the system, unable to decouple using internal commands. For good measure, Vanessa also blocked the device control supervisor, making it impossible for him to communicate with any mecs.

Then she went back to the other room, called Finnion outside, and explained what had happened. "It's Kevin," she said. "Something in the van downstairs is still operating. He's linking through from the lab back at Neurodyne. But I dialed in and fixed the software to stop him coming off the machine. So we can figure out what to do with him later, after I talk to Martin. In the meantime, it doesn't change the main business. We take care of that first. It's almost time. Do you want to bring Phil?"

For a while, Kevin was too numbed by what he had heard to know what to do. The talk seemed to have stopped. He risked another peek from Michelle's pocket and saw that Vanessa, the mustached man whom he now knew to be Garsten, and the thickset one they called Andy, had left. Michelle didn't seem to be in any immediate danger. While things were quiet, he could exit quickly and warn Eric via his car phone. He called down the Control menu and flagged the exit option to decouple. Nothing happened.

He tried again. Again the system didn't respond. Something was suddenly very wrong.

When he tried reconnecting to the mec, that was dead too. Desperately he selected alternate channels to the other mecs that they had left in Garsten's office. Nothing. He tried activating others that were still in the van, development models in the lab around him, and models in other parts of Neurodyne. Nothing.

And that was when he panicked. His father was about

to be murdered, and apart from Michelle, he was the only person who knew. But he was trapped, unable to move, with all his senses and motor functions locked into a machine. In effect, paralyzed—until somebody released him from the outside.

to be more annoyed apart from Mishell, who was the only person who broke free. But he was trapped inside, however, with all his costs and oh it's television asked into a machine, it's a clear, painted—and somebody released him from the outside.

CHAPTER THIRTY

Corfe's forebodings had grown progressively worse while he sat in the back of the Seattle city police cruiser outside Garsten's office, waiting for a representative from the security company to arrive. The van that he said had been stolen was not outside; neither was the beige Cadillac or any other vehicle. There had been no answer at the door, and an officer who toured around the outside of the building had found no sign of life. By that time, Corfe's own suspicion that he had made a mistake must have shown, and the two officers who had brought him had decided there was no evidence of an emergency sufficient to justify a forced entry. Corfe's attempt to confess that he and the missing woman had broken in already hadn't helped—especially when the security company reported no alarms and nothing amiss on their internal TV monitors. Well, it wasn't actually "they" who had broken in, he'd tried to explain, but little machines.

"Machines, huh?" The officers had just barely refrained from asking openly if they'd come out of a UFO that landed on the roof.

When the opened vent that Corfe told them they'd find at the back of the house turned out not to be, with no trace of the things he said would be inside the pipe, that hadn't helped much either. Now, from the way they had been exchanging gossip in the front seats for the last ten minutes and practically ignoring him, it was painfully clear that they had written him off as a crank and just wanted to see this business through, then go find themselves a coffee and donut shop.

A black Lincoln came along the street, turned off onto the parking strip, and drew up beside the cruiser. Corfe stared at it, now totally confused. It was too much of a coincidence not to be the same Lincoln that he had seen drive away ahead of the van. What in hell was going on?

A red-haired man in a brown parka emerged from the Lincoln. The officer who appeared to be the senior of the two, whom the other called Des, got out to talk to him. There was a brief exchange that Corfe didn't catch, accompanied by gestures in his direction. Then the two who were outside the car walked up to the house. The man in the parka opened the door, and Corfe saw him switch off the alarm panel in the entrance foyer. He disappeared inside, Des following.

Well, yes, Corfe thought to himself: If the mecs had triggered an alarm that he'd failed to spot, it made sense that it would have alerted the security company. But how had Garsten's security company known about the van? He still couldn't understand that part.

Unless . . .

He felt sick suddenly, as something that should have been obvious all along finally occurred to him.

"Officer?" The officer still sitting in the driver's seat turned his head. "Could you tell me the name of the security company that this person is from?"

The officer checked a notepad clipped on a rest

between the front seats. "An electronics company out Redmond way takes care of it—Microbotics."

Of course! Corfe groaned and slumped back in the seat. Garsten worked for Payne. No wonder Corfe had failed to spot any internal alarm systems when he was in there. If he'd stopped for a moment to think that Microbotics might be handling Garsten's security, he would have guessed there would be nothing obvious. Sophistication was their business.

And if Payne was the one behind this, that was where they would have taken Michelle.

"They're the ones who've got her," Corfe said.

"Who?"

"Microbotics. The owner of the company has a house across in Bellevue. That's where she'll be—and the van. We're at the wrong place."

The officer eyed him skeptically in the mirror. "Security companies don't snatch people off the streets. They'd call us. Do you know who the owner of that outfit is?"

"Sure, Martin Payne. I used to work for them. I just told you, that's where she is."

"Oh, you don't say?" The officer's tone carried a note of conviction that fell somewhat short of total.

The two who had gone into the house reappeared. The man in the parka stayed by the door, while Des came back to the car. "Nah, it's clean inside, Greg. Nobody." He waved a hand at Corfe. "There isn't anything in there like what you said. You wanna come and see for yourself?"

Corfe shook his head wearily. "It's okay. I know."

"He says we're at the wrong place," the officer who had stayed in the car said.

The one outside called back to the house. "It's okay. You can close it up." Then, to the car again. "What?"

"Now he thinks the Microbotics security people

grabbed her. He says they took her to Martin Payne's house, in Bellevue."

Des reached inside the car and lifted the radio handset off its hook. "Oh, man," he sighed resignedly. "Here we go for the weekend. Let's just wait in there for a minute, okay? I gotta get instructions on this."

The DNC software only communicated with the mec control subsystem. It couldn't access the phone lines, the e-mail, the Internet, or any other means Kevin could think of for possibly getting a message to the outside. He tried again to activate any of the mecs around him in the lab with the idea of using one of them to call Emergency on a regular phone, but it was no use. Every channel was dead. He would have sobbed with the fear and frustration if he could. But he had no bodily sensations or feelings, no impression of possessing physical extent in space. Although he could still think and move virtual limbs in mec-software visual space, his connection to the external world was suspended in a kind of limbo—an electronic sensory deprivation tank. He felt emotions inside, but there was no way to express them.

The full horror of what he had overheard hadn't penetrated fully. He was conscious of it, but in a detached way, as if he were watching somebody else thinking it. A defense mechanism in his mind was delaying the impact somehow, almost as if it knew that he couldn't afford the distraction of dwelling on it right now. But even that realization made his despair worse. Distraction from what? What else was there for him to do that he needed to focus undivided attention on?

He pictured Vanessa again, in the VR suit—probably testing it. What could go under a hotel-room door? she had asked Michelle. That was how they had killed

Jack Anastole in the hotel—with some kind of specially modified killer mec directed from another room. And they were going to do the same thing with Eric tonight in his hotel. There was time to warn him yet, if only Kevin could find a way. . . .

So would they have somebody installed in another room in the resort at Barrow's Pass? Or maybe they had developed a relay that could be operated remotely, like Taki's. Kevin thought of the killer mec being there right now in Eric's suitcase and Eric not even knowing, and somehow he virtually shuddered. . . .

No, that was unlikely he decided. The Microbotics mecs were still pretty crude, non-DNC types—the body suit was evidence enough of that. Although, given the kind of equipment that was sure to be available at a place like Microbotics, they would still have more-than-adequate capabilities when it came to communications. . . .

Wait a minute, Kevin told himself. Back up, back up. Like a man fallen overboard from a boat waving frantically before he went under, something in Kevin's already-fading train of thought was trying to get his attention. He tried to think back. . . . Why was it so difficult to track strings of thoughts and associations back in the reverse direction?

It was something to do with Eric's suitcase—suitcase in the car—maybe a mec in the suitcase. . . . So what was the significance of that? Mec in the suitcase, in the car. . . .

Mec in the car! Eric was using the Jaguar. Kevin had hidden two mecs in it—Tigger and Mr. Toad. If he couldn't get to the phone, maybe he could use one of the mecs in the car to warn Eric. But how could he, if he had already established that his communication with mecs wasn't working either? The answer was surely right there, if only he could find a way. . . .

He knew the hardware and software of Neurodyne's in-house system well enough to be aware how improbable this kind of failure mode was. The software channel drivers were modularized; for all of them to fail together was inconceivable. The only place where a malfunction could disable all channels simultaneously would be at the level above that where they all interfaced with the device control supervisor.

An anticipatory excitement bubbled up suddenly from somewhere in Kevin's subconscious, as even before he had fully followed the line through, an instinct told him that here was the solution.

The fault had to be in the device control supervisor. Specifically, that meant in the regular Neurodyne supervisor that handled the codes that all Neurodyne mecs operated on, because that was the supervisor they had been using. They had used the regular Neurodyne supervisor because the mecs they had sent into Garsten's office and the remaining ones in the van were regular Neurodyne production or research models. And, indeed, the others that Kevin had tried to activate in the lab where he was were all regular Neurodyne patterns too. But Toad and Tigger were special "battlemec" types that Kevin and Taki had modified, which used different codes and required a different version of the device control supervisor program. *And Kevin kept a copy of that supervisor in the general Neurodyne system!* He had put it there so that he could operate his own mecs in the firm's labs.

Maybe there was a way! If he could switch that version of the supervisor in place of the regular one that wasn't functioning, then maybe he would be able to access any of his own mecs that he could get a link to, even if he was shut off from the firm's. Praying that he wasn't building himself up with false hopes, he called down the Control menu and activated SYSCONF.

Kevin was standing before a yellow wall with a general system schematic showing as an organization chart of colored boxes with interconnections appearing as patchcords. He expanded one of the boxes to reveal its inner structure, then zoomed in to locate the high-level control subsystem. He isolated the device control supervisor by unplugging its virtual connecting cords, and exchanged it for the box representing the modified program, which in his last expedition to this part of the system he had left hanging conveniently on a virtual nail sticking out of the virtual wall. He repatched the cords to install it, and the box for the Channel Assignment Table, which until now had been blank, activated to display available options. He knew then that this was going to work.

His excitement rising, he selected the code assigned to Taki's relay in the trunk of the Jaguar, and attempted a test link. The entry line in the box changed color, and an icon lit up, confirming a connection. He reset to operator mode, checked the two choices that were offered, and selected Mr. Toad. Moments later he found himself in a dark recess surrounded by plastic tatters and foam rubber. There was distant wind noise and the sound of tires humming on road.

Vanessa sat down before the console and dialed the number to interrogate the Jaguar's satellite-referenced positioning system. The response showed as a cursor on a map of central Washington state being presented on one of the screens. The door of the room opened, and Finnion came back in with Garsten.

"He's just coming to the winding part where the cliffs are," Vanessa announced. "Just a couple more minutes. . . ." The other two said nothing.

Vanessa attached the interface lead to the body suit, donned the helmet, and activated the system. She flexed muscles and moved her head, and after a few seconds of adjustment "became" the assassin bug in the box that she had left in the car.

She was looking up out of a deep, rectangular pit. Far above was the foreshortened shape of a car window, streaked by raindrops driven in the slipstream. "It looks as if it's raining there," she remarked. "This is perfect. Accidents happen on wet days in places like that all the time."

For several seconds Kevin lay motionless, soaking up the feeling of relief as if it were sunshine. Then he extricated himself from the hiding place at the back of the trunk and crawled through the gap in the rubber sealing to the space behind the rear seat. He climbed out of the canyon of fuzzy vine-mesh walls onto the seat, and waded through grass toward the smoother expanse of leather lining the front edge. The vault of the car's interior curved high above like a sky within the sky. The one outside looked gray and stormy, with streaks of rain running down and back across the windows. The sound system was playing an aria that sounded like Mozart. A briefcase lay on the back seat, and two open cardboard boxes containing a variety of objects were wedged below on the floor.

Before him, the leather back of the driver's seat towered like a Himalayan wall, the blond waves of Eric's hair above the headrest forming a distant, lofty summit.

Then something moved below, right at the edge of Toad's broad-angle cone of vision. Kevin looked down. Something was coming up out of one of the cardboard boxes.

Kevin moved forward onto the rounded bulge at the edge of the seat. It was a mec unlike any that he had seen before—black and insectlike, with six legs articulating from a horizontal body, and a low, tapered head flanked by short pincers. Everything about the way it came up out of hiding and seemed to creep with slow, purposeful menace triggered an instinct that sensed evil. The beetle-like creature crawled over the edge of the box and fell out of sight to the floor; seconds later, it came into view again, climbing up the back of the plinth below the armrests of the two front seats. It got to the top of the plinth, crossed the gap to the fabric-covered side of the driver's seatback, and began ascending, inches below and behind Eric's elbow.

That was when Kevin realized he'd been wrong. The plan had never been to repeat Jack Anastole's hotel-room mishap at all. This time it was going to be a car accident. "They"—his stepmother; her lover; whoever—were doing it right now!

From that point, Kevin was not really in control. Pure reflex took over. He flung himself off the seat, arms and legs spread like a freefall parachutist, and landed sprawled along a cardboard ridge formed by a lid flap bent down inside the box. For a moment he clung precariously, a drop to the floor on one side, a compartmented plastic tray containing paints and craft materials on the other. Then he got his grip and scurried along the ridge to the corner. Trusting to the feel that hours of playing battle games had given him for mec-world physics, he leaped across to the plinth, avoiding the detour of going down to the floor and back up again as the killer beetle had done.

Although the beetle had the superior grasping ability of six legs, whoever was operating it was moving more carefully. Even so, it still had a lead. It seemed to be heading for the top of the driver's seatback. Kevin could either rely on his speed advantage to try and overhaul it, or go forward over the utility top between the two

front armrests and hope he could alert Eric. If he opted
for the latter and failed, there would be nothing to
stop the beetle; and in any case, even if he did manage
to get Eric's attention, there would still be the problem
of trying to communicate the situation. He crossed
the gap from the plinth to the seatback and began
climbing after the black shape moving high above,
clinging to the russet, fur-covered Eiger.

By the time the beetle reached the top, Kevin had
halved the distance between them. When Kevin
finally scrambled over the edge, the beetle was a
matter of inches away—at mec scale, a couple of car
lengths. He could see clearly now that it was of a
pattern unlike anything that had ever come out of
Neurodyne. It had more external linkages and
piezoelectric fiber attachments, and the leg design
and jointing arrangement was a different concept.
Close-up, the purpose of the sting-like protrusion
at the front of the turret head was chillingly plain.
It was moving across the top of the seatback, in the
space below the headrest. Through the gap, Kevin
could see part of Eric's collar and neck, and an ear,
his head swaying to the music as he drove. The road
ahead plunged into a tight, leftward curve, wet rock
rising on one side, a drop disappearing into mists
on the other.

Vanessa crouched on the seatback, checking the scene
ahead through the windshield. The road was treacherous,
no other traffic in the vicinity. She bunched, preparing
to spring.

There was no time to form any strategy. Kevin
launched himself as the beetle arched itself to leap
onto Eric's shoulder. They collided like metal wasps,
Kevin trying to use surprise and his momentum to tear

the beetle off and hurl it away. But momentum was of limited value at that scale, more than offset by the gripping power of six legs. The assassin bug held on, turned and parried him, and they rolled over and over along the top of the seat in a tangle of interlocked limbs and appendages.

It was like wrestling with a lobster. Not knowing the situation, Kevin had picked the wrong mec from the two in the trunk. Toad had been built more as a testbed for variable vision than as a fighter. If only he'd brought out Tigger instead, with its gigantic chainsaw, things would have been very different. But it was no use wishing now.

He grasped one of the assassin's legs to try dislocating it at a joint, but each of his arms was countered by another leg, both of them stronger. Another leg seized his head and started to twist. He turned his body, kicking one of the beetle's supporting legs away, and it fell to one side, partly releasing its hold to right itself. He feinted, ducked, and went again for a foreleg, locking close with the assassin for an instant, head to head like boxers in a clinch, and found himself staring into the monster's black, impenetrable eyes. He loosened an arm and tried to dislodge a leg that was forcing him over . . . but he was four limbs trying to fight six; and then he saw the pincers coming in from the side, ducked away . . .

But not quickly enough. An instant later his vision dimmed and lost depth, and he realized that one of Toad's eyes had gone. The other pincers struck; Kevin tried to ward them off, but his thumb had been snipped off before he realized that he could no longer judge distance. Seconds more, and he would be reduced to helplessness. Desperately crooking an arm around the black, angulated carapace, he heaved, straightened his legs, and hurled himself off the edge, taking the killer with him. To the sounds of a contralto singing Mozart filling the air, they tumbled together and landed in the craftworking box behind the seat.

Kevin was on his back in the plastic tray that he had looked down over from the top of the box. Around him were paint tins the size of oil storage tanks, and reels of embroidery thread that looked like drums of marine cable. He righted himself and began clambering over a pile of shiny, hexagonal pencil-logs that rolled and fell, making him lose his footing. The beetle was nowhere in sight, but he could hear scraping sounds coming from the adjacent compartment in the tray.

A pair of steel scissors resting on an edge of the tray offered a convenient ramp. Steadying himself against the dividing partition, Kevin moved cautiously up and peered over. Most of the space beyond the dividing wall was taken up by massive, pipelike pens and brushes. At the far end were several truck-size squeeze-tubes lying on their sides, their ends tapering into cones and capped. The beetle had wrested the cap off one of them, and even as Kevin watched, was maneuvering a gigantic brush—in reality probably about as big as a nail-polish applicator—under the blob of clear goo that was beginning to ooze from the opening. Chemical warfare.

The beetle looked and obviously saw him. Kevin was half blind and had no defense. Yet instead of retreating, he scaled the partition wall and advanced. The beetle turned, brandishing the glue-filled brush, and for a second or two hesitated as if suspecting a trick. Then it came forward and lunged.

Kevin's left arm was pinned by the first swab, powerless to move against the thick, sticky bond. The next blow caught the right side of his head, and in seconds his neck and shoulder joints were stiffening. The beetle circled at a distance, assessing the effect.

Then, evidently reassured, it moved in again and plastered his hips and legs. Kevin felt himself wading slower and slower through congealing molasses, then halting completely. The beetle came closer, and Kevin's last impression was of almost sensing its operator gloating. . . .

All just as Kevin had intended. It was a diversionary tactic to keep the beetle occupied for just a little longer.

For it was obvious that Toad was done for. But that had ceased to be of relevance, since by the time the beetle closed in to complete its work, Toad was no longer registering anything.

Kevin had switched channels.

Tigger was already on its way.

The man who had come to the front door was small and balding, and wore a lightweight maroon jacket with white shirt and a dark tie. "No, sir, I'm afraid that Mr. Payne is away and not expected back until Monday," he informed the officers. There were four of them with Corfe now. The gray-and-blue Seattle cruiser had arrived at Payne's residence accompanied by a white-with-navy-stripe car of the Bellevue police. "Apart from myself and two other members of the domestic staff, the house is empty at present."

Corfe felt ill. Again there was no sign of the van outside, no beige Cadillac. The two Seattle officers glowered at him, while the one from the local force, who had put the question, looked back at the man in the maroon jacket. "And you are who, exactly, please?"

"My name is Vogl, sir. I'm the house steward."

"And there haven't been any callers in the last hour?" the Seattle officer who was called Des said. "We're looking for a woman in her late thirties, tall, slim, long fair hair, wearing a light blue coat."

"Nobody has been here I'm afraid. I know nothing of any person of such a description."

"I see."

"You are welcome to come inside and check the house for yourselves if you wish."

The four officers looked at each other. Des from Seattle shook his head. The Bellevue officer turned back to Vogl. "Thanks, but I don't think that'll be necessary. We appreciate your cooperation. Sorry to have taken up your time."

Five pairs of feet retraced their steps to the two police cars parked in the forecourt. Corfe knew he wasn't doing himself any favors, but there was no other way. "Then there's no other place," he remonstrated. "She must be at the firm. They've taken her to Microbotics."

"Mr. Corfe, why don't you give it a break?" Des advised.

"Look, I'm not crazy," Corfe said. "I know how this must sound, but it's only a couple of miles away. I'm telling you, a person's life is in danger. These people have killed before. If I'm wrong, okay, you can charge me with wasting your time or whatever. But what if I'm not wrong? Do you want that on your record?"

The senior man from the Bellevue car held up his hands. "Well, I guess you won't be needing us anymore. That's over our line. Good luck, guys." He motioned to his companion, and they got back into their car.

Des looked at Corfe long and balefully, as if making sure his face would be permanently filed for future reference. "Get in," he said, and walked around to the other side of the car. "Okay, Greg, let's move out," he told the driver. "I'll call the Redmond dispatcher to have someone meet us there."

CHAPTER THIRTY-ONE

Garsten's voice rose, close-by yet at the same time in the background, dissociated from what Vanessa was seeing. Its note of alarm grated on her nerves, distracting her. "Vanessa, what is it? What's happening? What do you mean, someone else is there? How can there be?"

The surprise of encountering the intruder had been too great for her to stifle her reaction. It could only be Kevin. How he was doing it or where the other mec had come from, she had no time to think about now.

"Vanessa, will you please tell us what—"

"Shut *up!*"

"Phil, just cool it for a moment," she heard Finnion murmur. She concentrated on visual and tactile space, closing out reminders of her actual physical surroundings.

The intruder was permanently immobilized now. Its sudden appearance, just when she had been at her most keyed-up, had left Vanessa in a strangely obsessive shocked condition. She was conscious of one goal only: to complete the task that she had embarked on. Where the intruder had come from and how it had gotten there; how much Kevin knew; who else was a party to it—all of those things could wait. The obstacle represented by Eric symbolized everything. If she failed to eliminate that now, she would forfeit all.

She dropped down from the top of the cardboard box to the floor as before, and climbed the carpeted base of the plinth supporting the front-seat armrests. Finding holds in the seamwork and stitching, she scaled the leather upholstery to the level space at the top. From there, the sides of the two front seatbacks soared up on either side of her like the World Trade Center towers, while in front, the utility top with its sunken recesses for maps, cups, and change extended away like a city street between the walls of the two armrests. Vanessa moved left to the driver's seatback and stared up at the climb for the second time. Reflexes conditioned in a different realm still made it visually daunting, but she knew from experience that the actuality was effortless. She cast a last look back down into the cardboard box that she had come from, just to be certain. The odd, froglike mec with the enormous eyes, one of them gouged into an empty socket, was standing motionless as she had left it, the sticky, congealed, entrapping mass already setting hard. This time, then. She turned back to commence the climb. . . .

And then something yellow, moving fast, came at her out of nowhere. Metal flashed in an arc through the air. Although there was no sound, the pulse of vibration as Vanessa's arm flew away registered as an acoustic buzz to her senses. Momentarily too shocked to react, she stared in stupor at the severed stump of metal. The blade sliced downward again, and half of one of her center legs was gone. She stared in disbelief at the striped shape already closing again, raising some awful, scintillating weapon, the size of which alone evoked pure terror. Although the features were devoid

of expression, its precise, purposeful movements left
no doubts as to its intent.

Vanessa turned, tried to escape between the
armrests, but another of her legs went, and she canted
over. Then a pair of her pincers disintegrated before
her eyes. There was no pain, but the sight of herself
being physically dismembered triggered terror
reflexes that it was impossible to control, and she
screamed.

"*What the hell is it?*" Garsten's voice yelled, coming
from a different world.

Vanessa tumbled over, out of control. The tiger-like
apparition loomed over her; its blade shimmered and
grew larger.

"*Aghh! No—ooo! . . .*"

"*What is it, Vanessa?*"

Everything went blank, and then the helmet was
being lifted away. Finnion was standing in front of her,
holding the unplugged interface lead. For several
seconds Vanessa couldn't react, unable to shake off
the horror of the image. Finnion slapped her cheeks
once each in rapid succession, hard enough to sting.
"Are you okay? What happened? Say something," he
snapped.

Vanessa blinked, rubbed her face in bewilderment
as she reorientated. Then she stood up and began
peeling off the body suit. "Get my clothes," she said
in a voice trembling from a mixture of remnant fear
and confusion. "Forget everything. Something screwed
up somewhere. It's off. The whole thing's over."

As Mozart's aria swelled to its crescendo, Kevin lifted
the blade from the partly severed head. The saw wasn't
built for hardened mec alloy, and hacking off the limbs
had dulled the teeth. This would do all the same, he
supposed.

He planted a triumphant foot on the carcass, raised his saw in a victory salute, and switched off the blade.

"Nifty," he pronounced, with deep satisfaction. "Definitely nifty."

"What's ha—" Finnion began, but Vanessa cut him off.

"It's that boy again. He wasn't just snooping around here. He was there in the car too—controlling other mecs. I don't know how."

"I thought you said you dialed in over the phone line and fixed him," Finnion accused. "How—"

"I just told you, *I don't know* how. But it's obvious that he knows everything." Vanessa took the clothes that Garsten had brought from the room at the back where she had changed. "Get Martin on the line," she told him. Then, to Finnion again as she began dressing hurriedly, "Kevin may be onto us, but it doesn't mean that anyone else is—yet. He may still be immobilized physically in the machine. . . ."

The phone rang just as Garsten was about to pick it up. He answered it and blinked in surprise. "It's Martin for you," he said, handing the phone to Vanessa.

"Yes, Martin?"

"Vogl just called me from the house. The police were there with Corfe, looking for the lawyer. They could go there, to the firm next. You have to get her out."

"Oh God, that's all we need."

"Why do you say that, Vanessa? What's happened?"

"The hit messed up. Look, Kevin knows everything. He's at Neurodyne . . ."

"Christ, no!"

". . . but—and don't ask how, just now—there's a good chance that right now he's stuck in the system there and can't decouple. If we can get to him before anyone else does, we might still find a way to save things somehow."

"Christ . . ." Payne said again. There was silence for a few seconds. "Does anyone else know?"

"No, I don't think so. Could Andy send somebody down there? It would give us more time, anyway."

"Is Andy there with you?"

"Yes. I'll put him on." Vanessa handed Finnion the phone. "Martin wants to talk to you," she told Finnion needlessly. She finished dressing while Finnion listened for most of the time, nodding with occasional interjections.

"Yeah. . . . Okay. . . . That's what she says. . . . Sure, they're here. . . . Okay. . . . Okay. . . . I'll get on it right now. We'll call you when we're on our way." Finnion depressed the hook, released it again, and punched in another number. "We're sending Ollie and Royal down to Tacoma for the kid," he told Vanessa and Garsten while he waited for an answer. "The rest of us are going straight on to the boat, and they'll meet us there. The lawyer comes with us for insurance. . . ." He looked away and spoke into the phone. "Hello, Kyle? This is Andy. Put Ollie or Royal on. I got another job for them. It's urgent. . . ."

The would-be slayer was slain, but Kevin hadn't solved the problem of getting himself out of the machine. He still couldn't access any regular communications services, and the thought of being trapped in Neurodyne until Tuesday was far from appealing. There was only one thing he could think to try.

Leaving the dead killer beetle on the utility tray between the armrests where it had fallen, he went back to the base of the driver's seatback and climbed it until he could drop onto the padded top of the armrest. From there he scaled the hillside of Eric's elbow encased in a windbreaker sleeve, and followed along the ridge of folds and creases toward the hand resting on the steering wheel.

Vanessa and Martin's whole, elaborate plan had almost been unnecessary. A new thought struck Eric just as he was going into a slippery hairpin, and he almost forgot to straighten out of it.

If the mass-increase with velocity that was observed in laboratories was really just an indication of approaching an asymptotic limit to the rate at which a disturbance could propagate through an electromagnetic field— analogous to the limits of acoustic waves in material media—then it wasn't necessarily an absolute limit on the velocity of mass-energy at all, so much as a limit that applied to the velocity of electrical *charge*. All the experiments conducted had relied on information carried by electromagnetic means; and all the mass-velocity experiments were carried out in accelerators that operated on charged particles. Nothing in the literature had considered what happened in the case of *neutral* carriers. . . .

At that instant something crawled off his sleeve onto his hand and broke his train of thought. A wasp? . . . He moved his other hand from the wheel to flick it away—but then realized there was something odd about it, looked again . . . and almost went off the road for the second time in as many minutes. It was a mec— one of Kevin and Taki's battlemecs.

Was Kevin operating it? But how? . . .

Whoever it was must have seen that it had Eric's attention, for the mec started waving with one of those dreadful weapons that they hunted insects with and thought Eric didn't know about. He slowed the car, spotted a flat stretch of verge ahead, and pulled over, at the same time opening the window to give the car a change of air. If it was one of the boys' mecs, it would have had a microphone added. He picked it up between a finger and a thumb, and set it down on the fascia above the dashpanel. It was the one they called Tigger, if he wasn't mistaken.

"Kevin?" he said. The figure nodded, trailing the saw in one hand and emphasizing its response with an up-and-down motion of its free arm. "Yes, it's a good trick, and I'm impressed. You can tell me how you did it when I get back. Now, if you'll excuse me, I must get on. The weather here is—" He stopped as the mec dropped its saw and waved both arms above its head frantically.

"Are you in some kind of trouble?" Up-and-down again, with both arms: *Yes.* "Are you at home?" The arms made wide, over-the-head, crossed movements: *No.* "At the lab?" *Yes.* "Look, you know my number. If it's something urgent, why don't you just call?" Both arms extended sideways. *Can't.* "Is Doug there?" *No.* "Can't you contact him?" *No.* "Why not?" Response unintelligible. "Are you saying you need me to help?" *Yes.* "Do you want me to call somebody?" Again, unintelligible. "Surely you're not asking me to come back?" *Yes! Yes! Yes!* "But I'm on my way to an important conference." *I can't help that,* or, *You don't understand,* or, *Too bad.* Eric stared at the tiny figure perplexedly. "Can't Vanessa help?" *No! No!* The mec picked up its saw again, seemed to point at it, and then waved it in Eric's direction. Eric could make nothing of what it was trying to say. He sighed. "Very well, Kevin. But I'm warning you, this had better be good."

Eric used his car phone to call the resort at Barrow's Pass and told the conference secretary regrets, but there was an emergency and he had to cancel out. He also left a message of apology for the people that he

had arranged to meet for a late lunch. Then he turned
the car around to head back for Seattle. Just before
he closed the window, unseen by him, a blue-brown
butterfly drifted in and settled down by the rear seat.

As the car pulled away, Tigger turned and sat itself
down on the top of the fascia, apparently to take in
the view. But after a while, the mec ceased responding
to Eric's remarks. He reached out and picked it up,
but it was inactive. Evidently Kevin had tuned out.

Eric's frown of worry deepened. Despite the road
and the weather, he picked up the phone again as he
drove, and telling himself he should have done this
before, punched in Doug Corfe's personal number.

It was Eric's asking Kevin if he was at Neurodyne
that had alerted Kevin to the danger he could be in,
which he hadn't had time to give any thought to so
far. He knew that Vanessa was part of whatever group
had planned this; and they now had the van. So, even
if they hadn't worked out who, exactly, was operating
Tigger, they would quickly deduce that whoever it was
had to be physically coupled in from Neurodyne. And
from what Kevin had seen of the way they'd picked
up Michelle, it wouldn't be long before another
deputation showed up in Tacoma. There wasn't time
to wait for Eric to get back. But what else could he
do? The exit routine was blocked as solidly as ever.
He forced himself to stay calm and tried to think.

The only mec-connection capability he had, apparently,
was to the modified ones that he and Taki used, not
any of the regular Neurodyne models. The only way to
get out of the coupler, by the look of things, would be
to have somebody switch off the system from the outside.
If Eric was still hours away, and nobody else knew of
his predicament, then the only logical alternative was
to get a mec here to do it. Logical, yes. But how was

he supposed to translate that into practice? His mecs were at the house, not here—and in any case, they were all shut up in boxes or clipped immovably into racks. And the mecs at Taki's place were always locked away even more securely because the house was permanently overrun by children. Kevin wished now that he had lent one to Avril when she asked. At least she lived in Tacoma, which would have been a lot nearer. . . . But that wouldn't have done any good, anyway—hadn't she said something about going off on a hike in the mountains today? But maybe they'd canceled it on account of the weather.

He thought back again to when Avril and Janna had visited the house—had it really been only last Sunday? The parachuting mec had gotten caught in the tree, and they'd had to send Ironside up to free it. Strangely, he couldn't recollect anything more about Ironside after that—certainly not of returning it to its normal place in the lab at the house. So what had he done with Ironside? Where was it? . . . He couldn't remember. He and Taki had had this same problem before with the mec that had gone lost and turned up in Vanessa's bag. Well, he knew the simple way to find it this time.

He pulled down the Control menu, disconnected from Taki's relay in the trunk of the Jaguar, and rerouted to the system in the basement of the house. Ironside was listed as one of the available channels. He pointed with a virtual finger and selected "Activate." . . .

And found himself underneath what seemed to be a wooden bridge, wedged among empty soda cans about the same size as himself, and a mountain of balled-up, soggy paper. He wriggled his way out, feeling as if he were emerging from a garbage pile, and straightened up. The floor he was standing on was also of wood, curving upward on either side of him to become an enormous wooden canyon with the open sky above. A boat? His boat. That was right! Now he remembered—he had put Ironside under the seat when he, Doug, and Taki took the girls for a trip across the inlet, and then forgotten all about it. Ironside had been there, out in the boat, ever since.

He scrambled up onto the seat and peered over the side. The boat was moored at the dock, and he could see the familiar view of the house through the trees from the bottom of the rear slope. He could get other mecs out of their boxes and racks now—Ironside was big enough and strong enough to accomplish that. But this was still a long way from Tacoma. He stared up at the trees, and memories came back of flying up over them with Taki and looking down at the house. . . . And the beginnings began forming in his mind of what was surely one of his craziest ideas yet.

But hadn't this all been a crazy week?

The mooring line was as thick as his thigh. Wrapping both arms and legs around it and hanging sloth-like, he launched out over the water and began hauling himself toward the shore.

CHAPTER THIRTY-TWO

The Seattle city police car followed the Redmond city police car slowly past the front of Microbotics, then between the main office building and the laboratory block to circle through the employees' parking area at the rear.

"There, that's it! There's the van!" Corfe exclaimed, pointing from the back seat. Garsten's beige Cadillac was there. So was the black Lincoln. "She'll be here this time. Now will you believe me?"

"He's identified the three vehicles," Des said into the mike that he was holding. "The Dodge van, the Cadillac, and the Lincoln."

"Okay, let's check it out," a voice from the car ahead answered from the speaker.

"We're right behind you."

The two cars completed their circuit and halted outside the front entrance to the main building. "You'd better come in with us," Des told Corfe.

The glass doors were locked, it being a holiday. A young security man in a blue shirt came over from the receptionist's desk and let them in. The senior of the two Redmond officers asked who, on the premises, was in charge of security.

"Mr. Finnion's chief of security. He's here right now." The young security man reached for a phone. "Can I tell him what it's about?"

"Andy Finnion? Oh, sure, we know him," Des said. "Tell Andy it's Des Olesh from across in the city. We've got a guy here who thinks that a missing person might be on the premises. Also, a vehicle that he claims is stolen is parked at the back of this building—gray Dodge van, registration 437 ECH. We just want to straighten it all out."

"I'll see if I can get him."

Seconds ago, Corfe had thought things were about to turn his way at last. Now he was assailed by misgivings again. These people were all on the same side. But there was nothing for it now but to see it through once more. Finnion was not a complete stranger to him either. He had been in charge of security when Corfe worked at Microbotics—although Corfe had never had any occasion to get to know him particularly well.

While the Redmond officers stayed by the desk, the two from Seattle wandered around the lobby area, casually inspecting wall plaques, framed certificates of merit from various trade and engineering institutions, a plan showing the layout of the building. To one side was a glass-topped display case showing some of the company's products. A section of it was devoted to Microbotics's line of VR-driven micromecs. Des indicated them and grinned at Corfe. "Are they like the machines that you went into Mr. Garsten's office as?"

"Yes, as a matter of fact."

Des scowled and turned away with the look of somebody whose joke had fallen flat.

A double door opened at the rear of the lobby area, and Vanessa stepped through, followed a moment later by Finnion. She gave Corfe a cold glance, showing no sign of familiarity at seeing him. His premonition worsened.

"Hi, guys." Finnion nodded briefly at the policemen, his eyes settling finally on Des. "It's been a while now, Des. How's it all going?"

"Oh, up and down. You know, the usual roller coaster," Des said. Greg moved back to join them.

"Still crankin' 'em in for those retirement points, eh?"

"Well, we try. What else can you do?"

Finnion indicated Corfe with a raised eyebrow. "So, what have we got?"

"Well, this is Mr. Corfe, who says he worked here at one time. . . ."

Finnion nodded. "Yes, I recognize the face. I was trying to place the name."

"He's looking for a somebody by the name of Michelle Lang, and he says he has reason to believe she's being held here on the premises."

Impatience clouded Finnion's face. "Oh hell, not that again. I thought we'd cleared it up. First it was supposed to be Garsten's office, right? Didn't my duty supervisor talk to you there about an hour ago—Kyle Welsh? The place was clean. There were no alarms." Finnion showed both palms. "That's all we know. What else can I tell you?"

"You sound as if you know Mr. Garsten," one of the Redmond officers commented.

"Phil Garsten? Of course I do. He works for the boss here, Martin Payne. We're old friends." Finnion nodded toward Corfe and lowered his tone, suggesting confidentiality. "Look, I think you should know, this guy has had a grudge against the company ever since he was fired. He's always giving us a hard time. I don't think he's exactly . . . 'stable,' know what I mean?"

Corfe's eyes widened. "I was never—" he started to protest, but Des gave him a withering look.

"So this Michelle Lang isn't here?" Des said to Finnion.

Finnion's voice rose again. "No, for chrissakes! Why should she be? Who is she, anyway? I never heard of her."

"Then, ah, perhaps you can explain the van?" the Redmond officer who had spoken before invited.

Vanessa stepped forward. "That's easy, officer. It's mine. I drove it here."

Corfe shook his head wildly. "That's not true. I've had it since—" Des quieted him with a wave.

"Wait a minute, wait a minute. Are you telling me that—"

"But I borrowed it from—"

"Mr. Corfe, are you the registered owner of that van?"

"Well, no, not exactly. That is, not legally, but . . ."

Des turned to Vanessa. "You are who, ma'am?"

"Vanessa Heber. The van belongs to my husband and me. Mr. Corfe is employed by my husband's company, and yes, it's true that he does use it sometimes. Eric—my husband—gave him a job out of . . . loyalty, I suppose you could say." She hesitated, as if uncomfortable at what needed to be said. "As Mr. Finnion says, he sometimes tends to . . . 'do things' like this."

Corfe looked wildly from one policeman to the other. "She's lying. They're both lying. . . . I—"

"*Shuddup!* . . . Thank you. . . . Mrs. Heber, so the van is yours, registered in your name?"

"Yes. . . . Well, Eric's to be precise."

"And you are not reporting it as stolen?"

"Of course not."

"So you don't know anything about this Michelle Lang being taken from it?"

"That's ridiculous."

"Do you know who this Michelle Lang is, Mrs. Heber?"

"Yes, I've met her once or twice. She's a lawyer who works for a corporation that we're considering entering into a joint venture with."

"Do you know of any reason why she should be missing?"

Vanessa bit her lip for a second. "I can only suggest that it's probably a personal matter of Mr. Corfe's," she replied.

"*You bitch!*" Corfe breathed, unable to contain himself.

Des's mouth clamped tight. "Thanks," he said to Finnion and Vanessa. "I don't think we need detain you people any longer. Take care, Andy. Mrs. Heber. Enjoy what's left of the weekend, eh?" He cut Corfe off with a curt sweep of his arm before Corfe could say anything more, and motioned him out of the building. The two Redmond officers nodded at Finnion and Vanessa, and moved to follow. Corfe knew an expression that had reached boiling point when he saw one, and didn't argue.

"Mr. Corfe, you do realize that willfully diverting the police from their duties is an offense," Des began as soon as they were outside. "Now, we do have your complaint on file. If you have anything to add to it, let us know. In the meantime, we've done all we can. If you wish, we'll take you back to the station and put you down at the door there."

Corfe acknowledged defeat with a tired nod and thrust his hands into his pockets. Trying to continue this would be more likely to get him arrested than achieve anything useful. As they walked back to the two police cruisers, Corfe toyed with the keys in his pocket. Two sets of keys: his own keys; a set of spares from Eric, for the van. The van was still there, around the back of the building. He still didn't know what to do about Michelle, but whatever he decided, he needed to remain mobile. In any case, dammit, he'd borrowed the van legitimately. He wasn't about to walk back to Tacoma, or catch a bus. Let Vanessa try explaining it to Eric on Monday. Eric would know a lot more by that time than he did right now. Corfe would make sure of that.

"It's all right, I don't need a ride," he said, mustering an offended look. "I'll get myself back. Just call me a cab, will you?"

"As you wish, Mr. Corfe." Des didn't seem inclined to argue either. He passed the request to the local officers, who put out a call.

"There's a Brown-and-White on its way," one of them reported. "It'll meet us at the 520 intersection in ten minutes."

To protect and serve. You have a nice day too, officers, Corfe thought sourly to himself.

Ironside reached the house, stalked by a baffled and bemused tabby cat from the next house along the lakeside. It had occurred to Kevin that he might be able to communicate to Harriet to get a message to somebody, but her car was not there. Okay, then, he decided, back to Plan A.

There was a flap in the bottom of the workshop-lab door for Batcat to get in and out—although why it was needed Kevin had never really understood, because cats could get from one side of a wall to the other by osmosis. Kevin let himself in and, improvising a handy strip of timber as a ramp, crawled up it to undo the door latch from the inside.

Next, he hauled two aluminum strips down from a rack and positioned them as rails sloping up from the

floor to the top of the bench where he had left the
KJ-3—the model plane that he and Taki had added
"manual" controls to. He climbed via one of the rails
to the bench top and began his preparations by checking
the plane's tank and topping it up from a can of fuel
on the shelf above. Next, he cut several feet of nylon
cord from one of a row of reels dispensing wire and
other sundries, mounted on the wall at the back of
the bench.

He attached the ends of the cord to the tail of the
KJ-3, pushed the plane across the bench to the rails
that he had positioned, and carefully paid out the line
to lower it nose-first to the floor. He followed it down,
detached the cord, and wheeled the aircraft out through
the doorway to the rear yard. So far, so good, he
thought.

By now, he could feel Ironside getting low on charge.
Should he play safe but lose time by stopping now to
replenish? There wasn't much more to do here, and
when he finished, Ironside's part in his plan would
be over. There was no way the KJ-3 would lift Ironside's
weight. He decided to press on and risk it.

Going back inside, he climbed via a box to a stool,
and from there up onto the other bench to get to
where the mecs were kept. He selected Lancelot,
one of the small battlemecs, to fly the plane. But that
on its own wouldn't be enough. He needed to take a
more substantial one along too, but not too heavy
for the plane to carry. He settled on Dreadnought,
an intermediate four times bigger than Lancelot but
only a quarter the height of Ironside. And he had
no choice but to hope that his judgment was good:
Seconds after he released Dreadnought from its
restraining clip, Ironside ground to a halt, its charge
exhausted. Kevin now had to get the other two mecs
outside to the plane. Two separate trips weren't

necessary. Coupling through to Dreadnought, he picked up the inert form of Lancelot, tucked it under his arm, and hopped and jumped back down to the floor and out the door.

The next part was going to call for a little neuro-coupled channel-juggling. He carried the small mec over to the plane and pushed it into the cabin. Then he switched channels to "become" Lancelot, clambered behind the controls, pulled the rubber band that he and Taki had rigged as a seat harness securely over himself. A mec the size of Lancelot was necessary as the pilot: Dreadnought wouldn't have fitted in the seat or been able to work the controls, which were built to a smaller scale. But Lancelot had no way of starting the motor, which needed an external flip of the propeller. That was why Dreadnought was needed too.

Switching back into Dreadnought, Kevin walked around to the front of the plane and reached up with both arms to grasp one of the blades. . . . And something sent him sprawling face down in the dirt.

He rolled over and looked up, bewildered. A head the size of a car was staring down at him, its mouth gaping and showing saber fangs. Next-door's tabby was still there. . . . Kevin sat up, started to rise, and a giant paw knocked him flat again. This could go on for hours, he realized fearfully.

Then a low, menacing growl came from the direction of the house. Kevin turned his head. Batcat had come out of the lab door and was contending its territory. The tabby backed and turned to face the new threat. Kevin scrambled to his feet, reached up again, and jerked the airscrew. It kicked, the engine coughed, but nothing happened. A quick change back to being Lancelot at the controls, an adjustment of the fuel line; then he was Dreadnought outside once more. Another try. . . .

A splutter . . . dying, then recovery. And the motor burst into a roar.

Quickly, switch back to being Lancelot. Hold the controls in that position, tight on the brake. *Freeze!*

Dreadnought again. Run back to the cabin, step up on the wheel, clamber aboard. Squeeze into the niche behind Lancelot's seat—between the wings, preserving balance.

And then Lancelot yet again, one last time. Brake off, open throttle. Moving. . . . Picking up speed, getting bumpy. Hold that stick. Glimpse of the tabby streaking away between trees. Ease the stick back, gently. . . . *Liftoff!*

A tree opened out ahead. Kevin banked, made a climbing turn over the water, and came back with the house sailing by below. Harriet's car was just turning into the driveway.

Stage One accomplished, Kevin told himself. But it was still just a start. The KJ-3 didn't have the range to make it all the way to Neurodyne. And even if it could, there would be a dead zone where the mecs were out of range of the locally boosted signals from the house, but not yet close enough to the direct transmission from the lab. The only way, then, would be to hitch a ride.

He came around onto a course following the road eastward, in the direction of the I-5 Interstate leading to Tacoma.

"I've changed my mind. Can we go back, please?" Corfe said to the cab driver. They had gone about a mile, and both the police cars were out of sight.

"Pardon?"

"Can we turn around? I want to go back to Microbotics."

The driver shrugged, exited at the 405 intersection and crossed over 520 to take the approach ramp back.

Just as they rejoined the eastbound lane, the phone in Corfe's jacket pocket beeped. It was Eric.

"Doug, what's going on back there with Kevin? Do you know what he's up to?"

The question took Corfe by surprise. "What? Er, I'm not sure what you mean. What about Kevin? What's happened?"

"He's at the firm, and in some kind of trouble. Where are you now?"

"I'm in the city," Corfe answered vaguely. "What do you mean, some kind of trouble?"

"I'm not sure. But he's been operating a mec somehow that's appeared in the car here, and doesn't seem able to decouple from the system for some reason. He's insisting that I come back, so I've canceled out from the conference and am on my way. But now he isn't responding at all, and I'm worried. Can you get down there and see what's going on?"

Corfe was too confused to want to get into complicated questions and answers just at that instant. He needed time to think. "Sure. . . ." he mumbled. "Sure, Eric, I'll see what I can do."

"Thanks very much, Doug. Sorry to impose, and all that. But I'm sure you understand. Call me back when you know anything, will you? Otherwise I'll call you again when I'm a bit closer."

"Sure," Corfe said again. Eric hung up.

Corfe's apprehension increased. He was still not even back at Microbotics, and when he got there he might not find it so easy to pick up the van. If he was spotted, there could be arguments, all kinds of trouble. Come to that, the van might not even be there. There was no guaranteeing that he would be able to get back to Tacoma before Eric at all. But if Kevin was in trouble, they couldn't just leave him for hours. He racked his mind, thinking. . . . There was another possibility, he realized. He took the phone from his coat pocket again and called Hiroyuki's house. Nakisha answered.

"Hi, this is Doug Corfe. Is Taki there?"

"Hello, Mr. Corfe. I think my brother just set himself on fire with something. . . . Oh no, he's okay now. One moment. I'll fetch him."

Taki's people could move now, without risk of more delays. And they were close to Tacoma. Of course, there would have to be explanations later. But hell, a lot of explanations were going to be called for anyway.

"Hi, Doug. Taki here. How's it going?" Taki's voice was low, with a hint of apprehension. That was understandable—he knew what was supposed to have been happening at Garsten's today.

"It all went wrong," Corfe said.

"Oh, my God! How?"

"I can't go into details now, but I just talked to Eric. He's on his way back. Kev's in some kind of trouble at the lab. I don't understand what, exactly, but it seems he can't decouple from the machine. I don't know for sure when I'm going to be able to get back. Can you get Ohira over there and check the situation? Eric's worried."

"This is terrible," Taki gasped. "But if I ask Ohira, he's going to have all kinds of questions. How much can I tell him?"

"Anything he wants to know," Corfe said tiredly. "The whole thing's going to come out now, anyhow."

"Are Payne's people on their way there too?" Taki asked. "Do they know about Kevin?"

Corfe hadn't thought of that. He didn't immediately see how they could—but then, his faculties hadn't exactly been working at their best for the last hour or more. Vanessa knew that the van had been involved. Anything was possible. "I don't know. Maybe. They could, I guess," he replied.

"I'll see what I can do," Taki promised. "Shall I call you on your personal number when I know something?"

"I might be in an awkward situation. Best if you wait for me to call you."

"Check. Will do. Operation Intercept-Bad-Guys signing out."

Corfe told the cabbie to drop him off a hundred yards from Microbotics, and walked the remaining distance. Keeping well to the side of the front parking area, he followed the fence past the main building to the rear. The van was still there, although both Garsten's Cadillac and the black Lincoln were gone. To his mild surprise the rear parking area was deserted, and nobody appeared when he got into the van and started the motor. He backed out from the slot and drove out through the side gate without interference. His first priority was to put a respectable amount of distance between himself and Microbotics.

Which way to go then? He wasn't sure. But the absence of the two cars told him with reasonable certainty that Michelle was no longer out here. With Ohira mobilized in Tacoma, Corfe could get back to trying to get a lead on where Payne's people had taken her. And now that he had the van back with its equipment for linking to mecs, he no longer needed the help of the police to accomplish that.

CHAPTER THIRTY-THREE

The two cars headed west along the Evergreen Point Bridge, back in the direction of Seattle. Michelle had no idea where they were heading now. She was in the back of the Lincoln, one of her two inseparable shadows next to her and the other in the passenger seat up front, both as communicative as crash dummies. The red-headed man called Kyle was driving. Finnion was with Garsten and Vanessa in Garsten's Cadillac ahead. At least that way they didn't have to deal with her questions and protests, Michelle supposed. Not that she was any longer of a mood to sustain much in the way of protest. She had been running on tension since the previous day, and after the calamity at Garsten's had gone into a state of nervous collapse that left her numbed and exhausted. To make it worse, she had lost her one means of possible contact through which she might have made her whereabouts known: Vanessa had taken not only the phone from Michelle's purse but also the mec that had been in her coat pocket—although by that time it had ceased being active. Vanessa had made no attempt to disguise it as a casual search; she had obviously known the mec was there—maybe from spotting it in one of its sorties to try and

336

follow what was going on. That meant that she would very quickly have deduced who was operating it, and very likely, Michelle imagined, where from. What those facts in turn portended, she wasn't sure.

As to questions, she still had plenty of those in her head if not the energy to direct them at anyone just at the moment—which would have been pointless in any case. Principal among them was to know just what was going on. For it was plain that everyone around her was overreacting—overreacting, that is, to the facts of the situation as far as Michelle was aware of it. Even if there were condemnatory evidence to be found in Garsten's office, Corfe and Michelle hadn't found it— and nobody, strangely, had gone to any great lengths to establish if they had, nor what they had been looking for. In any case it would have posed little threat as things had turned out, because, as Garsten would be fully aware, nothing obtained in such a way could have been used in any prosecution. Its only use would have been in furnishing proof to warn Eric, as had been the intention. So, with the law fully on their side, all that Garsten and his associates had needed to do was have Michelle arrested and file charges against her and Corfe for trespass, technical illegal entry, attempted theft of information, and a list of other things that could hardly be contested and would probably put an end to both Michelle's and Corfe's careers. Instead, they had already laid themselves open to charges of assault and abduction, perjured themselves to avoid involving the police, and were now evacuating in panic. The only conclusion to be drawn was that a lot more was going on than Michelle knew about. As much as she thought in the drive from Redmond, she had been unable to form any guesses as to what. Now she was too exhausted to think.

❖   ❖   ❖

Corfe called Eric from a roadside pull-off at the last intersection on 520 heading west before the east shore of Lake Washington. The whole story would obviously have to come out now, and it seemed to him that delaying it could only make things worse. He told Eric about the suspicions concerning Vanessa and his plan with Michelle and Kevin to seek evidence in Garsten's office in order to avoid having to bring anything to Eric's attention until they were sure. But they'd blown it, Michelle had been seized, and now Corfe didn't even know where she was. Kevin ought to have been okay since he was back at Neurodyne and away from it all, but after Eric's call Corfe had mobilized Ohira to get over there and check out the situation. Corfe had tried to get help from the police but managed to blow that too. Corfe was sorry to have to dump it on Eric like this. That was the way it was. He realized as he finished speaking that his motive had been a confession in need of absolution, as much as anything.

Eric was still sounding dazed when Corfe finished. Clearly he was struggling to absorb it all. "My God, I can't . . . How sure are you? I . . . You're right. There's nothing more you can do about Kevin. Ohira will take care of it. . . . You need to try and find where Michelle is. Do you have any ideas?"

"No, but I'm trying to use the van's couplers to link into the mecs that disappeared from Garsten's office. If I can figure out where they are, my guess is that's where she'll be too."

"Yes . . . yes, of course. Try that," Eric agreed.

"I haven't had any luck from where I am now, which is west of Bellevue, coming to the bridge. I don't think she's this side of the lake. So I'm going across to the city now to try from a more central location."

"Maybe we can try talking to the police again, too,

when I get back," Eric said. "They might listen more to both of us—especially if you get something before then. I'll probably be about another hour. I've tried calling the firm again, but there's still no answer from Kevin."

"I'll call you back if there's any news," Corfe said. "Okay, Doug."

Corfe cut the call, started the van again, and pulled back onto 520, heading westward toward the Evergreen Point Bridge.

The flatbed tractor-trailer heading north on I-5 was passing the Lakeview exit south of Tacoma. In one of the hollows on top of its load of timber planks stacked in bales, the KJ-3 swayed precariously, a dab of color among the pine. While they were passing through the dead zone where the two mecs aboard the KJ-3 temporarily died, Kevin had briefly reactivated Tigger to let Eric know that his situation hadn't changed, but he had learned little new apart from that Eric was an hour away and driving riskily for the conditions. Then the truck came within the lab's signal range, and its two stowaways resumed functioning.

Once more at the controls as Lancelot, Kevin primed the fuel and got ready for startup. Coordinating the two mecs would be trickier this time. There would be no run-up to takeoff speed since they were moving already—and in any case there wasn't room. A step of sawn endgrain buttressed the plane's tail, and ahead of it the slope of the boards led up into the full force of the truck's slipstream. The best he could hope for would be a catapult launch at maximum power, trusting that the air flow would create enough lift to hold the plane until the motor took over. Kevin wasn't sure if he had figured out the aerodynamics accurately, but he was about to find out now. This was about as close to Neurodyne as they were going to get.

He switched channels to become Dreadnought, already standing outside, hanging onto the airscrew for balance on the lurching mountainside of wet wood. Wind roared through gaps in the timber higher up; unseen wheels sizzled on the roadway far below. He straightened up, worked a foot tighter into the crack that he had found for anchorage, and jerked down hard with both arms. . . . The motor fired first time.

Channel select, back to Lancelot.

The plane was already trying to lift and break loose—he had visions of being swept into the wooden step behind. . . . Need maximum thrust *now* to clear. What about Dreadnought? . . . The wings were lifting, catching air stream. *No time!* . . .

Full throttle, ride the flow. An invisible river of wind hammered up under the flimsy plane, snatching it away. It veered to the right, went into a nose-up stall, and pitched down toward the southbound highway. Kevin fought to steady it, holding a power dive until he felt he was up to flying speed again, and pulled up just in time to avoid a swerving pickup coming the other way in the fast lane. He eased into a climb, moving closer to the timber-laden truck again and rising past it. He had a brief glimpse of Dreadnought standing motionless among the topmost planks, and then it disappeared behind the wing. Kevin picked out the landmarks that would guide him to Neurodyne, banked into a turn to bring them sliding slantwise around behind the airscrew spinning in front of him, and then leveled out.

He wasn't sure what he intended to do now that he no longer had Dreadnought. Lancelot's only role in his plan had been to fly the plane to get Dreadnought to Neurodyne in order to turn the computer off. Almost certainly, Lancelot wouldn't be big enough.

However, one thing at a time, he told himself. At least he was still on his way.

It wasn't any of Ollie's business to know what was going on, but sometimes you couldn't help wondering. It seemed that the woman they'd picked up at Garsten's was another lawyer who had been somehow remote-controlling a break-in from the van into Garsten's computers. Lawyers! They were no different from the rest, he told himself. Next thing, they'd be shooting each other in back alleys too. Ollie wasn't sure what the other woman who'd been at the company that morning had to do with the kid they were supposed to bring in from Tacoma, but according to Kyle she was Payne's girlfriend. What was this kid doing on his own on some other company's premises that were supposed to be closed for the holiday, anyhow? Probably, he'd sneaked in to fool around with stuff he'd been told to stay away from, Ollie guessed. It sounded like some rich people's kid. Ollie decided he might quite enjoy this. He didn't like smartass, spoilt-brat rich kids.

"This it?" Royal said from behind the wheel. "Gowan Avenue—just past the construction, right?" They had slowed down and were passing a stretch of road with barriers and warning beacons, mounds of earth, and stacks of concrete pipe sections waiting to be laid. Silent earth movers and other machinery stood off the road to one side. Ollie consulted the sketch and directions that Andy Finnion had scrawled.

"Should be a gate with a sign somewhere along here," he confirmed.

They came to it almost at once: NEURODYNE. That was all it said. Royal pulled over and picked up the car phone. The lots in the office park were practically lost among the trees in the rain just starting to fall. "Let's just check it one more time." They had called Neurodyne's number on the way in. Royal listened for perhaps ten seconds, then shook his head. "There's nobody answering today. Okay, let's go."

They drove in through the gate and stopped outside the main entrance. Royal produced the keys that Andy had given him. Ollie read the directions for when they were inside: "Stairs up to the second floor. Corridor left. Third door on the left." They got out of the car. And that was when they became aware of the odd droning sound coming from somewhere in the direction of the Interstate, still distant but getting closer.

They exchanged puzzled looks. "What the hell's that noise?" Royal said.

"Dunno. . . . Chainsaw?"

"Not unless someone's running with it. . . . Anyhow, that's gotta be someplace up in the sky."

They stood outside the doors, scanning, looking more perplexed. Suddenly Ollie pointed. "There!"

They watched in astonishment as a toy airplane, yellow and red, came out from among the treetops. Their puzzlement turned to alarm as the plane descended toward the gateway, clearly heading for the Neurodyne building. Then it was just nose and wings with a tail fin behind, coming straight at them like fighters on strafing runs that Ollie had seen in war movies. He yelped, ducked, and without thinking pulled his gun from the hip holster at the back of his jacket.

But there were no bullets, and the toy plane veered and turned away. Then it swooped and made another pass, uncannily as if the pilot were checking them out—which was stupid, of course; what was in there to do any checking? Then it circled. Somebody, somewhere was presumably figuring out what to do.

Royal was standing tensed, his head jerking first one way then another, scanning the surroundings. "Where are they? Who's got the button for that thing?"

"I don't see anybody."

"Whoever it is has to be around here somewhere."

"What the hell are they doing?"

"How should I know?"

And then the plane climbed away over the parking area, turned above the gate, and headed back toward the building. Its engine note rose; it lined itself up, came in on a dive over the heads of the two men watching open-mouthed below . . .

And crashed into one of the second-story windows.

Kevin squirmed from beneath the motor and the wreckage of the nose, now crushed back into what had been the cabin, and clambered out over broken spars and shredded fabric. The rest of the plane was tilted almost vertically above him like an upended airliner, its nose inside the shattered window pane, crumpled wings impaled among jagged fingers of glass. He climbed over shards piled like smashed icebergs, and stopped at the edge of the sill to check his bearings. He was in the Test Lab, where he'd intended; there, a short distance away in one of the development couplers, was his real body—where the awareness that he was experiencing at this very instant was actually located. It was still an eerie sensation, even if hardly new. But there was no time for dwelling on things like that now. The two men with the blue car— who could only be henchmen of Payne's—were only a short corridor, a flight of stairs, and the thickness of the front doors away. But what was Lancelot supposed to do? Moving the spring-loaded On/Off switch would be like trying to turn the gun turret of a tank.

Still without a plan, he ran along the window sill until he could jump down onto the lab bench by the wall, and crossed its acreage of jungle-vine wires and tools standing like cranes to the far end. The rack containing the processors and DNC hardware that he was using was now standing immediately across from him. But a sheer chasm plunging hundreds of feet to the floor separated it from the bench. It was like looking across a Manhattan avenue at a skyscraper, except that it was built from gigantic planes of metal with exposed galleries of green, glasslike walls, and connected to other parts of the city by traceries of cable hanging in fantastic inverted arches. Beyond the rack, he could see himself in the coupler, serene and unmoving, with no visible hint of the turmoil raging within. He ran along the end of the bench frantically, searching for a way.

A bridge! A power conduit led from a service panel at the back of the bench to a distribution box mounted farther along the wall. About halfway along, a bundle of communications cables coming up from below grazed the conduit and then bent to run horizontally into the rack of equipment that Kevin needed to get to. He leaped, scrabbled at the top of the conduit with his arms, but started to slide on the painted metal. Then his fingers found the edge of a seam, and his grip held. He hauled himself up onto the conduit and followed it to where it passed above the cables. There, he faced a jump down, the height of a house. He judged the fall carefully and launched himself off, landing among the cables. A curving bow of trunklike cords hanging in space descended before him, then rose again toward the steel cliffs.

Through the empty building he heard the doors

downstairs bang open, and raised voices echoing. He forged ahead, down to the lowermost part of the bridge, then up toward overhangs of green-gold beryllium alloy. Footsteps clattered in a distant stairwell.

Kevin passed through a gate in a castle wall made of metal, into a courtyard lined with enormous cylindrical shapes and colored sculptures. Beyond, he moved through parallel canyons formed between planes of city blocks standing on edge. He recognized electrical couplings and connections all around him, but there was no indication which of them might be vital. In any case, the circuits were like tramlines, the wires as thick as mains plumbing, connector leads like armored power cable. There was nothing that he could hope to break or budge. He came to the edge of a precipice and stood looking around helplessly. The floor that he was standing on vibrated like a catwalk in a ship's engine room. He looked down.

Below him, a shiny, convex, black wall bulged out from beneath a steel bridge clamped to the structure by bolts that stood up like telephone poles. Silver pipes ran from terminal posts the size of fire hydrants to cylindrical forms outlined vaguely in shadow. He was inside the power subsystem. The pipes he recognized as wires from the mains transformer secondary winding, feeding the rectifiers and d.c. supplies for the entire cabinet.

There was only one thing he could do. Measuring the distance, stretching his arms and legs out wide to bridge the gap, he jumped. . . .

And his world changed to the Test Lab at normal size, with the echo still ringing in his ears of an explosive bang somewhere near his head. His senses took several seconds to readjust to the different dimensions of acoustics and feeling. Then he began fumbling at the headset, his limbs cold and cramped from being still for too long. An acrid smell touched his nostrils. Smoke was wafting from the power control rack of the cabinet next to him where the mec had fried, carried by silent cooling fans freewheeling to a halt. He struggled out of the DNC collar and stood up.

They came through the door from the corridor when he was halfway across the lab, one in an overcoat, the other in a gray parka. "Hey kid, it's okay. We just wanna talk," one of them called. Kevin wasn't persuaded and didn't stick around to debate the point. The one in the gray parka was waving a gun.

He ran between the benches and equipment cubicles, through the connecting doors to the Training Lab, and out into the corridor. Not to the center of the building, he told himself. They could come back out through the doors from the Test Lab and cut him off. He went the other way, to the emergency stairs at the end of the building, stopping on the far side of the door to uncoil an armful of hose from the fire point and drape it around the door handle and supply valve nearby. Guessing that it might gain him maybe half a minute at most, he raced down the stairs. Muffled thuds and sounds of the door being shaken came from above; then the sound of footsteps running back inside the building to the main stairs. Kevin reached the emergency exit, pressed the bar, and emerged outside the building.

He ran to the corner, from where he would have to cross the front parking area to get away. The blue Ford that the two men had come in was parked out front, and for a moment Kevin thought of going for it. But there wasn't time. He didn't have enough driver's confidence to be sure of a quick getaway—even if the keys were there, which he doubted. He sprinted instead for the gate.

Halfway across the parking area, he heard the main

doors of the building being thrown open. "Hey! . . . Hey, you! Stop! I told you it's okay. We just wanna talk." Kevin ran, not looking back, convinced that the gate was receding as fast as he approached. He heard car doors slam behind him, then the motor starting. Even if he got to the gate, he thought breathlessly, what then? There were acres of empty office park out there and nobody for a mile. He'd be overtaken in minutes whichever way he ran. Gasping, his chest pounding, he ran anyway. What else was there?

But the gate did get closer. And as Kevin came to it, who should he see but Taki on the other side, waving him on encouragingly. A hallucination, he decided. Warning of imminent terminal cardiac collapse. But Ohira's car was there too, with Ohira standing by it talking into a phone. Only then did Kevin become aware of the deeper, throatier chugging, growing louder than the sound of the car engine gaining on him from behind. Only as he swung through the gateway did he see the earthmover coming the other way, black smoke puffing from its standpipe, manned by two of the innumerable relatives.

Royal, his foot hard down, didn't see it at all until it was too late. The Ford went through the gate with its tires squealing—there was a metallic *clang-gg-gg*, followed by the rending of crushed hood and a *hiss* of stove-in radiator—and was pushed ignominiously back in again by the huge blade. The earthmover halted, barricading the gateway.

Kevin leaned an arm on Ohira's car and stood panting and shaking as the strain and sudden exertion after hours of being immobile took effect. Taki walked up to him and grinned.

"Knock-knock."

"You wouldn't dare," Kevin wheezed murderously. Ohira nodded in satisfaction and came back from the gate. "So you listen next time when I say you need help, okay?" He clapped a hand lightly on Kevin's shoulder and indicated the car. "Get in. My cousins will take care of those two. Now we have more work to attend to."

CHAPTER THIRTY-FOUR

The Lincoln followed the Cadillac south on the Interstate when they reached the city, passing a few blocks from where Michelle lived on the east side of Lake Union. They exited west, passing the Naval Training Center at the southernmost tip of the lake, and then headed north along the west shore until they came to a white building near the water's edge, with palms and colored lights in the windows, and a large, neon-bordered sign declaring it to be the "Shoals." Michelle knew the place: an exclusive marine club opened a year or so previously on Westlake, frequented by the local celebrities and millionaires, actual and aspiring. Despite her proximity across the lake, it wasn't a social scene that had ever held much appeal for her personally.

The cars drew up at a chain-link gate to one side of the building, and Garsten said something to an attendant in the box. The windows of the Lincoln were tinted one-way, making it pointless for Michelle to have tried attracting attention. The gate opened, and they drove through a short access road to a quay running along the rear of the building. A maze of piers and jetties with boats at their moorings stretched away in

349

both directions, masts swaying and lines flapping in the breeze that was building up. Immediately in front of them, a large, sleek motor yacht, easily the most impressive of all those in sight, was berthed stern shoreward, alongside one of the docking piers. A sign above the fishing cockpit looking down on the swim platform at the stern read: *Princess Dolores*.

The two cars parked among a scattering of other vehicles in slots along the service quay. Michelle's guards ushered her out, and they joined Vanessa, Garsten, and Finnion from the Cadillac. Michelle remained mute, resigned to whatever lay ahead. It was clear that nothing she might have to say was going to alter anything, and her reserves of energy were at an ebb. They walked out along the dock, Vanessa and Garsten ahead, Finnion and Kyle following with Michelle between them, and the two spooks bringing up the rear. Finnion had a folder of documents that he had brought from Microbotics. One of the escorts behind was carrying a large leather briefcase that Garsten had taken from the Cadillac.

A gangplank led up from the dock to the fore part of the vessel, and a set of steps provided access amidships. There seemed to be some kind of consternation around the steps. A half dozen or so people were standing around on the dock, with much hand-waving going on, and raised voices; more figures, similarly excited, were visible above on the deck. As the arrivals approached, three girls who looked to Michelle like hookers—high-class and expensively turned out, to be sure, but none the less mistakable for that—came down the steps carrying shoulder purses and garment bags, preceded by a crew member in a white mess-jacket. Vanessa and Garsten led the way through without ceremony and began ascending to the boat. Snatches of words reached

Michelle's ears from either side as she and the others followed.

"What does he mean, it's been canceled? We were invited. Tell him you want to talk to Martin right away."

"What kind of emergency? . . ."

"Of course it's not the weather. We don't have to go anywhere. . . ."

Michelle recognized Payne straight away when he reached the deck: yellow hair and bronzed features, wearing navy dungarees and a buff duffel jacket. He was with a dark-skinned, mustached man who looked like the captain, talking to some people standing in a semicircle, but excused himself when he saw Garsten and Vanessa. His eyes moved to Michelle and assessed her silently for a moment. Vanessa moved forward and murmured something to him that Michelle didn't catch. On the quay below, the hookers were getting into a red BMW.

"Later," Michelle heard Payne say. "First I need an update from you and Phil." He started to turn away, but caught Michelle's eye in the process. Michelle still didn't think it would do much good, but this was the time to try, if only for form's sake. Here was the boss, after all.

"Martin Payne, isn't it?" she said. He stopped and looked back. "Look, I'm not alone in this. You have to know that what you're doing is crazy. Why are you doing this? You've run up enough charges already to risk going away for a while, regardless of anything we've done. It's not making sense. Why let it get any worse?"

He seemed to only half hear, as if distracted by more pressing things. "Put her down in the salon with your two guys and keep everybody else out," he told Finnion. Then, nodding at Michelle, "I'll talk to you in a minute."

"What do you want me for?" she demanded, unable to prevent her voice from rising as Finnion took her elbow.

"Come on, you heard the man," Finnion said, guiding her firmly.

They took her down some stairs to a wood-ceilinged room with elaborate ornaments and furnishings, where cocktails and a buffet meal had been set but evidently abandoned in a hurry. Finnion posted one of his men by the stairs, the other inside the door at the far end, leading forward.

"Sit down and relax," he told them, waving a hand. "It's supposed to be a party. Have a sandwich or something. It looks like the guests won't be using this." The one carrying Garsten's bag set it down on the floor and surveyed the food laid out on the large table.

Finnion looked at Michelle and must have read the question still written on her face. "Don't worry," he said to her. "You're just in case we need a bargaining chip getting out of here. They'll put you off in a boat when we clear the limits." He turned and disappeared back up to the deck, closing the door at the bottom of the stairs behind him.

Michelle didn't believe him. But she poured a hot coffee and picked out a couple of rolls with cheese and meats anyway. Even people on the verge of nervous exhaustion had to eat.

"This stuff's not bad," one of the two left with her murmured through a mouthful of caviar, scooping crab paté with a finger of toast. "I'll take leftovers like this any time."

"Pity they didn't leave the girls too," his companion answered.

Michelle hunched down on one of the bench seats and sipped her coffee. It tasted good and was warming after the gray weather outside. One of the two men looked at her curiously, as if amenable to opening up a little and talking now that the mission of getting her here was accomplished. She avoided his gaze, and he turned away.

Corfe left the Interstate at the Convention Center and drove a few blocks east toward First Hill, oddly enough not too far from Garsten's office, where the day's whole crazy chain of events had begun. He parked the van in a quiet side street and was about to call Eric to let him know where he was, when an incoming call arrived first.

"Yes?" Corfe acknowledged warily.

"Doug, it's Kevin."

"Hey, Kev! What's been the problem there? We—"

"Doug, you don't understand. I'm on my way north with Ohira now, doing some low-flying on the Interstate. We had it all wrong. It was *today!* You understand me? They had it set up for today."

Corfe shook his head protestingly. "That's impossible. Michelle said—"

"She was a lot righter than she ever knew. There was a killer mec planted in Vanessa's car—the one Dad's using."

"But, but . . . I talked to him . . . it couldn't have been twenty minutes ago. He was okay. What are you saying? . . ."

"He didn't even know about it. Don't worry about that part, Doug. It's over. We just talked to him too. He says you've lost Michelle."

"I was just about to start trying to locate her."

"Ohira just got to the firm in time. They sent a couple of their heavyweights down to pick me up. So they know everything." The alarm in Kevin's voice sharpened. "It means she's in danger, Doug. *You have to find where she is.*"

Corfe gulped and nodded into the phone. "I'll do what I can." He gave Kevin his location and cut the call, then scrambled into the rear of the van, activated one of the on-board couplers again, and began frantically scanning the channels.

There was something familiar about the drapes high on the wall opposite, and the windows with the rounded corners, Michelle thought. She looked around and took in the round-backed chairs and couch, the sculptures and art works, rich carpeting, and marble-topped bar with mirrors below a long window at the far end. She looked the other way and saw two doors in the end wall, and between them the centerpiece with the crest carved in wood and the ship's name. It was the room that she had seen on the tape, she realized—the tape Kevin and Taki had made from the mec that had inadvertently found its way into Vanessa's car. Near Michelle's elbow was a furled U.S. flag secured to the wall, and beyond it the end of a wooden cabinet. From what Kevin had said—assuming nobody had come across it—that mec should still be there, up on the top of that cabinet somewhere. She forced herself not to look up and risk showing too much curiosity.

So what was Finnion talking about? Getting out of here, clearing the limits? . . . A party obviously canceled at short notice. It sounded as if they were intending to leave the country suddenly. All because somebody had been found trying to snoop into Garsten's office? Surely not. It made no sense. The situation was getting crazier by the minute.

Then something else in the corner of her eye caught her attention—just for an instant. She turned her head to look at the large briefcase of Garsten's that one of the guards had carried on board and put on the floor just below one end of the table. Michelle was sure it had moved. She watched it while she nibbled on a roll, trying not to stare too conspicuously. It did it again. The whole briefcase didn't move; but a bulge appeared for a moment part way along one side. Something was moving inside it.

After her experiences this week, the first thing that came to mind was mecs—they seemed to be involved in everything, whichever way she turned. She frowned. What could be going on this time?

The briefcase had come out of Garsten's car. When Garsten left the parking lot where Michelle had been seized, before he reappeared later at Microbotics, he'd said he was going to check his office. At Microbotics, Michelle had overheard Finnion saying something over the phone about the office being "clean." That had to mean Garsten's office. "Clean" probably meant that the signs of interference had been cleaned up— although why they would want it that way, Michelle couldn't imagine; she'd have thought Garsten would rather have left it as was, for evidence. But nothing today was making any sense. So if Finnion *had* meant that the mecs were no longer in Garsten's office, where were they? That had to be it. Michelle was looking at them. They were in the briefcase that Garsten had brought with him.

Excitement gripped her suddenly for the first time in hours as she realized the implication: It meant that the van was out there somewhere in the city, and Corfe or Kevin—or conceivably both of them—were still operational. Which in turn meant there was still a possibility of letting the outside world know where she was.

Before her eyes, a lump appeared in the side of the briefcase again, stretched to become a peak, and then a gray metal blade thrust itself through and began sawing its way down toward the floor. Michelle almost choked; then she sat forward hurriedly, putting her hand to her mouth as one of the guards glanced at her. She was not immediately sure what she meant to do, but obviously, to let anything come walking out onto the open floor would be guaranteeing disaster.

Yet even as she watched, a metal hand grasped one side of the rent and pulled it aside. Sure enough, one of the beer-can-size mecs that had been in Garsten's office began squeezing its way out. Michelle was on her feet reflexively. The guard who had eyed her before looked up questioningly. For a moment she stood, confused; then she wiped her brow with a flick of her hand and took off her coat. "It's hot. I need to get out of this." The guard looked away and resumed eating, smacking his lips noisily. The mec was outside the bag, and from the angle of its head Michelle could tell that whoever was operating it had seen her. She wasn't sure if that model registered sound or not. Surreptitiously, behind the cover of her coat, she made a quick "hold-it" gesture, showing her open palm and rocking it sideways several times.

She looked to one end of the room, then the other. "Is there a bathroom anywhere I can use?"

The guards looked at each other, as if to ask why nobody had thought to brief them on something like that. The one farthest away shrugged and nodded. The other moved past Michelle and opened the door in the left side of the end wall—the one opposite that through which they had entered. Beyond it, stairs led down to a corridor leading aft. He checked the doors opening off from it. "There's one right here."

As Michelle passed the end of the table, she let her coat slip off her arm, seemingly accidentally, to fall across the briefcase. As she stooped to pick it up, she scooped the mec with it, at the same time pushing the sides of the tear together so that it wouldn't be instantly obvious. She straightened up, collected her purse from the seat where she had been sitting, went down into the bathroom, and locked the door.

It seemed to Corfe that he couldn't move without walking straight into some kind of trouble. Listening for a while through the acoustically equipped mec that he had included in the complement at Garsten's had revealed nothing. Then, when he activated one of the larger telebots and tried looking outside whatever it was he had found himself shut up in, he'd had quick impressions of being on the floor in some kind of room, Michelle looking worried and flashing a warning signal at him, and then himself being bundled up inside something constricting and being moved. Since any further action on the telebot's part seemed not to be in order for the moment, he transferred to one of the smaller mecs still inside whatever the telebot had emerged from, and used that to gain another peek through the gap that he had made.

There was carpeted floor, the under parts of a table, and a pair of legs terminating in men's shoes. He crawled out and looked back to see that the mec had been in a large leather briefcase. There was something familiar about the place he was in, he realized. After a few seconds he recognized it, from this unfamiliar angle, as the main salon of the *Princess Dolores*. The *Dolores* was normally kept at the private dock behind Payne's house in Bellevue, yet when Corfe had stopped less than a mile from there before crossing back over the lake, he hadn't made contact. He could only conclude that the *Dolores* had been moved to some location nearer Seattle center.

Michelle had gone, and the surroundings looked clear. Deciding it would be prudent to spread his options around, he walked the mec farther back under the table, into the space between the edge of the carpet and the wall. Then he switched back to the telebot and remained inert, awaiting developments.

He felt the circus tent in which he was wrapped being set down on something solid. Then part of it was lifted aside, and a hand brought him out onto a shiny orange terrace by an empty swimming pool. Above the pool was an enormous mirror wall edged by lights. There were two Michelles, one reflected in the mirror, the other looking at him directly. He was in a bathroom, standing on the side of a marble washbasin.

Michelle's lips were moving. He made a side-to-side horizontal movement with an arm, indicating that he couldn't hear her. She seemed to understand. Corfe could see her biting her lip, thinking frantically. He walked across the surface and pointed at a chrome dispenser holding facial tissues. Michelle nodded, rummaged in her purse, and produced a felt-tipped pen.

She pulled out the top tissue, wrote on it, *Doug? Kevin?* and held it in front of him like a poster. Corfe indicated who he was, then pointed at the pen and made writing motions. Michelle gave it to him and held the tissue flat while he used both arms to write, moving the pen like a broom.

YACHT WHERE?

Michelle took the pen again and wrote: *Shoals club, Lake Union. Believe sailing soon. Fetch help.* Corfe signaled that he understood and would do his best. Michelle asked: *You have the van?* He nodded. In similar fashion he answered that he had contacted Eric and that he didn't know what the situation with Kevin was.

Michelle looked at the door suddenly as if someone was knocking or calling, then back at the mec, indicating by showing a palm and pointing that she was out of time. Corfe got the pen back and wrote hastily: *LEAVE MEC HERE* and pointed at the floor. Michelle stared for a second, then nodded. She took the pen, gathered her purse and coat, and set him down beneath the washbasin. Then she turned the light off and left, leaving the door cracked open.

Corfe waited a half minute, then moved cautiously across the floor and widened the gap till he could see out. He was looking along the corridor leading aft to the engine compartment. In the other direction, a short flight of steps led up to the salon. There was no sign of anyone nearby. He wasn't sure what he planned to do, but he needed to move the mec to a place where it would be less conspicuous. He walked it out of the bathroom, across the nearest stretch of passage, into the dark space beneath the stairs. Then he deactivated it, exited from coupler space, and was instantly back in the van. He took his personal phone from his pocket and called a number in Seattle Police Department headquarters.

"Hello, Lieutenant Shelvy? This is Doug Corfe again. I'm the guy who was there earlier, about the woman who had been abducted—the one I thought was at the lawyer's office."

"Yeah. I just heard the reports." Lieutenant Shelvy didn't sound very amused today.

"Look, I know that I've given you guys the runaround, and I know how this must sound, but you have to believe me. I *do* know where she is this time."

"Surprise me."

"She's on his yacht, Martin Payne's yacht: the *Princess Dolores*. It's at the Shoals club on Lake Union." There was an ominous silence. Corfe got nervous, and his mouth went onto automatic. "I mean, I've just been there. I saw her there myself not five minutes ago."

"You were on Martin Payne's yacht, Mr. Corfe?"

"That's right. . . . Well, not exactly on it myself, but—"

"Don't tell me. You sent one of those little machines there, the same ones that weren't in Phillip Garsten's office, right?"

"Yes, exactly. Except I didn't—"

"Mr. Corfe, if I hear one more word about this, you *will* be arrested and charged with obstructing the police. There will be no further warning." The line went dead.

Corfe called Eric and updated him on the situation. "You've got to stall things and stop that boat from sailing," Eric said.

"How?"

"Figure out something, Doug."

Corfe cleared down and stared at the console, thinking. The only way he could see of influencing anything that happened on the yacht was via the mecs. He recoupled to the system and activated another of the ones still inside the leather briefcase, and peered out. He was in shadow. Michelle had gotten the message and put her coat down over the bag. Corfe ran an inventory. In addition to the mec already free below the table and the larger telebot under the stairs, he had another telebot, five smaller Neurodyne models, the Keyboard Emulator, and the experimental acoustic model. Also, there was the almost run-down one that Kevin had left up on the cabinet, which was also acoustic. Corfe began moving them out to spread them around better.

Somebody else from police headquarters called Finnion a few minutes later. The tone was low and confidential. "Andy, it's Gus. Look, I don't know what's going on, but your boss's name has been buzzing all day here. Whatever it is, you guys had better cool it. Just a friendly word of advice, huh? Be careful, understand?" Finnion passed the word to Payne.

"Get everybody except Vic, Norbert, and the rest who are staying, off the boat now," Payne instructed Michaelis Ellipulos, the captain. "We're sailing as soon as you're ready."

CHAPTER THIRTY-FIVE

Wrapped in a heavy, hooded overjacket, Vanessa stood to one side of the bridge of the *Princess Dolores,* tight-lipped and saying nothing. Payne was pacing restlessly in front of the chart table to the rear, periodically checking his watch and sending nervous glances toward the shore. Ollie and Royal had stopped answering the phone. The conclusion had to be that something had gone wrong in Tacoma. After a quick conference, Payne had agreed they couldn't wait any longer. Now they had switched over from shore-based power to the ship's generators; the gangplank and the steps were up. But they still weren't moving.

Victor Bazhin appeared on the foredeck below. "Hey, Martin, what's going on?" he called up. "I thought we were supposed to be pulling out. Nothing's happening."

Payne leaned out of the starboard wing station window, to the side of the bridge. "There's a glitch with the electronics. We're looking into it now."

"Is it anything serious?"

"It can't be—everything checked out just fine this morning. It's always the way when something urgent comes up." Payne looked across to the communications and electrical racks on the rear wall of the bridge, where

Mike Ellipulos, the captain, and Nick, seaman and electronics specialist on the crew, had opened up the main breaker panel and were probing among the wires at the rear. "Mike, how's it going? What've we got back there?"

Ellipulos looked mystified. "I don't understand it. It wouldn't reset. The replacement module didn't work either. Now we find this." When they went through the pre-sailing checks, they had found an entire distribution subsystem dead, disabling the satellite-driven plotter and navigation system and one of the radars.

Payne strode over and looked down. "What?"

Ellipulos gestured. Nick was examining several stubs of cable protruding from the connectors. "Half the wires are gone at the back. They look like they've been cut."

Vanessa came across and looked past Payne, but still she said nothing. Payne shook his head, nonplussed. "That's crazy, Mike."

"I know."

"You're sure it was okay this morning?"

"Tested it myself."

Payne jerked his head from side to side, as if asking the world to judge if he deserved the things he had to endure. "Well, can we fix it?" he asked.

"I could replace the cables, no problem, but it would take a while," Nick said.

Vanessa moved closer behind Payne. "You don't need computers to move a boat," she muttered. "Fix the problem when we're at sea. Corfe's still loose in the city somewhere, and I don't like it. We need to get out of here."

"Forget that for now, Mike," Payne said. "Take her out manually. We've still got Loran backup."

Ellipulos straightened up and used a hand-held

intercom to talk to the first mate, who was out aft on the boat deck. "Zed, get ready to cast off. We're moving out now." Nick left the bridge via an outside ladder to go forward. Ellipulos moved into the captain's chair at the wheel and alerted Cole, the engineer down below. "Is everything set down there? We're casting off now."

From the boat deck behind the bridge, Zed's voice called orders to Nick and the other seaman, George, who was at the stern.

Vanessa was still staring dubiously at the opened breaker panel. "So what's Mike saying?" she demanded curtly, looking at Payne. "Are we supposed to have a saboteur on board, or something?"

Payne could only show his hands. "I don't know. It's like I said—crazy. One thing at a time, Vanessa. If you want us out of here, we're getting out of here, okay? We'll take care of that problem when we're clear."

Vanessa looked at the cut wires again. Impossible thoughts flew through her head. She walked over to the bench seat by the chart table where she had put down her shoulder bag, picked it up, and opened the flap. Back at Microbotics, she had, as a precaution, bound the mec that she had taken from Michelle's pocket tightly in adhesive tape to immobilize it. . . . But no, that wasn't it. The mec was still there in her bag, wrapped like a miniature mummy. Puzzled but still suspicious, she put the bag down again and went back to the opened panel. Payne, standing next to Ellipulos, was looking baffled. Ellipulos frowned and pressed the button again. "I don't get this. The starter's dead too."

"This isn't real," Payne breathed, shaking his head.

"Can't you start it from up on top?" Vanessa shot across at them.

"I wouldn't bother trying," Ellipulos answered. "The fly bridge controls are farther down the circuits from here. If we're dead, it's a certain bet it will be up there too. The only other way is to use the local starters on the engines."

"Do it, then," Payne ordered.

Ellipulos used the intercom to rouse Cole again. "Use the engine-room starters. Both engines, right away."

"What in hell's going on?" Cole's voice squawked from the speaker.

"We'll look into it when we get clear. The boss says we move now."

And then the shrill *woop-woop-woop* of an alarm sounded somewhere in the depths of the vessel, echoed by a repeater in the bridge monitor panel. Ellipulos sprang up and moved to quieten it, checked the status displays. "We've got a fire in the galley!" he told Payne. "This whole day's getting insane." Running footsteps sounded, and Zed appeared in the doorway from the boat deck. "Get below and give Trevor a hand," Ellipulos told him. Zed disappeared down the inside companionway, while doors opened and slammed below, and voices shouted. Bazhin and Garsten appeared on the foredeck below, looking alarmed. Then the engine room intercom buzzed. Ellipulos flipped a switch. "What is it, Cole?"

"I can't start it," Cole's voice said from the speaker. "We just had a bang down here."

"What do you mean, a bang? What went bang?"

"It sounds like something shorted out in the starter. There's smoke, and a breaker's out. I'll have to check it."

"I'm coming down there." Ellipulos snapped off the intercom and headed for the stairway that Zed had taken. Vanessa had swung the breaker panel wide open, torn the bundles of cables aside, and was searching determinedly around the back of the uncovered racking. As Payne started to turn to follow after Ellipulos,

Vanessa seized something inside and straightened up triumphantly to brandish it at him.

"*There!*" she exclaimed. "There's your saboteur, Martin!"

It was an intermediate-size mec, maybe an inch high. One of its grasping limbs was detached, hooked to its utility belt, and had been replaced by a pair of scissorlike cutting blades.

Payne stared at it incredulously. "How . . . ? I don't understand."

Vanessa marched to the open window at the wing station and threw the mec far out over the water. "Oh, don't you see? It's that woman. This wasn't the only one that she had. Come on."

They left the bridge and went below through the day cabin. Gray, choking smoke filled the passage leading forward to the galley. In the middle of it they could make out the figure of Zed in the galley doorway, directing a fire extinguisher. Trevor, the cook, was waving his hands and remonstrating to Ellipulos. "I know it was oil all over the stove, but I'm telling you there wasn't any oil open or anywhere near it. Hell, Mike, you think I don't know how to run a galley, for chrissakes? . . ." Ellipulos cut off the alarm, which had been drowning out the voices and other noises coming from around the boat. Vanessa led the way aft past the dining room, toward the main salon, Payne following.

One of the two guards that Finnion had left was hovering at the forward entrance to the salon, trying to gauge the situation, when Vanessa and Payne came in. Michelle sat on the bench seat farther back, doing her best to seem detached and contemptuous of the fiasco going on around her. Vanessa came over and stood in front of her, face flushed, eyes blazing, looking as if she was barely able to prevent herself from attacking Michelle physically. "Okay, how many are there, and where are they?" she grated.

Michelle eyed her distastefully, refusing to show any comprehension. "What are you talking about?"

"You know what I'm talking about. What other ones have you got?"

"What other what?"

"Give them to me!" Vanessa's voice rose as she finally lost control. Payne caught her arm to restrain her, but she shook him off.

At that moment a man in crew's dress appeared from the stairs at the rear of the salon, going down to the corridor leading aft past the bathroom. Michelle guessed he had come from the engine room. He was holding something between his fingers and looking mystified. "What do you make of this?" he said, addressing Payne.

"What is it?"

The engineer showed it. Payne turned it over and passed it to Vanessa without comment. The engineer went on, "It was jammed across the starter solenoid. That was what shorted it out. How'd it get there? I never saw anything like that before." It was another inch-size mec—or what was left of one. Its casing was blackened, and an arm and a leg had been partly melted.

"These!" Vanessa hissed, turning on Michelle again. "The rest. Where are they? Who's working them?" She spotted Michelle's coat, snatched it up, and began searching through the pockets, pulling out the contents and scattering them on the table top among the plates and buffet dishes.

And then more yelling and commotion broke out forward of the salon. There was a crash, the sounds of footsteps running, more banging, and then somebody fired a shot. The guard who was by Michelle wheeled, producing a gun reflexively; the other, at the forward end, was backing from the door, aiming his pistol low toward the floor. A metallic parody of a face appeared above the sill at the bottom of the door, followed by an approximately cylindrical, can-size body equipped with arms in the act of bracing themselves to haul the contrivance over. It was one of the telebot prototypes that Michelle had seen in Garsten's office. The guard fired at it, splintering wood from the sill, and the bullet ricocheted out of the room evoking more outraged yells forward.

"Hold it, you idiot!" Payne shouted.

The telebot seemed to reassess the situation, ducked back out again, and disappeared off to one side just as a heavy ornamental brass from one of the walls crashed into the spot that it had occupied. A man that Michelle didn't recognize appeared framed in the doorway briefly, flailing with a fire ax to the crunches of tearing woodwork.

"It's going for the stairs," Finnion's voice yelled from somewhere behind him.

"What in hell is it?" somebody else demanded from somewhere.

There was a mêlée of bodies trying to get past each other and go in different directions at the far end of the room. Then Garsten materialized from among them and strode on in, looking from side to side and around the floor. "That was the same as the one in my office," he muttered. "Which one of you had my bag? Where is it? . . . Ah, there!" He stooped as he saw the briefcase, and grabbed it up. *"Jesus!"* He showed it to Vanessa and Payne, pointing at the rent cut vertically down one side.

He cleared the end of the table and tipped out the briefcase to produce a heap of cords and cables; bits of string, wood, and plastic; a carpenter's measuring tape; and an assortment of metal items in various forms and shapes. "They're gone!" he exclaimed, gesturing. "All the bugs and walking junk they had in my office was in here. Look, they must have got out through here. Christ, they must be all over the ship!"

Ellipulos came in, looking around demandingly from face to face. "What is that thing? What's going on aboard my ship?"

Payne showed him the burned mec. "Little machines. There's more like this around. Get your men looking. Look everywhere."

Vanessa looked back at Garsten. "How many were there?" she asked, paling.

He spread his hands. "Hell, I don't remember. It wasn't exactly a time to be stock taking. I just—"

Vanessa seized the neck of Michelle's sweater and dragged her to her feet. Her mouth compressed into a tight gash on a face bloodless with rage. *"Who's controlling them? Where from?"*

"You're the scientist. You find out."

Vanessa took a glass from the table, smashed the rim against the edge, and held the jagged edges close to Michelle's face. "I'm warning you. . . ." Michelle was paralyzed, unable to react in any way.

Garsten raised a hand, looking alarmed. "Hey . . ." he cautioned. Payne took a step forward and caught Vanessa's arm.

And then something dropped from among the figurines and trophies along the top of the wall cabinet, onto Vanessa's head. She screeched, dropped the glass, and began tearing wildly at her hair. . . .

Corfe felt as if he were in one of those nightclub acts where the performer gets lots of china plates spinning on top of flexible canes that have to be tweaked periodically to speed the plate up again before it falls off. By the end, the act reduces to a nonstop panic of running frantically back and forth across the stage, rescuing one platter after another seemingly just on the verge of crashing.

Having eleven mecs scattered through the boat was all very well, but there was only one of him in the van to operate them. Besides cutting equipment cables up on the bridge, shorting out the engine starter, sabotaging the galley, and deploying his other troops, he had kept his audio system tuned to the mec up on top of the cabinet in the salon in order to listen in on what was happening with Michelle. But there was a limit to how much he could keep up. It had been bad enough when he could switch from one to another and move them into place surreptitiously, before anyone on the boat—other than Michelle—knew what was going on. Now that things were happening, he was losing track of which mec was where and their different situations; and as often as not, there simply wasn't time to coordinate his moves, even when he did know.

So far he had lost two and was about to lose another. The one he had left in behind the main breaker panel on the bridge had stopped responding; one, he had sacrificed to short the starter in the engine room; and the one he had just thrown off the cabinet in the salon had been almost out of charge anyway.

He had to get back to the telebot that he'd managed to get outside and left hidden temporarily behind a rope locker by the entrance foyer in order to intervene with Michelle, even though it was being chased, shot at, and obviously in a tight spot. He rolled and clutched to entangle himself in Vanessa's hair, pinched at her fingertips when they came clawing at him, and then switched back to the telebot's channel. . . .

Only to find himself cartwheeling through the air,

then falling toward shifting hillocks of wind-jostled water. There was a shock as he hit resistance, a brief impression of sinking through green, opalescent light. Then nothing.

Three gone. Then the noise from the salon faded in his ears and died. Corfe transferred his audio input to the remaining acoustic mec, lodged under the bedside table in one of the guest staterooms. It brought sounds of too many voices yelling at once, with banging and noise in the background, for anything to be comprehensible. No time to wonder about that: Check back with Michelle.

He activated the mec still tucked behind the edge of the carpet under the salon table. It showed Payne trying to help Vanessa disentangle the mec from her hair, Garsten turning away to meet another figure approaching from the far-end door. Michelle had moved back, away from Payne and Vanessa—she seemed okay for the moment. A chance for a quick review elsewhere. Corfe juggled channels frenziedly.

The KE was posted as a lookout on a ledge in the corridor leading aft from the salon. All was quiet there.

Back to the surviving telebot, which he'd left below a life preserver on the boat deck just behind the bridge. A crewman was rampaging around in the wheelhouse, obviously searching, moving closer. Situation getting risky.

Meanwhile, the audio continued bringing voices from the stateroom area midships:

"Look at this. It's cooked."

"That's what we're looking for. You two take that side. Start looking everywhere."

"You mean there's more of them?"

Feet thumping; objects moving; doors slamming.

Corfe had a general tool-utility mec in the engine compartment, which had climbed part of the way up to a fuel supply line. Could he afford the time to move it the rest of the way?

"Hey, guys, what's that? Look, is that one? I think I found one."

Corfe groaned. It had to be the one that he'd been forced to leave at the base of a wall while he attended to another emergency. He hastily switched channels to it and found he was being nudged by a wooden mainmast leading up to a huge figure looming silhouetted against light. He was prodded out onto an open expanse of floor; then the heel of a huge boot was coming down on him like a swooping dragon.

Five gone.

Too much to do. There wasn't enough time for anything. He was overwhelmed. . . .

Then everything went blank, and Corfe found himself suddenly back in the coupler station inside the van. The rear door was open; figures were clambering in. He blinked, stupefied. His concentration had been so total that he had lost all track of time.

Kevin slid quickly into the station next to him and put on the headset and collar. Taki was getting into the third, on the other side behind Kevin. Ohira was at the door. "Stay there," Ohira told Corfe, extending an arm. "Just give me the keys." Corfe found the keys in his pocket and handed them over. Ohira tossed them to one of his kinsmen, who ran around to the front and climbed in the driver's door. A car filled with more Oriental faces was pulled up close behind.

"They've got Michelle on Payne's boat—Shoals, on Lake Union," Corfe gasped.

"I know. Eric told me. We're going there now," Ohira shouted. "He's heading there too. Keep stalling them." He slammed the doors. The motor started, and moments later Corfe felt the van moving, then pulling away fast and cornering. He and the other two buckled themselves tight into the seats—once neurally coupled, they would have no functioning reflexes to stop themselves being thrown around.

"Okay, then, Doug, what have we got? Initiating now." Kevin scanned the displays, his fingers racing over switches and keys.

"We're losing mecs," Corfe said. "There's only six left functioning on the boat."

"That's okay," Taki said from behind. "I brought a box of them in the car."

And now there were three operators.

"Right." Corfe smiled for the first time that day. That ought to even things up a bit. "Kev, there's a telebee in trouble up near the bridge that you can pick up on," he said. "Taki, I've got a critter in the engine room that needs to move." He switched them all through to the common audio channel, then reentered coupler space himself.

"Got it," Kevin's voice said on the circuit.

"Active," Taki confirmed a couple of seconds later.

"I'm forward of Taki, in the salon where Michelle is," Corfe told them. "She's going to need help pretty soon. The KE is along the passage to the left leading aft. Kev, the general utility on Channel Three is at a switchbox farther forward. It's sawed halfway through the main input power line. Can you handle that one too? . . ."

CHAPTER THIRTY-SIX

One of Finnion's men had found a medical kit containing scissors, and Payne was trying to cut the mec out of Vanessa's hair. It seemed to have lost all life but was hopelessly entangled. She shook with the effort of containing her fury and trying to keep still. "Get it off me, Martin! Get that thing *out!*"

The room was in pandemonium with passengers and crew searching along shelves, shaking out drapes, tearing up seat covers and cushions. Garsten crouched to probe around where his briefcase had been set down, then yelled in alarm and recoiled back as something scurried up the outside of his jacket sleeve. He swatted with his other hand, missed, and lost his balance twisting and trying to grab it as it burrowed under his shirt collar.

Then there was a noise that sounded like an explosion from somewhere forward, and the salon lights went out. More shouting and consternation erupted in the darkness. Michelle, still on her feet, edged to the table where the buffet was laid out, found the end, and heaved it up hard to be rewarded by a tremendous din of crashing china and shattering glass. She lunged at the forms of Payne and Vanessa outlined in the darkness, and shoved them toward where Garsten had gone down on his hands and knees. They reeled and went down, and another shadowy figure loomed and tumbled over them. Michelle threw a chair in on top for good measure, and in the confusion moved to the end of the room where the two exits were, one leading up, the other down. Someone was coming down the companionway to the right. Michelle slipped into the passage on the other side that she had been in briefly earlier, leading aft.

Closets and doors lined both sides. Her only choice was to continue toward the stern, where the lights were still on, and hope that that part of the boat would be empty of people for the moment. She figured the engines were that way, and the engineer was still in the salon. On a vessel this size, there seemed a good chance that he worked alone.

The passage ended at a bulkhead door leading through to the engine room. Michelle peered in warily. To the right, immediately past the door, was a cubbyhole partly partitioned off from the rest of the compartment, with a chair, a tiny steel desk, and several shelves of charts and manuals. Opposite, on the left, was an open kit locker with steel steps leading up to what looked like a hatch out to the deck. Beyond was the engine room proper, built around the two main diesels standing parallel with a walkway between them. At the far end, past the engines, a steel ladder surrounded by more machinery led up to another hatch, which Michelle judged had to be near the stern somewhere.

As she was debating which way to go, a movement on a ledge near her head caught her eye. It was a mec— in fact, the peculiar one that Corfe called a "KE," with a socket like a hat on top of its head, that plugged into computer cords. It was waving at her. There was no time for quizzing. She picked it up and set it on the palm of her hand. It jabbed an arm several times, pointing in the direction of the engine room. She went through, among valves and housings, generators, batteries, banks of electrical gear. It was hot and noisy, with one of the generator systems running, but at least the engines were quiet.

Gesturing like a tiny, animated compass, the mec guided her to a point up among a tangle of pipes and valves, where she found another mec. It was wielding what looked like a miniature saw blade, working at one of the pipes like a logger sectioning a felled trunk. The KE in Michelle's hand pointed and gesticulated frantically, but she was too tense and fearful to grasp what the gestures meant. Then she heard shouts and voices behind her as the door above the stairs at the far end of the passage she had just come along was thrown open.

Michelle had a fraction of a second to make a choice. There were two directions she could take to a hatchway out. The one to the left, from the locker space, was closer but meant going back, toward whoever was approaching. She hurried the other way, between the main engines, scrambled up the steel ladder, and pulled herself through the stern hatch. Outside on the deck she froze, her head inches from the opening. A voice grew louder in the engine compartment below, calling back to somebody, but Michelle was unable to make out the words against the noise of the generator and auxiliary machinery.

Michelle eased back from the hatch opening and looked cautiously around. She had come up in the fishing cockpit, extending across the stern below the fantail extension of the after lounge, which sat above the engine room aft of the salon. Although she could hear voices and activity higher up and forward on the boat deck, the after superstructure hid her from view from all angles, unless somebody should come to the rail at the extreme end of the fantail, immediately above her.

Steps led up to the fantail, but that way was out of the question. The dock looked just a little too far away and too low to step across onto easily—and besides, seemed horribly exposed. Two gates through the stern rail of the fishing platform seemed to lead down even lower.

Voices sounded again from inside the hatch. "Hey, Cole, did you see that woman who was with the boss? She's gone someplace."

"Well, she ain't in here."

"How's the starter? Can you rig it?"

"Nearly done."

Michelle eased herself quietly across to one of the gates in the fishing cockpit rail. Below it, a short ladder led down to a swim platform that formed the stern, riding just a few feet above the water. And there, pulled up on the swim platform, was a small, outboard-driven, three-person inflatable. Her way off the yacht was right there. Well, it was about time, she thought to herself. By now, she deserved a break.

She checked quickly that no one was close, then turned and backed feet-first through the gate and down. The inflatable was tied by a line to a handrail. Michelle put her hands against the craft's bow and gave it a test push. It moved more easily than she had expected. She slid it down off the platform into the water and threw after it one of several paddles from a rack. Then she turned, kneeling on the edge of the platform, and prepared to follow. Just as she was about to lower herself into the boat, a roar started up inside the yacht, and the hull shuddered. The diesels were running.

Michelle found the floor of the boat with a foot and steadied it. . . .

And then she realized what the KE mec had been

trying to convey to her in the engine room. The pipe
that the other mec had been trying to cut—probably
a fuel line—was too big. The KE had wanted her to
break it with something. Now, after everything, because
Michelle hadn't understood, Vanessa, Payne, all of
them, were about to get away.

Michelle stood agonizing, with one foot in the boat.
She could write it off as a lost cause and get herself
away at least; or she could go back, now that she knew
what was needed, and at least try to do something.
The water beneath the stern of the *Princess Dolores*
began churning, almost settling her decision by
throwing her out of the boat. A voice called from the
direction of the bridge, "Cast off aft." Footsteps
sounded from the far side of the fantail above.

Michelle hung on and turned her head, looking down
and then back. . . . And as her eyes roamed over the
docks behind her as if seeking guidance, an astonishing
sight greeted her: Ohira's car was pulling onto the quay,
the wreckage of the chain-link gate still trailing from
one side of the hood. There seemed to be some
commotion back along the access road, where the gate
attendant was out of his box, waving his arms, other
figures turning and shouting. Even as Michelle stared
in astonishment, Eric's van appeared where the gate
had been, with another car following behind.

Somehow, they were here! They just needed a few
more minutes.

Still not certain what she intended doing, Michelle
reversed direction and hauled herself back onto the
swim platform. As she released her grip on the handrail,
the KE mec fell away into the boat bobbing below.
Michelle had completely forgotten that she was still
clasping it. She climbed back to the fishing cockpit,
crawled across the deck to the hatch, and lowered her
head to look into the engine compartment.

Even just turning over, the diesels drowned any noise she might have made. The space between the engines was clear, but she could see the shadow of the engineer moving at the far end, near the cubbyhole that she had passed by, and the locker space where the other hatch was.

Then a sudden *whoosh* sounded from somewhere above. A crimson glow erupted on the far side of the ship's launch stowed on the boat deck, and a cloud of pink smoke rose from the vicinity of the bridge. Voices shouted above, and seconds later a bell began ringing in the engine compartment below. Michelle looked inside the hatch again, in time to see the engineer turn away, talking into a phone headset, and then disappear to the side in the direction of the locker space ladder and hatch, apparently going up to the deck to see what was happening.

Michelle didn't really make the decision; some kind of higher self that had assessed the situation faster and more accurately took over. Dropping down through the hatch, she made her way forward between the engines to the place where the KE had guided her before. The mec with the saw was still there but no longer moving. Michelle looked around, spied a bench and rack with tools, searched along it. . . . She picked up a hefty-looking wrench and weighed it experimentally. There seemed to be plenty of clout there. She selected a bend in the pipe that the mec had been tackling, near a joint that a hard blow or two would stand a good chance of opening, aimed, steadied, and swung with both hands. The pipe didn't break away clean, but the joint ruptured enough to send liquid cascading out over the floor. For good measure, she broke a set of glass spirit gauges full of reddish liquid to send that spurting over the engine compartment too, then dropped the wrench and retreated back up through the hatch.

There seemed to be a fire up above, with figures running about in consternation on the boat deck. An alarm siren began sounding somewhere along the lakeside. Figures were running along the quay. Something fell from above where Michelle was crouching and clattered across the deck. She looked up and had just glimpsed the metal face peering down from beneath the fantail rail when a voice called her name from the direction of the dock. She looked across and realized that the *Dolores* had begun to move.

An Oriental was running forward on the dock, waving to her—one of Ohira's people. He was swinging a nylon sports bag as if to throw, and signaling for her to catch it. Behind him, several others were wheeling out one of the shoreside gangplanks. Michelle ran to the nearside rail and caught the bag. It was full of mecs. Even as she watched, one of them—a telebot—came to life and scurried along the deck to the object that had fallen from above. It looked like a gun. The other mec was climbing down after it from the fantail. The two of them began dragging it between them, while another emerged from the bag.

The gangplank touched the side of the cockpit, but at once the gap started opening again. "Ms. Lang! Come quick." The Japanese who had thrown the bag waved frantically. It was her only chance now. The inflatable tied below the stern was pitching crazily in the turbulence from the screws.

But as Michelle was about to move, another figure dropped down the stairway from the fantail. It was one of Finnion's guards. He hadn't seen Michelle, who was back under the edge of the fishing cockpit, but he had seen the Japanese holding the gangplank.

Misinterpreting their intentions and thinking they were trying to board, he produced his gun and aimed. Michelle hit him full-force from behind, throwing all her weight. He doubled over the rail and went down into the water between the boat and the dock. Michelle caught herself before she went in after him, steadied herself, and then jumped to the gangplank. It was rolling back again before she was halfway down.

Vanessa ran forward from the salon to the bottom of the stairs going up to the bridge. Smoke was engulfing everything above. Garsten, in the doorway behind her, had torn his shirt off to shake the mec out of it. Ellipulos disappeared upward, hauling a fire extinguisher. Payne came down out of the smoke, his eyes red and cheeks streaming.

"What is it? What's happened up there now?" Vanessa shrieked.

Payne shook his head, groggy and bewildered. "One of them set off a distress flare behind the bridge somehow. The boat deck's alight. . . . I don't know. . . ."

Victor Bazhin and Norbert Dunne were blocking the door from the dining room and forward lounge, looking aghast. Zed shouldered his way through from behind them. "Where's Mike?" He spotted Payne. "Chief, somebody's overboard."

"Who?"

"I think it's one of Andy's guys—went in off the stern."

Finnion, holding a flashlamp, came through from the darkened salon aft of them. "A bunch of guys just showed up in two cars—Japanese or something. They've just crashed through the gate. That gray van of yours is there too."

Vanessa closed her eyes and inhaled slowly, her jaw tight. Now she saw their mistake in all its ghastliness. The van left unguarded; Corfe loose. And now Ohira was involved too—which no doubt had a lot to do with whatever had gone wrong in Tacoma.

Kyle, holding a gun, came out of the salon behind Finnion. "The lawyer—she's off the boat," he announced. "They got her off."

"How? Where is she?" Vanessa whispered.

Kyle gestured behind him with the gun. "Fished her off on a gangplank. They're landing her on the dock now."

"Why didn't you shoot her, you fool?" Vanessa seethed.

"Hell, it's not up to me. I just—"

"*Give me that!*" Vanessa's tone was enough to make Kyle let her take the gun from his hand. She went back through the salon, heading for the stern.

"Christ, she can't! There's people coming from all over out there," Kyle said.

"Wait!" Payne called after Vanessa, but she took no notice. He started after her. At that moment, the engines died.

"Get up on deck," Finnion snapped at Zed and Kyle. "Head her off outside."

Vanessa stormed through the salon, down the stairway at the end and along the passage, and burst into the engine room. Cole was wielding a wrench, grappling to stem fuel pouring from a broken pipe. His clothes were soaked; the floor was awash.

"What the hell now?" Vanessa shouted. "What happened to the engines?"

"Can't you see this? . . . Major emergency situation. The sight glasses for the tanks are wrecked too. We're not going anywhere. Get everybody off, fast!"

Then movement farther along the compartment caught Vanessa's eye. Two telebot mecs working together were dragging something along the floor in the aisle between the engines. They must have dropped it down the ladder from the hatch at the far end. It had a barrel, and looked for all the world like a cannon being trundled between them.

"Cole. What's that?" She pointed. The engineer looked back. His eyes widened into whites.

"*Jesus!*" He dropped the wrench, seized her, and pushed her down the aisle, virtually throwing her over the top of the mecs. "*Get up that hatch! . . .*"

"What—"

"*JUST GET OUT!*"

But Vanessa would need precious seconds to scale the ladder. Cole turned to run back to the locker-space hatch and collided with Payne coming the other way. Finnion was coming down the stairs along the passage behind Payne.

"*GET OUT! IT'S A FLARE PISTOL! EVERYTHING'S GONNA BLOW!*" Cole bawled at them.

Payne dived sideways for the locker-space hatch. Cole kept on going and flew up the stairs after Finnion, who had hurriedly reversed direction.

Probably, Kevin shouldn't have done it. The intention had been simply a scare tactic to keep the engine room off limits. But after his experiences of fighting the assassin bug in Eric's car, getting Lancelot to Tacoma to free himself from the machine, a wild ride with Ohira, and finally the crazy act to stop the *Dolores* from sailing while the van careened across Seattle, his adrenaline had taken charge.

And, being coupled into mec space, he hadn't known at that time that Michelle was off the boat and safe; she had been climbing down to a rubber boat at the stern at one point, but now the KE mec was there but Michelle was not. Then, seeing Vanessa brandishing the gun. . . .

And no-one was actually in the engine room itself by that time. . . .

He would agree with Eric later that it was an overreaction, unjustified by the circumstances, going too far. But he never really meant it. The feeling it gave him later, every time he relived the moment, was something that he would remember always and wouldn't have missed for the world.

He pulled the trigger.

The main blast came up through the side hatch that Payne had just emerged from, carrying him over the side and into the water on the side of the boat away from the dock. Black, oily smoke followed, boiling up also out of the stern hatch that Vanessa had come out of and shrouding the afterdeck. She clutched the rail by the starboard gate down from the fishing cockpit, coughing and retching. The *Dolores* was drifting, dead in the water. People were coming out onto the quay from the back of the Shoals club building, others gathering on its second-floor terrace. Someone had thrown a lifebelt to the figure struggling in the water between the boat and the dock. Sirens of approaching fire trucks wailed along the waterfront. Flames erupted from somewhere near the stern on the far side, and another figure jumped into the water. Orange tongues were also licking from the side hatch that Payne had escaped through. There was no way for Vanessa to go forward.

Payne was swimming toward the stern. Vanessa looked down and saw the inflatable boat tied to the swim platform, which was what he was making for. Black smoke from the burning diesel fuel and pink clouds from the flare blazing on the boat deck above were mingling to blot out the whole scene. The inflatable, she realized, could also be their way out of this.

She turned and climbed down to the swim platform.

As her head came level with the fishing cockpit deck, she noticed the nylon sports bag with another mec just in the process of crawling out. It came to the edge and peered down, watching while Vanessa dropped into the rubber boat and helped Payne in over the side. When she turned to untie the line, the mec flew down at her and landed on her coat. Literally—it had wings. She gave a shout, more from ire than fear, tore it off and threw it down.

"What is it?" Payne gasped as he sat up.

Vanessa untied and used a paddle that was already there to push them clear of the *Dolores*'s stern. "Those things. They're everywhere."

Payne lowered the outboard into the water and ran out the starter cord to turn the motor. But before he could let the cord back in for a real starting tug, another mec leaped from the floor, grabbed ahold of the cord with all four of its limbs, and wedged itself tight in the outlet. Payne pried at it with his fingers but couldn't budge it. "It's stuck. I can't move the cord."

"Damn!" Vanessa looked around desperately. The pall of smoke was descending around them from above, while confusion spread along the dock. A fire truck was stopped behind the van at the top of the access road, lights flashing, blaring to get past. Two more fire trucks appeared behind the parked cars, hoists, and slipways in an adjoining yard, while figures ran ahead to open a gate connecting through to the quay behind the Shoals building. A fire tender launch was also moving out farther along the shore of the lake.

On the far side of the *Dolores* from the dock was a floating pier connected to the quay by a wooden bridge. Beneath the bridge, a narrow channel led through to the next basin, which fronted the adjacent yard that the fire trucks were moving through. Vanessa pointed.

"Never mind the motor. Just get us through there. There'll be a way out somewhere in all that."

"What then?"

"I don't *know*. One thing at a time, Martin."

With Payne paddling canoe fashion, they moved away from the stern through the smoke, under the bridge. Looking back, it seemed that the whole aft section of the *Dolores* was ablaze. Lines had been thrown from the quay to stop it drifting farther. More figures were jumping to join those in the water. As the inflatable came out behind the boats moored at the next dock, the sounds of approaching police sirens added to the whooping of fire trucks and wailing of the dock siren. As far as they could tell, their getaway had not been detected. Other small craft were putting out here and in the basin they had left, and nobody seemed to have singled them out.

Payne brought the craft to a wooden jetty leading to steps going up, and steadied it while Vanessa got out. He threw a turn of line around one of the mooring stanchions and followed her up. At the top, Vanessa stopped dead, too stunned to say anything for several seconds.

Eric had arrived. Not fifty yards away, the maroon Jaguar was screeching to a stop among the other parked vehicles, trailing a procession of police cruisers flashing red and blue lights and making noise like a sabbath of banshees. Eric jumped out, and without waiting or even turning his head, strode through the gate that had been opened for the fire trucks, toward the commotion taking place at the back of the Shoals building, around the burning vessel. The police cars halted in disarray, doors flying open, uniformed figures leaping out and chasing after him.

"My God! What's happening?" Payne breathed. "How did he get here?"

Vanessa didn't answer as she took in the situation, her mind racing feverishly. Everyone was focusing on the burning boat and the crowd on the quayside in front of it. The Jaguar was in the next yard, outside that periphery of attention. She felt in her coat pocket. Her keys were there. She showed them to Payne and indicated the Jaguar with her eyes. He followed her glance, understood, returned a nod.

They walked across quickly to the car. Vanessa climbed into the driver's seat, closed the door, and started the motor. Payne dropped down in the passenger seat moments later, dripping and squelching. She backed up and turned, conscious of the risk that somebody left in one of the police cars might notice and intervene—but there was no other choice.

Nobody noticed, however. Vanessa kept her speed down as they left the dock area, then accelerated along Westlake not minding the direction, anything to get away from the general area.

CHAPTER THIRTY-SEVEN

Taki thought it was "sen-super-sational."

"Decidedly memorable," Kevin agreed.

Neither of them had seen a large ship afire before. Orange flames were consuming the stern and midships section, and a tower of smoke writhed upward and spread into the gray overcast of the sky. The rain farther south hadn't reached the north side of the city yet. Kevin could feel the heat beating at his face, even from the van, now down on the quay. Hoses were being directed into the blaze and over the as-yet untouched forward half from several fire launches on the far side as well as from trucks drawn up on the quay, but even so, every now and again something inside the boat would flare up or explode with a muffled concussion and cause a fresh outbreak.

Corfe was sitting on the tailboard of the van, looking exhausted, his bearded features suggesting something out of Hades in the flickering red glow from the police cars parked haphazardly around. The officer in charge had talked to Eric and was now supervising the questioning and note-taking going on among the yacht's bedraggled company, some wrapped in blankets, others being tended for scrapes and bruises by crew from the ambulances that had arrived in the wake of the police cars. Two other officers were talking to Ohira. Michelle was standing to one side with Eric. She had seemed confused and disoriented when Kevin first emerged from the van, but was recovering rapidly. Kevin, preoccupied with the visual feast of the burning vessel, only partly heard what they were saying.

"Michelle, you should have *told* me! Do you think I couldn't have dealt with it, for heaven's sake?"

"We were going to. But we just wanted this final piece of evidence to show you, to clinch it. It wasn't exactly the kind of thing I'm used to springing on people every day."

"You make it sound as if I need some kind of . . . of support team to manage my life."

"But Eric, you *do*. You're in a different reality for most of the time. You need people around you to handle this one for you. Don't get me wrong—it's not a criticism. That's what lets you be what you are. But look at us even right now . . ." Michelle swept an arm, "standing here philosophizing, in the middle of what looks like an air-raid. Doesn't that underline what I'm saying?"

There was a short pause. Then Eric looked her up and down and asked, "Are you sure you're all right? You look as if you've been in an air-raid, anyway."

"I'll be fine." Michelle sighed. "Doesn't anybody around here have any coffee?"

Ohira turned from the open door of his car, a few yards away. "Just coming up." He produced a flask and some Styrofoam cups.

"I didn't know you read minds too."

Ohira grinned craggily. "Ancient Japanese custom."

"Eric?" Michelle inquired. He nodded gratefully. She took two of the cups, and held them while Ohira filled them.

Corfe accepted a mug of something from an ambulance man and shook his head in answer to some question. He seemed to be regathering his wits and showing more interest in what was going on. Kevin went over to him.

"Hi, Doug. Are you okay?"

"Aw, I figure I'll make it." Corfe took a long swallow from the mug, wiped his mouth with a knuckle, and looked at Kevin curiously. "So what happened to you down at the lab? When we couldn't get any answer on the phone, I was starting to get really worried."

"Oh, there was trouble. It's really been one of those days that you hear about."

"I thought some of Payne's people might have gone there."

"They did. But the Tacoma cops have got them now."

"Why were you stuck there? How come you couldn't decouple?"

"I'm not sure."

"Hell. . . . So tell me what happened."

Kevin frowned and tried to think back, but before he could go into it, Eric joined them.

"You're looking better, Doug. I think I'm just beginning to get an idea of how much I owe you. I—"

Corfe raised a hand tiredly. "Not now, Eric. There'll be plenty of other times for all that." He looked around them and shook his head. "I don't know. . . . How did you do it? I was trying all day to get the police to take it seriously, and they wouldn't even talk to me. You show up with a posse of them in tow. What's the trick? Scientific intellect? German charisma?" He frowned. "Come to that, when did you even talk to them? You couldn't have had time."

Eric grinned and accepted a cup of coffee from Michelle as she rejoined them. "I didn't have to. It's amazing what happens when you come up the Interstate at a hundred and ten. They appear from everywhere. You know that as well as I do, Doug. It works every time."

Corfe stared at him in astonishment. "You—" Then he caught sight of another figure close by. "Ah, Lieutenant Shelvy, I do believe. Lieutenant, let me introduce Ms. Michelle Lang—real and in the flesh. Alive and well too, thanks to *these* guys."

The lieutenant held up both hands. "Okay, okay. All I can say is that situations like today aren't exactly part of the manual. What else can I tell you?" He looked away as another officer approached. "Excuse me. What is it, Des?"

"Everyone seems to be accounted for except two: the owner, Mr. Payne; and one of the guests, a Mrs. Heber."

"None of the boats picked anyone up on the other side?"

"No. I just checked."

Eric lowered the cup from his mouth and turned to stare at the inferno. "Oh, my God!" he whispered, genuinely horrified, despite the circumstances.

Shelvy's eyes flickered over him uncertainly for a second. "I take it she is your wife, Mr. Heber?" he said. His voice was professional, detached, but in an appropriately lowered tone. Eric nodded, his eyes invisible behind the flames reflecting off his spectacles.

There was a moment of heavy silence. Then Shelvy said, "Look, there's really nothing more you can do here. I understand what you people have been through, but we will be needing full statements and some other details cleared up back at headquarters. If there's any further news, you'll be informed right away."

Eric looked away, then nodded again. "Yes, of course. I understand. Will it be all right to use my car?"

"Sure. I don't think we need worry about that. You

can follow one of our guys. Des, can you find someone to go back with Mr. Heber?"

"Sure." The other officer called to somewhere past the van. "Hey, Stan, can you get over here?"

"Kevin, Doug, Michelle, you can ride with me." Eric looked inquiringly at Shelvy. "I assume that's all right, Lieutenant?" Shelvy nodded, and then was called away to take a radio call. "Maybe you'd better stay with your uncle," Eric told Taki. Taki nodded. The officer called Des turned back to them.

"Which is your car, Mr. Heber?"

"Oh, it's back that way in the other yard—a maroon Jaguar." Eric indicated with an arm. They began walking in a group toward the gate. "What about the others?" he asked Des.

"Oh, they'll all show up there too in good time. It's gonna be a busy evening." He laid a hand lightly on Kevin's shoulder in a way that was intended to be comforting. "Sorry about your mom, son. But it's not all over yet. Give it a bit more time. You can never be too sure of these things."

"She's my stepmother," Kevin said.

"Oh. . . . Okay."

"Which way?" Michelle halted, then looked back at Eric.

Eric pointed, then stopped and looked about as if he might have made a mistake. He shook his head bemusedly.

"What?" Corfe said.

"It's gone."

Michelle looked around. "It can't be, surely not."

Eric pointed. "It was there. I'm certain of it."

Kevin walked forward and stared down at the space that Eric had indicated. A trail of puddles and wetness on the concrete led toward the edge of the quay. He followed it to the top of steps leading down, then turned

and waved for the others to come over. At the bottom
of the steps was a jetty with an inflatable outboard
tied up loosely to a stanchion. Painted along the front
was the name *Princess Dolores*.

Eric gazed at it, then back at where the car had been.
He dipped his hand in his pocket and produced his
keys. The others stared at them. Eric waited silently,
inviting them to form their own conclusion.

If he still had *his* keys, it could only mean . . .

Vanessa clipped a red light at the west end of
Nickerson Street, prompting a blast on the horn from
a pickup that had been just moving off. "Ease up, for
God's sake," Payne rasped at her irritably. "We're clear
enough now. All we need is to get hauled up for a
speeding ticket after all this."

"Who's left to give us one?" Vanessa shot back. "Every
cop in Seattle is at the boat."

"That's still no reason to go asking for trouble."

She had headed westward on the south side of the
Ship Canal not with any particular destination in mind,
but simply to put distance between them and the Lake
Union area. In fact, they would more likely want to
end up going the other way, either to get on the
Interstate or carry on across to Bellevue or Redmond.
Not wishing to retrace her route now, she got into the
lane for the Ballard Bridge in order to circle back on
the north side. She drummed her fingers impatiently
on the wheel while a Volvo dawdled in the approach
ramp ahead of them, finally putting her foot down and
cutting around it.

"For Christ's sake ease up!" Payne snapped.

"Martin, why don't you try thinking about what we're
going to do, instead of carping at me all the time? If
those fools of yours had known how to run a security
business, none of this would have happened."

"My people? Hey, don't you go blaming them. You're the one who told them to bring her back to the firm."

"Did you expect me to wait until she threw a fit out on the street? There was no problem with that. What on earth possessed Phil to bring those things back with him to the boat?"

"That wouldn't have been a problem either, if you hadn't made them a present of the van."

"How was *I* supposed to know they'd just let Corfe walk in and take it? God, Martin, you call that security?"

"You were there; you were supposed to know what they were doing. If I was there, *I* would have known."

Vanessa gripped the wheel tight and released a long, exasperated sigh as she strove to control herself. They came off 15th onto Market, going east.

"Martin, this isn't doing any good," she said curtly. "We need to decide where we're going. What do you want me to do?"

Payne dropped the sodden handkerchief that he had been using to mop his hair and neck down onto the floor. "Get far away, of course. We'll need papers, some cash. . . . I need a change of clothes." He took his phone from his coat pocket, looked at it oozing water, and threw that on the floor too. "Take 520," he said as he reached to unhook the vehicle's phone. "We'll go to Bellevue and do it now, while everything's still up in the air. We'll probably have to get your papers and things too."

"Harriet will probably be there—the housekeeper."

"Well, it's not as if you need to ask her permission, Vanessa. Just take what you need and go. In fact, you could mention something about having to go up to Canada at short notice—that's what everyone will be expecting. Instead, we get an evening flight to El Paso, pick up a rental, cross into Mexico. Or we could make it Miami, hire a boat, and head for the islands." He looked over at her. She didn't speak. "Well, got any better ideas?" he challenged. Vanessa shrugged, shook her head. Payne punched in a number.

"Oh, Vogl, it's me. I'm on my way now, and I'll be needing some things in a hurry. First, a change of casual clothes and a weekend bag packed. Passport, personal documents, and ten thousand in cash. Spare pocket phone and the laptop. Got all that? . . . Yes. . . . No, I don't know how long for. And if anybody calls, you haven't heard from me, okay? . . . Ten minutes at most. . . . Fine." He hung up.

"I still don't understand how he—the boy—got out of that coupler," Vanessa said. "I had it locked out. There's *no* way he could have decoupled from the inside."

Payne made a face. "Why ask me? That's your department. Those Japanese must have gone there and gotten him out."

"The same question applies. How could *they* have known he was there? He had no way of communicating."

"All I know is that somebody must have got in the way of the two guys that Andy sent down there." Payne waved a hand. "What were they looking for in Phil's office? If it was the codicil, how did they know about it? How does Eric show up here instead of where he was supposed to be? There's a whole lot been going on that we don't know about, Vanessa."

They were now going south on Roosevelt, approaching University Bridge. The road immediately in front was clear, but the cars farther ahead were slowing to a halt before the warning barrier, which was down and flashing red lights. To the left, a schooner was moving out along the channel, sails furled, running on its auxiliary engine. Beyond the barrier, the hinged center sections of the bridge had begun rising.

Vanessa emitted a vexed sigh and eased up on the gas.

"What's this?" Payne picked up a small object off the top of the dashpanel. For a moment, before touching it, he'd thought it was a wasp. It was about the same size and had yellow and black tiger stripes.

At the sight of it, Vanessa lost the control that she had been fighting to preserve. She had forgotten the mec. They were here too, in the car. In an instant, all her recollections of grappling with it and being cut to pieces came pouring back. She stabbed at the button to open the passenger-side window. "Throw it out," she shuddered.

"What? I don't—"

"Just get rid of it, Martin!"

And then something else, with wings, rose up from behind the seats and brushed her shoulder. Vanessa screamed and swatted at it with her hand.

Limenitis Lorquini, or Lorquin's Admiral, a common butterfly of western North America and Canada, dark blue and brown with white markings. Stirred by the rush of air, it fluttered, confused for a moment, and then vanished out the window. Payne laughed. "Just a bug, Vanessa. What's this? You're getting too jumpy. It's not like—"

He broke off as he saw her eyes widening in shock, her mouth open in a silent shout of protest, the look of horror spreading across her face. "What? . . ."

Vanessa raised her hand from the utility shelf between the front-seat armrests. Something was sticking to her palm—something black, long and pointed like an insect, sinister- looking. Most of its legs were missing or reduced to stumps. It was fastened to her skin by a sharp, needlelike sting attached to its partly severed head.

Payne shook his head. He knew, but his mind refused to accept. "No! Pull over. Stop the car. . . ."

Vanessa tried to speak but could only gurgle. The

toxin was already taking effect. As the muscles in her leg contracted, straightening it against the gas pedal, her last voluntary act was to jog the wheel and avoid the line of stationary traffic. The windshield iced as they crashed through the barrier, accelerating hard.

"Vanessa! . . ."

The Jaguar cleared the top of the upward-hinging ramp and somersaulted as its front went down into the gap. It hit the end of the opposite section roof first, dead center, the momentum caving it in like a karate-chopped soda can, ends buckling, fountains of glass exploding out in all directions. The car hung for several seconds, tipping back slowly as the angle of the bridge steepened. Finally it broke free and plunged into the green-gray water.

It was night by the time salvage boats, working by floodlights, brought the wreck up again. This time, Vanessa's condition wasn't virtual. And what was left of Payne had to be buried without a head.

EPILOGUE

The tour bus looked vaguely like a stretched, big-wheels version of a golf cart with a transparent bubble top. It had seats for a driver and six passengers, slung high above four roundwall tractor treads independently suspended for rugged terrain. The driver had a blue uniform with cap, white shirt and tie, and looked the part of somebody in charge. Seated in pairs behind him were a man in a sweater and slacks, one in a jacket, another in shirtsleeves, two women in skirts and one wearing jeans—representative of a mixed vacation group that could have been found anywhere. Except that they all had immobile features and oddly proportioned bodies, and their clothes and faces were painted on.

Amy Patterson, feature writer for Time-Life, was at the back on the right. The rendering of a tan check two-piece with yellow, high-necked blouse was a little on the staid side of anything she would have picked herself, but the other reporters and journalists "occupying" the figures around her were hardly interested in matters like that. It was special preview day for the press at Seattle's just-completed *MICROCOSM* test site, which would open to the public tomorrow. A half dozen more were planned at major U.S. cities in the next six months, and two in Japan. It didn't need to be the kind of large, centralized undertaking that would require visitors by the thousands and parking lots measured by the acre to justify it, like a Disneyworld. A few square yards of any kind of environment—natural, synthetic, subterranean, aqueous—could be created anywhere. So they could more appropriately be offered as smaller, local attractions comparable to the neighborhood park or the mall movie theaters. Eventually, the information package circulated by the new corporation said, there was no reason why individuals shouldn't acquire their own to use as they chose, like personal computers.

"Now, here are some more protozoans that are kind of interesting. If you look down in the water just outside to the right, you'll see a bunch of what look like green goldfish squirming around—or should that be greenfish?"

They had stopped on a rock shelf by a grotto formed under a roof of scaly arches sprouting leaves the size of tennis courts. The voice of the young man—Amy had judged him to be about fifteen or sixteen—came over the audio circuit that they were all tuned into, its youthful quality contrasting with the visual effect of the surrogate's painted mustache. But he was doing a good job, Amy thought.

"They belong to the class known as flagellates, on account of the filament that they use to propel themselves along, which you might just be able to make out. This particular kind is called *Euglena*, typically five to ten thousandths of an inch long. They're responsible for the green scum that you get on ponds, when they get too numerous. They live by photosynthesis. The red patches are rudimentary eye spots that enable them to seek light."

"What are those?" The sandy-haired man in the gray

sweater at the front waved a hand painted china-doll pink. He was really a newsman from NBC, and had a ginger beard.

The driver shifted in his seat to look back. "Where?"

"There, a bit farther out—the Tinkertoy beach balls." There was no need to carry a camera on this assignment. Everything they saw through their micromec eyes could be recorded automatically at the push of a virtual button. The NBC man was pointing at a cluster of what looked like spherical cages, each a foot or so across. Their surfaces consisted of greenish blobs stretched into five-pointed stars by bars attaching to their neighbors, the result being a lattice of triangles.

"They're pretty interesting too," the driver answered. "*Volvox.* It's a colony of thousands of flagellates similar to *Euglena,* embedded in the surface of a jelly ball. The flagella form a kind of fuzz around the outside, but you can't see them too well from here. They move the ball about through the water. What's interesting is that the same side is always forward when it swims, so it's got a definite front and a back. The only way to explain that is that the activities of all the members are subordinated to the colony as a whole. Nobody really knows how that works. If they all just did their own thing independently, the ball would never get anywhere."

"You could view that as the beginnings of individuality, maybe," somebody commented on the circuit.

"That's exactly what it is—a first step toward what you see in the higher animals—distinct individuals made up of millions of cells."

"Where did you learn all this at your age?" Amy couldn't help asking.

"You gonna be a biology major?" the NBC man asked.

The bus pulled away and followed below a wooden cliff on which spiky and squirmy life-forms were moving beneath fungal circus tents of brown and orange. "As a matter of fact my specialty is computers and electronics. But you get into just about everything when you've got a scientist for a father, especially one like Eric—even tour guiding." There were a couple of laughs.

"Anyhow, this ride will have given you an initial feel of what it's all about. I'm going to stop a little farther ahead, and we'll zap you all back to the theater for a coffee break and a presentation on the technology. We thought it would help you frame questions if you'd had a chance to sample the experience first. Then, after that, we'll come back down here, and that's when you'll be able to get out and walk around. We'll use the bus to visit a few places where we've got some short hikes prepared. . . . Okay, are there any other points for now?"

There weren't. Everyone seemed content just to gawk. Amy pointed at an icon on the top edge of her visual field as they had been briefed, and it unrolled a choice of simple command options. She indicated *Commentary* to switch her speech input from the common circuit to a private channel, and resumed recording.

"Well, just a few more impressions before we go back for a technical session. I'm still not sure I really believe this. I have to remind myself that the lake we're driving past is probably less than a yard across, and those aren't really mountains on the other side.

"In front, we're approaching what I can only think of as some kind of primordial jungle—the kind you imagine pterodactyls flying over, and dinosaurs crashing around in. It's not anything like trees as we know them, but gigantic, curving trunks all twisting together, and huge, leathery plates of leaves, much higher up above than you ever see trees. The light is peculiar too, in that . . . Oh, my God, there is a dinosaur! It's even bigger than the trees, staring down over them at us like a Tyrannosaurus." Amy called down the command menu again and hovered a finger warily near EXIT. "It's got a flat, pointed head and enormous black eyes made up of thousands of lenses. I think it's a praying mantis. . . ."

Kevin watched from the back of the auditorium as Corfe gave his talk, "Introduction to DNC," accompanied by slides, charts, and demonstrations. It seemed to be going over well, with a lively flow of questions from the audience. Ohira was sitting to one side, decked out formally in a black suit with bow tie for the occasion.

"So can we take it that this technology has a clean bill of health now?" somebody asked from the front. "Weren't there some scares going around about, oh, six months or so ago? Something about it being able to mess people up in the head?"

Corfe nodded knowingly. "That's all been put to bed now. It was exposed as a malicious campaign initiated by hostile commercial interests that stood to lose in a big way. You see, the *MICROCOSM* venture—we still call it 'Bug Park' among ourselves here—is really just a side line. The big-money applications are in science and industry."

"So there's no truth in those allegations?"

Corfe smiled faintly and shook his head. "Not a scrap. It was all investigated officially. They all went away."

A modest auditorium the size of a local movie theater was all that was needed—another could always be added next door if the demand called for it. The couplers were luxurious compared to the ones Kevin was used to; it was the electronics that constituted the biggest capital outlay. The park itself was a square twenty feet on a side out back. That could always be enlarged, and more variety added as needed, too.

Somebody tapped him on his elbow. He turned to find Avril there. She motioned with her head at the doors behind, leading through to the lobby area. Kevin nodded and followed her out.

Taki was outside, among the staff attending to final chores, and contractors cleaning up and making last-day finishing touches to the decor. Janna was with him, holding a phone. "What's the plan for the girls this evening?" Taki asked Kevin. "Are they staying in town or going back to Tacoma? Janna's folks need to know." Neurodyne was hosting a dinner in town for the guests that night.

Kevin was surprised that Taki should even ask. "Coming with us, of course. They're part of the firm now." Avril and Janna had made their debut as tour bus drivers too that morning, and seemed to have enjoyed it. Unofficially, they were becoming quite proficient small-game hunters also.

Taki looked at Kevin while Janna relayed the information into the phone. "A guy in the group that I was with just now wanted to know if we'd thought of starting a flying school—teaching people to fly planes, using mecs. It sounded like a great idea. What do you think?"

Kevin shrugged. "Why not? Put it on the list." New suggestions were pouring in all the time. "Where did he hear about that, anyway?" Kevin asked.

"I think your dad mentioned it when they were talking over the phone," Taki answered.

"Why just planes?" Avril put in. "Why not let people have a try at the flymecs?"

"I don't thing they're ready for going public with yet," Taki said.

"But they're getting better all the time."

"One thing at a time," Taki said. "Learn to think like an engineer."

"You have to think ahead too. I've got lots more ideas. Wanna hear 'em?"

"Where is Dad, anyway?" Kevin muttered, looking around.

"I'd rather have something to drink," Taki said. "Why does neurocoupling make you thirsty?"

"I've got change. I'll get them," Avril said. "What do you guys want?"

"Coke," Taki answered.

"Orange," Kevin said.

"Want to give me a hand, Jan?" Avril said.

"Sure." Janna put the phone in her purse and followed after Avril in the direction of the vending area.

Kevin spotted Eric with Michelle, over by the door to the briefing room—unlike a movie theater, there would need to be some introduction and familiarization for first-time users. Harriet, looking smart in a navy dress trimmed with white, had just left them and was coming over to where the two boys were standing. Michelle gripped Eric's arm, leaning to say something close, and they both laughed together.

"So, how is everything going?" Harriet inquired. Kevin got the feeling that she had seized the moment to leave discreetly.

"Pretty good," Taki replied.

"When are we going to sign you up as a guide too?" Kevin asked her. They had persuaded Harriet to try the mecs finally, but that was about all. Kevin didn't think there was much danger of a lifetime addiction developing. Taki's sister was evidently not alone.

"Oh, I think I've gotten too used to being the size I am to want to go changing it now," Harriet told him. "I like things looking the way they are." She studied Kevin for a moment, then turned to follow his gaze.

Eric was off in another world again, but this time it was shared, not one purely of his own.

Harriet looked back at Kevin. His face had an odd, distant grin. Her voice fell to a confidential note. It didn't matter that Taki was listening—he had long been family. "And if you ask me," she said, "from the way some other things are shaping up, it might not be long before you have to start getting used to having a new stepmother all over again."

Kevin couldn't pretend that it came as a total surprise.

Michelle had been showing up at the house and the office too often for that; there had been too many days with just her and Eric going off somewhere together, too many evenings of cozy dinners and late-night dancing. Kevin nodded and grinned in a way that he hoped conveyed the wisdom and worldliness that seemed to be appropriate.

"Oh, I don't think I'd have too much of a problem dealing with it this time," he said. He looked at Taki and raised a quizzical eyebrow. Taki solemnly nodded approval.

A burst of enthusiastic applause from the auditorium door behind them endorsed it.

END

THE WORLDS OF CHARLES SHEFFIELD

Reigning Master of Hard Science Fiction

"He has the scientific grounding of a Clarke, the story-telling skills of a Heinlein, the dry wit of a Pohl or a Kornbluth, and the universe-building prowess of a Niven."
—Spider Robinson